THE WAR THAT NEVER WAS

MICHAEL A. PALMER is the 1988 recipient of the Samuel Eliot Morison Award for Naval Literature and is the critically acclaimed author of numerous naval histories. He teaches history at East Carolina University in Greenville, North Carolina, where he lives with his wife and two children.

AVAILABLE NOW

Termite Hill
By Tom Wilson

Vietnam: A Reader
By the Editors of *Vietnam* magazine

Operation Vulture
By John Prados

Company Commander Vietnam
By James Estep

Helmet for My Pillow
The General
March to Glory
By Robert Leckie

Samurai!
By Saburo Sakai with Martin Caidin
and Fred Saito

Zero
By Masatake Okumiya and Jiro Horikoshi
with Martin Caidin

Fork-Tailed Devil: The P-38
The B-17: The Flying Forts
By Martin Caidin

The World War II Reader
By the Editors of *World War II* magazine

The Civil War Reader: 1862
By the Editors of *Civil War Times Illustrated* and
America's Civil War

What They Didn't Teach You About The Civil War
What They Didn't Teach You About World War II
By Mike Wright

Manhunt
By Peter Maas

THE WAR THAT NEVER WAS

MICHAEL A. PALMER

ibooks
new york
www.ibooks.net
DISTRIBUTED BY SIMON & SCHUSTER

To Fritz,
who never gives up

An ibooks, inc. Book

ibooks, inc.
24 West 25th Street
New York, NY 10010

The ibooks World Wide Web Site address is:
http://www.ibooks.net

ISBN: 0-7434-7451-1
First ibooks printing July 2003
10 9 8 7 6 5 4 3 2

Share your thoughts about *The War That Never Was*
and other ibooks titles in the ibooks virtual reading group at
www.ibooks.net

Contents

PROLOGUE
The Tenth Anniversary Game 1

THE NOVEL
The War That Never Was 11

EPILOGUE
The War That Was 345

Abbreviations 355

Tables of Organization 358

MAPS
The Northern Flank 24
Libya and the Central Mediterranean 49
Greece, Turkey and the Aegean 68
The Indian Ocean and Persian Gulf 87
The Western Pacific 100
Korea and the DMZ 117
The Atack on the Tbilisi 144
The Front in Germany 155

THE TENTH ANNIVERSARY GAME

Yuri Grigorevich Sinsukin felt strangely calm as the aging Tupolev airliner taxied down the Moscow airport runway. He twisted his neck so that he could peer out the small window for what might well be his last look toward the city. He was about to leave his birthplace, the land of his ancestors. Yuri's children were grown and married; his wife was dead; his business interests took him increasingly to the United States. "Why not just move to the States?" a friend had asked after his last trip. "Indeed, why not?" Yuri had answered.

"Sir?"

The voice startled Yuri. He turned quickly and nearly bumped heads with the smiling flight attendant.

"Your seat, please. It must be upright for takeoff."

Yuri returned the young woman's smile, staring at the pretty attendant as he felt for the button on the armrest. At last he found it and his seat shot forward.

"Good springs," she remarked.

"Just like the ones in our watches," Yuri replied.

The attendant appeared confused.

"You know, our Russian watches," Yuri joked, "they run faster than anyone else's."

Yuri laughed but the stewardess just smiled politely before making her way up the aisle. As he watched the young woman, he couldn't help but notice the sheen on the seat of her uniform and the runners in her stockings. "Shabby, so shabby," he thought to himself as his glance returned to the dirty window, "just like the rest of this damned country!"

Russia, poor Russia, so run down, so shabby, so . . . so poor. Yuri could remember the old days, the days of his youth, the last years of the old Soviet Union. Things had been bad then, but there had still been a vitality of sorts to the place. Or was it just that Yuri had been younger, more vital? He had been a man of importance, a naval officer attached to military intelligence. He had power. He traveled freely. In fact, in those days, with a few words to the right person, he could have had that young attendant for a night when the plane arrived in Washington. But what did it matter now? And what fascination was there in spending a night with an unwilling flight attendant who didn't even own a decent pair of stockings? Yuri shifted his weight, trying to get comfortable. He let out a long sigh, the sigh of a troubled soul, a soul about to leave its body. But that's what souls did when their body died, wasn't it? Besides, Yuri wasn't a Russian. He was a child of the Soviet state, a state that no longer existed. Neither he, nor his parents, had ever known Russia. Yuri considered himself a man without a country, a free agent, to use an American sports term. And Yuri enjoyed sprinkling his excellent English with properly used American idioms.

Yuri liked Americans; he liked America. He had decided to leave Russia one night when it dawned on him that he had spent far more of his adult life living in the United States than he had in Russia. Yuri, who was born in 1945, spent sixteen of his first forty-four years living in the United States. And he had spent two of the last ten years in America as well. In many ways, he felt more comfortable being an American than he did being a Russian. He knew what it meant to be an American. He knew what people expected of him. But, Yuri had begun to ask himself, what was expected of a Russian? What was he to do? The answer to that question had come far more quickly than he expected. He wrestled with it for a few weeks, but he knew all along what he would ultimately decide. He would emigrate to the United States; he had his book—his key to success in America. Yuri, who had spent years portraying himself as an American, would now actually become an American. And then he would fly his family to the States, if that was what they wanted, and take his grandchildren to see the Statue of Liberty.

The Tupolev was on the runway now. The pilot brought the nose of the plane around to port. There was a pause. And then Yuri felt the engines throttle up. The airliner raced down the runway. Yuri could feel the power driving him into his seat. As the wheels left the ground, he took one last look at Moscow, and then he turned his glance forward. He had expected to feel emotional at this point. Perhaps, he had speculated, his eyes would water. But instead he just felt a wondrous sense of relief. He felt lighter as the Tupolev's pilot allowed the Gs built up during the takeoff to bleed off. Yuri felt . . . he searched his mind for the proper Americanism . . . Yuri felt born again!

Thirty minutes later, with the Tupolev cruising at 35,000 feet, Yuri was hard at work, with a double-vodka and an American notebook computer at the ready. He hit the power switch and the PC booted up, loading Windows 6.2, and popping Yuri into his appointments for the next day. At 0800 he would join his American literary agent—Fred Hanson—for breakfast at the Vista Hotel. And then at 0930, the two men would meet with Annie Taft, the reporter from the *Washington Post*.

★ ★ ★

It was 0940 when Yuri's cab pulled up in front of Hanson's Georgetown townhouse. Yuri was tired, suffering from jetlag and the innumerable vodkas he had consumed the night before in the Vista's lounge. He had called Fred and cancelled the breakfast. Yuri had needed sleep more than he had needed food. He stumbled up the steps. Before he could ring the bell, Fred opened the door, shook Yuri's hand, and led him into the dining room. Yuri could smell the fresh coffee brewing and his head felt instantly better. As he entered the room, a woman that he assumed, correctly, to be Annie Taft, rose and offered him her hand. He shook it and gestured for her to sit. He then plopped himself into a chair and immediately reached for the coffee pot. Fred beat him to it, pouring Yuri a cup.

"I appreciate your taking the time, Mr. Sinsukin. You must be tired after the flight."

"Please, call me Yuri. And yes, I'm tired, but that's how it is. Now, what would you like to talk about?"

"Well, your new book, obviously."

"Of course, but what . . . angle? And allow me to ask a question. Have you read it?"

"Yes, I have. And I enjoyed it. I found it very interesting."

"Good. Good. Okay, ask your questions."

"Well, first, just how did you manage to gather all of the information in the book? There have been some reports that you were an intelligence officer? Is that true?"

Hanson had forewarned Yuri to avoid answering that one. Yuri had spent the better part of two decades studying, and sometimes spying on, the American military, especially the U.S. Navy. But Hanson made it clear that Yuri should not play up that part of his career. "Focus on your time at Newport," Fred had recommended, "we'll save the spy angle for your next book."

Yuri dodged the question.

"The information was drawn entirely from open sources, I assure you. The technical databases appended to the official report are quite extensive."

"And the report itself, what was its genesis?"

Yuri was relieved that Taft hadn't pressed the point.

"Well, in 1998 and 1999, I was the first 'Russian' naval officer to attend the U.S. Navy's Naval War College at Newport, Rhode Island. Since I had been involved in the late 1980s and early 1990s in war planning, I decided that it might be interesting to write a comparative study of Soviet and American war plans from that period for my research project."

"Was access a problem?" Taft asked.

"No," Yuri replied. "The Russian government had released the bulk of Soviet-era documents in the mid-1990s, so that wasn't a problem."

"What about the American plans," Taft asked.

"Well, that proved to be a bit more difficult. At first, the Department of Defense refused to declassify the relevant documents, but, after some arm twisting, as what they called a sign of the new spirit of Russian-American cooperation, they granted me nearly complete access, although with a catch."

"And that was?"

"I had to work with an American Naval War College student and prepare a joint Russian-American report. So the War College assigned a U.S. Navy captain, John Griggs, to work with me."

Yuri then proceeded to explain how, in the course of their research, he and Griggs had discovered the system and database tapes for the Naval War College's last Global Wargame to pit NATO against the Warsaw Pact. Then, during a research trip to Russia, the two officers had ferreted out the hard copy—the printouts of the database—of the corresponding Soviet computer simulations. Excited by their finds, Griggs and Sinsukin proposed that they reconstruct the Global Wargame, circa 1989, using both Soviet and

American data. The two officers believed that the exercise would provide some indication of a how a conflict might have unfolded, and would also illustrate the different Soviet and American approaches to the art of war.

"And it all went smoothly?" Taft asked.

"Smoothly? No, not really. The whole project just kept getting bigger and bigger. And the price tag kept rising."

Yuri explained that while the Naval War College supported the idea, funding for the increasingly ambitious proposal remained a problem. Dollars were short because of budget cuts and neither of the officers involved had the computer expertise to do the job. Fortunately, the proposal gained support as it made its way up the U.S. Navy chain of command, but it also grew increasingly more elaborate. What had been a fairly straightforward, if somewhat involved student project, ultimately became a diplomatic extravaganza.

CHINFO, the U.S. Navy's office of the Chief of Information, was the first Washington organization to seize on the Griggs-Sinsukin proposal as an excellent opportunity to play up improved Russian-American relations. DOD's public affairs office followed suit. The December 1998 emergency aid package for Russia, the fourth annual "Christmas bailout," and the unofficial, but widely reported, Russian-American defense talks concerning continued instability in the Balkans, Persian Gulf, and East Asia, made a display of cooperation attractive. Then came the proposal that retired high-ranking American and Russian military personnel be invited to play themselves at Newport. When the Defense Department expanded the list of invitees to include representatives from those nations that had been allied to the United States and the former Soviet Union in the late 1980s, the scenario was nearly complete.

"Whose idea was it to invite the high-ranking civilians?" Taft asked.

"Your State Department," Yuri explained. "Afraid that the focus on conflict would send the wrong signal concerning the current direction in which Russian-American relations were heading, State suggested that the Global Wargame take place under the guise of a gathering of former military and political leaders to celebrate the tenth anniversary of the fall of the Berlin Wall and the end of the Cold War. Hence the name 'The Tenth Anniversary Game.'"

When the increasingly complicated proposal finally found its way to the desk of the President of the United States, the chief executive gave it his wholehearted support. But the White House, also, suggested further changes. The president offered to fly former Soviet President and Communist Party Chairman Mikhail Gorbachev and American President George Bush to Newport to play themselves.

"So finally everything fell into place," Yuri continued, "and for two weeks, between the seventh and twentieth of November 1999, an international group of retired military officers and former civilian policymakers gathered in Newport and fought a hypothetical Third World War. It was quite a show, very impressive. I remember overhearing one retired admiral, an American admiral, explaining to a reporter that he had come to Newport 'to fight the hot version of the Cold War, the war that never was.'"

"And that's where you got the idea for your title—'The War That Never Was?'" Taft asked.

"Yes, it just stuck in my mind."

"And what about the idea for the book?"

"Well, the contest, though only a simulation, was extremely intense. You can imagine with Bush and Gorby leading their respective teams, with rumors of nuclear release sweeping the rooms, I'll tell you, it seemed at times as if there really was a war taking place outside the walls of the Simulation Center. And then, when it all was over, and the analysts had pored over the data and had written their reports, all we had to show for the effort were a set of thick tomes, full of dry analysis, with innumerable charts and graphs, backed up by indecipherable appendices, all of which we knew would soon be dumped in file cabinets where they would likely remain for eternity.

"So, I asked myself, how could the report of such an interesting exercise turn into such incredibly boring pap? Why couldn't someone capture the intensity of the game. What might a popular writer—someone like Tom Clancy or Cornelius Ryan do with the report?"

"I know Clancy, but who was that second guy?" Taft asked.

"Cornelius Ryan," Hanson interjected. "He was a journalist turned military historian. You know, he wrote *The Longest Day*, *A Bridge Too Far. . . .*"

"Oh, yea, I've seen the movies."

"Well," Yuri returned to his point, "I thought that perhaps I could do it. I could take the report and make it come alive. Change it from a boring document into an exciting history, a history of a non-event if you will, a history of. . . ."

"A war that never was."

"Right, Ms. Taft."

"Call me Annie."

"Okay, Annie."

"And, so, what did you do next?"

"Next? I got myself an agent."

Yuri turned to Fred who smiled and said, "and when I heard Yuri's idea, I knew we had a possible best seller."

The tape on Taft's recorder popped. As she flipped the cassette, Yuri poured himself a second cup of coffee.

"Annie?"

"Sure, thanks," she responded as Yuri refilled her cup.

"Yuri, what about the copyright on this report. Doesn't the U.S. government have any control over it?"

"Good question, Annie," Fred Hanson replied, "but the answer is no. The report was never classified. And as a government document it can't be copyrighted. So anyone has the right to take it and do whatever they want with it."

"What about the American officer, whatever his name was?"

"Griggs," Yuri answered, "John Griggs. I asked him if he wanted to work with me but he's still in your navy and he can't, for reasons that I'm not sure I understand."

"You see, Annie," Hanson explained, "since Griggs is still serving, he's a Federal employee, so he can't make a profit off the work he performed as a government worker. He's covered by a variety of ethics in government acts. But Yuri, being a Russian citizen, isn't."

Taft turned to Yuri and asked the obvious question.

"Doesn't the Russian government have similar regulations?"

Yuri just smiled. "No. At least not yet."

"And besides," Hanson added, "since Yuri has resigned his commission, he wouldn't be covered in any case."

"So, Yuri, all these royalties you're earning, don't have to be shared with anyone, right?"

"Ha! I wish. I give Fred 15 percent."

"But no one else?"

"Other than the taxman, no, no one else."

Taft scribbled a few notes and then checked her way down the page of her notebook.

"Now, Yuri, some people who've read the book have wondered, since you were a naval officer, and this whole thing took place at the Naval War College, why does the book open on the ground in Germany?"

"Good question, Annie. One of the first problems we had developing the scenario for a Third World War involved how it might get started. There was quite a bit of disagreement over that, especially among the Americans. But finally we—the Russians—convinced them that it really didn't matter. However the war started, and by that I mean whatever the causes of the war might have been, the war would have begun in the same fashion—with a blitz attack in Germany."

"So what we have here is what they used to call the 'bolt from the blue?'"

"No, not exactly, Annie. There was quite a debate about the question of surprise. Just how complete would it have been? Ultimately, we compromised. We agreed with our American colleagues that the war would have probably developed out of some crisis and that as part of its usual crisis response, American forces, especially naval forces, would have had about two weeks to move to more forward positions. In return, the Americans yielded to us near-total operational and tactical surprise. If I recall, we worked on the assumption that NATO detected our movements toward the front in Germany only a few hours before the attack began."

"What about the situation elsewhere?"

"It didn't matter, Annie. You see, our military planning process was controlled by army officers and everything, everywhere, was tied to the start of the war along the inner German border. Nothing would be done at sea, in space, or anywhere else that risked compromising tactical surprise in Germany."

"And that's why the book starts in Germany?"

"Right, with Soviet mechanized forces crossing the border, with NATO troops, in fact, American troops, trying to slow that advance."

THE WAR THAT NEVER WAS

"He that commands the sea is at great liberty,
and may take as much and as little of the war
as he will. Whereas those that be strongest by land
are many times nevertheless in great straits."

FRANCIS BACON, 1597

THE WAR
THAT NEVER WAS

ONE

There was already a hint of dawn in the eastern sky. Streams of light soon would silhouette Russian armor along the horizon for the "Dragoons" of the U.S. 2d Armored Cavalry Regiment. Ordered to delay and to gauge the strength of the Soviet advance directed through the Hof Corridor, forward elements of the regiment's 2d Squadron raced toward the border.

War had come to Germany. Ten minutes earlier, at 0300, all hell had broken loose along the "trace" dividing West from East. Rockets and artillery had pounded Camp Hof—wisely evacuated by the 2/2 ACR's mission reaction team two hours earlier—and the observation post's two platoons had escaped the war's opening barrage intact, thanks to alert NATO intelligence assets that had detected the Warsaw Pact concentrations. West of Hof, a small Bavarian city nestled along the Inner-German Border (IGB), the scout platoon's M-3 Bradley fighting vehicles took up a blocking position at the intersection of the E6 and E62 autobahns, while the tank platoon, less a single M1A1 that had thrown a track, moved through Hof to take up positions north of the city along the roads from the East German towns of Gera and Plauen.

As the tanks reached the crossroads on the northern outskirts of Hof, SGT Newell Donohue knew what was coming. 1LT Jack Harradin's familiar voice suddenly came over the radio. The platoon commander announced that the tanks would split at the intersection. Harradin would lead a two-tank section along the Gera road; Donohue would have to patrol the road from Plauen solo.

Donohue fervently believed that armored cavalry regiments ought to have five-tank platoons, whatever "the organization of the rest of the damned U.S. Army." There were always multiple axes of advance to cover, and invariably one of a platoon's tanks was out of commission. Two tanks operating together were far more than twice as powerful as one.

"Off to a shitty start," Donohue remarked over the radio.

"Sorry," Harradin responded. "Button up Bravo 24. Good hunting."

Donohue lowered himself into the cupola and closed the hatch, although he preferred operating as tank commander from an open turret. A lecture given at Fort Knox by an Israeli armored warfare expert had long stuck in Donohue's mind—"a buttoned up tank loses 65 percent of its efficiency." But until it was clear whether or not the Russians were using chemicals, it was smart to keep "Battlin' Betty" airtight.

At forty-five mph the Abrams zigged and zagged through the fields alongside the road while Donohue kept a close eye on the terrain ahead through his commander's independent thermal viewer (CITV). He watched the sector from twelve o'clock to three o'clock; his gunner, PFC Rick McGill, the sector from nine o'clock to twelve o'clock.

Speed was one of the Abrams' premier defensive attributes. Inside a range of a mile, Soviet tanks could not traverse their main guns quickly enough to track an Abrams, while the M1A1's stabilized turret allowed it to fire accurately on the move. But at such speeds, an Abrams could also blunder into trouble. "Battlin' Betty," unsupported, would have no section-mate to cover a withdrawal.

As the Abrams sped northeast toward the border, Donohue noted movement in his CITV. "Rick, tank in sector right two!" Donohue centered his sight on a Russian T-80 and hit the target designator button. The tank's computer instantly began slewing the turret to starboard, bringing the gun and the gunner's sight into alignment with Donohue's CITV. "Gunner, battlesight, tank, sabot!"

"Identified!" McGill responded.

"Up!" yelled the loader, Dan Conte, as he rammed the sabot round into the breech.

"Fire and adjust!" shouted Donohue. As he began searching for the next target, he heard McGill shout "on the way" as the 120-mm Rheinmetal smoothbore gun boomed and sent a sixty-pound projectile through the air at over six thousand feet per second. Two seconds later the gunner howled, "Target! Brewed that sucker!"

Donohue had already identified and designated another T-80, then remembered to hit the contact button on his battlefield management system, an electronic display that indicated the positions of the tanks in his platoon. LT Harradin would know that Bravo 24 was engaged and perhaps could wrangle some help for the isolated Abrams.

"Target creamed!" came the call from McGill as the second Soviet tank exploded.

As Donohue scanned ahead looking for more tanks, he noticed a distant muzzle flash followed by a nearby explosion. "Back her up!" he yelled into the intercom. Driver Steve Heil soon had the tank in reverse as Donohue fired the smoke mortars to cover "Battlin' Betty's" retreat. The smoke screen would blind the Russian tanks while the M1A1's thermal sight and laser rangefinder would allow Donohue to continue the engagement.

"Gunner, identify!" Donohue screamed, spotting at least a half-dozen more tanks. "Holy shit, there's at least a company out there. Fire! Fire!" A third, fourth, and fifth T-80 were soon burning wrecks and Donohue had thoughts of maneuvering offensively to finish off the Russkis when a tremendous explosion shook the Abrams. He was thrown hard against the CITV.

Conte screamed hysterically, "I'm bleeding; I'm bleeding!"

"Damage?" Donohue yelled. The Abrams had been hit in the right rear by a missile that had blown off the track, but otherwise left the tank intact. The impact had thrown Conte against the breech. His head was split wide open. Donohue had already spotted the culprits—Soviet armored personnel carriers (BMPs) on the right flank—and ordered Heil to replace the mortally wounded loader. As the turret slewed around he fired off more smoke mortars and prepared to engage the "Bimps."

The first round clearly hit a lightly armored BMP and stopped it, but McGill noted a muzzle flash from its 30-mm cannon. "Shit, that round ripped clear through him, Newell." Donohue ordered Heil to switch to heat and McGill's second round left the Soviet BMP a flaming wreck. Two additional BMPs and a BTR-70 reconnaissance vehicle shared a similar fate before a tank round struck "Battlin' Betty's" turret.

The tank began to fill with smoke. Although he couldn't see flames, Donohue switched on the halon extinguishers and called for a damage report. The Soviet 125-mm round had failed to penetrate "Battlin' Betty's" Chobham armor, but the gun was out of commission and the turret would no longer traverse. Conte was dead. "All right," Donohue yelled, "time to book. Rick, open the escape hatch."

Four hours later, Donohue, McGill, and Heil emerged from a battered, hot-wired Mercedes Benz at the headquarters of 2/2 ACR, the Warner barracks in Bamberg. "Battlin' Betty" was a smoldering ruin but so were five Soviet T-80 tanks and four BMPs. Assigned an old M60A3 and a new loader, Donohue received congratulations on his impressive kill ratio, and warnings not to lose a second tank "because there are no more replacements."

★ ★ ★

Donohue's engagement with the advance elements of a Soviet tank battalion along the Plauen-Hof road was in many ways typical of the situation facing NATO forces along the East German and Czechoslovakian borders in the early-morning hours of 14 July. From the Baltic Sea to Austria, heavily outnumbered NATO units were destroyed where they fought or fell back under heavy pressure, but generally only after inflicting significant casualties on attacking Soviet mechanized forces.

Despite these losses, the Warsaw Pact juggernauts pressed ever westward toward the Rhine over the following days. In many sectors, Soviet operational maneuver groups (OMGs) drove deep into the allied rear and threatened to break the cohesion of the NATO line. After a week of such heavy blows, the NATO front seemed ready to collapse.

In Moscow, the initial victories along the German front, reported in spectacular if exaggerated fashion by Soviet television, fed a growing sense of excitement. Economic hardships and political disagreements were forgotten. A Swedish diplomat in the Russian capital reported that "the people seem to step with a new pride and no longer grumble while standing in their interminable queues; they speak enthusiastically of the news from the front."

The same sense of euphoria infected many senior military leaders. Chief of the General Staff Marshal Aleksei Posokhov spoke openly of "the coming victory." COL Sergei Kaganovich, an aide to Warsaw Pact CINC Marshal Vladimir Kubitskii, was caught up in a ritual of handshaking and backslapping as reports of new advances reached the headquarters of the high command of the combined forces of the Warsaw Pact. Kaganovich often found himself standing mesmerized before the situation map in the war room at Warsaw Pact headquarters.

By the end of the first week of the war, elements of the Northern Front's Second Guards Tank Army had reached the Kiel canal and the lower Weser River. Lübeck, Kiel, and Hamburg were isolated. Bremerhaven had been taken by a coup de main on 18 July. The Third Shock Army had crossed the Elbe-Side canal and established a bridgehead over the Weser between Bremen and Hanover. The Twentieth Guards Army had broken through elements of the I British and I Belgian Corps between Hanover and Kassel, had crossed the Weser at Hameln, and had driven southwest as far as Paderborn, where the Belgian 1st Mechanized Infantry Division checked the Soviet advance.

Only on the right flank of the Central Front's advance, between Kassel and Bamberg, in the sectors of the III West German and the V U.S Corps, had NATO limited Soviet advances. Further south, the First Guards Tank Army had exploded through the Hof corridor and had reached Nuremberg. Czechoslovakian and Russian divisions from the Soviet central group of forces had fought their way across the Danube at Regensberg and Passau. Warsaw Pact spearheads had captured Donauwörth and Augsburg, although they had been driven from the latter city by a prompt West German counterattack. Canadian troops had hastened forward to halt the advance of Czechoslovakian units along the upper Isar River. The Bavarian capital—Munich—was in danger of becoming surrounded.

Vindication of the Soviet concept of operational art seemed at hand, even though Warsaw Pact losses had been significantly higher than anticipated, the rate of advance—about fifteen kilometers a day—half of that expected, and West German and American forces had stalled the Pact drives in Hesse and northern Bavaria. Despite continued resistance and occasionally successful local counterattacks, NATO forces were on the verge of disintegration. The collapse of the northern and southern flanks of NATO's central front appeared imminent.

COL Kaganovich also dutifully monitored the maps that charted the progress of Soviet and Pact forces on the northern flank, in the Balkans, and in Anatolia. Red arrows, squares, and triangles marked the positions of Russian and Warsaw Pact ground and naval units. Progress on the flanks was important, for Soviet planners had not staked everything on a single throw of the die. The ultimate success of the Warsaw Pact campaign did not depend solely on a successful blitzkrieg to the Rhine.

The offensive launched on the morning of 14 July by the Warsaw Pact High Command's Northern and Central Fronts against NATO forces in Germany was the operational centerpiece of a Soviet strategy that sought to engage and defeat NATO's military forces before the alliance's full economic and manpower resources could be mobilized. Soviet leaders understood that in the initial stage of a war they would enjoy a preponderance of force. The proper strategic approach was to seek decisive results as quickly as possible while delaying Western, especially American, mobilization and deployment. There were thus two main theaters of conflict—Germany, where the principal NATO ground and air forces were deployed, and the North Atlantic, across which the United States would have to move its forces should NATO survive the initial assault.

The Soviet general staff had assigned each of the fronts operational goals consistent with this strategy. For the forces of the critically important Western Strategic Direction (TVD)—the Northern and Central Fronts deployed in the German Democratic Republic and Czechoslovakia—the primary operational objectives were to smash NATO forces and to drive to the Rhine within a fortnight. But the general staff also understood that despite its best efforts to employ its forces in line with lessons drawn from the scientific study of military history, it could not be certain of success: the offensive could falter. That being the case, the plans developed for the fronts of the Western TVD included provisions for a more extended campaign in which follow-on forces would ultimately overwhelm exhausted NATO defenders.

In the Northwestern and Atlantic TVDs the Soviets sought to gain positions from which they could interdict the sea lines of communication (SLOCs) between North America and Europe. Success on the northern flank would provide the Warsaw Pact with a second, perhaps even a third chance to destroy NATO forces on the central front by preventing American reinforcement and resupply.

Front headquarters in the Southwestern TVD had prepared

plans to seize the Turkish straits, to secure the Aegean littoral, and, in coordination with a Southern Front offensive against eastern Anatolia, to force Greece and Turkey out of the war. Unless the Islamic fundamentalist regime in Teheran invited the Soviets to send troops into Iran, the general staff had no intention of attempting a drive toward the Persian Gulf. Soviet naval forces deployed in the Indian Ocean were considered expendable. Their destruction would at least tie down American naval units.

In the Far Eastern TVD, Soviet forces prepared to wage an air and naval war in the western and central Pacific that would prevent the movement of U.S. naval assets to the Atlantic. Moscow hoped to forestall the entry into the war of South Korea and Japan, but with American bases in both nations, the ultimate involvement of those countries was thought likely.

Soviet strategic plans attached great importance to operations around the Eurasian periphery. Soviet planners did not suffer from the central front mindset that affected many Western analysts. "The West has become so enamored of our operational concepts," COL Kaganovich had concluded in one pre-war report, "that they have missed the strategic significance of the developing correlation of forces on the flanks."

Indeed, Soviet forces were not concentrated on the central front. Only the operations of the navy's Baltic Fleet had any relationship, though indirect, to the ground war in Germany. The fleet's primary mission was to support amphibious operations by the Baltic Front against Denmark, part of NATO's Northern European Command (NEC), with control of the Baltic exits to the North Sea and the Atlantic being the ultimate goal. The Northern, Black Sea, and Pacific Fleets were oriented toward support of operations around the Eurasian periphery.

Of the Soviet Union's 10,000 military aircraft, the air defense command controlled 2,200 interceptors committed to the protection of the Soviet homeland. The strategic nuclear forces commanded about 800 bombers. To the extent that these Blinders, Badgers, Backfires, and Blackjacks were committed to conventional operations during the course of the war, most found themselves playing a maritime strike role on the flanks. Soviet naval aviation (SNA) controlled another 1,700 aircraft which were likewise committed to strike and support roles on the flanks. Of the remaining 5,300 frontal aviation assets, only 2,000—38 percent (20 percent of all military aircraft)—were actually deployed on the central front.

Nor was the Soviet army concentrated in central Europe. The 63 divisions in East Germany, Poland, and Czechoslovakia represented but 30 percent of Moscow's ground strength. Of the 157 Soviet and Warsaw Pact divisions deployed in the three European TVDs, only 91—58 percent—were ranged opposite West Germany.

Given the cost of naval and air forces, the Soviet Union clearly spent considerably more for the high-tech forces deployed on its flanks than it did for the relatively low-tech forces operating on the central front. Soviet strategists understood the significance of the campaigns on the flanks to the final military defeat and political dissolution of NATO, as well as to the ultimate outcome of a potentially extended campaign on the central front.

TWO

MG Dimitrii Malygin, commander of the 76th Guards Airborne Division, smiled when one of his young officers made the thumbs-up sign. As the Il-76 Candid air transport carried the general and his staff over neutral Sweden, Malygin noted the mixed expressions on the faces of his officers. Only minutes before their drop over Bodo, Norway, a few were excited, almost exuberant. Most appeared serene, lost in thought. Several seemed petrified. Malygin wondered who would perform best—the smilers, the thinkers, or the fearful?

Malygin himself was apprehensive. His division was being dropped seven hundred kilometers behind the NATO front. The 76th Guards was to capture the airfield at Bodo, an important NATO airbase as well as a tourist center with a population of about thirty thousand, and the headquarters of Commander, North Norway (COMNON) at nearby Reitan. The Soviet paratroopers would then move inland and cut the E6 at the head of the Salt Fjord. Plans called for the Soviet Sixth Army's relief column to reach Bodo in ten days, but Malygin expected that his men would have to hold out for at least a fortnight, if not longer.

What troubled him most was that Northwest Front only had sufficient air transport to lift two battalions of the division's 234th Regiment on D day—14 July. The regiment's third battalion and most of the heavy equipment would be flown in on the fifteenth. Thereafter, two fully equipped battalions would land at Bodo each day, the transport of the entire division being completed by D + 4— 19 July—well before the American 4th Marine Expeditionary Brigade (4 MEB) could spearhead any NATO drive from the south. But what if the situation in the air deteriorated and delayed the transport of the 237th and 239th Regiments to Bodo? Unsupplied and unreinforced, Malygin was unsure how long he could hold out.

At the final commanders' conference held at Murmansk on 12 July, Malygin had made his concerns known to a surprisingly sympathetic Northwest Front commander. GEN Georgii Golikov had listened patiently as Malygin had voiced his doubts about the plan. The relief column had too far to come. There were too many mountain passes, too many bridges, too many ferrys to be seized. "Dimitrii Ivanovich," Golikov had assured his airborne commander, "I wish we could lift your entire division on the fourteenth. I have begged Moscow for more assets, but demands elsewhere leave few transports for our theater. I'm sorry. I recognize the risks involved, but only an ambitious plan offers any prospect of success."

Golikov had only been appointed to command Northwest Front on 6 July following the front's establishment the previous day by the general staff. The new high command superseded the old Arctic Detached Front, a low echelon headquarters that had lacked the authority to coordinate the operations of the strategic, air defense, naval, air force, and army assets on the northern flank. Various staff exercises and studies had demonstrated the impracticality of attempting to coordinate operations in the far north from Moscow, as had been intended. "The command should have been upgraded years before," Golikov had told Malygin at their first meeting, "but the Navy during its heyday under Gorshkov resisted a reorganization and our political leadership balked at the move, afraid it would not conform to our stated policy of 'lessened tensions' up here in the north."

Golikov understood that while the last-minute reorganization improved the Soviet control structure on the northern flank, many of the long-standing problems of coordination and cooperation remained. He was no stranger to the northern flank. He had commanded the 45th Motor Rifle Division (MRD) at Pechenga in 1978–1979 and had headed the Arctic plans division of the general staff in the early 1980s.

To Golikov, the conquest of north Norway posed more difficult strategic problems than overrunning Germany. The main line of resistance in Norway lay five hundred kilometers from the Soviet border. Only two roads—the E6 through north Norway and the E78 through Finnish Lapland—crossed the difficult Arctic landscape. The warm summer weather in the far north was a mixed blessing. The climate was more bearable, but the terrain remained as imposing. Frequent rains made off-road movement impossible, even more so than in the winter when the ground was frozen and firm. After reaching the main Norwegian defensive position, known appropriately as Fortress Norway, Russian troops would confront NATO forces entrenched in mountainous terrain along a front that stretched less than forty miles from the Lyngen Fjord to the Swedish border.

Codenamed RINOK-CAD, the Soviet plan was designed to break the Lyngen position by preventing NATO reinforcement of the Fortress region and enveloping the left flank of the Norwegian defenses. The RINOK forces included the 76th Guards Airborne Division, the Leningrad Military District's Air Assault Brigade (LAAB), and the 63d Marine Brigade. The drop of the 76th Guards at Bodo would prevent the movement of reinforcements north along the E6 from southern Norway. The LAAB would seize the airfield at Evenes and the bridge at Skanland which connected the mainland to Hinnoy Island. The five battalions of the 63d Marine Brigade would land on Hinnoy and capture the port of Harstad, link up with the air assault brigade, and mount a division-sized drive that would threaten both the port of Narvik and the airbase at Bardufoss. Soviet frontal aviation assets would attack northern Norwegian airbases, both to reduce the sortie rate of NATO interceptors and to prevent the movement of reinforcements by air into the Fortress region. The Soviet Northern Fleet, after escorting the marine brigade to Harstad, would establish at least temporary control in the northern Norwegian Sea and prevent the landing of NATO amphibious forces in north Norway.

The CAD forces included the ground component of the Soviet

invasion force—the Sixth Army's 45th and 54th MRDs. The 45th MRD would cross the Norwegian border, seize Kirkenes, and drive south along the E6. The 54th MRD would push from Kandalaska through Finnish Lapland to the E78 and drive along the Finnish Wedge into Norway. As the CAD forces approached Skibotn, where the E6 and E78 converged, Sixth Army would launch a concentric assault by the two MRDs, the marines, and the air assault brigade. Isolated and denied reinforcements, the Norwegian units would be hard pressed to defend the Fortress region whatever its inherent strengths.

Golikov had ended his 12 July commanders' conference by exhorting his subordinates to drive hard and fast. "I know that some of you think that this is a secondary theater, and that you would rather be in Germany. Believe me, if the war lasts more than two weeks, our success or failure here, up north, will prove decisive." Golikov then rose to his feet as aides entered the room and poured vodka into the glasses set before each officer. "Gentlemen," he began, purposefully avoiding the use of *comrades*, "a toast. To victory!"

★ ★ ★

Malygin's dry mouth would have welcomed another toast. He reached for his canteen, but noticed that the transport's yellow warning light was lit. He immediately unbuckled, stood up, and made his way toward the door, determined to be the first man to jump. The commander of the 76th Guards believed in leading from the front—literally. His deputy division commander and chief of staff would fly into Bodo on the 16th. As Malygin hooked his chute to the wire, he noticed that his senior political officer, new to the world of paratroopers, was right behind him. "Good, good," Malygin shouted, pounding the man on the shoulder. "When you jump you have to yell Geronimo." The door open, the light green, Malygin leaped from the Candid.

The drop was well executed. Malygin's headquarters section landed with the 1st battalion of the 234th Regiment (1/234) along the coast west of Lake Solöi and north of Bodo. By 0415 Malygin had the battalion formed up and ready to move. He was in radio communication with the 2/234 which had landed southeast of the lake between Bodo and the small town of Hopen, which lay along the road that ran from Bodo to the E6. After sending a company east along the road to cover the attacking force's rear, 2/234 was ready to move out as well.

At 0520, as the two battalions converged on Bodo, Malygin received word that his second battalion was being bombed by four Norwegian F-16s. "Where the hell is our air support?" Malygin wondered. He immediately contacted Northwest Front headquarters at Murmansk and demanded air cover, dismissing protestations from the controllers that it was difficult to provide support so far from Soviet bases in the Kola. "You dropped us here with a promise of support. Now deliver."

By 0600 both battalions were advancing again, although the 2/234 had suffered heavy casualties. About 0730, the 2d battalion reported that it was under mortar fire. Malygin held up the advance again and called for air support. At 0815 a half dozen Su-24 Fencers arrived and, misguided by the forward controllers with the 2/234, bombed and strafed Soviet positions for twenty minutes.

Enraged, Malygin decided to press south along the coast with the 1/234. Intelligence reports indicated that the garrison at Bodo was no larger than four hundred men. Assuming the reports were accurate, the Norwegian commander had overcommitted himself to the defense of the airfield's eastern approaches. A quick move from the north might well overrun Bodo.

At 0930, 1/234 reached Bodo. With fewer than eight hundred paratroopers, Malygin quickly moved through the town and seized positions from which the airfield could be brought under observation and mortar fire. To Malygin it appeared that the Norwegians were in the process of evacuating all the aircraft they could. He ordered an immediate advance and after a brief, relatively bloodless firefight, the key NATO airbase was in Soviet hands.

Throughout the afternoon, Malygin consolidated his position around Bodo. With the 2/234 battered, he decided against any immediate move east to cut the E6. That would have to wait until additional forces and some BMD troop carriers arrived on the 15th. Malygin was further disappointed to learn that while the Spetsnaz detachment assigned to his division had surprised the NATO headquarters compound of COMNON at Reitan, Norwegian LTG Torbjorn Bjol and several senior staff officers had escaped capture.

Nevertheless, Malygin was relieved, if not entirely pleased, with his success. His men had fought well and overcome difficult circumstances.

At Evenes, further north along the coast, the Soviet paradrop was a complete success. The 2d battalion of the LAAB landed on open ground about three miles northeast of Skanland. After detaching a company to seize the bridge that connected Hinnoy Island to the mainland, the battalion moved south for the assault on Evenes. The 3/LAAB landed three miles east of the airbase. One of its companies moved eastward as far as Bogen along the road toward the E6, while the remainder of the battalion marched west toward Evenes. The small garrison force—about 160 men—was quickly overrun. By noon, with the airfield secure and the bridge at Skanland firmly in Soviet hands, the air assault brigade's paratroopers began moving east in battalion force toward the E6 and Narvik.

***

As paratroopers glided to the ground at Bodo and Evenes, tanks and mechanized infantry of the 45th and 54th MRDs crossed into Norwegian and Finnish Lapland. Sixth Army commander LTG Aleksandr Berdiaev had instilled the need for speed on his two division commanders, BGs Fedor Muratov (45th MRD) and Mikhail Pisarev (54th MRD). Berdiaev had taken the two brigadier generals aside after the Murmansk conference and promised to promote instantly to major general whichever one first reached Bodo. Pisarev had joked: "We ought to be thankful for glasnost: in the old days, whoever failed to reach Bodo on schedule would get a bullet in the back of the skull!"

Despite heavy losses, Muratov's 10th Motor Rifle Regiment (MRR) bulled its way through Kirkenes on 14 July, all but destroying the Norwegian battalion-sized South Varanger Garrison. Muratov had no time to waste. Under the CAD timetable, the 45th MRD had to reach the bridge over the Tana River near Seida—seized by the airmobile 1/LAAB on the morning of the fourteenth—within forty-eight hours. At 2200 on 15 July, elements of the 45th MRD's Tank Regiment reached the bridge. Small contingents of Norwegian regulars and reservists nevertheless continued to harass traffic along the E6 between the border and the Tana River.

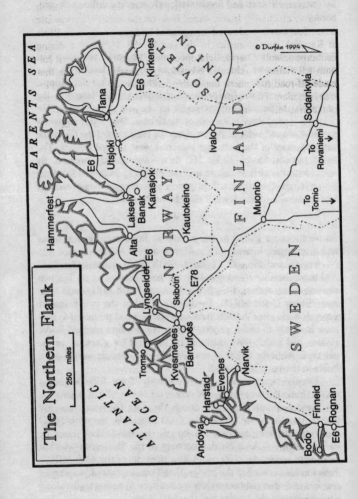

© Durfée 1994

The Northern Flank

250 miles

BARENTS SEA

SOVIET UNION

Kirkenes

E6

Tana

E6

Utsjoki

Hammerfest

Karasjok

Lakselv

Banak

Alta

Kautokeino

FINLAND

Ivalo

To Rovaniemi

To Sodankyla

Muonio

To Tornio

NORWAY

Lyngseidet

Skibotn

E6

E78

Tromso

Kvesmenes

Bardufos

ATLANTIC OCEAN

Andoya

Harstad

Evenes

Narvik

SWEDEN

Bodo

Finneid

E6

Rognan

Muratov's 61st and 253d MRRs crossed the neutral Finnish border south of Lake Inarii, seized Ivalo on the Arctic Highway late on the fourteenth, and raced for a second bridge over the Tana River at Karasjok, seized earlier in the day by the 3/253 in a daring heliborne assault. Despite light opposition, Muratov's southern column fell victim to vehicular breakdowns, marshy conditions that made off-road movement impossible, and delaying actions by Finnish irregulars. Forty-eight hours into the advance, the lead elements of the 61st MRR were still 25 kilometers from Karasjok.

The decision to violate Finnish territory had been made by Soviet planners in the late 1940s. They had recognized early on that a drive limited to a narrow front along the E6 would be stopped in its tracks.

As Golikov's troops crossed the Finnish border, Soviet diplomats in Helsinki presented the Finns with an ultimatum—acquiesce in the movement of Russian forces through Lapland, or face an invasion of the more populated southern regions of the country. With an entire Soviet corps poised along the border for a drive toward Helsinki, the Finns were expected to submit to the limited violation of their neutrality.

The Soviets did not seek a wider Scandinavian campaign. Even if Finland rejected the ultimatum, its armed forces were weak, it was vulnerable geographically, and could be dealt with quickly. The concern in the Kremlin was that such a campaign could lead to Swedish intervention. With its Scandinavian neighbors Denmark, Norway, and Finland under attack, the Swedes might feel compelled to enter the fray. Unlike Finland, Sweden could not be overrun quickly without the deployment of significant airborne and amphibious assets that were already committed elsewhere. Nor were the Soviets eager to see the Swedish navy and air force supporting NATO in the Baltic Sea.

Presented with the Soviet demand for uninterrupted passage, the Finns looked to NATO and Sweden for help. The NATO alliance could offer little but sympathy and a plea for the Finns to stand up for their rights as an independent nation. The Swedes offered no immediate assistance and preached caution. But Stockholm nevertheless lodged a formal complaint through its ambassador in Moscow, ordered the mobilization of its forces, and began moving reinforcements north.

Finnish President Veikko Honkanen held no illusions about Finland's position, existing as it did in the shadow of the Soviet colossus. But whereas his predecessors might well have given in to Moscow's demands, Honkanen was one of a new generation of leaders whose views of Russia had changed as political unrest, especially in the Baltic states, forced a rethinking of the ultimate meaning of Finnish sovereignty. Honkanen had no desire to take any actions that might provoke a full-scale invasion of his country, but he had no wish to appear as an accomplice in the invasion of neighboring Norway. He hoped to avoid his dilemma by ignoring the Soviet ultimatum. To avert a direct confrontation with the Russians, he prohibited air force activity north of latitude 66 and ordered the Lapland Jager battalion and border guard detachments to pull back toward Tornio.

To Finnish forces in Lapland, withdrawal in the face of overwhelmingly superior Soviet forces was nothing more than an order to implement accepted doctrine. To cover their retreat, Finnish units routinely destroyed bridges, felled trees, and mined roads, actions that slowed the Sixth Army's advance and enraged Russian troops. Soon, reports of massacres of captured border guards and indiscriminate shooting of civilians by Russian soldiers, began to reach the world.

Nevertheless, the Soviet advance continued. The stronger right-hand column of the 54th MRD—the 81st and 337th MRRs and 54th Tank Regiment—drove along the axis Kuolayarvi-Sodankylä-Kittila-Muonio. There, Pisarev's troops would reach the E78, which would carry them through the Finnish Wedge to the Norwegian border west of Skibotn. The left-hand column—the 118th MRR—drove along the axis Kemijärvi-Rovaniemi-Tornio, to protect the left flank of the division if the Finns attempted to move forces north to interfere with the Soviet advance.

By the night of 15 July, Pisarev's formations were deep into Lapland, although they were well behind schedule. The 81st MRR was still fifteen miles from Kittila, and the 118th MRR nearly twenty miles from Rovaniemi, to which the Finnish Jagers had retired. In his evening report to Sixth Army headquarters, Pisarev failed to mention Finnish efforts to retard the Soviet advance, attributing the delays to the continual breakdown of Soviet tanks and vehicles along narrow roads, the impossibility of off-road movement in the vast marshy areas of Lapland, and flooding caused by torrential rain on the evening of the 13 July. But the Finns knew better.

THREE

At his Murmansk headquarters on the morning of D day, GEN Golikov was satisfied with the early progress of the CAD forces in Lapland and the Norwegian county of Finnmark. "The maxim that plans rarely survive initial contact with the enemy," Golikov liked to point out, "is not foreign to the Soviet officer corps." Although the situation confronting the 76th Guards Airborne worried the Northwest Front commander, when word reached Murmansk in the early afternoon that Bodo had finally been taken and secured, Golikov immediately boarded a waiting helicopter and flew to the headquarters of the Northern Fleet at Severomorsk.

Golikov was less than fully comfortable in his role as joint commander of the northwest TVD. He controlled not only all ground forces (excepting the KGB border detachments) and frontal aviation assets, but also the bulk of the Northern Fleet. Golikov was familiar with the strengths and weaknesses of the Soviet army and air force, but most naval matters were foreign to him. He had taken all the proper joint staff courses and understood how the navy could support frontal operations in a TVD, but he did not really understand how the navy worked. He knew how far one could push troops, and for how long air crews could be expected to maintain high sortie rates. But how much was too much to ask of the naval service?

Professionally, Golikov got along well with ADM Boris Obnorsky, the Northern Fleet commander, but considered him a man overburdened by responsibilities who frequently seemed to speak a different language. Obnorsky served two masters and was saddled with three missions. His Northern Fleet had to support both Golikov, the front commander, and Marshal Pavel Goncharov, who commanded the strategic forces in the Northwest, Atlantic, and Arctic TVDs. Protecting Soviet strategic assets, such as the Northern Fleet's ballistic missile submarines (SSBNs), from NATO attack was Obnorsky's primary duty; supporting the advance into Norway was secondary. Obnorsky also bore a tertiary responsibility for control of naval operations in the Atlantic and Caribbean. In the weeks before the war, the naval staff had ordered him to reinforce the Soviet Mediterranean squadron with Northern Fleet submarines.

In the final days before the war, a troubled Golikov had watched Obnorsky concentrate the bulk of his surface striking and ASW forces in the Norwegian Sea, while he was forced to scatter his principal strength—the submarine arm. Of the Northern Fleet's 119 nuclear and diesel-powered attack and guided missile submarines, 22 were detached to protect the SSBNs, 23 were in or on their way to the Mediterranean, 5 were in the Caribbean, 6 were off the North American coast, 3 were in the south Atlantic, and 13 were operating along the North Atlantic convoy routes south of the Greenland-Iceland-United Kingdom (GIUK) Gap. With 18 submarines in the yards for repair or modernization, only 29 were available to support operations between the GIUK Gap and the Arctic.

To avoid the possible conflicts inherent in the command structure, Golikov had argued that the Northern Fleet had to seize and to maintain the initiative at sea. Obnorsky had agreed, but faced with qualitatively and quantitatively superior NATO naval forces, had remained pessimistic about the ultimate outcome of the campaign. "I will control the Norwegian Sea for the first forty-eight hours," Obnorsky had warned Golikov, "but after that, I guarantee nothing."

By the morning of 14 July, Obnorsky had nevertheless achieved a major concentration of Soviet surface forces in the northern Norwegian Sea. RADM Ivan Keistut's Surface Strike Group 1—which included the carrier *Tbilisi*, the *Kirov*-class cruiser *Kalinin*, two additional cruisers, a pair of destroyers, and the replenishment ship *Boris Chilikin*—formed the centerpiece of the Soviet naval presence about 250 miles northwest of Tromso. An additional surface strike group and an anti-submarine warfare group—together consisting of another three cruisers, five destroyers, and two frigates—brought the number of Soviet surface combatants in the Norwegian Sea to seventeen.

RADM Keistut's primary mission was to cover the movement of the amphibious force that was scheduled to land at Harstad late on 14 July. Gunfire Support Force 1—the *Slava*-class cruiser *Mar-*

THE WAR THAT NEVER WAS

shal Ustinov, an additional cruiser, and two destroyers—and Landing Force 1—five frigates, fourteen amphibious ships (carrying three thousand men and eighty-two tanks and other vehicles of the 63d Marine Brigade), eleven minesweepers, and the submarine depot ship *Ivan Kolyshkin*—were rounding the North Cape as the war began.

Only two weak NATO surface forces were within striking distance of the Soviet groups on the morning of 14 July. They caused Keistut little concern. At 0400, the Northern Fleet's air arm had successfully mined Tromso's Olavsvern naval base. Until Norwegian minesweepers and hunters cleared a channel, RADM Tor Hammer's squadron—the frigates *Narvik* and *Bergen* and sixteen missile-armed *Hauk*, *Storm*, and *Snögg* fast attack boats—were unlikely to sortie. SNA reconnaissance aircraft had located Standing Naval Force Atlantic (STANAVFORLANT or SNFL) about 250 miles southwest of Narvik. West German RADM Jürgen von Korckwitz, flying his flag in the destroyer *Lütjens*, commanded the multinational task force which included the destroyer *Iroquois* (Canadian), and the frigates *Pieter Florisz* (Netherlands), *Capodanno* (U.S.), and *Phoebe* (British). Although von Korckwitz was steaming northwards, Keistut considered the five-ship force too distant and too weak to intervene effectively.

Keistut was primarily concerned about the threat posed by NATO submarines, an uncertain number of which prowled the waters of the Barents and Norwegian seas. Northern Fleet intelligence knew that at least four Norwegian diesel boats (SSs) were operating off the coasts of Finnmark and Troms. Reports from a variety of human and technical sources regarding departures from major NATO naval bases led Obnorsky's intelligence staff to conclude that no more than six NATO nuclear attack submarines (SSNs) were in the Norwegian and Barents seas.

Despite the forced dispersal of his submarine force from the Arctic to the South Atlantic, ADM Obnorsky had concentrated more submarines than NATO in the area north of the GIUK Gap. But with two SSs detached to land Spetsnaz units on Jan Mayen and Svalbard, and six nuclear and four diesel boats patrolling the Gap, only eleven SSNs and cruise missile-armed SSGNs and two diesel boats remained to screen Soviet surface forces off the Norwegian coast. NATO had, in fact, concentrated six Norwegian diesel boats and eleven British and American SSNs in the Norwegian and Barents seas.

RADM Keistut was also concerned by reports from the Soviet intelligence ship *Bakan* which throughout the thirteenth trailed a U.S. Navy carrier task force operating between six hundred and seven hundred miles southwest of Narvik. The *Forrestal*, escorted by three cruisers (including two Aegis), two destroyers, and accompanied by the replenishment oiler *Milwaukee*, posed a potential major threat to Soviet operations.

The *Forrestal*, over three decades older than the *Tbilisi*, was nevertheless a far more effective ship. Forty of the American carrier's eighty fixed wing aircraft (and six helicopters) were capable fighters—F-14 Tomcats and F/A-18 Hornets. Another twenty were A-6E Intruders, all-weather strike aircraft. With the carrier's additional suite of E-2C Hawkeye AWACS (airborne warning and control aircraft), KA-6D tankers, EA-6B Prowler electronic support measures (ESM) aircraft, and SA-3 Viking ASW patrol planes, the *Forrestal*'s Carrier Air Wing 6 was a formidable force. The *Tbilisi* carried a dozen each of navalized Su-27 Flankers and Yak-38 Forgers, and fifteen KA-27 Helixs, several of which were modified to serve as airborne early warning platforms. But only the Flankers were effective interceptors and strike aircraft. The VTOL (vertical take off and landing) Forgers were still far inferior to NATO aircraft and were not in any way comparable to the AV-8B Harriers. And the Helixs were less effective than the Hawkeyes. With only a thousand miles separating the Soviet and American carrier task forces, and with the *Tbilisi* already operating within range of dangerous NATO ground-based aircraft, Keistut was as concerned about the air picture as he was about the subsurface situation.

Northern Fleet headquarters had closely monitored the movements of the *Forrestal* task force in the Norwegian Sea. Based on the *Bakan*'s reports, Obnorsky's fleet command post (KPF) at Severomorsk vectored two submarines—an *Oscar II*-class SSGN and a *Victor III* SSN—from positions east of Iceland into contact with the *Forrestal* task force.

At 0315 on the fourteenth, after receiving a prearranged extra low frequency radio message to begin hostilities, the Oscar fired a pair of Type-65 wake-homing torpedoes at the *Forrestal* at a range of forty-five miles. The American carrier had just completed replenishing her supply of JP-5 from the *Milwaukee* and had increased speed to thirty knots to put as much distance as possible between herself and the *Bakan*, which had a top speed of less than twenty knots. As a result, the unfortunate *Milwaukee* had fallen behind and into the carrier's wake. Both Soviet homing torpedoes struck the replenishment vessel which disappeared in a massive explosion of stores and fuel. Although damaged only moments later, the destroyer *Conolly* miraculously survived a Type-65 attack when the influence detonator on a torpedo fired by the *Victor III* exploded prematurely.

The Americans were quick to respond. The *Richard E. Byrd* directed its two 5-inch guns against the *Bakan* and turned it into a blazing hulk. A trio of the *Forrestal*'s SH-3G Sea King helicopters detected, kept at bay, and after a two-hour hunt ultimately sank the *Oscar*. The *Victor III* evaded an attack by the *John Rodgers*'s SH-60B Seahawk LAMPS III, but was driven to the south of the American task force. Doing so put her squarely in the path of the Royal Navy SSN *Talent*.

This *Trafalgar*-class nuclear attack boat had departed the 2d Submarine Squadron base at Devonport, near Plymouth, on the morning of 11 July to reinforce NATO submarines already in the Norwegian Sea. At 0306 on the fourteenth, the *Talent*, trailing its communications buoy, had received a coded VLF message—hostilities had commenced. Aware that the course of the *Forrestal* task force would shortly converge with that of the *Talent*, CAPT Alan Maunde, not eager to risk an attack by "overanxious or jumpy American ASW types," decided to slow his passage north and allow the Americans to pass.

At 0420, the *Talent* was heading northeast, course 045, at five knots, depth 300 feet, tucked in for safety beneath a strong thermal layer at 270 feet, when sonar reported a contact bearing 315. Maunde held his course, speed, and depth steady. By 0442 the sonar solution had improved. The contact was running at about fifteen to twenty knots, on a nearly perpendicular course about four miles ahead. At 0444, the *Talent*'s chief sonarman reported that the contact was a Soviet *Victor III*, holding a steady course and speed—140 at seventeen knots. The *Victor* was headed southeast at the best speed possible with its towed array sonar deployed.

Maunde immediately increased his speed to ten knots and gave the first of a series of rudder orders that would bring him onto the same course as the Russian submarine. "If he keeps up at that speed his sonar will be fairly deaf and I'll be able to pull into his baffles," an excited Maunde told his executive officer. Once into the baffles, a sonar blind-spot created by the turbulence of a submarine's propellers, Maunde could conduct a stealthy approach. By 0502 the *Talent* had achieved a good firing position with a 78 percent sonar solution. "I wish it was better," Maunde admitted, "but the Russian's pulling away." Maunde did not want to risk losing his towed array this early in the war, but he was afraid that he might lose contact if he took the time to reel it in. Maunde decided to attack. At 0504 the *Talent* fired a pair of Marconi Tigerfish torpedoes. The range was about three miles.

Even with the *Talent* in its baffles, the *Victor's* sonar was good enough to detect the sound of compressed air ejecting the British torpedoes from their tubes. Alerted, the Russian commander immediately increased speed, tearing off his towed array in the process, and fired a torpedo blindly along the bearing of the threat.

Maunde maintained a steady course and speed, still unwilling to lose his towed array or sever the wires that guided his Tigerfish. About three minutes later, the *Talent's* sonar detected the approaching torpedo, zigging and zagging, passively searching for the *Talent*. As the torpedo zigged, Maunde increased speed to fifteen knots and zagged, turning to port. The maneuver failed. The sonarman reported the torpedo homing, active. "Damn, it has us!" Maunde exclaimed.

The control room was deadly still for what seemed an eternity. Maunde at last broke the silence. "My God, boys, it's so quiet I can hear your assholes clinching." The crewmen broke into smiles, albeit strained ones. Then Maunde gave orders for a turn back to starboard, allowing the torpedo to approach from directly astern.

When sonar reported the torpedo at a thousand yards, Maunde released a noisemaker and altered course to port, hoping that the torpedo would be fooled and that the maneuver would not snap the Tigerfish's guidance wire. When sonar reported the torpedo passing astern and turning to begin a starboard search, the sense of relief was unbelievable.

Maunde ordered the helmsman to return the *Talent* to its original course. The Tigerfish fortunately were still under control and had begun to close on the target. It was now the turn of the *Victor* to maneuver to avoid destruction. The Soviet submarine released a noisemaker and turned hard to starboard. "Damn, our torpedoes have been fooled," Maunde cursed. "Not yet, captain," the sonarman answered. On the computer console he could differentiate between the noisemaker and the Soviet submarine and steered the torpedoes right to the target.

The first Tigerfish struck the *Victor* squarely amidships, starboard side, and a moment later the second British torpedo hit near the same spot. The initial explosions were followed shortly by a third. The wreckage of the *Victor* began slowly to sink toward the ocean bottom.

★ ★ ★

As the pair of Soviet submarines tangled unsuccessfully with the *Forrestal* task force, NATO submarines concentrated against Russian surface forces in the northern Norwegian Sea. A half-dozen Norwegian diesel boats were operating in the numerous fjords of the counties of Troms and Finnmark, to the south and east of the Northern Fleet's surface groups. From the southwest and west, six British and American nuclear attack submarines moved to intercept the Soviets. To the northwest, the American *Permit*-class SSN *Gato* and the British *Churchill*-class SSN *Conqueror* moved south from positions along the fringe of the Arctic ice cap.

The NATO submarine concentration was but one element of a prewar operational concept developed to crush, in a series of concentric attacks, Soviet surface forces in the Norwegian Sea. The movement of the Norwegian squadron from Tromso, STANAVFOR-LANT from Trondheim, air strikes from north Norwegian bases and from an American carrier, were expected to check any Soviet surface force that had rounded the North Cape.

But the Northern Fleet deployed far greater forces into the Norwegian Sea than NATO planners expected. The aggressive Soviet effort surprised British GEN Sir Owen Peirse, Commander-in-Chief, Allied Forces Northern Europe (CINCNORTH). After reviewing an intelligence report, Peirse admitted to an aide: "The Russians have been talking defensively for so long, I didn't really think they would come out and give us the opportunity to destroy them. I expected them to send a surface force around the North Cape, but didn't think they'd send their fleet. Frankly, I don't know that we're prepared for that."

The NATO effort was further handicapped by the mining of the approaches to Tromso's Olavsvern naval base which delayed the planned departure of RADM Hammer's squadron, and by the destruction of COMNON headquarters at Reitan. Although Bjol himself was not captured, his air and naval deputies and their staffs were. Accordingly, the coordination of the operations of the Norwegian squadron at Tromso and of Norwegian and British air squadrons based in north Norway, both of which were COMNON responsibilities, suffered throughout the first days of the war.

On the morning of 14 July, with the *Forrestal* out of range to the south and Norwegian air squadrons fighting for the survival of their bases, the task of defeating Soviet surface forces in the Norwegian Sea fell to NATO submarines.

Their attacks gained in intensity throughout the day. Off the North Cape the Norwegian diesel boats *Kunna*, *Stord*, and *Kaura* attempted to penetrate the screen of the Soviet amphibious group. A *Victor I* SSN ambushed and torpedoed the *Kunna*. A Soviet frigate drove off the *Stord*. But at 0715, the *Kaura* sank a *Ropucha*-class LST. About five hours later, she scored again, sinking a second *Ropucha*. The persistent *Stord* torpedoed the *Alligator*-class LST *Sergey Lazo*. The damaged LST, its speed reduced to seven knots, quickly fell behind as the Soviet landing force pressed on toward Hinnoy.

American attack boats had mixed success. The *Gato* ran afoul of a patrol line of Soviet SSNs established to screen the movement of Soviet ballistic missile submarines from their Kola bases to their Arctic bastions. A pair of Soviet SSNs destroyed the *Gato* after a nine-hour engagement. Further south, the American SSN *Greenling* contacted the advance ship of ASW Group 1, the southernmost of the Soviet forces in the Norwegian Sea. The old *Permit*-class submarine torpedoed but failed to sink the *Marshal Vasilevsky* before being driven off by the *Udaloy*-class destroyer's Helix helicopters.

★ ★ ★

By the afternoon of the fourteenth, NATO air reinforcements were reaching Norway. At Orland, a major NATO base near Trondheim, ground personnel worked desperately to accommodate the new arrivals—F-15 Eagles of the U.S. Air Force's 53d Tactical Fighter Squadron, Phantoms from the RAF's 43 and 111 Squadrons from Leuchlars, and Buccaneers of 12 and 208 Squadrons from Lossiemouth.

LTG Torbjorn Bjol also arrived at Orland on his way to Bardufoss to establish a new forward COMNON headquarters. Reports from the north, particularly those concerning the continued progress of the Soviet amphibious force, alarmed Bjol. Over the protests of the RAF squadron commanders, Bjol ordered the Buccaneers of 12 and 208 Squadrons to conduct an immediate strike against the Russian landing force, led and escorted by Norwegian F-16s from 338 Squadron.

Because Bjol's air deputy and staff had been captured at Reitan earlier in the day, the strike plan was marred by hasty and amateurish staff work. The presence of the *Forrestal* task force was either completely forgotten or ignored. Not surprisingly, the poorly planned attack failed. Su-27 Flankers from the *Tbilisi* intercepted the attackers and forced them to abort. The Flankers destroyed six Buccaneers. Only a single Su-27 was lost, shot down by a Norwegian Falcon.

While Bjol may have overlooked the presence of the *Forrestal* in the Norwegian Sea, ADM Obnorsky did not. By 1100, it was apparent that the two Soviet submarines trailing the American carrier had been sunk. Obnorsky, concerned by the continued northerly movement of the task force, ordered LTG Viktor Nekrasov, Commander, Naval Aviation, Northern Fleet, to attack and destroy the *Forrestal*.

At 1255, Nekrasov presented Obnorsky with a detailed plan for a two-regiment Tu-22M Backfire strike supported by Tu-16 Badger (ESM) aircraft, escorted by a regiment of long-range interceptors. Obnorsky immediately approved the plan, contingent on the allocation of fighter support. The Northern Fleet, despite its extensive aviation assets, controlled only the fighters on board the *Tbilisi*. "This is asinine," Nekrasov complained to Obnorsky.

"Whenever we need interceptors to escort our maritime strike missions, we have to go begging to Northwest Front for the strategic defense force's support. It's just ridiculous!"

The disgruntled Nekrasov next presented the plan to GEN Golikov, still at Northern Fleet headquarters. At 1325, he gave his approval but frankly told Nekrasov that the frontal aviation assets under direct command lacked the range to escort the Backfires the nearly nine hundred miles to the *Forrestal*.

Golikov instead called GEN Vasili Struve, commander of the Archangelsk Air Defense Sector, while Nekrasov listened on another line, prepared to jump in and provide technical details if necessary. But none were required. Struve was less than sympathetic, and pointed out that his regiments of long-range MiG-31s and Su-27s had spent the morning not protecting the strategically important bases in the Kola, but escorting Golikov's air transports to Bodo and Evenes. The Russian pilots were exhausted and dozens of planes were down for maintenance. Struve offered to make available what planes he could, but only if Golikov cancelled the air transport missions scheduled for the morning. This Golikov refused to do. The buildup of the 76th Guards Airborne Division could not be delayed.

When Nekrasov suggested that Golikov go over Struve's head to the general staff, the Northwest Front CINC just shook his head. Asking Moscow for help would just waste more time. Denied fighter escort, Golikov gave Obnorsky the option of cancelling the strike. The admiral looked distraught, and seemed ready to call off the attack. But then he stood up, placed his hand on Nekrasov's shoulder, and said "We go." The time was 1355.

The Backfires began to launch from Olenogorsk at 1540. To take full advantage of the speed and range of the Tu-22Ms, the plan for the strike was changed at the last moment. The subsonic Badgers were left behind and the Backfires flew a longer, more circuitous route over the Atlantic to evade detection by the Norwegian Air Defense System or the NATO AWACS flying from their forward base at Orland. Nekrasov hoped to attack from the northwest, along an unexpected axis to surprise the Americans.

Indeed, RADM Hugh Barnhart, commanding the *Forrestal* task force, had pushed his Hawkeyes and Aegis cruisers as much as 50 to 150 miles ahead of the *Forrestal* along the expected threat axis to the northeast. But the task force's left flank was covered by a U.S. Air Force E3A Sentry of the 552d Airborne Warning and Control Wing flying from Keflavik, which detected the approach of the Soviet armada—thirty-seven Backfires, preceded by a single Tu-95D Bear reconnaissance plane.

The destruction earlier in the day of the *Bakan* and the submarines trailing the *Forrestal*, placed the burden of tracking the American carrier on Soviet naval aviation's reconnaissance aircraft. The Bear's mission was to locate the *Forrestal* and provide data to the Northern Fleet KPF that would allow it to vector the Backfires to the target. The Bear's Big Bulge radar could detect large surface vessels such as the *Forrestal* at ranges up to 200 miles. While the AS-4 Kitchen air-to-surface missile carried by the Backfire had a range of 250 miles, the bomber's own Down Beat radar had an effective range of less than 175 miles, and that under ideal conditions.

While the Backfires were still over six hundred miles from the reported position of the *Forrestal*, the Bear detected heightened radar emissions and increased air activity around the carrier, including a strengthening of the CAP (combat air patrol) screen to the northwest. Nekrasov deduced that the Americans knew the strike was coming. When subsequent reports reached the KPF of radar jamming, apparently by EA-6B Prowlers from the *Forrestal*, and that the American surface ships had adopted emissions control (EMCON), Nekrasov smelled an ambush and recommended an immediate abort of the mission. The Northern Fleet's SNA commander knew that he could not afford to lose two regiments of Backfires. They were as irreplaceable to the Soviet navy as carriers were to the American navy. Obnorsky and Golikov, who had been following the progress of the attackers, agreed, but the order came too late for the crew of the Bear, destroyed by a Phoenix missile fired from a *Forrestal* Tomcat.

★ ★ ★

As the Soviet surface groups made their way south along the Norwegian coast, RADM Hammer at Tromso recognized that if his squadron remained idle much longer, the opportunity to strike the Russian amphibious ships before they disembarked their marines would pass. Throughout the morning, the *Varanger*, one of the Nor-

wegian navy's new double-hulled, air-cushioned, surface effect mi-
nehunters, the old American-built minesweepers *Sira* and *Vosso*,
and a pair of Coast Guard helicopters which towed old barges along
the channel, had worked desperately to clear a path from the Olavsvern base. Despite the fact that the channel was still judged "unsafe,"
Hammer ordered his squadron to get under way. Remarkably, no
ships were damaged. Hammer's squadron left the Malangen Fjord
and stood on a direct course for the Soviet amphibious squadron.

The Northern Fleet KPF, apprised of Hammer's departure, directed two regiments of Tu-16G Badgers to an area 300 miles west
of Tromso. As the Norwegian squadron exited the fjord, Soviet
reconnaissance aircraft tracked Hammer's ships and vectored the
Badgers into attack positions. The force of thirty-eight Badgers
launched as many as sixty AS-6 Kingfish SSMs at the Norwegian
squadron, heavily damaging the *Bergen*, and sinking the *Narvik* and
nine missile boats. Undaunted, Hammer continued his approach.
The squadron next had to run a gauntlet of escorting Russian destroyers and frigates. The damaged *Bergen* and the remaining three
missile boats were soon destroyed, but not before the *Hauk*-class
missile boat *Jo* managed to launch six Penguin Mk3 SSMs, four of
which turned the *Alligator*-class LST *Ilya Azarov* into an inferno.

LTG Bjol had reached his newly established COMNON headquarters at Bardufoss in the late afternoon only to learn of the total
destruction of Hammer's squadron. Bjol, already facing rear-area
threats from Russian *desant* (airborne) forces at Bodo and Evenes,
believed that a successful Russian amphibious landing would unhinge his entire defensive position in north Norway. He appealed to
CINCNORTH for assistance, but other than supporting Bjol's continued demands for air strikes from Orland, there was nothing
Peirse could do to remove the threat to COMNON's sea flank.

Sir Owen supported Bjol's demands that the British Bucca-
neers at Orland launch a second strike against the Soviet amphibi-
ous group. The plan called for a coordinated attack by Orland-based
Falcons and Buccaneers, supported by additional F-16s from
Bardufoss and American aircraft from the *Forrestal*'s Carrier Air
Wing 6.

Unfortunately, the second air attack, although well planned,
fared no better than the first. Shortly after 1900, the Bardufoss
Falcons, preparing to support the Orland strike, had to scramble to

intercept Soviet Badgers escorted by MiG-29 Fulcrums. The attack heavily damaged several runways and, most importantly, left no planes available to support the strike against the Russian amphibious squadron. Almost simultaneously, an American AWACS detected a large force of Soviet bombers about 1,100 miles NNW of the *Forrestal*. The Backfires were actually on their way to attack a NATO convoy west of Iceland, but their course paralleled that of the afternoon strike against the *Forrestal*. RADM Barnhart, commanding the *Forrestal* task force, diverted to CAP duties the Hornets and KA-6D tankers earmarked to support the Orland strike. Bjol nevertheless refused to cancel the attack. Flankers and Forgers from the *Tbilisi* again intercepted and drove off the British and Norwegian aircraft before they could close to within missile range of the Soviet transports. Four Buccaneers were lost as well as a pair of Norwegian Falcons. Two Forgers failed to return to the *Tbilisi*.

With the defeat of Hammer's squadron and the failure of the second strike from Orland, the only forces that could prevent a Soviet amphibious landing were those of ADM Sir Benjamin Le Q. Hill-Norton's Eastern Atlantic Command. Both Bjol and Peirse spoke directly with CINCEASTLANT and stressed the importance of the destruction of the Russian LSTs. But there was little that the three-hatted Hill-Norton could do. He was also Commander-in-Chief of the Royal Navy's Home Command, as well as Allied Commander-in-Chief Channel (CINCHAN), which left him both a subordinate and an equal of the Supreme Allied Commander Atlantic (SACLANT). In the late afternoon, STANAVFORLANT had been attacked by a regiment of Badgers. Fortunately, the strike was conducted at extreme range and of the score of missiles released, only one found a target, striking and severely damaging the German destroyer *Lütjens*. Hill-Norton had promptly given RADM von Korckwitz permission to change course and to seek protection under the CAP umbrella of the *Forrestal*.

The growing concentration of American and British nuclear attack submarines remained the sole means of destroying the Soviet amphibious squadron. Ably directed by British RADM David Livesay, Commander, Submarine Force Eastern Atlantic (COMSUBEASTLANT), the NATO SSNs sparred throughout the evening with the ships of KPUG 1, the ASW group covering both the *Tbilisi* and the amphibious squadrons. By morning, three of KPUG 1's four ships had been sunk—the cruiser *Nikolayev* and two *Udaloy*-class destroyers, the *Admiral Spiridonov* and the damaged *Marshal Vasilevsky*.

Unfortunately, the NATO successes came too late. In the early hours of 15 July, a Russian gunfire support force began bombarding the Norwegian naval base at Ramsund. At 0200 the LSTs of OV 1 approached the shore. A pair of Norwegian *Nasty*-class torpedo boats attacked from a hidden anchorage along the coast west of Harstad. The *Knurr* put two torpedoes into a *Polochny*-class LST which sank off shore, but the Norwegian boats were soon destroyed by well directed gunfire. At 0240, troops of the 63d Marine Brigade began landing on Hinnoy Island.

★ ★ ★

The commander of the 63d Brigade was MG Ivan Ganenko, a six-foot-five-inch, forty-two-year-old Ukrainian. Ganenko's somewhat unconventional, personal style of leadership was foreign to many Soviet officers. He was often heard to rail against "the military scientists who are giving us a corps of managers who don't know how to fight." LTG Berdiaev, the Sixth Army commander, considered "Vlad," as Ganenko was known to his men, "a cowboy." But the men loved him and his impact on their morale and efficiency was marked. Ganenko was a hard man to dislike.

Ganenko's reputation was legendary. In the late 1980s he had been instrumental in having the official term used to describe the Soviet Union's soldiers of the sea changed from *naval infantry* to *marines*. "That's what we are," Ganenko had argued in *Red Star*, "so that's what we should be called." He had continued to push for a reorganization of the Soviet Union's naval infantry along lines similar to the U.S. Marine Corps.

Only Ganenko's physical presence saved the Hinnoy landing from disaster. As the 63d Marines landed on either side of Harstad—elements of the 1st, 2d, and 3d battalions to the west, the 4th and 5th to the east—units were intermixed and the men were shaken by the losses suffered at sea. NATO forces had failed to prevent the landing, but en route to Hinnoy the Soviets had lost a cruiser, two destroyers, and four amphibious ships, including one of two large *Alligator*-class LSTs. A second *Alligator* had been torpedoed and, continuing on course at reduced speed with an escort of a single frigate, would be sunk at 1023 on 15 July by the Norwegian submarine *Stadt*. Of the 3,000 men and 82 vehicles embarked at Pechenga and Murmansk, only 1,800 marines, 20 tanks, 4 armored personnel carriers, 3 self-propelled artillery pieces, 7 trucks, and 2 command vehicles reached Harstad. Amid the chaos, Ganenko's personal presence was all important. Vlad was everywhere, rallying the men, getting them forward, directing fire.

Ganenko's most pressing problem was coordinating the two-pronged advance on the port area. Many of the tanks had been lost, along with most of the communications vehicles. Ganenko, who landed with the 1/63, had to relay messages to his 4th and 5th battalions through the gunfire support ships off shore, losing precious minutes.

And time was of the essence. The 63d Brigade's prime objective was to capture Harstad before the Norwegians could destroy the port. Ganenko had impressed upon everyone the importance of speed, because the supplies and heavy equipment for the marine-airborne drive on Narvik had to be unloaded at Harstad. In his instructions to Ganenko, Golikov had ruled out an air strike or shore bombardment from the gunfire support group for fear of collateral damage.

Seizing the town of 22,000 in an infantry assault proved more difficult than expected. Soviet intelligence had correctly estimated that only a single company of regulars from Brigade North garrisoned the town. But the capture of the Skanland bridge by the air assault brigade on the morning of 14 July had trapped about a thousand reservists on Hinnoy Island, mostly men due to report to units at Narvik. By the morning of 15 July, the garrison commander had concentrated nearly 1,200 men in and around Harstad.

As the marines of the 63d began to land, the Norwegians began the systematic and planned destruction of Harstad's port area. From his command post west of the town, Ganenko could see explosions across the harbor at the Norske Olje tanker facilities. Minutes later the Norske Shell fuel storage tanks went up in flames. Ganenko turned toward an aide and cursed the commanders of the 4th and 5th battalions, promising to relieve them of their commands, or worse. Although only the 1st Battalion was thus far ashore west of the town, Ganenko ordered an immediate attack. The Norske Esso tanker wharves on the western edge of the port were soon in Soviet hands, captured undamaged.

The fight now moved to the center of town and the important cranes, dry docks, and other repair facilities of the Harstad Stälindus and the Kaarbos Mechanical Works. Ganenko's marines fought from house-to-house and street-to-street—Stalingrad on a small scale. Norwegian and Russian soldiers were soon locked in a vicious struggle for a large mobile crane. Ganenko personally directed the fire of an assault gun while one of his battalion commanders led a squad of marines in a successful attack on the crane, which was then driven out of the line of fire.

By 1530 the shipyard had been captured, relatively intact, but Norwegian troops still controlled the eastern sections of the port where they completed their demolitions. Recognizing that most of what remained in enemy hands had been destroyed, Ganenko called for fire support from the *Marshal Ustinov*'s 130-mm guns. By 1700 the battle had ended. Over 750 Norwegians were taken prisoner. Soviet casualties totalled 54 killed and 292 wounded. Ganenko immediately ordered the newly appointed commander of the 5th Battalion to commandeer whatever Norwegian vehicles he needed for a drive to link up with the airborne forces. At 1940, elements of the 5/63 relieved the company of the Leningrad Front's air assault brigade at the Skanland bridge. The last of the RINOK objectives had been seized.

FOUR

▰▰▰▰▰▰▰▰▰▰▰ "They're airborne, sir." VADM Vladimir Makarov, chief of staff of the Black Sea Fleet, nodded an acknowledgement to his young aide then looked at the clock. It was 0350. Two regiments of Badgers, with an escort of Air Defense Force MiG-31 Foxhounds, had taken off from Crimean bases and were forming up over the Black Sea. In ten minutes they would enter Turkish airspace as they raced toward attack positions south of Cyprus. Their objective was an American carrier task force off the Levant coast. Nervously, Makarov grabbed a cigarette and struggled with a pack of matches. The aide produced a lighter, and a steady hand.

Makarov had been over the details of the plan a hundred times and each time he disliked it even more. The fighters had to open a corridor through Turkish air defenses for the Badgers, an operation considered problematic by the fleet air staff. And if everything went as planned, if everything went perfectly, the strike planes would still reach their intended attack positions, six hundred miles distant, a full hour after hostilities had commenced in the eastern Mediterranean.

Soviet anti-carrier doctrine called for coordinated strikes by surface groups, submarines, and land-based Soviet naval aviation forces. Badgers and Backfires would launch their air-to-surface missiles at maximum standoff range—from 100 to 250 miles. Soviet surface ships, in sensor contact with the American task force, would provide terminal guidance and direct the missiles to their targets. These surface ships, along with missile-armed Soviet submarines, would simultaneously launch attacks of their own. Combined action would thus flood American air, missile, and gun defenses, even the vaunted Aegis system, and destroy the targets.

Unfortunately, in the eastern Mediterranean combined action was impossible. The Soviet Defense Council had decided, at the recommendation of the Ministry of Defense, that the war would start at 0300 hours, central European summer time (0400 in the eastern Mediterranean). At that instant, Soviet units would cross the inner-German border, and strike aircraft would penetrate NATO airspace in an attempt to catch as much of NATO's air force on the ground as possible. While Soviet planners doubted that their assault would achieve strategic surprise, they nevertheless expected to attain operational and tactical surprise. Accordingly, the general staff ruled out any violation of NATO airspace before the offensive began in Germany. Since the Black Sea Fleet's strike aircraft based in the Crimea could not reach the eastern Mediterranean without overflying Turkey, all such raids had to be delayed until 0400 (local time). The general staff considered the prospects of an undetected passage through the NADGE, NATO's air defense ground environment radar warning system, impossible and certain to trigger a NATO alert, thus sacrificing the element of surprise not only for Soviet units in Germany but also for the naval forces in the Mediterranean.

As a result, the options for the Black Sea Fleet were few. Surface and submarine forces could delay their attacks until the arrival of the strike aircraft from the Crimea, or the forces in the eastern Mediterranean could conduct the initial attack on their own. ADM Semen Presnitski, commander-in-chief of the Black Sea Fleet, had concluded that operational and tactical surprise was more important, although, he admitted to Makarov, "the entire Soviet naval system of combined action has come unraveled before the war's even begun." Makarov agreed, commenting aloud, "what an awful way to begin a war."

The timing of the initial attack was but one of many problems confronting the staff of the Black Sea Fleet. The Soviets had five task forces in the Mediterranean, isolated from their Crimean bases until Warsaw Pact troops seized the Turkish Straits and cleared the Aegean littoral of NATO forces. The Black Sea Fleet's recent plans had not envisioned such large-scale operations. The American naval buildup of the 1980s, and the shift in Soviet thinking from nuclear to conventional war, had led Soviet planners to consider sustained naval operations with a fleet divided into mutually non-supporting parts as suicidal. Lack of bases and air cover mattered little in a nuclear war that would be concluded in hours. But in a struggle lasting weeks or months, such factors almost guaranteed defeat.

As a result, the Black Sea Fleet had scaled down its plans for naval operations in the Mediterranean. In peacetime, fewer surface vessels cruised the Middle Sea and plans called for the withdrawal of the main elements to the Black Sea in the event of a crisis leading toward war. The Black Sea Fleet planned to rely on small, expendable surface forces, Arab proxies such as Libya and Syria, air strikes from Crimean bases, and attacks by submarines to keep American nuclear-capable carriers and cruise-missile equipped surface and subsurface combatants at bay, that is, out of range of the Soviet Union proper. Only after Warsaw Pact forces had opened and secured the Straits would the fleet sortie into the Aegean and, conditions permitting, the Mediterranean.

Unfortunately, as the crisis developed, ADM Presnitski found himself forced to alter his plans and to shift significant naval forces to the Mediterranean. The Americans reinforced the Sixth Fleet in an attempt to display resolve to their allies in the region, as well as to convince Libya and Syria to remain neutral. As a result, Arab leaders in Tripoli and Damascus became less than anxious to play their assigned roles in Moscow's scheme for war. To ensure Libyan and Syrian participation, the Soviet general staff ordered the Northern and Black Sea Fleets to send additional submarines and surface ships into the Mediterranean.

By D day, twenty-five Soviet major surface combatants and seventeen diesel and nuclear submarines were in the Mediterranean. KPUG 2, built around the old helicopter-carrier *Moskva*, escorting two amphibious transports carrying over six hundred Soviet marines, had just exited the Sea of Marmara. KUG 3, the cruiser *Slava*, two destroyers, a frigate, two replenishment ships, with a small landing force, was off Tartus, Syria. KUG 2—the cruiser *Azov* and two frigates—operated from Benghazi, Libya. KUG 1—the carrier *Minsk*, battlecruiser *Kirov*, and two destroyers—was in the southern Aegean, trailed by KPUG 1, built around the *Leningrad*.

From his KPF at Sevastopol in the Crimea, ADM Presnitski directed VADM Leonid Gudkov, overall commander of the Soviet Mediterranean Squadron (SOVMEDRON) with his flag in the *Kirov*, to concentrate his surface strength in the eastern Mediterranean. The Syrian flotilla from Latakia, the *Slava* group from Tartus, and the *Minsk-Kirov* and *Leningrad* groups coming from the Aegean, now forced to operate without the support of the Black Sea Fleet's SNA assets, would engage and destroy American forces off the Levant coast and support Syria in the event of Israeli intervention. Gudkov would then move west to rendezvous with the *Azov* and *Moskva* groups, to engage NATO forces as they moved eastward from the central Mediterranean, or to retire into the Aegean to operate in conjunction with Pact ground forces as they moved south, hopefully opening the straits in the process—a task expected to be completed within a fortnight.

★ ★ ★

The U.S. Navy was similarly poorly deployed to initiate hostilities and win "the battle of the first salvo." The outbreak of war found two American carrier task forces at risk of defeat in detail.

Concern for the security of the eastern Mediterranean was the raison d'etre for an American presence that dated back to 1946. Just as long-standing was apprehension for the safety of carrier task forces operating in the eastern Mediterranean where they could be overwhelmed by Soviet air attack, or isolated from their main base at Naples in the Tyrrhenian Sea and from reinforcement through the Strait of Gibraltar. VADM Harry Turner, commander of the U.S. Sixth Fleet, hoped to begin the war with his carriers in the central Med. "I'd planned to feel, and fight, my way east," he told his staff the morning of D day, "but instead, well . . . what can I say: this is a helluva way to start a war."

The developing crisis made an American naval presence in the eastern Mediterranean necessary. Carrier Striking Group 1 deployed to "Bagel Station," an unmarked rendezvous off the coast of Israel long frequented by U.S. naval vessels. This powerful and flexible American group consisted of a carrier task force that included the *Theodore Roosevelt*, the Aegis cruisers *Shiloh* and *San Jacinto*, a third cruiser, a destroyer, a surface action group (SAG) built around the battleship *New Jersey*, and a small amphibious task force—the *Guam*, *Ponce*, and *Manitowoc*, transporting the three thousand marines of the reinforced battalion-sized 22d Marine Expeditionary Unit.

Ominous signs of Libyan involvement in the central Mediterranean led to a second concentration in the Tyrrhenian Sea. Carrier Striking Group 2 included the carrier *John F. Kennedy*, the Aegis cruisers *Cowpens* and *Yorktown*, and two destroyers. The major American amphibious force, Task Force 61—the ships *Nassau*, *Whidbey Island*, *Portland*, *Fairfax County*, *Sumter*, *Harlan County*, *Raleigh*, and *Trenton*—carried the marines of the 26th MEU, which had been held in the Mediterranean after its relief by the 22d, and a reinforced battalion of the 6th Marine Expeditionary Brigade. The remaining personnel of the brigade would be transported by air from the United States. Most of the MEB's heavy equipment and supplies were already in the Mediterranean aboard the ships of Maritime Prepositioning Ships Squadron 1, steaming east between Rota and Sigonella.

Sixth Fleet's submarine force, Task Force 69, deployed seven nuclear attack submarines in the theater: *Baltimore* and *Dace* in the eastern Mediterranean; *Memphis* and *Boston* in the central; *Philadelphia* in the western; and *Batfish* and *Trepang* at Rota.

Turner's inability to concentrate his two carriers left the *Theodore Roosevelt* dangerously exposed in the eastern Mediterranean. The *John F. Kennedy* was not poised to strike east, but to strike south against Libya which, situated as it was on the Sixth Fleet's flank, could threaten American lines of communications. To Turner, the threat of Libyan participation changed the whole strategic picture in the Mediterranean. Until the Libyan navy and air force were neutralized, the *Roosevelt* would be on its own.

The navies of the United States' Mediterranean allies also mobilized as the summer crisis deepened. In the eastern Mediterranean, the navies of Greece and Turkey monitored Soviet movements in the Aegean. NATO's Naval On Call Force, Mediterranean (NAVOCFORMED), commanded by Royal Navy RADM E. Gordon Smith-Humphreys, cruised off the northern coast of Crete to demonstrate the alliance's commitment to its eastern members. Smith-Humphreys's four destroyer group included the flagship *Exeter* (British), the *Hayler* (U.S.), the *Rommel* (West German), and the *Audace* (Italian). Further south, the small Israeli fleet prepared for potential hostilities.

In the central and western Mediterranean, the Italian navy had nearly completed its preparations for war and had already begun trailing Russian and Libyan submarines.

The French navy was at full alert status. On 13 July, the commander-in-chief of the Mediterranean fleet, VADM Jean-Claude Ricaud, had raised his flag in the aged carrier *Foch* at Toulon. Several submarines and destroyers had already deployed to the south. But the French, while still members of the North Atlantic Treaty Pact, had withdrawn their military forces from the NATO command structure decades before the current crisis. The extent to which they would choose to cooperate remained to be seen.

The same was true for Spain, which was also a NATO nation, but one whose forces remained outside the alliance command structure. Fortunately, the Spanish and American militaries had a long history of cooperation. As Spain's ships and aircraft monitored Soviet movement through the Strait of Gibraltar and in the western Mediterranean, Madrid passed the information to the appropriate NATO commands.

On the morning of 14 July, the Mediterranean was an armed lake, with the greatest concentration of naval resources anywhere on the planet. ADM Turner told his staff: "Our fleets are tightly intermixed. The process of unmixing's likely to be bloody. So hold on to your hats, because here we go."

★ ★ ★

RADM Dwight "Triple Sticks" Reece III, commander of Carrier Group 1 in the eastern Mediterranean, expected war. "I don't know why," he told an aide, "but I just know it; I can feel that this time it's gonna happen. I just pray we're ready for it." Aware that there were several Soviet task forces bearing down on him from east and west, Reece maneuvered to prevent the Russians from achieving a deadly concentration in an opening salvo.

His force was more powerful than any one of the Soviet or Syrian squadrons preparing to assail him. His SAG—the *New Jersey*, *Biddle*, *Kidd*, and *Semmes*—packed a powerful punch. But protecting both his carrier and amphibious assets was no easy task. He chose to maintain a central position throughout 13 July and to maneuver toward one of the groups as dawn neared on the 14th. "In other words," Reece told his staff, "we're surrounded."

Reece was well supplied with timely and accurate intelligence. American E-3A Sentry AWACS aircraft monitored the movement of all Soviet forces except the small squadron that slipped out of Tartus under emissions control. Israeli reconnaissance drones detected that departure and relayed the information promptly to the *Roosevelt*.

As the Soviet net began to close, Reece headed north, toward the southern coast of Cyprus, ostensibly right into a Soviet trap. But he was determined to keep the Russian squadrons from linking up, or from positioning themselves to launch simultaneous attacks on his force. At 0330, local time, he turned east, toward RADM Pyotr Ulamski's *Slava* group, the movement of which was being monitored by E-2C Hawkeyes from the *Roosevelt* and by the carrier's F/A-18 Hornets and A-6E Intruders on surface combat air patrol (SUCAP). Reece hoped to keep his distance from the two Soviet squadrons coming from the west—the *Minsk-Kirov* and *Leningrad* groups. At 0402, he learned that the offensive had begun along the IGB.

A minute later, sensors detected incoming SSMs, launched by the *Slava* group. Electronic counter-measures and defensive missiles foiled the attack. As SSMs from the first Soviet salvo detonated in the air, plunged into the sea, and passed harmlessly overhead, a second, totally uncoordinated and undirected Syrian-launched bar-

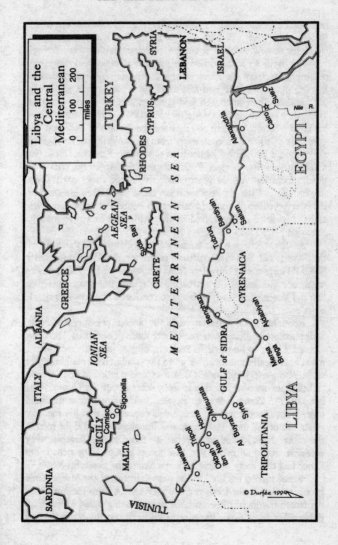

rage was on its way. Sensors promptly detected this follow-up strike. Reese's ships responded by turning off their active sensors upon which the somewhat older Soviet-built Syrian missiles were homing.

The Syrians had launched their attack at maximum range expecting ships from the *Slava* group to provide terminal guidance. But the Black Sea KPF had lost touch with the Syrians after they left Latakia. Their approach had gone undetected on the *Slava* as well. After launching his own attack, RADM Ulamski remarked to his chief of staff, "Where the hell are the Syrians?" and then ordered his ships to turn east, away from the Americans. The Syrian strike should have failed as badly as that of the Russians. Unfortunately, several Styx surface-to-surface missiles struck the *Guam* in quick succession. A massive explosion ripped the vessel apart. Over five hundred of the six-hundred-man crew, and fifteen hundred of the over seventeen hundred marines on board the amphibious assault ship were either killed in the explosion or subsequently drowned.

As the wreckage of the burning *Guam* illuminated the horizon, the Soviet and Syrian squadrons raced for the Levantine coast. SUCAP Hornets and Intruders from the *Roosevelt* fired several air-to-surface missiles at the retreating attackers, but scored no hits. Nor did Reece's SAG, which failed to conduct a SSM counterattack of its own.

Reece had good reason to resist the obvious pressure to execute an immediate retaliatory strike. "These kinds of decisions," he commented, "have to be made in seconds, almost instantly, and aren't made analytically, but intuitively." In the combat information center of the *Roosevelt*, Reece noted that everyone seemed to be in shock. "I heard the men whispering to each other about the *Guam*. 'Was it a nuke?'" Commanding an isolated task group over a thousand miles from friendly waters, Reece was concerned that his shooters might fire off all their Harpoons and Tomahawks, and if the men in the other ships looked as nervous as those in the flagship, they probably would all miss. Two task forces escaped untouched, but Reece had two more to deal with, including the powerful *Kirov*.

Reece turned his SAG to the west to intercept the *Minsk-Kirov* group, while a strike force prepared for launch from the *Roosevelt*. An Israeli flotilla of fifteen missile boats, having failed to intercept either force from Syria, likewise raced to the northwest in hope of joining the Americans in action. Altogether, a formidable concentration of allied warships bore down on VADM Gudkov's surface strike group.

At 0445 local time, a confused action began south of Cyprus as the Americans and Israelis joined battle with Gudkov's force. Again, the Soviets launched first. One SSM struck the replenishment ship *Detroit*, inflicting minor damage. The Americans focused their effort on the *Minsk*, a concentration that reflected more the American faith in aircraft carriers, whether Soviet or American, than the true capabilities of that ship compared to the battlecruiser *Kirov*. A half-dozen Harpoons smashed into the vessel, the *New Jersey* and other Tomahawk-armed American ships saving their longer-ranged missiles in the close-in fight. The Israelis launched their attack a few minutes later and five Gabriel missiles hit the *Kirov* killing Gudkov. As the crew of the heavily damaged *Minsk* struggled to contain fires, probably fuelled by unspent missile propellant, sensors detected another barrage of incoming missiles. A half-dozen Harpoons fired by the *New Jersey* struck the *Minsk*, totally devastating the ship, and forcing its abandonment. The *Minsk* sank the next day. While the surface action raged, Soviet, Syrian, Israeli, and American aircraft fought confused battles over the eastern Mediterranean. Russian and Syrian MiGs covered the movement of their task forces. Israeli F-15s, Kfirs, and F-4s escorted a strike by venerable A-4 Skyhawks against the retiring *Slava* group. American F-14 Tomcats and F/A-18 Hornets guarded a squadron of A-6E Intruders that attacked Gudkov's ill-fated squadron.

Massive "furballs" developed—raging aerial duels that ebbed and flowed over "Bagel Station." Fifteen Soviet and Syrian planes and a single American Hornet were downed. A-6Es streaked in to attack the *Kirov*. The Intruders were armed with standoff Harpoon missiles. The air defenses of the Soviet task group seemed formidable enough to rule out a more risky, if more accurate, bombing run. Effective employment of electronic countermeasures by the Soviets deflected the missiles from their intended target, but seven Harpoons struck the *Sovremenny* which was operating a blip enhancer, a device that mocks the radar return of larger vessels, totally wrecking the ship's superstructure. The destroyer sank in less than twenty-five minutes. The Israeli strike failed to penetrate Syrian-based Soviet combat air patrols that covered the withdrawal of Ulamski's squadron and that of the Syrians to Tartus and Latakia.

While the loss of the *Guam* and nearly two thousand sailors and marines was a tragedy, Reece's task group had weathered the Soviet "first salvo." The damage to the *Detroit* was minor, although the ship was slowed. The *Roosevelt* remained unscathed, despite the enormous number of Soviet missiles targeted in its direction. In return, the *Minsk* and *Sovremenny* had been sunk; the mighty *Kirov* damaged.

Most important, Reece had prevented the Soviets from concentrating their forces and had engaged them consecutively, rather than simultaneously. Ulamski, in the *Slava*, had been directed by the Black Sea KPF to continue westward after his attack and to join Gudkov, steaming eastward with the *Minsk-Kirov* group. Unable to find his way around the American task group, he had turned about to return to Tartus to reload empty missile tubes. Likewise, Gudkov's deputy commander, RADM Dimitri Penza, after assuming command in a damaged flagship of a shaken division, had been forced to turn north, nearing the coast of Cyprus, before being able to head east again. The delay placed his own squadron, as well as RADM Anatoly Filopov's *Leningrad* group beyond the effective range of Syrian-based CAP. The loss of the *Minsk*, with her squadron of Yak-38 Forgers, left these ships exposed.

The devastation of the *Minsk* squadron had other unforeseen results. At 0515 the SNA strike force of MiG-31 Foxhounds and old TU-16 Badger attack and ESM aircraft flying from the Crimea reached the eastern Mediterranean west of Cyprus. The ships of Gudkov's group which were to have vectored the strike planes to their targets—the American task group operating south of the island—were by then fleeing north under emissions control. When COL Vladimir Kirrilin, commander of the strike force, failed to contact the *Minsk*, the Black Sea KPF directed him to return to base. As the Badgers made a sweeping clockwise turn, several surface contacts appeared on their radars at a range of about ninety miles to the south. Kirrilin, who had no intention of flying all the way from the Crimea to return home empty-handed, ordered a course change preparatory to an attack. But seconds later, at least a dozen aircraft were picked up on radar. By this time the escorting MiG-31s, low on fuel, had been forced to return to base. Kirrilin ordered immediate missile release and led his strike group home.

The surface contacts were Egyptian—neutrals. The squadron of two frigates and a dozen missile boats were heading south, seeking cover from Egyptian F-16s flying from Matruh. Six of the eight missile boats and the frigate *Qena* were sunk by the unexpected Soviet attack. On his return to Saki, Kirrilin was ordered to Sevastopol where he was court-martialled and shot.

★ ★ ★

At 0710, RADM Reece dispatched a liaison team to Israel headed by Navy CAPT Roger Davis to coordinate operations in the eastern Mediterranean, especially the establishment of an American "carrier haven" off the Israeli coast. Reece recognized that Israeli cooperation would be critical to American survival off Bagel Station.

Davis found Defense Minister Lev Cobin eager and fully prepared to cooperate. The Israeli inner cabinet had met secretly on the evening of 12 July when intelligence officials had concluded that war was imminent and that Syria would probably fight as a Soviet ally. Cobin told his fellow cabinet members: "It's clear our fate is tied to that of the Americans. If they lose, we lose. We've little choice but to join the fray." By the time Davis arrived, the Israelis had an agenda worked out and were prepared to tell the Americans exactly what they could and could not do. Israeli troops had already attacked Syrian forces in Lebanon and along the Golan.

By 1130 Reece had in hand a detailed Israeli-American airspace management plan for Bagel Station. The *Roosevelt,* the Aegis cruiser *Yorktown,* the amphibious transports, and the replenishment ship *Detroit* steamed southeast for the Haifa haven and the protective umbrella of the Israeli Air Force. The SAG, commanded by CAPT Calvin Lewis, steamed north to engage Soviet forces in a surface action.

After the morning engagements, Soviet squadrons in the eastern Mediterranean sought to regroup and to replenish. The Syrian flotilla filled its empty missile tubes at Latakia. At 1405, RADM Penza, now commanding the *Kirov* force, turned and destroyed the shadowing Royal Navy frigate *Amazon.*

Lewis, in contact with the *Amazon,* was too far off to be of assistance. Nevertheless, he pressed on to the north. At 1420, the destroyer *Semmes* detected and sank a Soviet *Victor III*-class submarine, apparently covering the eastward movement of the *Lenin-*

53

grad group. By 1500, Lewis's SAG was within sensor range and in a concentrated SSM attack heavily damaged the helicopter cruiser. Fearing air attack, Lewis promptly turned back to the south.

By late afternoon, it was clear that the Americans held the initiative on the surface and in the air in the eastern Mediterranean. Throughout the morning and afternoon, aircraft from CVW 8, the *Roosevelt*'s air wing, and Israeli Phantoms and Skyhawks attacked bases in western Syria. Harpoon-armed Intruders sank a pair of Syrian missile boats in Latakia harbor. A dozen Syrian fighter-bombers and eighteen Soviet MiG-23s from the regiment at Tartus were downed or destroyed on the ground. A half-dozen Israeli and two American aircraft failed to return.

At 1930, with the air situation improving, Reese directed Lewis's SAG, which had regrouped with the *Roosevelt*, to move north to cover Israeli missile boats preparing to strike Soviet surface forces at Tartus. About seventy-five miles west of the Syrian coast, Lewis again contacted RADM Filopov's group, nursing crippled ships towards the safety of the Syrian port. A prompt Harpoon attack sank the destroyer *Sposobny* and further damaged the cruiser *Kerch*, victim of an earlier submarine attack. Minutes later, Israeli missile boats caught the *Kirov* group at anchor. Israeli SSMs struck the battered battlecruiser as its crew worked to reload missile tubes. Torn by massive explosions, the *Kirov* came to rest on the harbor bottom.

Reports of the loss of the mighty *Kirov* shocked Black Sea Fleet headquarters at Sevastopol. Presnitski heaped abuse on his commanders in the Mediterranean and ordered an immediate SNA strike against the American SAG. VADM Makarov protested: "Shit, by the time we organize the attack and the planes fly the seven hundred miles to the Syrian coast, the American and Israeli forces will be gone!" Presnitski nevertheless refused to countermand his order.

Shortly after 2200, the attack began when a lone Su-27 Flanker that somehow had managed to evade detection downed one of the *Roosevelt*'s Hawkeyes operating northwest of Reece's task group. About 2215, nineteen Flankers engaged the *Roosevelt*'s CAP Tomcats. As the outnumbered F-14s struggled to fend off the Soviet interceptors, strike planes—Badgers and Backfires—penetrated the protective CAP umbrella.

LTC Dimitrii Yazin, who commanded the lead Backfire regiment, considered the situation terribly confused. The Americans were jamming the Soviet radars and had deployed decoys and blip enhancers. Yazin knew that the Americans had only one carrier. Yet his radar picture indicated that there were multiple large targets. Yazin ordered that missiles be launched along the bearings of the contacts, hoping that the terminal guidance systems of Kitchen and Kingfish ASMs would find actual and not bogus targets.

Of the hundred-plus Soviet ASMs launched, only nine struck American ships. But those nine wrought terrible havoc. Four ASMs hit the cruiser *Biddle*; three hit the destroyer *Semmes*. Both ships sank. A single ASM struck and heavily damaged the amphibious ship *Ponce*. The *Manitowoc* was hit by an AS-4 which passed through the ship's forward funnel but failed to explode.

As the Soviet attackers flew north toward their Crimean bases, an exasperated Reece reestimated the situation. The Soviet strike aircraft had obviously overflown Turkey, again. Reece had hoped that the Turks would be able to seal off the eastern Med from air attack. Apparently they were not. Feeling exposed and isolated at Bagel Station, Reece decided to tuck his ships into the carrier haven off Haifa and adopt a more defensive stance. "If the Russians keep attacking," he told the Israelis, "I just hope they run out of planes before I run out of ships."

Reece believed he had reason to be optimistic. Reports from his pilots indicated that Soviet losses had been heavy. Seventeen Flankers and a score of Badgers and Backfires were reportedly downed. Unfortunately, these claims were exaggerated. Russian losses had totalled five Flankers, three Backfires, and four Badgers.

Reece also received direction via Sixth Fleet from the Joint Chiefs of Staff. He was to order his amphibious commander to disembark the survivors of the 22d MEU immediately at Haifa. Earlier in the day, the Soviet amphibious ship *Vilkov* had sailed from Tartus and landed a token detachment of marines in Beirut to fight alongside the Syrians. By landing American marines in Haifa, the message had read, "the US Govt will provide Israelis evidence of American commitment their security and stiffen their resolve." Reece had no problem with the directive, because he knew that the safest place for his marines was ashore.

★ ★ ★

As RADM Reece sparred throughout D day with enemy surface and air forces, allied ASW units established a protective screen around Bagel Station that Soviet and Syrian submarines failed to penetrate. At least one Russian SSN, a *Victor III*, was destroyed in the attempt, ambushed by the Israeli submarine *Gal*. When he learned of the sinking, Reece admitted to his staff that "the ASW guys, and that includes the submariners, have to keep doing a great job, because if we have to contend with subsurface, as well as the surface and air threats, we're gonna be overwhelmed."

In addition to their ASW role, allied submarines also struck at Soviet surface forces which, as they raced for Tartus, had to pass between Cyprus and the American and Israeli forces operating northwest of Haifa. In a series of attacks during the fourteenth, the SSNs *Torbay* (British), *Baltimore* and *Dace* (U.S.), and the diesel submarines *Gal* and *Rahav* (Israeli), all but destroyed RADM Filopov's *Leningrad* group as an effective fighting force. About 1600, the *Los Angeles*-class attack submarine *Baltimore* torpedoed and sank the damaged helicopter cruiser *Leningrad*. As Filopov's group continued east, the Israeli submarines *Gal* and *Rahav* sank the cruiser *Admiral Golovko*, the destroyer *Bedovy*, two missile boats, and damaged the cruiser *Kerch*. Allied losses included the *Dace*, torpedoed in the morning by a *Kilo*-class diesel submarine off the west coast of Cyprus, and the *Torbay*, the sole Royal Navy submarine in the Mediterranean, an early afternoon victim of a homing torpedo launched by one of the *Leningrad*'s Hormone ASW helicopters.

Despite the destruction of two powerful NATO SSNs, Black Sea Fleet headquarters considered the performance of the six Soviet and three Syrian submarines operating in the eastern Mediterranean disappointing. When ADM Presnitski reviewed the reports of the first day's operations at 2300, he just sat there and shook his head. "What is wrong with our submarines, Makarov?" he asked. The Black Sea Fleet's chief of staff had no answer.

★ ★ ★

In the western Mediterranean and the Atlantic approaches, the Soviets relied almost exclusively on their submarine arm to contest NATO sea control. The nearest Russian surface group was at Benghazi, steaming eastward, not westward. The intelligence ships and frigates that had monitored the movements of western ships, especially American men-of-war, had all been located and sunk by noon on D day. Soviet and Libyan aircraft based in Tripolitania and Cyrenaica were kept on the defensive by aggressive allied attacks. Crimean-based long-range SNA assets were committed to supporting operations in the Aegean and the eastern Mediterranean.

On the morning of 14 July, three Russian submarines were in the western Mediterranean and one diesel and one nuclear attack submarine were in the Atlantic, patrolling the approaches to the Straits of Gibraltar. The Soviet commanders had sailed from their Northern Fleet bases with orders to conduct offensive operations against allied warships in the vicinity at commencement of hostilities. The Black Sea Fleet KPF expected that aggressive undersea operations would prevent the concentration of NATO strike and amphibious forces in the central Mediterranean.

To counter the threat posed by the five Russian submarines, ADM William "Mike" McMichaels, Commander-in-Chief, Allied Forces Southern Europe (CINCSOUTH), in cooperation with the French and Spanish Mediterranean commanders, committed significant allied assets to an ASW effort that stretched from Cape St. Vincent to the Tyrrhenian Sea.

The Soviet submarine campaign in the western Mediterranean began promisingly enough at 0345 when a *Kilo*-class diesel boat torpedoed the French destroyer *Aconit* off the northern coast of Sardinia. The *Aconit* survived the attack and received prompt assistance from a nearby Breguet Atlantique of Maritime Patrol Squadron 24F. To avoid the determined French counterattack, the *Kilo*'s commander attempted to escape through the Strait of Bonifacio, between Sardinia and Sicily. But the passage was patrolled by the Italian diesel submarine *Guglielmo Marconi* which sank the *Kilo* with a single Whitehead A-184 wire-guided torpedo. The *Kilo* had been one of two Soviet submarines the Black Sea Fleet command had positioned to intercept the French carrier *Foch* if it sortied from Toulon. Informed by an ELF transmission that the war had begun, an *Alfa*-class nuclear attack boat, patrolling off the west coast of Corsica, began to move slowly and quietly northwest. At 1330, based on satellite intelligence, the Black Sea Fleet KPF successfully vectored the undetected *Alfa* into an attack position. Evading four

French escorts, the *Alfa* fired a pair of wire-guided torpedoes at the French carrier, only one of which hit the target. Struck on the port side, the *Foch* quickly took on a list that made flight operations impossible. Its crew fought valiantly to save the immobile carrier, expecting at any moment to be struck a second time by a Russian torpedo. After several hours work, counterflooding had corrected the problem, and the *Foch* was again underway at a reduced speed of fifteen knots.

As damage control teams worked to save the *Foch*, the French conducted ASW sweeps that located, but failed to destroy the *Alfa*. The *Alfa*, capable of submerged speeds of more than forty knots, fired a second pair of Type-65s at its pursuers, turned and raced to the northeast as French destroyers, frigates, and helicopters conducted desultory counterattacks.

The Black Sea KPF vectored the *Alfa*, now in the Tyrrhenian Sea, toward Italian warships moving south from the Alto Tirreno base at La Spezia. About 2200, Soviet sensors detected several surface contacts—ships of the Italian 3d Naval Squadron escorting amphibious transports carrying the San Marco marine regiment. In shallow water, made dangerous by the active maneuvering of the Italian escorts, the Soviet commander only hesitantly pushed his attack and failed to achieve an ideal firing position. The Italian ships were not even aware that two Type-65 torpedoes had been fired at them. The *Alfa* again sped off before the Italians were able to counterattack and headed for deeper water and safety.

For the Spanish navy, the Third World War began at 1040, when five *Descubierta*-class frigates of the 21st Squadron from Cartagena detected a *Tango*-class diesel south of Majorca. Before the Spanish could prosecute an effective attack, the Russian commander turned the tables and torpedoed and sank the *Cazadora*. The *Tango* then broke contact and headed south.

CDR Richard Sharples's American SSN *Philadelphia* had left Rota for the Aegean on the evening of 12 July. At 1100, as the *Los Angeles*-class submarine made a prearranged shallow run with her antenna extended, Sharples received a "heads up" from Commander, Submarines Mediterranean that a Spanish-Russian engagement was going on to the north. Sharples went deep and slowed to fifteen knots, extending his towed array sonar. About 1120 the *Philadelphia*'s sonar picked up a submerged contact.

But was it Soviet or Spanish? Sharples knew that at least two Spanish submarines—the *Delfin* and *Siroco*—were in the area. Operating under restrictive, if sensible, rules of engagement, he delayed his attack until his sonarmen could make a definitive identification. Sharples had some new men at the consoles, and despite the wonders of modern technology, much of what had to be done required a degree of experience that was simply lacking. No sooner had the *Philadelphia* identified the contact as Soviet and fired a Mk-48 wire-guided torpedo at the *Tango*, than sonar picked up the sound of an approaching torpedo. Nervous Spanish ASW operators in the *Vencedora* had mistakenly attacked the American submarine. The *Philadelphia* maneuvered successfully but the guide wires of the Mk-48 snapped. Sharples broke off the attack. But the persistent Spanish continued to work their original contact. Finally, at 1940, the *Infanta Elena* and *Infanta Cristina*, located, attacked, and forced the *Tango* to the surface, where it was dispatched by gunfire from the *Diana*.

At 2300 on 13 July, the Soviet intelligence ship *Zond* had reported the departure from Rota of VADM Joaquin Luis Martín-Ortega's Grupo Aeronaval Alfa—a task force that included the carrier *Principe de Asturias* and three *Santa Maria* (Perry)-class frigates. The Black Sea KPF immediately vectored two Soviet submarines that were in the Atlantic about 200 miles west of Rota—a *Foxtrot*-class diesel, and a nuclear-powered *Charlie II*—into positions for attacks on the Spanish force.

Throughout the morning of 14 July, VADM Martín-Ortega's group, supported by Spanish and American P-3 Orions and British Nimrods, patrolled the approaches to the Strait of Gibraltar to prevent the expected movement of Soviet submarines into the Mediterranean. At 1330, a British Nimrod from Gibraltar located what it believed to be a Soviet submarine. Based on the Nimrod's report, Martín-Ortega immediately launched a half-dozen Sea King and Sea Hawk helicopters. On reaching the area of the reported detection, the Spanish helos began dropping patterns of sonobuoys. Between 1440 and 1850, contacts were frequent but intermittent, as relays of Spanish helicopters worked the area. At 1945, one of the Sea Kings attained a good contact and dropped a Mk-46 torpedo. Ten minutes later, the *Foxtrot* broke the surface, its crew abandoning ship.

The second Soviet submarine, a *Charlie II* commanded by

CAPT Alexis Kizevetter, survived a day of harassment at the hands of American P-3C Orions. Kizevetter headed south as night fell, hoping to gain a brief respite. Shortly after 2200, his sonar revealed a high-speed surface contact bearing down on the *Charlie* from the northeast. Kizevetter assumed that the contact was a Spanish frigate, detached from the Rota squadron. He fired a pair of ET-80A torpedoes, both of which fortunately missed their target—the Moroccan frigate *Lieutenant Colonel Errhamani*. When word of a Moroccan diplomatic protest reached Black Sea Fleet headquarters in Sevastopol at 2330, the staff responded glibly, given the likely impact of Moroccan intervention. But ADM Presnitski was not amused. Of the five Russian submarines in the western Mediterranean and off Gibraltar, three had been sunk. "And what have we gained for these losses?" Presnitski, his voice booming, asked his staff. "I'll tell you what we've gained: shit! Nothing but shit! We've sunk two stinking frigates and nearly brought a neutral into the war. And you fools laugh?"

As Soviet and Syrian forces battled the Americans and Israelis in the eastern Mediterranean, RADM Arkadi Filiminov's KPUG 2 initiated operations to secure the Aegean. At dawn, the *Alligator*-class amphibious transports *Donetsky Shakhter* and *Aleksandr Tortsev* began landing six hundred Soviet marines on the St. Barbara beach at Myrina, a small port on the west coast of Limnos. Overhead, specially modified army attack helicopters flying from the *Moskva* supported the invasion as the guns of the cruiser *Ochakov* pounded the old Genoese fort that overlooked the harbor. By noon, the island at the entrance to the Turkish Straits was in Soviet hands.

At 1220, the Black Sea Fleet KPF directed Filiminov to steam south to engage and destroy Turkish forces in the northern and central Aegean while Soviet submarines kept the Greek navy and NAVOCFORMED at bay. ADM Presnitski was also anxious to cover a small force of two frigates and a tanker. Originally part of the *Leningrad* group, the tanker carried fuel for the SOVMEDRON but, plagued by engine trouble, had been left behind by RADM Filopov in his haste to reach the eastern Mediterranean. The three vessels had anchored off Samos during the 13th, technicians had repaired the problem, and the ships were now heading north. Eager to secure what could become a very valuable supply of naval fuel, Filiminov left four fast attack boats at Limnos to protect the LSTs and the cargo transport *Onda* and raced south with two cruisers, four destroyers, and a frigate.

But the Turks struck first. At 1345 a S-2E Tracker patrol plane located the small Russian force northwest of Samos. Twenty minutes later, seven F-100 Super Sabres of 111 Filo (Squadron) flying from Eskisehir sank the frigates *Rezky* and *Rubin* and the tanker *Kola*. Further north, the Turkish submarine *Cerbe* penetrated Filiminov's ASW group west of Lesbos and at 1430 torpedoed the cruiser *Ochakov*. The *Cerbe* avoided detection, penetrated deeper into the Soviet formation, and at 1545 fired four torpedoes at the *Moskva*. Three missed but the fourth struck the destroyer *Admiral Zakorov*. According to Soviet accounts, the commander of the *Zakorov* ran his ship into the torpedo's path to save the helicopter cruiser.

Under cover of these attacks, Turkish naval forces at Izmir escaped to the south. VADM Yuksel Sancar's squadron—the *Anittepe*, *Adatepe*, and *Gayret* (all late 1940s' vintage American-built destroyers), the frigates *Yavuz* and *Gemlik*, four *Dogan*-class fast attack boats, and three minesweepers—was too weak to challenge the *Moskva* group (the *Anittepe* mounted only guns). Sancar hoped to join RADM Smith-Humphreys off Crete.

Stung by the Turkish attacks, Soviet forces struck back. Hormone helicopters from the *Moskva* located and sank the *Cerbe*. A regiment of Crimean-based Badgers attacked VADM Sancar's squadron, sinking three fast attack boats, the minesweeper *Seymen*, and the old *Gayret*. But RADM Filiminov's KPUG, operating under the direction of the Black Sea KPF, inexplicably failed to contact the Turkish squadron which escaped to the south and ultimately rendezvoused with NAVOCFORMED off Crete on the morning of the fifteenth. Nor could the KPF vector Soviet submarines in the southern Aegean into positions to intercept the retiring Turkish squadron, although a *Tango*-class diesel boat stumbled across the Greek minesweeper *Dafni*, which it torpedoed and sank. By the end of D day, the Soviets controlled the northern and central Aegean, but had failed to bring the bulk of the Greek and Turkish navies to battle.

Nor had Russian submarines succeeded in preventing the movement of NATO reinforcements into the Aegean. A *Foxtrot* had torpedoed and sunk the Turkish submarine *Yilderay*, but not before the Type-209 boat had itself ambushed a *Charlie I* which the Black Sea KPF had stationed off the eastern end of Crete. Two Greek submarines evaded detection by Soviet submarines patrolling between Greece and Crete and entered the Aegean from the Adriatic to join the pair already operating southeast of Athens. At 2200, the American SSN *Memphis* passed Cape Spatha. By the morning of 15 July, a half-dozen NATO submarines, a small Greek squadron, and a reinforced NAVOCFOR-MED were operating in the southern Aegean.

On the *Moskva*, RADM Filiminov and his staff debated the sanity of the instructions that continued to emanate from the KPF in the Crimea. The ASW group's six ships, two of which were damaged, were too weak to clear the Aegean through offensive action against NATO naval forces. Far from being in an advantageous position, Filiminov's KPUG was trapped, surrounded by NATO controlled coasts to the north, west, and east, and by powerful NATO surface and subsurface forces to the south.

At 0035, Filiminov contacted Black Sea Fleet headquarters and asked for an estimate: when would the Turkish straits be in Warsaw Pact hands? Filiminov already knew the answer—ten days. The admiral then ordered that a message be sent to the KPF recommending that offensive surface operations be halted in the Aegean. VADM Makarov received the communication and informed Filiminov that headquarters staff had already reached the same conclusion and was shaping a new strategy for both the Aegean and the eastern Mediterranean.

Filiminov read the response and smiled. Then he asked for a folder of message traffic regarding the operations of the Soviet forces off Syria. As he read the reports and it became evident that no relief could be expected from that quarter, the admiral suffered a total loss of resolve.

As Filiminov left the bridge, he turned to CAPT Kamensky. "We Russian officers," he said, "must always maintain our sense of the tragic. You know the old French proverb, 'If you wish to learn to pray, embark on the sea.'" Filiminov then retired to his cabin and committed suicide. Kamensky later found Filiminov's service revolver in his right hand; a small cross in his left.

FIVE

At 0325 the report of RADM Filiminov's suicide reached Black Sea Fleet headquarters at Sevastopol. Makarov, who knew that Filiminov had been Presnitski's chief of staff when he commanded the *Kirov*, personally carried the message to the admiral. As the fleet commander read the communication his eyes moistened. "This is as bad as losing another cruiser, Makarov, such a waste. The admiral was a good man." Presnitski began to pack the pipe that he often smoked when he was troubled. "We must open the straits, or we'll lose all our ships before this is over."

Jumping suddenly to his feet, Presnitski grabbed a passing aide and asked for the dispatches from Southwest Front headquarters. When the young officer returned with a binder, Presnitski quickly leafed through the papers. "Good, very good, operations are ahead of schedule." Presnitski looked up and smiled, but all around him he saw only the somber faces of his staff. "Makarov," he said, "I would wager you that there are many smiles at Vinnitsa."

★ ★ ★

At Vinnitsa, the Ukrainian headquarters of the Warsaw Pact Southwest Front, COL GEN Gagik Kambarov and his staff were in fact astonished by the first day's successes. "Almost everything has gone perfectly," Kambarov wrote in his diary. The 103d Guards Airborne Division had landed in good order near Kandira, a town about sixty-five miles east of Istanbul. Turkish air opposition to the drop had been light and the units of the division had already captured all but one of their D day objectives. To the west, the Bulgarian offensive toward the Aegean and the straits had made rapid and surprising progress.

At 0400, units of the Bulgarian Second Army crossed the Rodopi range along the Bulgarian-Greek border and broke through the NATO frontier defenses. The Greek 11th Infantry Division halted the attack of the Bulgarian 17th MRD before Xanthi, which left the Greeks with a bridgehead over the Nestos. But by noon, elements of the 2d MRD were in Komotini, cutting the E55—the east-west road that connected Greek and Turkish forces. By nightfall, Bulgarian troops had reached the Aegean coast. Over 30,000 Greeks were cut off.

The Bulgarian Third Army launched a converging attack from the north and the west toward the crossroads of Babaeski where the E95 and the E5N—the main highway from the Bulgarian border through Edirne to Istanbul—converged. Throughout the morning, the Turks held their positions along the Meric River and the high ground of the Yildiz Daglari. But in the early afternoon, repeated airstrikes by Warsaw Pact ground support aircraft broke the back of the Turkish resistance. By midnight, the Bulgarian 3d MRD, supported by the 13th Tank Brigade, had taken Babaeski. The Turkish defenses in Thrace began to collapse.

The speed of the Bulgarian advance surprised Kambarov. The Southwest Front commander had grave reservations about the ultimate success of the campaign. Compared to central Europe, avenues of advance in Greece and Turkey were limited by the rugged terrain. European Turkey was like a funnel, with Istanbul at the narrow end less than thirty miles wide. At the Catalca position, forty miles west of Istanbul, lakes and coastal inlets reduced the front to about fifteen miles. The Greek-Bulgarian frontier was long, but its left rested on the Yugoslav border and the mountains of northern Macedonia. The Greeks had two excellent defensive positions in their rear—the 150-mile-long "Metaxas Line" dating from 1940 which ran along the Nestos River to the Aegean, and a 65-mile-long, more defensible line along the Sturma River to the south.

Fortunately for Kambarov, political considerations led both the Greeks and the Turks to keep their forces forward, along the border. Ever since the Greek army's redeployment following the Cyprus crisis of 1974, it had been positioned primarily to stop a Turkish drive from the east, not a Bulgarian drive from the north. Kambarov viewed the Turkish commitment to "forward defense" and the Greek preoccupation with the "threat from the east" as an opportunity. "If we can strike hard and fast and destroy Greek and Turkish forces along the frontier," Kambarov had told his staff, "and prevent them from withdrawing behind the Nestos and into the defenses of Istanbul, we have an excellent chance of securing a rapid victory." At Vinnitsa in the early hours of 15 July, that victory appeared to be at hand.

The Bulgarian successes of the first day had done much to equal the odds, for Kambarov's forces were outnumbered on the ground and in the air. The Greek and Turkish air forces controlled over eight hundred combat aircraft, the Romanian and Bulgarian only six hundred. Although often considered weak on defense issues, among NATO's sixteen nations in percentage of population under arms, the Greeks (5.9 percent) were second only to the Norwegians (7.7 percent). The Turks were fourth (3 percent). The Greek army consisted of fourteen divisions and seven brigades, plus the usual assortment of supporting troops. Turkey, with a population of eighty million, fielded a much larger army—sixteen divisions and twenty-four brigades—although only ten and fourteen respectively were available for operations in Thrace and western Anatolia. Other units were deployed in Cyprus and in eastern Anatolia along the borders with Syria, Iraq, Iran, and the Soviet Union. The Bulgarian army consisted of eight motor rifle divisions, of which three were cadres, and five independent tank brigades. The Romanian army, which would form the second echelon of the attacking force, consisted of two tank divisions, eight motor rifle divisions, and three mountain brigades. Only half of the Romanian divisions were fully mobilized as the war began.

The Soviet assets of Southwest Front were substantial, but few were available to support initial operations. Kambarov was fond of pointing out to anyone visiting his headquarters that, of all of the front commanders responsible for operations against NATO, only he had to rely primarily on non-Soviet forces. No Russian units were stationed in Bulgaria or Romania. The divisions of the Southwest Front's tank reserve and the Odessa and Carpathian military districts were hundreds of miles from the straits. The understrength category II and III formations would take weeks to mobilize and reach the front, by which time the war, if all went according to plan, would be over. The only units available to assist the Bulgarian-Romanian drive to the south were the Soviet 103d Guards Airborne Division, the Black Sea Fleet's marine brigade, and a pair of air assault brigades. Southwest Front also controlled over five hundred combat aircraft which, once the war began, would stage to forward bases in the Balkans. The SNA assets of the Black Sea Fleet—over two hundred aircraft of which half, however, were helicopters—would also be available to support operations.

One of Kambarov's most difficult tasks was combatting the widespread belief among his Soviet units that the war would be decided in Germany before they could reach the front. He stressed the importance of the Southwest Front's operations. Greece and Turkey were NATO members and had to be defeated. The Turkish straits had to be seized and opened for the divided Black Sea Fleet to survive. "And who among you," Kambarov asked his officers at staff meetings, "does not wish to be known as one of the 'conquerors of the straits'? Let us succeed where the Tsars failed; let us throw the Turk out of Europe and ensure that *if* we fail in Germany and the war continues, here in the south we will have smashed our enemies and secured other opportunities for victory."

An effective conquest of the Turkish Straits—one that would allow the passage of the fleet from the Black Sea into the Aegean—necessitated the control of both shores of a 200-mile-long waterway running along a northeast-southwest axis. At the Black Sea end, the Bosporus separated Istanbul from its suburb of Uskadar. The Dardanelles of World War I fame was at the Aegean end. In between lay the Sea of Marmara.

The Southwest Front's plan of operations sought the rapid destruction of NATO forces in Thrace and the early seizure of the Bosporus. To Kambarov, seizing the latter was much like capturing a bridge—best done from both ends at once. Accordingly, he supported an ambitious plan for airborne and amphibious operations on the Asiatic side of the Bosporus. ADM Presnitski and his staff balked, arguing that the Black Sea coast of Asiatic Turkey was unsuited for an amphibious landing and that inadequate port capacity would hinder a buildup of a beachhead. But Kambarov envisioned an airborne assault on D day that would capture the ports and thus make an opposed amphibious landing unnecessary. Additional supplies would be delivered by air. A successful division-sized airborne operation reinforced by the Black Sea marine brigade would prevent the movement of the Turkish Second Army toward Istanbul and, in conjunction with the Bulgarian-Romanian offensive in Thrace, would lead to the rapid dissolution of Turkish defenses. With the Bosporus open, Southwest Front would stage airborne, airmobile, and amphibious operations along the coast of the Sea of Marmara to support the movement of Romanian and ultimately Soviet forces in their drive to control the southern shore.

★ ★ ★

At dawn on 14 July, MG Denis Panferov's 103d Guard Airborne Division began landing west of the Sakarya River. By noon, paratroopers had captured Kandira and the small ports of Karasu and Kefken, at which the Black Sea marine brigade was to land the following day. With his left resting firmly along the Sakarya, Panferov directed separate columns toward Uskadar, Izmit, and Adapazari.

After securing Kandira, the 393d Guards Airborne Regiment pushed east along Route 25, paralleling the Black Sea coast. By 2030 when the drive halted, the paratroopers had advanced nearly twenty miles in the face of increasing resistance including, late in the evening, elements of the Turkish 2d Infantry Division.

At 1300, the battalions of the 583d Guards Airborne Regiment began their drive along the thirty-four kilometers of road that ran southwest from Kandira to Izmit—Panferov's primary D day objective. The capture of the town of 150,000, along with Kandira, would sever all the roads between Anatolia and Istanbul. The Turkish 39th Infantry Regiment slowed, but could not halt the paratroopers' advance. By midnight the 583d Guards were fighting in the town and by dawn on the fifteenth, the roads through Izmit, including the E5, were either cut or under Soviet fire. Nevertheless, Turkish resistance continued and the paratroopers began a slow, bloody, house-to-house contest to clear the town.

After securing Karasu and the left flank of the airhead along the Sakarya River with one battalion, COL Boris Latunov led the remaining two battalions of the 688th Guards Airborne Regiment south along the road to Adapazari. Elements of the Turkish 39th Infantry Regiment delayed the Russian advance throughout the afternoon. But at 1730, a Soviet battalion-sized maneuver group in BMD airborne assault APCs smashed their way through the Turkish defenses and sped along the road toward Adapazari. Outside of the town, two companies of the Turkish 5th Tank Brigade lay hull-down in ambush. The eight American-made M-48A5 tanks shot up sixteen of the twenty attacking BMDs. Only two Turkish tanks were lost, victims of Spigot ATGMs.

Despite the repulse at Adapazari, Southwest Front headquarters considered Panferov's D day operations successful. Izmit, the

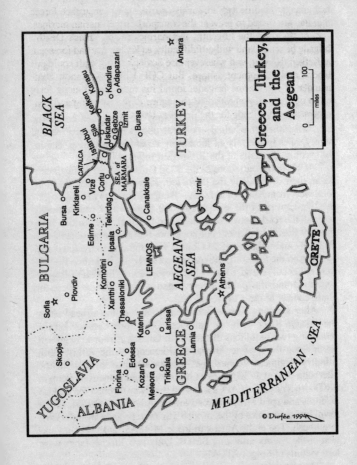

primary objective, was in Soviet hands. Black Sea ports and beaches had been secured. The Soviet fleet and the small Bulgarian Navy had engaged and destroyed Turkish surface and subsurface forces that had attempted to prevent the transport of the Russian marines.

At 0630 on the fifteenth, the marines of the "Black Death" brigade began to land without difficulty, as Kambarov had foreseen, at Kefken, Karasu, and wherever else Soviet landing craft could put troops and equipment ashore. But COL Villem Kirsanov, commander of the marine brigade, found his men spread along forty miles of coast. Kirsanov spent the entire day regrouping and concentrating the brigade for the drive on Uskadar.

Panferov's 393d Guards Airborne Regiment, minus a battalion ordered to reinforce the attack on Adapazari, spent the fifteenth on the defensive, fending off local Turkish probes. The 583d Guards Airborne Regiment continued its efforts to clear Izmit of Turkish troops and, at Panferov's order, sent a battalion east along the E5 toward Adapazari. This intended enfilading movement was itself taken in the flank when the Turkish 11th Infantry Brigade pushed north into the gap between Izmit and Adapazari. Still unsupported, COL Latunov's 688th Guards Airborne Regiment continued its drive on the town, but without success.

At his headquarters in Kandira, MG Panferov grew concerned by Latunov's inability to capture Adapazari. Turkish control of the town unhinged the left flank of the airhead. Around noon on the sixteenth, as Panferov fed additional battalions into the battle, he went forward to join Latunov at his command post. But the division commander's presence made little difference. Turkish resistance stiffened. Monitored Turkish radio transmissions indicated that additional formations had reached the front, including elements of the 16th and 20th Mechanized Brigades and the 6th Infantry Division. Five airborne battalions could hardly be expected to wrest the town from such forces. Nevertheless, Panferov ordered the attacks to continue. Only through offensive action could the larger Turkish forces be kept off balance. Panferov was determined to maintain the initiative for a few more days, by which time the Bosporus would be taken.

On the 103d's right flank, the marines began their drive west at noon on the sixteenth. Well supported by SNA Su-17 Fitter ground-attack aircraft, Kirsanov's men drove along Route 20 and the E5 toward Sile and Gebze, scattering the Turkish defenders and capturing both towns by nightfall. The advance continued the following morning and at 1830 the left-hand column of three battalions reached Kartal on the E5, less than fifteen miles from Uskadar. From the high ground northeast of town, Kirsanov could see the Bosporus.

The marine commander's splendid observation was interrupted when an aide handed him a dispatch from Panferov, to whom Kirsanov was subordinate. The marines would attack toward Uskadar at 0630 the next day, 18 July, a movement timed to coincide with the commencement of the Romanian army's offensive against the Catalca position. Kirsanov, who had intended to continue his advance the following morning, was nevertheless surprised that the Romanians were already in position to begin their attack. Southwest Front's plan of operations had not envisioned a direct attack on Istanbul before D + 9. Kirsanov jogged to his communication vehicle and put in a call to Panferov, who, as senior commander, was in direct contact with Front headquarters. Kirsanov learned that the campaign in Thrace had proceeded with such speed that the timetable had been advanced. Word had reached Panferov that Kambarov had ordered Warsaw Pact minecountermeasure vessels to prepare for operations in the straits. Kirsanov was determined that his marines would be the first to reach the Bosporus.

★ ★ ★

The Bulgarian Third Army reached the Sea of Marmara at Silivri, near the junction of the E5N and the E55, late in the evening of the fifteenth. At 0430 on the sixteenth, Southwest Front ordered the Romanian army to open its offensive toward Istanbul and directed the Bulgarian Second and Third armies to round up the Greek and Turkish troops pocketed in Thrace. A Greek infantry division, one infantry brigade, and two tank brigades were cut off west of the Meric. The collapse of the Turkish First Army had left one mechanized and four infantry divisions, and two tank brigades isolated in pockets north and south of the E55. Fortunately for NATO, the Turkish 3d Mechanized and the 33d Infantry Divisions had fought their way back into the Catalca position relatively intact.

The rapid collapse of his First Army before Istanbul dismayed Turkish GEN Vural Ersari, Commander, Allied Land Forces Southeastern Europe (COMLANDSOUTHEAST). The potential surrender of over a hundred thousand NATO troops, of whom seventy thousand were Turks, could shake the Alliance, but most certainly would be a stain on the national honor of the Turkish people. But Ersari believed that prompt, coordinated counterattacks could lead to the relief of most of the surrounded forces. "After all," he reasoned, "there are only a hundred thousand men in the entire Bulgarian army."

At Ersari's direction, the staff at LANDSOUTHEAST labored throughout the night of 15-16 July to draw up a plan for the rescue of at least some of the isolated formations. The relief of the small Turkish pocket south of Vize, given the movement of an entire Romanian army along Route 20, was considered impossible. But the larger Turkish pocket, isolated south of Babaeski, and the Greek pocket, west of the Meric, could, the planners believed, join forces and fight their way into the Gallipoli peninsula. LANDSOUTHEAST's plan consisted of three phases: the Greek forces coming from the west, and the Turkish from the east, would retake the bridge over the Meric at Ipsala; Turkish forces would cover the movement of the Greeks over the river; both forces would then retreat south along Route 6 into the peninsula.

Unfortunately, Ersari had no authority to order the Greeks, who had withdrawn from the NATO military command in August 1974, to cooperate. The Hellenic commander in the northeast, MG Constantine Patras, had a plan of his own which called for the trapped Greeks to attack to the west, while a relief force led by the 20th Armored Division drove east from Xanthi. Despite the intercession of Italian GEN Luigi Gasperis, Commander, Allied Land Forces Southern Europe (COMLANDSOUTH), the Greeks refused to coordinate their operations with the Turks. As a result, both relief efforts failed and a hundred thousand allied soldiers were doomed to march hundreds of miles along hot, dusty, Balkan roads to miserable, unsheltered, and soon to be disease-ridden prisoner-of-war pens in southern Bulgaria.

As the Bulgarian Third Army wheeled to the right, the Romanians took up the attack toward Istanbul, launching thrusts along Route 20 and the E5N. By the evening of 16 July, the Romanians had reached the Catalca line in the north, opposite Lake Derkos, where the attack came to a halt for the night, twenty miles from

Istanbul. On the morning of the seventeenth, the southern column reached Buyukcekmece along the E5N. The Romanians had closed up to the Catalca position along its entire length. The assault—the final drive for Istanbul—would begin the next morning.

SIX

At 0100 on 14 July, the American cruiser *Belknap* left Naples harbor. Aboard was VADM Harry Turner, Commander, United States Sixth Fleet (COMSIXTHFLT). The *Belknap* raced to the southwest at 30 knots. Turner intended to rendezvous with RADM John "Rug" Byrnes's Carrier Striking Group 2, which included the *John F. Kennedy*, off the northern coast of Sicily before dawn. "Intelligence reports seem to indicate," Turner told his staff, "that we're about to go to war."

But with whom and against whom? For days, Turner had reviewed the situation in the Mediterranean. "What we will do," Turner had concluded, "depends very much on how things shake out in the Med." Would Syria fight alongside the Soviets? Would Israel and Egypt come to the aid of the United States? And, perhaps most importantly, what course would Muammar al-Qaddafi, the Libyan leader, pursue? Libya's entry into the war would provide the Soviets with naval and airbases in the strategically important central Mediterranean.

As the war clouds gathered in June and July, the governments of the United States, Italy, France, and Egypt pressured the Libyans, diplomatically and with displays of military power, to remain neutral. The United States maintained the powerful *Kennedy* task group and an amphibious task force in the Tyrrhenian Sea. On Sicily, VMF/A-211, twelve F/A-18 Hornets, flew into Sigonella and two squadrons of air force F-16 Falcons of the 401st Fighter Wing arrived at Comiso. The Italians reinforced VADM Carlo Donello's 1st Naval Division, which included the light aircraft carrier *Giuseppe Garibaldi*, at Taranto. The French hastened the repair of the carrier *Foch* which had returned in mid-June from a lengthy Indian

Ocean deployment. The Egyptians, acting in concert with Morocco, Algeria, and Tunisia, suggested that the Libyans join a proposed North African league of neutrality.

These efforts to deter Libyan entry into a possible war appeared to have some effect. Despite the ongoing mobilization of forces throughout the Mediterranean basin, the Libyan military remained on its normal peacetime footing. To Turner in Naples it appeared that the "Libyan madman" had no intention of providing the allies with an excuse to attack. But Qaddafi's reluctance to place his military on a war footing irked Soviet leaders in the Kremlin, who had thus far relied on a crisis atmosphere to prompt mobilization by their allies-to-be.

At 2207 on 12 July, GEN Sergei Gloriozov, special representative of the Soviet general staff, arrived at Okbah ibn Nafi airbase, outside Tripoli. The Soviet ambassador to Libya had already arranged a meeting between the Russian general and the Libyan leader at 0700 the next morning.

At 0400, an aide woke Gloriozov: a plane was waiting to fly the special representative to Sciuref, a small village several hundred miles south of Tripoli. Gloriozov was puzzled, but the aide explained that ever since a U.S. Navy attack on his palace, Qaddafi had routinely changed locations every few days.

At Sciuref, the general was met by a member of the Libyan leader's personal bodyguard, who frisked Gloriozov, and then drove the Russian to a tent palace in the desert west of the village. To enter the tent, Gloriozov had to crawl on all fours through the only visible aperture. He found himself at last face-to-face with "the Tentmaker," as the Russians and East Germans serving in-country often characterized Qaddafi.

Learning that the Third World War would begin in less than twenty-four hours, and that the Soviet Union expected Libya to fight alongside the Warsaw Pact, Qaddafi's face remained expressionless. He stared blankly at Gloriozov and then got up and wandered off into the desert, accompanied only by a pair of Bedouin security men. After forty-five minutes, the Libyan leader returned. "We shall fight together," he told Gloriozov, "as socialist brothers." Qaddafi ordered the immediate alert of Libyan forces.

At 0302 on the bridge of the *Belknap*, VADM Turner's aide handed the Sixth Fleet commander a message. It confirmed what Turner already knew—that the war had begun. But as he handed the paper back to the aide, the addressee line caught the admiral's eye—COMSTRIKFORSOUTH. As of 0300 Turner's had become a NATO command—Naval Striking and Support Forces, Southern Europe.

Ten minutes later the *Belknap* picked up an SOS from an Exxon tanker torpedoed about 150 miles southeast of Malta. "Who do we have in that sector?" Turner asked. Earlier in the day an American P-3C Orion had tracked the Libyan *Foxtrot*-class diesel submarine no. 313—the *Al Ahad*—running on the surface. "Get McMichaels [CINCSOUTH] on the line," Turner ordered, "let's see if we have permission to retaliate against the Libyans."

At 0327, an aide handed Turner an affirmative response. CINCSOUTH reported that Libyan complicity in the attack on the tanker was certain. At 0322 Qaddafi had announced to the world that one of his submarines had struck a crushing blow against the U.S. Navy, sinking the *John F. Kennedy* as it steamed southeast of Malta on its way to cross the "line of death." Turner read the message and shook his head. "Can you believe this shit; he's the asshole who just crossed the line of death."

* * *

As NATO forces in the Tyrrhenian Sea moved south toward Tripoli, Soviet and Libyan naval forces moved not north, but east. The Black Sea KPF had directed RADM Yelizari Cherdantsev, with his flag in the *Azov* off Benghazi, to move his own KUG and the bulk of the Libyan squadron at Tripoli to the eastern port of Darnah, where a second Libyan squadron was based. Black Sea Fleet believed that such a concentrated surface force would be powerful enough to threaten any premature American move from the central Mediterranean to link up with RADM Reece's *Theodore Roosevelt* task group off the Levant coast, to check any move by NAVOCFORMED to the south, and to survive until the Soviet campaign in the eastern Mediterranean had been won and a regrouping of naval forces achieved. Russian and Libyan submarines operating south of Sicily would cover the eastward movement.

Responsibility for the defense of western Libya—Tripolitania—rested primarily with the Libyan air arm. It was, on paper, a substantial force of more than 550 combat aircraft. But over four hundred planes were in storage and many of the rest were flown by Syrian, North Korean, or Russian pilots. The Soviets also controlled the extensive Libyan air defense system. There were only about seventy-five fighters—miserable Su-20 Fitters and nearly obsolescent MiG-23 Floggers—combat ready in Tripolitania on the morning of D day. The Soviets had promised to supply pilots and to fly in additional aircraft in the event of a crisis. But in the midst of a global war, neither the Soviet Union nor any of its surrogates could afford to send hundreds of skilled pilots to Libya. Nor did a single Russian fighter reach a North African base (except for a handful of damaged aircraft that could not make it back to the Crimea) during the course of the war.

Over two hundred NATO fighters and attack aircraft were available to take on the Libyans during the fourteenth. RADM Byrnes's *Kennedy* task group alone carried eighty-six aircraft including twenty F-14A Tomcats, twenty F/A-18 Hornets, and twenty A-6E Intruders, a force numerically equal, and qualitatively superior to the Libyan forces based around Tripoli. The dozen AV-8B Harriers on the Italian carrier *Garibaldi*, and the sixteen Super Etendards and ten Vought F-8E Crusaders of the French carrier *Foch* would be available to support the *Kennedy*'s operations. NATO land-based air assets in Sicily included a dozen U.S. Marine Corps F/A-18 Hornets at Sigonella, thirty-two F-16A Falcons of the USAF's 401st Tactical Fighter Wing (TFW), 612th Tactical Fighter Squadron, at Comiso (the wing's 613th and 614th TFSs were scheduled to arrive on the fifteenth and sixteenth respectively), thirty-two Italian F-104G Starfighters of 37 Stormo at Trapani, and thirty G 91Ys of 32 Stormo that had staged from their base at Brindisi to Catania.

At 0900, the *Kennedy*, four hundred miles north of the Libyan capital, launched its first strike of the day, supported by American Hornets and Falcons and Italian G 91Y attack aircraft. Targets included Idris and Okbah ibn Nafi airbases, and radar and SAM sites around Tripoli.

As the strike planes headed south, Hawkeyes detected the launch and approach of approximately four dozen Libyan Floggers and Fitters. The E-2Cs orchestrated the opening stage of the ensuing air-to-air engagement, bringing Tomcats, Hornets, Falcons, and even the Italian Starfighters into intercept positions. The dogfight began at 1005 over the island of Lampadusa. By 1025, the skies were clear. At least half the Libyan fighters had been downed. NATO losses totalled three aircraft.

VADM Turner welcomed the Libyan's willingness to offer battle. "They're a hell of a lot easier to shoot down than they are to get at on the ground," he remarked to his staff. But the gutsy if foolish Libyan decision to come out and fight had forced CAPT Jack Lawler, the CAG (commander, air group) of CVW 3, to abort the planned strikes against Libyan air defenses. "Virtually all of my Hornets," Lawler informed Turner, "had to jettison their ground-attack ordnance to join the dogfight." That decision maximized the air wing's air-to-air capability in the aerial battle that followed, but made a continuation of the strike impossible.

At 1615, the *Kennedy*, now fifty miles west of Malta, began launching her second strike, again supported by ground-based aircraft flying from Sicily. This time the Libyans chose to rely on their air defense system, not their fighters, to repel the attack.

LT Thomas "Taps" O'Roark flew an A-6E from the *Kennedy*'s VA-75. His Intruder was loaded up with HARMs (high speed anti-radiation missiles) and a pair of decoys. O'Roark flew to a position about forty miles northeast of Tripoli, while Hawkeyes from the carrier, flying high overhead, beyond the range of Libyan SAMs, monitored air traffic and radar emissions. As they detected active search radars, the Hawkeyes directed the Intruders toward the targets. The Libyan SAM sites would either be destroyed or forced to shut down before the attack planes, only minutes behind, reached their targets.

As an EA-6B Prowler ECM aircraft jammed Libyan radars and communications, O'Roark flew with three other Intruders towards several pulse radar sites east of Tripoli. At a range of fifteen miles, each of the four Intruders released a decoy. As they flew toward the Libyan radars, the decoys, which emitted the electronic signature of an approaching strike aircraft, enticed the Libyans to "light up" their radars. The Intruders then released their HARMs which homed in on the active radar emissions. "You could see the Libyan radar sites go off the air one-by-one as our HARMs found their marks," O'Roark reported.

LT Dennis "Suds" Brewster, flew a similar mission west of Tripoli, but had a somewhat more trying experience. Brewster, in a VFA-136 F/A-18 Hornet, was flying due south toward the Libyan coast when a strong doppler radar suddenly began emitting, burning right through a Prowler's jamming. The SAM site had a lock on the Hornet. Still a hundred miles out, well beyond the range of a HARM, Brewster's radar picked up a missile launch. He had been warned that there might be some modern SAMs—Grumbles [SA-10s] and Gladiators [SA-12s]—in Libya, and the doppler was a giveaway. Both SAMs were capable of speeds approaching Mach 3 and were effective against low-level aircraft. Realizing that he had only seconds to react, Brewster turned hard to starboard, taking a course perpendicular to the approach of the SAM. Sweating profusely and jerking his neck back to pick up and then keep an eye on the SAM, Brewster waited until the last moment and released chaff. "The SAM flew right through the shit!" he exclaimed over his radio. The relieved Hornet pilot turned hard to port diving to no more than a hundred feet. Flying as low as he dared, nearly crashing into a patrol boat off the coast, Brewster approached the SAM site from the northwest. All kinds of radars were on, and when the range was inside 20 miles Brewster pulled up to 750 feet and started launching his HARMs, assuming that with the Libyan defenses all cranked up, the HARMs would find their way home.

The actions of Brewster, O'Roark, and other aviators from the *Kennedy* succeeded in suppressing most of the SAM sites near Tripoli. Hornets, Intruders, Falcons, and Italian G 91s, struck air defense installations and air fields around the Libyan capital. At least thirty aircraft were destroyed on the ground. NATO losses totalled two planes—an Italian G 91, and a navy Hornet.

At 2330, the *Kennedy* and Italian and American bases in Sicily began launching aircraft for the third major raid of the day, this time supported by Crusaders and Super Etendards from the French carrier *Foch*. The late-evening strikes met virtually no opposition from the Libyan Air Force. The few interceptors that had survived the earlier battles had scattered to airfields in the south or east. Those that remained in Tripolitania were caught on the ground as

NATO strike aircraft hit Libyan airfields, SAM sites, and command centers.

On the morning of the fifteenth, Carrier Striking Group 2, now designated as NATO Task Force 502.2, carrier striking force, struck Libyan air defense positions in the Gulf of Sidra. "We've plastered their IADS [Integrated Air Defense System] south of the 'Line of Death'," Rug Byrnes reported to ADM McMichaels, "while the guys from Sicily have cleaned up whatever was left in the Tripoli area." NATO aircraft knocked out airfields, radar, missile, and communications installations at Misurata, Sirte, Ras El Sidi, Ras Lanuf, and Mersa Brega. By the afternoon of the fifteenth, VADM Turner felt confident enough to report that NATO ruled the skies over two-thirds of Libya and that strike force south had cleared its right flank in the central Med.

★ ★ ★

The success of NATO strikes against Libya had diplomatic as well as military ramifications. The crippling of Libyan air power sped Egyptian entry into the war.

When the summer crisis spread to the Middle East in late June, the American president named former Virginia Senator Robert Southall as special ambassador to the Middle East. Southall, in Cairo on the morning of the fourteenth, went directly to the American embassy where, at 1000 local time, he spoke by phone with the president who charged Southall to pressure the Egyptians to enter the war, or at the minimum allow U. S. forces access to Egyptian bases.

Egyptian President Hosni Mubarak was reluctant to join or to support the American war effort in the region, although his military advisors, stung by the Soviet attack on the Egyptian naval squadron, and eager to settle scores with Libya, were willing, if not eager to enter the war. But Mubarak had less than complete faith in the capabilities of his military, especially his air force. He was concerned about his stature in the Arab world if he fought alongside Israel. And he was uncertain whether or not the Americans could sustain themselves in the eastern Mediterranean, or in the Indian Ocean.

Mubarak put off a meeting with Southall until the morning of 15 July. By the time the American ambassador reached the Egyptian presidential palace at 1000, reports of NATO successes in the eastern Mediterranean and in Tripolitania had alleviated many of Mubarak's fears. But not all. Southall found that he had a hard sell on his hands. So he told the Egyptian president that the United States had provided Egypt with billions of dollars in loans and military hardware, and that now it was the time for these IOUs "to be called in." Southall demanded that permission be granted to allow American forces to move into selected Egyptian bases as staging points for further moves into the Indian Ocean and into southeastern Europe. The ex-senator also suggested that he would find it very difficult to convince his former colleagues that they ought to continue to bankroll a state that had let down the United States in its biggest crisis.

Mubarak sat silently in his chair. He faced the most difficult decision of his life. If he chose wrong, the repercussions for his country, and for his own family, would probably be great. He had hoped to wait and see which way the war went before committing Egypt to any policy other than neutrality. But here were the Americans, twisting his arm.

Southall then made a grave tactical mistake. He told Mubarak that he needed the courage of a Sadat, who had signed the peace treaty with Israel.

"President Sadat," Mubarak reminded the American, "was assassinated!"

Southall did his best to recover from his faux pas. As he stumbled over himself, Mubarak rose from his chair and walked over to a window, framed in bulletproof glass. Then he turned to face the American.

"Fine, Senator Southall, I will allow American forces to use Egyptian bases, but if my country is to enter the war, what is it that you want us to do?"

"Attack the goddamned Libyans," was Southall's reply, "so we can move unhindered into the eastern Mediterranean."

To this Mubarak agreed, if the United States would provide intelligence assistance, air support for Egyptian operations in Cyrenaica, and the commitment of American ground forces to the campaign. Although such details had to be left to the respective military staffs, Southall agreed in principle and both men shook hands.

"If we capture Qaddafi alive," Southall asked, "who gets him?"

Mubarak smiled. "I believe," he replied, "that when the time comes, Allah will show us the way."

★★★

At 0530 on the morning of 16 July, Sicily-based U.S. F-16 Falcons joined carrier aircraft from the *Kennedy* and *Foch* in attacks against Libyan installations around Benghazi. Simultaneously, over a hundred Egyptian air force Falcons and MiGs struck bases in the Tubruq area. The Libyans were outnumbered in the air by ratios of three and four to one. By the end of the day, Qaddafi's air force had ceased to exist as the pattern of NATO success in Tripolitania was repeated in Cyrenaica.

At 0600, the 26th MEU/SOC (Marine Expeditionary Unit/Special Operations Capable) landed at Zuwarah, fifty miles west of Tripoli. In their amphibious tractors, landing craft, hovercraft, and helicopters, the American marines quickly established a beachhead and captured a nearby airfield. By noon AV-8B Harriers flying from the strip were supporting patrols moving east toward Tripoli.

At 0700, three Egyptian divisions—two armored, one mechanized—struck west toward Tubruq. A single Libyan armored division bore the brunt of the attack. Large but inconclusive tank battles continued until nightfall. The engagements resumed the following morning and by day's end the Libyans began to fall back.

The American and Egyptian attacks left Qaddafi in a difficult position. His army was, like his air arm, largely a paper force. Half of the tanks of the Libyan army were in warehouses. In addition to the irregular forces under arms, only three full strength formations were available to resist an attack—an armored division deployed along the Egyptian border, a mechanized division in reserve at Benghazi, and a second mechanized division near Tripoli. Qaddafi ordered the Benghazi division to reinforce the armored division along the Egyptian frontier. Determined to crush the American "invaders," he ordered the division quartered in and around Tripoli to eliminate the American bridgehead.

By noon on the seventeenth, the marines had taken a second

airstrip near Az Zawarah, soon a base for Cobra attack helicopters, and had advanced to within twenty-five miles of the Libyan capital. But LTC W. "Mike" Harris, commander of the 26th MEU, found himself "in some deep shit." Patrols reported that at least a brigade-sized force was deployed astride the coastal road. Another brigade was working its way around the marines' right flank. Harris halted the advance and the marines quickly set up defensive positions.

At 1330 the Libyans attacked. Hornets from Sicily, Harriers from Zuwarwah, and Cobras from Az Zawarah provided the assistance Harris's eight hundred men needed to hold off fifteen times their number. But casualties were heavy. Harris, who had had visions of "capturing Tripoli while the Marine Band played the Hymn," now thought only of the survival of his command. "If they hit us again before we're reinforced," he observed, "we're going to be a bunch of dead Jarheads, 'good marines' I suppose, from the Libyan point of view."

Nevertheless, Harris's successful stand east of Az Zawarah changed the course of the campaign. Qaddafi, determined to crush the American marines, ordered the Benghazi division to halt its advance toward the Egyptian border and to move west to the Libyan capital.

Qaddafi's decision thrilled the hell out of Marine Corps GEN George Gilchrist, Commander-in-Chief, Central Command (CINC-CENT) in his headquarters at McDill Air Force Base in Tampa, Florida. Egypt was in CENTCOM's area of responsibility (AOR) and on the morning of 18 July, Gilchrist was preparing to fly to Cairo to establish a forward headquarters to coordinate Egyptian-American operations against Libya. Gilchrist was literally headed out the door when a major shoved recon photos at him and insisted that he give them a look. Reconnaissance aircraft had brought back fabulous shots of an entire Libyan mech division stretched back for hundreds of miles, heading west, away from the battle. Given NATO's virtually total command of the air over Libya, Gilchrist considered the 600-mile march from Benghazi to Tripoli suicide. "The poor Libyans are nothing but Falcon fodder," he told the major.

Gilchrist's move to his CENTCOM forward headquarters in Cairo was preceded by the arrival of the first American ground troops in the theater—on the evening of the seventeenth, C-5A Galaxies transporting the 1st Battalion of the 75th Rangers, landed at a military airfield outside of Cairo. On the morning of the eighteenth, Military Airlift Command (MAC) transports began landing the 2d Brigade of the 82d Airborne Division at Zuwarwah, Libya.

Many senior American and NATO military commanders viewed the movement of American ground forces, especially a full regiment of the United States' only true airborne division, to Libya with some skepticism. Gilchrist insisted on the deployment, arguing that the only way to get the Egyptians wholeheartedly into the war was through the commitment of American ground forces. In Gilchrist's mind, Egypt also provided an excellent base for the United States' non-NATO earmarked forces, that is someplace where he could send units before the other CINCs grabbed his forces. From Egypt, Gilchrist could commit units quickly into the Persian Gulf if the Russians moved there, or north to support COMLANDSOUTH-EAST.

As the American paratroopers moved toward the front, B-52Hs of the Strategic Air Command's 5th Bombardment Wing struck Libyan concentrations west of Tripoli. Qaddafi's hopes that his forces could resume the offensive on the eighteenth were as shattered as his army.

The Libyan mechanized division had yet to recover when the 82d's 2d Brigade attacked on the morning of the nineteenth. Supported by Falcons and Hornets flying from Sicily, the paratroopers drove to within ten miles of the Libyan capital by nightfall. But the Americans, despite their successes, were unable to resume the advance. To LTC Harris, whose marines supported the paratroopers' advance, "the Libyan troops were terrible, but there were so many of them, just pushing them out of your way was exhausting." As the Americans rested on the twentieth, the air force bombed and strafed anything that moved.

While American troops pushed toward the Libyan capital, tank clashes raged along the Egyptian-Libyan border, site of innumerable engagements during the western desert campaign of the Second World War. The battle ebbed and flowed across the desert and coastal escarpment as both Egyptian and Libyan forces advanced and retreated. But by the evening of 18 July the battered Libyan armored division could no longer maintain the unequal struggle. An Egyptian armored drive through "Hellfire" (Halfaya) pass broke the Libyans along the old Via Balbo and early on the morning of the nineteenth, Egyptian mechanized troops entered Bardia. As the Libyans attempted to pull back along the few available roads, the columns were subjected to constant air attack by the Egyptian air force. The retreat soon became a rout. On the twentieth, the Egyptians attacked Tubruq, evacuated by the army, but defended by the loyal Jamahiriya Guard. The battle for Tubruq lasted for 36 hours and was marked by brutality and atrocity. But the town was in Egyptian hands and the advance to the west continued. The battle for Cyrenaica was over.

SEVEN

The campaign against Libya was but one of several waged within the United States Central Command's area of responsibility (AOR). On the morning of 14 July, all hell broke loose from the Red Sea to the Strait of Malacca. Four Russian "tankers" began dropping mines in the shipping channels of the Persian Gulf, while Soviet aircraft, surface combatants, and submarines staged dramatic attacks against allied and neutral ships.

Despite their initial successes, Soviet forces operating in the Indian Ocean were weak. The fleet command post in Aden vectored five nuclear attack submarines and three diesel boats toward allied and neutral ships. A surface strike group (KUG)—the small carrier *Kiev*, the cruisers *Chervona Ukraina* and *Admiral Isakov*, and the destroyers *Boyevoy*, *Simferopol*, *Okrylenny*, and *Admiral Levchenko*—cruised the Gulf of Aden northwest of Socotra. A dozen frigates, corvettes, minesweepers, and support ships rounded out the Soviet Indian Ocean squadron (SOVINDRON). Only a handful of Russian SNA and air defence force aircraft were actually based in the region, despite a last-minute reinforcement. The *Kiev* carried a dozen mediocre Yak-38 Forgers. Nineteen Il-38 Mays operated from Aden and about a hundred aircraft—Tu-16C Badgers (as well as a few models modified for electronic support measures, Be-12 Mails, Su-27 Flankers, and Su-24 Fencers—crowded the hangars and runways of the main airbase at Ras Kharmah, on the island of Socotra. But only the score of Flankers could be judged capable interceptors, and only the Badgers, armed with stand-off missiles, posed a threat to American surface forces. While the Ethiopians and the Yemenis were prepared to "fight at the side of their Socialist brothers," their navies were insignificant and their air forces were small, obsolescent, and poorly equipped to support maritime operations. Additional Soviet strike assets, including powerful Backfires and Blackjacks, operated from bases in the Caucasus and central Asia. While Russian planes had the range to strike targets deep in the Indian Ocean, it was a long, exhausting flight and, moreover, one that required the aircraft to overfly neutral Iran or Pakistan.

Soviet planners, well aware of these difficulties, recognized that the critical battles of an Indian Ocean war could well be those waged in the capitals of the neutral states. With the outbreak of war, Russian diplomats set out to convince the leaders of Iraq, Iran, and India that the time had come to drive the Americans from the Indian Ocean. The entry into the war of any one of these three countries had the potential to decide the course of the campaign. India possessed the largest navy in the Indian Ocean and its intervention would tilt the naval balance in the region against the Americans. Iranian entry would open the Persian Gulf to air attack and a possible offensive conducted by the Soviet Southern Front's airborne and ground forces. Iraqi entry would threaten the oil-rich and mostly pro-American states of the gulf's southern littoral.

But on the morning of 14 July, no one in Moscow knew how the major neutral states, nor any of the small, yet strategically placed countries of the region, would react once hostilities began. A Soviet Foreign Ministry official responsible for Indian Ocean affairs noted that "our projections are no more than intelligent guesses, so we're going to war with our fingers crossed, because without a major diplomatic break, our strength in the region is limited, very limited."

Soviet objectives in the Indian Ocean were ambitious, although clearly defined. The general staff directed VADM Constantine Anokhin, commanding all Soviet forces in the theater from his headquarters in Aden, to interdict Allied tanker traffic in the Indian Ocean. "Our purpose is not strategic, as some have assumed," Anokhin explained to his staff, "but practical, because much of the fuel for the American Sixth and Seventh Fleets comes from Persian

Gulf refineries. If we can staunch that flow, the impact on American naval operations will be marked."

But direct Russian attacks on tankers, virtually none of which were American, and the disruption of Middle Eastern oil traffic was likely to enrage the Arab states of the Gulf. Soviet military actions could very well prove diplomatically counterproductive, for under similar pressures during the latter stages of the Iran-Iraq tanker war, the Gulf states had worked closely with the Americans. Nevertheless, Anokhin and other senior Soviet leaders believed that early offensive successes achieved at American expense would ensure Arab neutrality, and induce several states to throw in their lot with the victorious Communist bloc. "We are engaged," a Soviet foreign ministry assessment concluded, "in a rather difficult balancing act."

Nowhere was that balancing act to prove more exacting than in Tehran. The Soviets opened their diplomatic offensive by demanding permission to move Russian troops through Iran to the gulf and to operate fighters from southern Iranian airfields. The Soviet ambassador in Tehran did not expect the Iranians to agree to such proposals, but while Moscow did not wish to drive Iran into the American camp, nor to risk an invasion that could easily become a second, gigantic Afghanistan, the Soviet leadership believed that the Iranians would and could do little to interfere with overflying Russian aircraft. VADM Anokhin believed that Soviet strike aircraft would be able to overfly Iranian airspace because their air force had yet to recover from the 1980s—a disastrous decade of revolution and war.

Until such time that Iraq, Iran, or India joined the campaign against the United States, the burden of operations in the theater rested primarily on Anokhin's shoulders. At his Aden headquarters, he considered his position unenviable. Anokhin had concentrated all of his surface assets and his three most powerful SSNs in the Gulf of Aden where they could operate under the CAP umbrella of Ras Kharmah. "But that leaves me only five submarines, including three diesel boats, to operate offensively in the remainder of what's an extensive theater," he lamented to his staff. Supply shortages, particularly of missiles for his ships and aircraft, also troubled Anokhin. The general staff had dispatched convoys to the Indian Ocean from the Crimea and the Far East weeks before the war, but on the morning of 14 July, neither had reached Socotra, where the principal anchorages and airfields were located. The Sevastopol convoy had cleared the Bab el Mandeb and was only a few hours from Aden and safety. But the Vladivostok convoy, six freighters escorted by three frigates and a pair of corvettes, was still nine hundred miles southeast of Socotra. Anokhin, unwilling to move the *Kiev* KUG far from the protection provided by Su-27 Flankers based at Ras Kharma, had no choice but to leave the second convoy out on a limb.

***

Throughout the thirteenth of July, American RADM Anthony Moore, Commander, Carrier Task Force 77.1, monitored Soviet naval movements in the Indian Ocean "hoping like hell that the Russian commander would bring his *Kiev* group out from under the damned Socotra umbrella to protect that convoy." With only a single carrier, and with no land-based support, Moore considered the prospects of simultaneous operations against the Soviet Indian Ocean Squadron (SOVINDRON) and Socotra problematic. "I'm all alone out here in a big, big ocean," Moore reminded Gen Gilchrist, "with little prospect of reinforcement. I simply can't afford to make a mistake."

Like Anokhin, Moore controlled a powerful but small force. His single carrier battlegroup included the *Nimitz*, the Aegis cruiser *Thomas S. Gates*, the cruiser *Arkansas*, the destroyers *Waddell* and *Hewitt*, and the fast combat support ship *Supply*. A sizable amphibious task force—the *Peleliu*, *Juneau*, *Denver*, *Tortuga*, and *Mount Vernon*, carrying four thousand marines of the reinforced 11th MEU—accompanied the carrier battle group (CVBG) about seven hundred miles northeast of Socotra. A second small task force—the Aegis cruiser *Hue City*, the cruiser *Gridley*, and the destroyers *Chandler* and *Ingersoll*—were in Raysut, Oman, on a port visit. Four additional American destroyers and frigates were dispersed throughout the Indian Ocean.

At 0900 local time on D day, the National Command Authority named Moore Commander, Joint Task Force Middle East (CJTFME), CENTCOM's on-scene commander in the AOR. Moore immediately assumed control over Middle East Force (MEF) in the Persian Gulf. RADM Jonas Sommers's command included the flagship *La Salle*, docked in Manama, Bahrain, along with a pair of minesweepers,

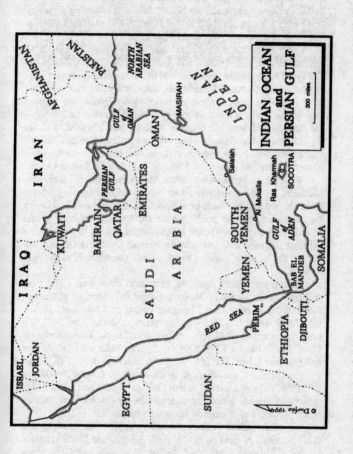

and five frigates patrolling the Gulf. The amphibious assault ship *New Orleans,* carrying seventeen hundred marines and six RH53D Stallion mine countermeasure helicopters, was escorting a convoy, along with a frigate, in the Strait of Hormuz and making a show of force and of minesweeping capability.

Other allied naval forces on hand in the Indian Ocean on 14 July included British, French, and Australian ships and submarines. The Royal Navy frigate *Hermoine* and the minesweeper *Brecon* were in Abu Dhabi. A small French task force at Djibouti included the destroyers *Jean Bart, Duquesne,* and *Duguay-Trouin,* the support ship *Marne,* and the minesweeper *Lyre.* An Australian task force—the destroyer *Hobart,* the frigates *Adelaide* and *Derwint,* and the replenishment ship *Success*—was off the southwestern coast of Sumatra. One British, one French, and one Australian submarine complemented the four American SSNs on patrol in the Indian Ocean.

With the outbreak of hostilities, Moore faced myriad problems. Militarily, he was uncertain about who would be fighting whom. Moore hoped that he would be able to depend on Bahrain and Oman for assistance, but he could not be certain that anybody would provide help, especially if the United States got off to a bad start. Without Bahraini assistance in the Persian Gulf and Omani support in the western Indian Ocean, Moore considered his position tenuous.

Moore also faced daunting command dilemmas. "The joint problems aren't too bad," Moore reported to Gilchrist right before the outbreak of hostilities, "because virtually all my assets are naval." MEF was a U.S. Navy headquarters, and the *Nimitz* CVBG, until the morning of 14 July, had answered to the Commander-in-Chief, Pacific Fleet. CENTCOM's U.S. Army units were mostly sent to Egypt and Libya. The U.S. Air Force assets in the Indian Ocean were minimal—a squadron of B-52s at Diego Garcia, another of F-15s that deployed to the Persian Gulf on 15 July, and a handful of tankers in-theater. Moore considered the geographic and international problems of command far greater headaches.

No allied Indian Ocean command, similar to the headquarters that controlled operations in the North Atlantic and Mediterranean, existed. The Arab states had always been rather reticent about working too closely with the United States, and those western powers with forces in the theater—Britain and France—had been unwilling to formalize any agreements for fear that it might appear to be some kind of "imperialist" command. Staff contacts and discussions had addressed many of the command issues that might arise, but, in Moore's view, "on D day the whole command thing remained rather inchoate."

Geography also posed special problems. The Persian Gulf and the Gulf of Aden were geographically remote and the problems the United States faced in the two areas were very different. "It's all well and good," Moore told Gilchrist, "to name me CJTFME, but in reality there's damned little I can do to direct operations in the Persian Gulf. I intend to stay out of CMEF's hair."

★ ★ ★

The Soviet offensive in the Indian Ocean began with well-timed and well-executed attacks on the morning of 14 July. As the Kremlin expected, the Iranians took no action to prevent overflights of their territory and Russian strike aircraft flew south from Caucasus bases throughout the day.

At 1010 local time, Tu-95H Bears bombed Diego Garcia. No American fighters were on hand to intercept the attack, although the island base's improved Hawk batteries downed nine of the Bears. While most of the bombs fell wide of the mark, several straddled runways, destroying a B-52 that had been about to take off. Although Navy P-3Cs continued their ASW patrols, not a single B-52 took off from the island until the following morning. Other Soviet bombers that overflew Iran struck shipping in the Persian Gulf. A dozen Tu-16 Badgers appeared over the Strait of Hormuz and attacked a pair of Panamanian tankers bound for Kuwait, sinking one and heavily damaging the other. The American amphibious assault ship *New Orleans*, passing through the strait no more than ten miles from the tankers, narrowly escaped destruction. The frigate *Klakring*, patrolling in the northern Persian Gulf, proved less fortunate, attracting the attention of no fewer than six Tu-22M Backfires. The commander of the *Klakring* saw the attack develop as Saudi E-3C Sentry AWACS aircraft passed data to the American frigate. But calls for assistance, passed by MEF to the Saudis, Kuwaitis, and Bahrainis, failed to elicit a response.

In the Gulf of Oman, four Socotra-based Soviet Badgers attacked the American squadron at Raysut, Oman. Despite American appeals for support, two squadrons of Omani fighters at the nearby Salalah airbase failed to intercept the attackers and, less than thirty nautical miles from Raysut, the Badgers launched their ASMs. The port's air defenses did join the Americans' efforts to destroy the incoming missiles, but two AS-4s found targets. A single Kitchen struck the cruiser *Gridley*, but, miraculously, caused only light damage. A second ASM hit the Omani missile boat *Dhofar* which exploded and sank.

About three hundred miles south of Karachi, Pakistan, a *Victor II* SSN began a day-long series of attacks against the U.S. frigate *Cook*, which, following the outbreak of hostilities and the early morning attacks on neutral shipping in the gulf, had taken a pair of Kuwaiti tankers under escort. For nine hours the Soviet submarine stalked the old *Knox*-class American frigate and her wards, sinking first one, and then the other tanker. Finally, at 1930, a Type-65 torpedo struck the *Cook* which sank seventy minutes later.

In the early afternoon, the Soviets attempted to follow up their morning successes with a second wave of air attacks throughout the theater. Tu-95 Bears returned to Diego Garcia, launching stand-off cruise missiles against the island's facilities. Effective countermeasures and air defenses diverted or downed the incoming missiles. In the Persian Gulf, a second wave of Badgers appeared over the Strait of Hormuz, and located and sank the *New Orleans*. Thanks to the rescue efforts of the Omanis, all but 230 of the ship's 1,700-man marine contingent were saved. Further north, Backfires conducted a surprise bombing raid against the Bahraini airbase at Muharraq, causing substantial damage.

Throughout the morning and afternoon of the fourteenth, allied forces responded slowly to the Soviet challenge. The *Nimitz* battle-group steamed west toward Socotra, screened by American and British SSNs. In the early afternoon, the Royal Navy attack submarine *Turbulent* damaged and drove off a *Charlie II* SSGN that had penetrated the *Nimitz*'s outer screen.

In the Persian Gulf, it was early evening before RADM Sommers, CMEF, had "gotten a handle on things." At 1530 Sommers recommended that all tankers, both allied and neutral, take shelter in the nearest port. By 1700, Sommers had concentrated his remaining American frigates off Bahrain. By nightfall, the sea lanes in the Gulf were rapidly becoming devoid of shipping.

The Soviets, aware of Sommers's moves, responded by focusing their efforts against Bahrain. At midnight, Russian bombers again struck Muharraq. A handful of Bahraini F-5s, aided by a half-dozen of Qatar's Mirage F-1s, surprised the attackers and downed seven Soviet bombers, although the strike further damaged the airbase.

A thousand miles to the south of Bahrain, aircraft from the *Nimitz*'s Carrier Air Wing 11 approached Socotra. The attacking aircraft—a Hawkeye, two Prowlers, six Tomcats, thirteen Hornets, fourteen Intruders, and two KA-6D tankers—made their way in small groups toward the Ras Kharmah airbase. At 2340, the Tomcats, six Hornets armed with air-to-air missiles, and a Prowler engaged about a score of Soviet Flankers and Fencers fifty miles from the island.

As the furball began, LCDR Richard Goldsmith and his bombardier, LT Randolph Mazyck, flying a lone A-6E, streaked undetected over the western coast of Socotra and headed for the main Soviet command and control bunker near Ras Kharmah. Goldsmith's Intruder carried a pair of standoff land attack missiles (SLAM), a ground attack version of the Harpoon. Goldsmith and Mazyck were to approach the island from the west at low altitude and to fly one of their SLAMs to the target. The Soviets had no Il-76 Mainstay in the Indian Ocean and if their ground control facilities could be knocked out, at least temporarily, the combat air patrols defending the island would be at a disadvantage.

At 2342, Goldsmith reported "feet dry," as his Intruder crossed the coast. Seconds later Mazyck fired the SLAM. "Good release," he informed Goldsmith, as the missile acquired the global positioning system satellite and headed toward the target. Two minutes later, Mazyck launched a second SLAM. As the missile fell from the wing, Goldsmith banked the aircraft to starboard and flew south back over the water. The second missile also successfully acquired GPS guidance.

At 2346, the first missile went active and began relaying signals to the Intruder's AWW-13 advanced data link pod. When Mazyck shouted "arcade time," Goldsmith knew that his bombardier-navigator was getting video from the missile. On his display screen, Mazyck could make out the target complex—a small bunker located between two larger buildings. He moved the cursor to the target, locked on the aim point, and waited. Seconds later, the SLAM closed on the target. The screen suddenly went blank. Mazyck knew that either the missile had been downed by a SAM or, more likely, had hit the target. When the second missile activated about ninety seconds later, the image confirmed Mazyck's expectations. The signal from the second SLAM came up on the CRT and he could see the bunker burning. He flew the second missile to the target just to make sure.

Denied effective ground control, the Fencers and Flankers were no match for an equal number of U.S. Navy Tomcats and Hornets. The U.S. Navy fighters downed at least twelve Soviet fighters, many before they could even engage the Americans. "We took quite a toll of the Russians on our way in with our Phoenixes and Sparrows," one Tomcat pilot radioed back to the carrier. No sooner had the Americans closed than the Soviets began to disengage.

As the American fighters drove off the Russian interceptors, pairs of U.S. Navy attack aircraft commenced a well planned and executed strike. While the Prowlers jammed Soviet detection and communications capabilities, decoy and HARM-armed Intruders and Hornets destroyed several SAM radars and forced many more to shut down. Maverick-armed Hornets then attacked the neutralized SAM positions, striking the radars and the launcher positions themselves. Other aircraft delivered guided and dumb munitions— French-made Durandals to destroy runways, fuel air explosives to destroy unprotected aircraft, and laser-guided bombs to hit storage bunkers, hangars, buildings, and fuel storage sites.

Thirty minutes after the strike began, another dozen Soviet aircraft were destroyed, one runway was virtually beyond repair, and a second and third were heavily damaged although serviceable. Only two of the attackers, apparently hit by SAMs, failed to return to the *Nimitz*.

★ ★ ★

As D day ended, neither the Soviets nor the allies had seized the initiative in the Indian Ocean theater. Soviet naval and air forces had disrupted tanker traffic, sinking three major and several small tankers. ASM-armed SNA strike aircraft flying from Caucasus bases had sunk the large amphibious transport *New Orleans* and two American frigates. Bomb and cruise missile-armed Soviet aircraft

THE WAR THAT NEVER WAS

had damaged strategically important facilities at Diego Garcia and Muharraq, although both airbases remained operational. But the SOVINDRON had lost one of its five SSNs. Soviet bombers and SNA strike aircraft, operating at extreme ranges from their bases, had suffered heavily—at least two dozen aircraft were lost during the day. The *Nimitz* battlegroup had successfully attacked Ras Kharmah, sweeping aside Soviet fighters and heavily damaging the base.

Moreover, the Soviet failure to gain a clear upper hand in the Indian Ocean fighting was a major diplomatic setback. Far from being cowed, the Arab Persian Gulf states of Kuwait, Bahrain, and Qatar sent their air forces into combat to protect Gulf tanker traffic from Soviet attack. The bombing of Bahrain not only failed to knock out the island's important airbase, but also drove the Bahrainis into the American camp. As darkness fell on the gulf, a squadron of U.S. Air Force F-15s of the 49th TFW began landing at Muharraq after long flights from Holloman AFB, New Mexico. Shortly before noon on D day, the Omanis, stung by the Russian strike against Raysut and the sinking of the *Dhofar*, had opened their bases to the Americans and that evening U.S. Navy P-3Cs began to arrive at Masirah, Oman. The adherence of Yemen and Ethiopia to the Soviet cause prompted Somalia to support the allies' efforts.

Most importantly, Iraq, Iran, and India chose to remain neutral, at least for the moment. The Indians began to mobilize and sent their fleet to sea to patrol the "Zone of Peace." New Delhi threatened to forcibly expel any belligerent naval or air units found within a hundred miles of the Indian and Sri Lankan coasts. The declaration actually served allied interests since neutral tankers were free to move through Indian waters in safety. The Iraqis, with one eye on the Iranians and another on the Arab Gulf states, adopted a wait-and-see attitude toward the war.

In Tehran, the war provoked an immediate and sharp political debate. Many Iranian leaders saw the conflict as the opportunity to go to war on equal terms with the Great Satan—the United States. But the interventionists were divided between those who were willing to allow the Soviets transit of Iran, and those who did not want Russian troops moving through the country or taking up positions along the Persian Gulf. The moderates in Tehran considered it suicide to join the Soviets in a war with the west. Iranian entry, they believed, would provoke an Iraqi attack, supported by the Arab

Gulf states, and ultimately American air strikes on Iranian ports and oil facilities. Even if the Americans lost the war, the Iranians would only be able to recover ground lost during the war by relying on Soviet forces. While the moderates favored neutrality, they, too, were divided between those who were prepared to take action against overflying Soviet aircraft, and those who thought it best to ignore the overflights. As the fourteenth ended, the Iranians continued to debate. In the interim, they privately protested Russian overflights but publicly denied that they were occurring.

EIGHT

As RADM Moore sparred with the Soviets in the Indian Ocean on the morning of 14 July, further east ADM Roger Cooper, Commander-in-Chief, Pacific (CINCPAC), stood sweating in full-dress uniform conducting a tour of Pearl Harbor for the visiting CINC of the navy of the People's Republic of China. At 1502 local time, still the thirteenth of July in Hawaii, a red-faced aide handed Cooper a message from Washington—the United States was at war. Taking leave of his Chinese guests, Cooper hurriedly returned to his headquarters, made sure that everybody "got the word," and then dispatched a coded message to all his commands "to execute CINCPAC Operations Plan 220-90."

OPLAN 220-90 called for U.S. forces throughout the Pacific Command (PACOM) to initiate conventional offensive and defensive operations against Soviet units and the Soviet Union itself. The plan assumed that neither power, at least initially, would have the assistance of any of its allies, other than the use of foreign facilities, such as Soviet bases in Vietnam and American bases in Japan, South Korea, and the Philippines. Cooper personally called the State Department in Washington to ensure that its diplomats "were doing their utmost to ensure that these host governments did not place any restrictions on the use of our bases." Cooper also set his staff to work in an attempt to divine the probable intentions of the United States' potential allies—Japan, South Korea, Taiwan, the Philippines, Australia, and New Zealand. The situation was confused, and at 1530 the only thing Cooper knew for certain was that the United States and its NATO allies were at war with the Soviet Union and its Warsaw Pact allies. All was quiet along the demilitarized zone (DMZ) in Korea, no Soviet aircraft had violated Japanese or South Korean air space. Routine Soviet air activity from Nha Trang, Vietnam continued, but Washington had yet to empower CINCPAC to conduct offensive operations against Russian bases outside the Soviet Union.

With Central Command taking control of most of the American assets deployed in the Indian Ocean, operations in the western Pacific were ADM Cooper's major concerns on D day. The Soviet decision to spare Japan and Korea from attack at least temporarily secured PACOM's ground and airbases. The squadrons of the Fifth (Japan), Seventh (Korea), and Thirteenth (Philippines) Air Forces suffered no Pearl Harbor-like air strikes. As each hour passed, PACOM's air strength grew. Reinforcements from the United States had already begun to reach the western Pacific. As the crisis had deepened, the National Command Authority had begun to move forces to the western Pacific. On the afternoon of 13 July, an alerted squadron of FB-111Ds of the 27th Tactical Fighter Wing from Cannon AFB, New Mexico, had reached Clark AFB in the Philippines. A squadron of Marine F/A-18s had joined the three attack squadrons already deployed at Iwakuni, Japan. Cooper thus controlled a formidable array of land-based air assets that included fifteen fighter and attack squadrons, Harpoon-armed B-52Gs of the 43d Special Wing at Andersen AFB, Guam, ECM aircraft, tankers, transports, AWACS, and command and control aircraft.

The absence of a North Korean assault across the DMZ on the fourteenth also pleasantly surprised Cooper. His biggest concern had always been that the North Koreans would strike out of the blue on D day and catch his forces off-guard. That they had not gave the Americans time to get everybody prepared. By the evening of D day, the U.S. Army's forces in Korea—the Eighth Army, principally the 2d Infantry Division—were fully alerted, although the JCS forbade any unusual troop movements for fear that such moves would provoke a North Korean attack. Nevertheless, back in CONUS, Hawaii,

Guam, and Okinawa, American marine and army troops were preparing to move to both Korea and Japan.

Whether the apparent Soviet policy of restraint in the Pacific theater would extend to the ocean remained to be seen. Cooper could imagine the Soviets going to war in the Pacific without attacking South Korea, although he doubted they would, or could, control the Koreans. And he could see them avoiding attacks against Japan, hoping to keep Japanese forces on the sidelines, although he considered such a course highly improbable and not necessarily to American disadvantage. But he had never figured out just how anyone could think that the United States could go to war with the Soviets at sea in the Atlantic but not in the Pacific. That just was not in the cards. And it was with the situation at sea that Cooper was most concerned. "The Pacific is a mighty big place," CINCPAC liked to tell pre-war audiences, "and the U.S. Pacific Fleet looks awfully small once you start spreading it around."

★ ★ ★

As the war began, American naval forces in WESTPAC were "spread around." Routine peacetime requirements and the nature of the Soviet threat in the region necessitated the dispersion of ADM Thomas "Jerry" Jernigan's Pacific Fleet. Jernigan did not have a carrier within two thousand miles of another carrier on D day. They were spread from the Aleutians to the Gulf of Aden, and CENTCOM immediately grabbed the *Nimitz*. "How's that for concentration?" Cooper asked his staff.

The nuclear-powered carrier *Carl Vinson* was in the South China Sea, about 350 miles east of the Vietnamese coast on D day. RADM Ralph Holmes's Carrier Task Group 77.2 included the Aegis cruisers *Antietam* and *Vincennes*, the cruiser *Harry E. Yarnell*, two destroyers, the replenishment ship *Roanoke*, and the SSNs *Pasadena* and *Springfield*. Soviet forces in the South China Sea included a surface striking group of four *Kashin*-class destroyers, and a replenishment ship at Cam Ranh Bay, as well as a pair of nuclear attack submarines. The Russians also had a mixed force of Tu-16 Badger strike aircraft and MiG-23 fighters at Nha Trang, north of Cam Ranh Bay.

Jernigan's second carrier battlegroup, RADM John Miller's

Carrier Task Group 77.3—the *Independence*, the Aegis cruisers *Princeton* and *Vincennes*, the cruisers *Reeves* and *Sterett*, three destroyers, VADM Edward Youman's Seventh Fleet flagship *Blue Ridge*, and oilers and replenishment vessels—were at Yokosuka, Japan. The "*Indy*" group was centrally positioned, able to move south to cover an amphibious move to the Korean peninsula, or north to support Japanese forces in Hokkaido, raid Soviet bases in the Kuriles, or strike against the major Soviet naval base at Petropavlovsk on the Kamchatka peninsula.

Jernigan's third carrier battlegroup was in the Bering Sea, having steamed from the northwestern coast of the United States under the cover of fog and bad weather fronts and having passed, hopefully unseen by the Soviets, through the Aleutians. The Third Fleet's Carrier Task Group 33.4, commanded by RADM Martin Carr, included the carrier *Kitty Hawk*, the Aegis cruisers *Bunker Hill* and *Mobile Bay*, the old nuclear-powered cruiser *Long Beach*, two destroyers, and the fast—twenty-five-plus-knot—replenishment ship *Camden*. CINCPACFLT operation plans called for the carrier to be in position to strike the Soviet base at Petropavlovsk early on 15 July. To support the strike, CINCPACFLT had deployed a pair of SSNs off Kamchatka and during the afternoon and evening of D day moved two squadrons of A-6s—one of Marine Aircraft Group 13 (VMA 121) from El Toro, California, and navy squadron, VA 196—to Adak where they joined four navy EA-6B Prowlers of VAQ 139.

Jernigan was concerned about the survivability of the *Kitty Hawk* group and wanted to send the *Independence* task group north to assist RADM Carr. On 10 July, two Soviet surface groups had left the Sea of Japan and sailed northwest, managing to avoid detection by hiding under the same weather fronts that hid the *Kitty Hawk* from Soviet satellite surveillance and aircraft reconnaissance. The stronger KUG included the small carrier *Novorossiysk*, the *Kirov*-class cruiser *Kalinin*, a cruiser, two destroyers, and an oiler. The smaller KUG included the *Kara*-class cruiser *Tashkent*, two additional cruisers, and a pair of destroyers. ADM Jernigan's concern "was that these groups might well be screening Petro and we might be walking into an ambush in the far north." ADM Cooper acknowledged the danger, but believed that the *Kitty Hawk* group, supported by the Intruders on Adak, "could deal with any Russian surface threat in the North Pacific," a view endorsed by RADM Carr.

Cooper was more concerned about the situation to the south and east of Japan. The Soviets had dispersed a half-dozen submarines throughout the East China Sea and the waters between the Marianas and Japan and a small KUG—three cruisers and a destroyer—had been reported off Taiwan. So positioned, these Russian forces threatened the major American sea lines of communication (SLOCs) and Japan's principal tanker routes.

In response, Seventh Fleet had concentrated formidable amphibious assets in WESTPAC. A sizable task force had concentrated at Okinawa—fourteen ships capable of lifting over twelve thousand marines of III MEF. Maritime Prepositioning Ships Squadron 3 lay anchored at Guam, loaded with equipment for 1 MEB, based in Hawaii (the 3d Marines). A six-ship convoy carrying additional equipment and supplies for the marines was at sea about 750 miles south of Okinawa. If the *Independence* group moved north, only about a dozen frigates, an SSN, and three squadrons of patrol aircraft would remain to protect these assets.

Cooper also worried that the Soviets might move their remaining surface assets from Vladivostok through the Tsushima Strait between Japan and Korea, link up with their KUG already in the East China Sea, and "devastate our poorly screened amphibious forces as they clear Okinawa." On the morning of 13 July, CINCPAC received a report from Japanese intelligence sources that a task force including the carrier *Baku*, two cruisers, a destroyer, four frigates, and several replenishment vessels would shortly depart Vladivostok. Unless the Japanese and South Koreans intervened, only limited American forces—the four marine squadrons at Iwakumi, Japan, the SSN *Tunny*, and the old diesel boat *Barbel*—were positioned to prevent a Soviet move through the Tsushima Strait.

Despite his concerns, CINCPAC deferred to his subordinate's judgment. To Cooper's mind, Jernigan was responsible for operations in WESTPAC, and the decision was his call. Either choice involved risks, grave risks. No one knew what the Russians were going to do, or for that matter the Japanese or Koreans, north or south. But Cooper was a proponent of what he considered a cherished naval principle—the initiative of the subordinate, trust and confidence. Cooper had no wish to overrule a subordinate's decision, especially one of his first decisions of a campaign. CINCPAC believed that a commander either placed his faith in a subordinate's judgment and capability, or replaced the man. Cooper had known Jernigan for twenty years and had complete faith in him. So the *Indy* went north, not south.

If uncertainty was widespread throughout American commands in the Pacific on 14 July, it was just as prevalent in the various Soviet headquarters. The general staff's pre-war directives to the various commands in the Far East called for the protection of the territory and the land- and sea-based strategic arsenal of the Soviet Union from atomic and conventional attack. But were such objectives to be attained strictly through defensive measures, or could they better be achieved through the conduct of offensive operations?

Soviet thinking about war in the Pacific had long suffered from four basic problems—the command structure in the Far East, doctrinal differences, geographic restraints, and the likelihood that Moscow would face an uncertain diplomatic picture in the theater.

For the Soviet Union, the Peoples' Republic of China, not the United States, posed the greatest military threat in the Far East. The fear that hordes of Chinese would pour across the long border that separated the two Communist giants permeated not only Soviet military minds, but also those of ordinary Russians. "To us," one high-ranking Russian diplomat wrote, "the 'yellow peril' was very real, very real indeed." Because a Sino-Soviet struggle would be principally a ground war, the control of all Soviet forces in the Far Eastern TVD had traditionally been vested in an army general—on 14 July GEN Igor M. Ilichev—with the Soviet navy assigned a subsidiary role.

Of course, on 14 July the Soviet Union went to war with the United States, not the PRC. The war plans that addressed this contingency accorded the Soviet navy a "leading role" in the conduct of all operations, both defensive and offensive, in what planners recognized would be primarily a maritime struggle. Nevertheless, the High Command of Forces (HCOF) in the Far Eastern TVD remained in army hands and the commander of the Soviet Pacific Ocean Fleet (POF)—ADM Pavel G. Ushakov—found himself op-

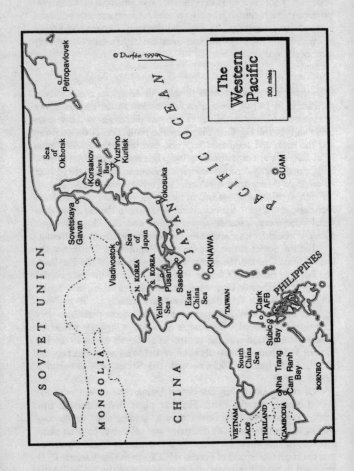

erating under a command setup designed principally to fight a China war, not to wage an oceanic struggle against the world's most powerful navy.

Not surprisingly, there were differences in approach to the problems the Soviets faced in the Far East. ADM Ushakov and GEN Ilichev went at things quite differently. Ilichev wanted to keep the naval forces close to the coast, in what he termed a defensive posture, and to wait for what he supposed would be a quick end to the war in Europe. Ushakov wanted to get his forces out to sea, through the straits and out of the Sea of Japan, to conduct offensive operations against enemy shipping, airbases, and forces as far from Soviet territory as possible. He hoped to keep the enemy off balance during the initial stage of the war, which he, too, hoped would be short.

For Ushakov, geography was everything to the POF. To reach the Pacific, Soviet naval forces had to break out of the Sea of Japan and the Sea of Okhotsk through the barriers formed by the Korean peninsula, Japan, and the Kuriles. Ushakov considered wartime passages through the Tsushima Strait between Korea and Japan, and La Perouse Strait between Sakhalin and Hokkaido "problematic." A contested passage through the Kuriles could also prove difficult. And of the major Soviet naval bases in the Far East—Vladivostok (Sea of Japan), Sovetskaya Gavan (Sea of Japan), Magadan (Sea of Okhotsk), and Petropavlovsk (Bering Sea)—only the last named actually fronted the open Pacific. "If we don't pass these barriers before the beginning of hostilities," Ushakov warned, "we will have a tough time fighting our way through once things heat up." And while Ilichev considered a two-week-war a short conflict, to Ushakov the prospect of a fortnight-long naval struggle in the Pacific seemed an eternity. "I'm convinced," he told Ilichev, "that given the mobility and striking power of American naval units, if the bulk of our surface forces are restricted to defensive operations in the Seas of Okhotsk and Japan, they will be trapped and destroyed."

Poor internal communications were another set of problems likely to dog Soviet operations in the Far East. The termini of the Trans-Siberian rail lines were Vladivostok and Sovetskaya Gavan, both major naval ports. But the bases at Magadan in the Sea of Okhotsk, the various minor naval and air facilities on Sakhalin Island and in the Kuriles, and the major base at Petropavlovsk on the southeast coast of the Kamchatka peninsula, had to be supplied by air or sea. ADM Ushakov liked to point out before the war: "It's generally overlooked, but we have our own SLOCs in the Pacific, and they are vulnerable, especially those running to Petropavlovsk." Ushakov was also responsible for the resupply of Soviet facilities in Vietnam, a task he considered impossible to execute.

Given these geographic handicaps, Ushakov had long argued for an offensive naval strategy in the Pacific. The year before the war, shortly after he had been named to command the Pacific Fleet, Ushakov had penned an article for the Soviet Union's professional naval journal—*Morskoi Sbornik*—in which he wrote of the need to develop an independent naval strategy for the Pacific theater and had recommended seizing the initiative at sea to keep war at arms length from the homeland. "How can we secure the SLOCs to Petropavlovsk and Cam Ranh Bay," he asked, "if we restrict ourselves to operations in the Sea of Japan and the Sea of Okhotsk?" He suggested that in the event of a crisis, the POF should pass the straits before the war began under the pretense of a large exercise and then conduct offensive operations east of Japan. Ushakov also compared his ideas for offensive naval warfare with the army's deep battle doctrine. "Such deep battle concepts," the admiral wrote, "are as applicable at sea, as they are ashore."

Unfortunately, for security reasons, *Morskoi Sbornik*'s editors rejected Ushakov's article. When the admiral persisted, making similar arguments in a speech delivered to naval cadets, he drew public rebukes from senior army commanders who wrote of Ushakov's flirtations with discredited "western navalist and imperialist pretensions" such as the idea that naval strategy existed independently from national strategy. Ushakov knew that only the outbreak of war saved him from prompt retirement.

Not surprisingly, when the summer crisis began, GEN Ilichev rejected Ushakov's request for permission to move the bulk of his fleet to sea. "Everything was geared toward achieving surprise in Germany," he recalled, "and Ilichev was afraid that naval movements of any significance would alert the Americans to the imminence of war." Only the intervention of the main naval staff in Moscow, working through the general staff, forced Ilichev to compromise and to permit Ushakov to send the *Novorossiysk-Kalinin* surface striking group to sea on 10 July.

Ushakov and Ilichev also disagreed over the conduct of operations in the Far East against the region's neutrals. To the commander of the Soviet Pacific Fleet, Japan was a bulwark blocking passage into the Pacific, and a base for American naval and air units. The prospect of waging a maritime war in the Pacific and allowing the Americans to operate from secure sanctuaries in Japan "was absurd." Ushakov, who believed that the Japanese would undoubtedly enter the war on the side of the United States, argued that Soviet forces should strike both American and Japanese bases in Japan on D day in an effort to catch the enemy off-guard and to seize the initiative, especially in the air.

Ilichev, and the general staff, disagreed. Soviet objectives in the war lay in Europe and senior Kremlin leaders, both civilian and military, had no desire to widen the war in the Far East. They pointed out that only the absence of a war in the Far East had saved the Soviet Union in the winter of 1941. Why open a second front?

Only days before the war began, COL Vitali Ignatiev, who served on the general staff's Far Eastern planning section, had flown to Vladivostok in an effort to head off a confrontation between Ilichev and Ushakov. Ignatiev informed both men that the general staff wished to avoid any conflict in the Far East. While that was unlikely, the general staff hoped to keep the war as restrained as possible. Soviet forces should defend their homeland and strategic deterrent forces—the ballistic missile submarines—until the army had overrun Germany and forced a ceasefire. To widen the war in the Pacific, and to push Japan into the enemy's camp, would only complicate the ultimate resolution of the conflict. Moreover, the wider the war in the Far East, and the more committed Soviet forces became, the greater the danger of Chinese intervention. Ignatiev stressed the fact that the general staff "shuddered" at the thought of going to war with the United States in the Pacific knowing that the massive Chinese Army lay on the flank.

The general staff rejected Ushakov's proposals on sound military grounds. The Soviet Pacific Fleet deployed about 40 strategic missile submarines (SSBNs and SSBs), 80 diesel or atomic powered attack submarines, 75 major surface combatants, and 250 fixed-wing combat aircraft, although not all of these forces were operational. In addition, a dozen ships, a half-dozen submarines, and about 75 aircraft were deployed in the Indian Ocean. Air defense force assets in the Far East included 600 modern interceptors, but these were stretched along a 3,000-mile arc from Novosibirsk to Kamchatka. Frontal aviation forces in the Far Eastern military district totalled about 390 aircraft, although most were based along the border with China. Thus, of the nearly 1,000 fighters deployed in the Far East, no more than 375 were deployed where they could support the Soviet navy in a maritime war in the Pacific.

The United States Pacific Fleet deployed about 270 major surface combatants and submarines, although on D day no more than 50 were in the Western Pacific, supported by about 350 land- and sea-based navy and marine aircraft, including about 100 fighters. The U.S. Air Force deployed another 250 aircraft in Japan, Korea, and the Philippines, mostly fighters. Japan's entry into the war would add 75 submarines and major naval combatants, 80 naval aircraft, and 360 aircraft of the Air Self Defense Force, including 260 fighters, to the allied order of battle. "With Japan by their side," Ignatiev warned, "the Americans will achieve parity in overall air strength and a marked superiority in fighter types."

Accordingly, the general staff was unwilling to support ADM Ushakov's calls for a D day assault against Japan. "We are not unaware of the possibility that the Japanese will intervene in any case," Ignatiev announced, "but we expect to win in Europe before that eventuality comes to pass."

Having concluded, Ilichev and Ignatiev, both army officers, looked to Ushakov. The admiral sat silently. Then he began to nod. "I have my differences with the general staff and the army," he told Ignatiev, "and I'll put them on paper for you before you return to Moscow. Nevertheless, I must admit that given our strategic position out here in the Far East, none of the options available are particularly attractive. So we'll do it your way."

Thus, on D day the Soviets began not a military, but diplomatic and public affairs offensives in Japan, South Korea, the Philippines, Singapore, Indonesia, and Taiwan. Soviet diplomats entreated and threatened each of these countries to remain neutral and to forbid the operations of American forces from their soil. Other Soviet officials, local communists, and their supporters initiated campaigns designed to divide public opinion and to persuade East Asians that they ought not to allow themselves to be dragged into a European war by the United States.

NINE

Shortly after 1100 Tokyo time (1500 at Pearl), reports of air battles over the Sea of Japan began to reach LTG James Bridges, Commander, Fifth Air Force, at his headquarters in Yokota, Japan. To the north, American F-16 Falcons of the 432d Tactical Fighter Wing (TFW), based at Misawa in northern Honshu, and to the south, F/A-18 Hornets of Marine Aircraft Group 15, based at Iwakuni, engaged Soviet MiGs and Sukhois in aerial duels to control the air space to the west of the Japanese home islands. The marine and air force pilots found themselves outnumbered and hard pressed. At 1335, Bridges called GEN Henry Eustace, Commander, Pacific Air Forces at Hickam AFB, Hawaii, over a secure telephone line and requested the release of the two squadrons of F-15 Eagles based at Kadena, Okinawa, which had heretofore been restricted to CAP missions between Japan and Taiwan. Bridges also recommended that Seventh Air Force assets in South Korea be fed into the battle. Eustace promptly gave Bridges complete authority over the 18th TFW at Kadena, but, fearing a North Korean attack across the DMZ, PACAIRFOR, with CINC-PAC's approval, continued to hold the South Korean-based Seventh Air Force's 314th Air Division in reserve.

The D day dogfights over the Sea of Japan pitted at least 150 Soviet against about 75 American fighters. Despite this disparity in strength, the American airmen quickly demonstrated their superior skills, tactics, hardware, and methods of airborne command and control. Only eight American fighters failed to return, while the Soviets lost over three-dozen fighters and as many as forty other aircraft, principally reconnaissance types.

Soviet and American fighters also tangled over the South China Sea. At 1137, a pair of Tomcats from the *Carl Vinson* downed a Badger flying a reconnaissance mission from Nha Trang. The Tomcats soon found themselves "bounced" by four Soviet MiG-23s. The F-14s downed two of the Flankers and gave up the pursuit of the others to a second pair of Tomcats who found themselves in a furball with Vietnamese MiG-21s a hundred miles from the coast of Vietnam. U.S. Air Force F-4 Phantom IIs of the 3d TFW from Clark AFB also tangled with Vietnamese MiGs over the South China Sea. These initial encounters were far from decisive. Few aircraft were lost—two Soviet and three Vietnamese MiGs, and the lone reconnaissance aircraft which before its demise reported the position of the American carrier. The most significant aspect of the engagement was the participation of the Vietnamese. At noon, RADM Holmes, commander of the *Vinson* group, requested permission "to strike Soviet and Vietnamese airbases before they strike at me." Within fifteen minutes, Holmes's entreaty, with CINCPAC's endorsement, had passed up the chain of command and received an affirmative response.

Holmes's staff had already worked the bugs out of a contingency plan for a coordinated attack by American aircraft flying from the carrier and Clark. Shortly after 1400, an E-2C Hawkeye coordinated a strike by navy Tomcats, Hornets, Intruders, Prowlers, and air force F-4s and FB-111s from the Philippines. Soviet and Vietnamese interceptors were quickly overwhelmed. The Tomcats and Hornets made quick work of the outdated MiGs, mostly Flankers and Fishbeds. More than a score were downed in air-to-air combat while strike aircraft devastated the SAM defenses around Nha Trang and destroyed as many as seventy-five aircraft on the ground. American losses totalled four aircraft.

Near disaster marred Holmes's success. While recovering its aircraft, a sudden wind change forced the *Vinson* to adopt a course alteration that threw into confusion the task group's ASW screen, including the SSN *Springfield*. While the group's ASW assets mistakenly stalked the *Springfield*, a pair of Soviet attack submarines—reportedly a *Yankee* and a *Victor II*—penetrated the screen and sank the cruiser *Vincennes* and the destroyer *Leftwich*, which took three torpedoes intended for the *Vinson*.

The Soviets gained even greater successes on D day in the North Pacific. Several hours before hostilities began, Soviet Bear reconnaissance aircraft located four American frigates convoying six container ships about nine hundred miles southeast of Hokkaido along the Seattle-Yokohama sealift route. Throughout the morning and early afternoon, the Pacific Fleet KPF vectored air, surface, and subsurface assets—the *Novorossiysk-Kalinin* group, a *Foxtrot*, an *Akula*, and SNA Backfires and Badgers—into strike positions. The attacks began at 1330 and lasted for three hours. All ten American ships were sunk. The Soviets lost neither a ship, a plane, nor a submarine. ADM Ushakov saw the sharp engagement as a vindication of his strategic ideas for Pacific operations. "This battle was," he reported to the general staff, "a classic example of our combined action naval doctrine and the most successful engagement fought by our naval forces on D day, anywhere."

For CINCPAC, the convoy debacle was one of those events in life that suddenly bring everything into sharp focus. The loss of the container ships, loaded with ordnance and spare parts for air force squadrons in Japan, placed an immediate burden on American air transport assets which had to be shifted from other missions to fly supplies to the western Pacific. The Soviet success also demonstrated the dangers of operating without air cover. ADM Cooper immediately saw the wisdom of ADM Jernigan's strategy. Allied land-based air assets in South Korea and Japan blocked the movement of Soviet strike aircraft to the south and to the east. Their only way out was to the north—between Hokkaido and Kamchatka. The only way to plug that gap was with naval air. Fortunately, Jernigan had his carriers closing in perfectly—the *Kitty Hawk* coming down from the Aleutians, and the *Independence* coming up from Yokosuka. But Cooper remained concerned: could two carriers fight their way into the gap and close it? Cooper hoped for the best. At least the *Kitty Hawk* continued to evade detection, while the Soviet attack, though successful, demonstrated that the *Novorossiysk* group was further south than CINCPAC had feared and posed no threat to the *Kitty Hawk* which continued to close the range on Petropavlovsk.

At Vladivostok, Ushakov used the successful afternoon attack on the American convoy to convince the Far Eastern commander, GEN Ilichev, to support a more offensive strategy at sea. Throughout the evening of 14 July, Ushakov and his staff worked to maintain the initiative in the North Pacific. About 2200, the *Novorossiysk* and *Tashkent* groups rendezvoused seven hundred miles east of Hokkaido and steamed at twenty knots toward the west. The *Baku* group had left Vladivostok and sped north along the Khabarovsk coast. If all went according to plan, the Soviet Pacific Ocean Fleet would catch the *Independence* task group, then steaming north from Yokosuka, "in a vise northeast of Hokkaido and annihilate the Americans with an overwhelmingly powerful combined attack."

But the *Baku* group's move north would also virtually denude the Sea of Japan of major Soviet surface forces. When an alarmed Ilichev questioned Ushakov's plan, the POF commander responded that with Japan neutral there was little risk. RADM Yevgeni Tarasov's KUG would be off Vladivostok by the evening of 15 July. That Tarasov was anywhere near the Sea of Japan was, in fact, principally Ilichev's doing. Ushakov had wished to use the cruiser-destroyer group as a raiding force in the East Indies. It had been the Far Eastern TVD commander who had directed Ushakov to order Tarasov to steam north from the Malacca Strait on 9 July. Unfortunately, engine failure in the flagship—the *Kresta* II-class cruiser *Admiral Makarov*—forced Tarasov to halt for repairs at Shanghai. Tarasov had just managed to complete his repairs and leave port six hours before the war had begun. Now the group raced north for safety and a potentially dangerous passage in wartime through the Tsushima Strait.

Of more immediate concern to Ushakov were alarming, though not surprising, reports that American attack submarines were patrolling off Petropavlovsk. Late in the evening of D day, the admiral proudly observed his staff direct a pair of *Victor III*s into an ambush that sank the SSN *Omaha* and almost caught a second American SSN, the *Pogy*.

Off the east coast of Honshu, the Pacific Ocean Fleet command post struggled to vector another *Victor III* and a *Foxtrot* into contact with the *Independence* group as it steamed north from Yokosuka. The decision taken by the Japanese Maritime Self-Defence Force (MSDF) to use Yokosuka-based Escort Flotillas 1 and 4 to conduct an ASW sweep ahead of the American carrier, ostensibly "to secure access to Japan's ports" in keeping with Japanese neutrality, complicated the Soviet effort. A Mitsubishi HSS-2B Sea King ASW helicopter from the destroyer *Shirane* located the *Foxtrot* and passed the information on to the Americans. A pair of SA-3 Vikings from the *Independence* were soon on the scene and hunted down and destroyed the Soviet submarine. Only by praiseworthy handling did the commander of the *Victor* achieve an attack position against one of the American screening vessels and torpedo, but fail to sink, the destroyer *Oldendorf*.

In the Sea of Japan, although aerial engagements continued throughout the day, surface and subsurface activity remained limited. Soviet intelligence correctly estimated that only two American submarines were active, although the eight Japanese boats at sea, and the loss of more than a dozen patrol aircraft, made effective tracking difficult and left Ushakov's KPF confused. The Pacific Fleet commander knew that the Japanese were conducting surveillance operations with their submarines and patrol aircraft and relaying the information to the Americans. Ushakov considered Japanese actions in the Sea of Japan, as well as the obvious screening conducted for the *Independence* as it sortied from Yokosuka, "troubling and hardly the acts of a neutral."

Late in the evening of D day reports reached Vladivostok that North Korean submarines were leaving their bases at Cha-ho and Pipa-got and taking stations in the Sea of Japan and the East China Sea. Ilichev wondered whether the North Koreans were about to enter the war? "The expansion of the struggle to the Korean peninsula," he warned Ushakov, "will greatly complicate our relations with Japan and the PRC, whether the invasion succeeds or not." Ushakov agreed. A Korean war would at the minimum "turn the Tsushima Strait into a battle zone" and threaten the movement of RADM Tarasov's group into the Sea of Japan.

Tarasov's sprint north from Shanghai had not gone unnoticed by the Americans, Japanese, or the South Koreans. All three nations moved forces into the Tsushima Strait during D day. RADM Kim Hyung Duk, commanding the South Korean Third Fleet, left Pusan and entered the waters of the strait with a force of fourteen ships. The four destroyers of Japanese Escort Flotilla 2 left Sasebo shortly after noon and the Maritime Staff Office rushed Escort Flotilla 3's five destroyers south from Maizuru.

Of course, neither South Korea nor Japan were at war with the Soviet Union and few American forces were available to challenge Tarasov's move through the Tsushima Strait. The marine Hornets at Iwakuni were fully committed to the air-to-air battle over the Sea of Japan. The Iwakuni-based marine attack squadron, the A-6Es of VMA-242, spent the day preparing for what proved to be an abortive strike against the *Baku* group as it left Vladivostok. The *Sturgeon*-class SSN *Tunny* remained docked at Sasebo, replacing its towed array sonar which had been lost in an accident with a Japanese fishing boat. Only the thirty-year-old diesel boat—the *Barbel*—was able to leave Sasebo during afternoon to take up a position in the southern approaches to the strait. At 2340, the *Barbel*'s commander achieved a firing position but "found the Soviet ships off Tori-shima mixed in with several large Japanese-flagged tankers." Unwilling to risk damaging the neutrals, he found his twenty-knot boat "quickly outpaced by the Russians as they raced north at over thirty knots."

That same evening, the *Barbel*'s sister submarine, the *Blueback*, had much better hunting in La Perouse (Soya) Strait. A large Soviet convoy of fifteen corvettes escorting ten freighters, which had left Sovetskaya Gavan bound for Petropavlovsk earlier in the day, neared Kaiba Island (O. Moneron) about 2000. At 2013, Fitzgerald executed a perfect attack, firing all six bow torpedoes at two merchant ships, sinking both. Before the *Blueback* could reload its tubes, Soviet patrol aircraft began dropping sonobuoys in a pattern between the convoy and the American diesel boat. Fitzgerald felt compelled to break off the attack and the convoy subsequently passed safely through La Perouse Strait.

The bitterest fighting on the evening of D day occurred in the South China Sea. Following the successful afternoon raids, RADM Holmes continued to steam closer to the coast of Vietnam intent on "taking out the Russkies as quickly as possible so I can get back up to the North Pacific before the action up there is over." Holmes's aggressiveness caused some raised eyebrows on the Hawaii staffs. Reason for concern seemed justified when a message reached CINCPAC that a third ship of the *Vinson* task group, the destroyer *Thorn*, had been torpedoed and badly damaged.

Undaunted, Holmes persisted in his plans. At 2330, a second joint attack began. As navy F-14s provided cover, air force Phantoms, FB-111s, and B-52s struck SAM installations around Cam Ranh Bay, while the *Vinson*'s Hornets and Intruders attacked the Soviet surface squadron which, to Holmes's surprise, still lay at anchor. Having destroyed SNA assets in Vietnam, Holmes now intended to eliminate the threat posed by Russian surface forces based at Cam Ranh Bay.

Vietnamese MiGs vainly attempted to drive off the attacking American aircraft. Tomcats of the *Vinson*'s VF 111—the Sundowners—"hosed" at least a dozen MiGs. Soviet-manned SAM installations scored somewhat better results, destroying five B-52s early in the raid. But the strike succeeded in knocking out more than half the SAM sites and destroyed several key command and storage centers. Attacking navy aircraft sank two *Kashin*-class destroyers and the replenishment ship *Vladimir Kolechitsky*.

RADM Yevgraf Blaghoi, commander of the KUG, had resisted recommendations from his staff and suggestions from the Pacific Fleet KPF that he should steam into the South China Sea and attack the American CVBG. Blaghoi believed such a course would take his destroyers beyond effective CAP and lead to his force's destruction at the hands of American aircraft. He had remained anchored at Cam Ranh Bay in the belief that Soviet and Vietnamese fighters, and an extensive SAM defensive system, would protect his ships from air attack.

The successful American raids in the afternoon and evening of 14 July left Blaghoi's KUG exposed. As the KUG commander surveyed the damage to his force, he received a sighting report from one of the Soviet submarines stalking the *Vinson* that placed the carrier task group no more than 150 miles from the Vietnamese coast. Blaghoi, with half his force and his support ship sunk, now decided to sortie from Cam Ranh Bay.

At 0200 on the fifteenth, Blaghoi's two destroyers, under complete emissions control and making thirty-six knots, closed undetected to within SSM range of the American task group. At Blaghoi's command, the *Kashin*s fired off their entire load (four SSMs each) of Styx missiles. Effective countermeasures, the *Antietam*'s Aegis system, and good fortune foiled the attack. Holmes ordered an immediate counterattack by the *Thorn*, *Yarnell*, and *Antietam*. The more sophisticated American Harpoons found their targets. Within minutes, the *Reshitelny* and *Smyshlenny* were afire and Blaghoi was dead.

As the *Yarnell* picked up survivors, American ASW helicopters detected and shortly thereafter sank a *Victor III*. At 1534, COMSEVENTHFLT relayed a message to Holmes from the *Springfield* that the SSN had sunk a second Soviet attack submarine. "As far as I'm concerned," Holmes radioed Hawaii, "that's it. Sovs are finished in the South China Sea. Unless Vietnamese want to take us on again, it's time to head north."

TEN

The Vietnamese were not, in fact, anxious to continue hostilities with the United States. Hanoi had found itself a participant in the conflict less by design than by accident, when Soviet ground controllers sent Vietnamese MiGs into action against American fighters over the South China Sea during the afternoon of D day. The successful American strikes against Nha Trang and Cam Ranh, the rapid destruction of most of the Soviet air and naval assets based in Vietnam, and the loss of nearly fifty of their own fighters stunned the Vietnamese. Worse yet, late in the day reports reached Hanoi that Australian FB-111s had begun to arrive at Singapore and that Chinese troops were mobilizing along the Vietnamese border. Despite the protestations of the Soviet ambassador who proclaimed it a socialist duty for the Vietnamese to "tie down imperialist American forces in the South China Sea," Hanoi decided to approach the United States through the government of India. The Vietnamese offered to halt immediately all Soviet operations if the Americans would refrain from further attacks. When the president contacted ADM Cooper for his opinion, CINCPAC responded: "We have no designs on Vietnam, and with the Sovs all but eliminated from Cam Ranh, no reason to reject Hanoi's offer." The expansion of the war to Southeast Asia had been contained.

★ ★ ★

Not so in Northeast Asia. At 0300 on 15 July, North Korean forces crossed the DMZ and attacked South Korea. The spread of the war to the Korean peninsula dramatically changed the face of the conflict in Asia. What had been a European war that had overflowed into the Pacific now became an Asian war.

For the Soviet Union, there were several benefits to North Korean intervention. Demands expanded on already overstretched American resources in the Pacific theater. Moreover, if the North succeeded in overrunning the peninsula, the southern flank of the Japanese-South Korean bulwark that enclosed Soviet East Asia would be unhinged.

Nevertheless, the Kremlin had not pushed Pyongyang to enter the war and had attempted, obviously without success, to persuade the North Koreans to remain neutral. As the Soviets had expected, Beijing responded sharply to the spread of the war to the mainland and, fearing an increased Soviet role in the peninsula, accelerated its mobilization in Manchuria.

To the Chinese, a renewed Korean war was a lose-lose proposition. Shiv Vaipul, the Indian ambassador in Beijing, noted that "the Chinese didn't want to see the North Koreans lose, since that might bring the capitalists to the Yalu, but neither did they want to see the North win, since that would cement closer ties between Pyongyang and Moscow. No, the war in the peninsula confronted the PRC with a no-win situation."

To Beijing's chagrin, the war also strengthened the relationship between the United States and the Nationalist regime on Taiwan. The Nationalists viewed the North Korean invasion as "a second June 1950," an opportunity to repeat history and to forge closer ties between Taipei and Washington. "The time is at hand to prove our worth to the Americans as allies," a Nationalist diplomat declared. Two hours after the Korean attack, Taiwan declared war on both North Korea and the Soviet Union, opened its ports and airfields to United States military forces, and began operations against Soviet submarines patrolling in the East China Sea.

But the most significant impact of North Korea's intervention came in Japan. Throughout the day, left wing and neutralist protestors demonstrated outside the Diet building in Tokyo and at the gates of American bases throughout the country. They demanded "the immediate halt of U.S. militarist operations from Japanese soil" fearing that their country would be "dragged into a U.S.-European war." The most violent demonstration occurred at Yokosuka where two policemen and six protestors were killed in a melee. An investigation later determined that the march was organized by the Chae Ilbon Choson In Ch'ong Yonhaphoe, the General Association of Korean Residents in Japan, a North Korean front organization.

The protests heightened the sense of crisis that gripped Japan on the fourteenth. The Diet deliberated throughout the day, debating the course a nation that found itself in the middle of a theater of war ought to take. Should Japan intervene alongside the United States, or remain neutral? And if the latter, how should that neutrality be defined?

Prime Minister Tomozuki Inoguchi favored intervention. He had been a Diet member during the security debates that had preceded the U.S.-Japan Joint Communique of May 1981 and had been in the forefront of those who spoke of a "U.S.-Japan alliance" and wanted Japan to play a larger defense role in Asia and the Middle East. Inoguchi knew that most of the members of the House of Councillors likewise favored intervention, but whether such a consensus existed among members of the lower, but more powerful elective body—the House of Representatives—remained to be seen. Wisely, Inoguchi remained noncommittal throughout the debates that began in the late afternoon of 14 July and continued into the early morning hours of the fifteenth. He listened patiently as members argued for a variety of courses that corresponded to the views of the various political factions in Japan. Even as his aides conducted straw polls on the Diet floor, Inoguchi came to the conclusion that Japan was "too divided politically" to risk intervention.

But that mood changed suddenly at 0310 when the exhausted Diet members received word of the North Korean assault. The impact was immediate. As a Japanese Defense White Paper had concluded: "Historically, the Korean Peninsula holds the key to Japan's security. To this day, the peace and stability of the Korean Peninsula remains a vital factor in Japan's national security." To a majority of the Diet members, the North Korean assault across the DMZ directly threatened Japan.

At 0340, Inoguchi finally rose to speak. He confirmed the reports of the North Korean attack. He mentioned that he had received word that Taiwan would soon declare war. Then he reviewed the options available to Japan. He dismissed the arguments of the extreme neutralists who wished to demand the halt of American operations from all bases in Japan. Such rights had been granted in the U.S.-Japanese Security Treaty and could not be denied. Then Inoguchi moved the debate to the question of intervention.

> What are the interests of our country? Are concerns about Europe peculiar to the Americans? How well will Japan fare in a world dominated by the Soviet Union? Where, I would ask, are our markets? Do we want to see Europe overrun by the Soviet army? Do we want to see the Americans defeated and humbled militarily? And

what about the communist attack in Korea, a dagger aimed at Japan? Our Middle Eastern oil supplies have stopped flowing. What are we to do about the war going on all around us? I would ask you to go back to the Diet debates in the early 1980s, look at the record. We spoke then of a U.S.-Japan Alliance. We claimed to be the Americans' equals—partners in Asian security. Now it is time to pay for that partnership and to bear that burden, not in the interest of the United States, but in the interests of Japan. Is this a war that originated in Europe? Yes, certainly. But, I ask you, who started the war? The United States? No, the Soviet Union. And again, I tell you to look at the record. We have sized our defense forces on the assumption that any war in which we would be involved would be a war that originated in Europe and hence would leave us facing only a portion of the Soviet Union's forces. The war we now see is the war for which we have planned. The time has come to act, and to act in our own security interests. Ask yourselves this question: Will Japan's security be improved or diminished if the United States is defeated? To me, the answer is obvious. We must stand by the United States; we must stand by the South Koreans. We cannot afford to stand aside.

After completing his speech, Inoguchi remained at the podium, looking out over a deadly quiet chamber. Then, suddenly, a deputy in the rear sprang to his feet, faced east, threw his hands into the air, and shouted "Banzai!" Soon, other members joined in the cheering, making clear to Inoguchi that the majority of the Diet supported the Prime Minister. At 0440, Japan declared war on the Soviet Union and its allies.

ELEVEN

The North Korean strike south on 15 July involved direct assaults across the border, operations by special forces units that emerged from a half-dozen tunnels under the DMZ, airborne and seaborne commando raids into the South Korean rear, and attacks by North Korean agents and indigenous communist forces in cities and throughout the countryside.

Fortunately, the outbreak of war had brought the allied defenders to full alert status and the North Korean attacks, while they were executed with the expected vigor, were dealt with fairly successfully by South Korean and American military and security forces. A half-dozen South Korean senior officers, including the commander of the Second Army, were assassinated, but raids against the country's political leadership and LTG Wade Freeman, Commander, U.S. Forces Korea (COMUSKOREA) and commander of the ROK-United States Combined Forces Command (CFC), failed miserably. The South Korean navy's First Fleet, operating along the eastern coast, and Second Fleet, along the western coast, intercepted and destroyed all but a handful of the small North Korean raiding craft and three submarines that ventured south. Likewise, South Korean and American interceptors downed the vast majority of North Korean transports that attempted to carry paratroopers or commandoes south. The few North Koreans who managed to get ashore or jump to safety were contained and eventually rounded up by the Republic of Korea (ROK) Second Army in the lower half of the peninsula, and by the rear echelon elements of the First and Third Armies further north.

But the principal threat to South Korea, and the main North Korean effort, came directly across the DMZ. Three powerful North Korean corps led the assault. The North Korean I Corps, with four divisions in the initial assault, drove south along the east coast out of the "Punchbowl" and along the coastal roads. In the area between the "Iron Triangle" and Sangnyong, the V Corps—six infantry, one armored and one mechanized division—drove south along the traditional route of invasion—the Uijongbu corridor toward Seoul, the South Korean capital. The North Koreans concentrated their II Corps—four infantry and one armored division—between Sangnyong and the coast for the direct drive along the axis Kaesong—Munsan—Seoul.

Although the North Korean general staff had planned the I Corps offensive as a subsidiary attack designed to force the commitment of ROK reserves along the east coast, North Korean infantry divisions, heavily supported by armor, made rapid progress south and the ROK First Army, holding the eastern half of the DMZ, lost ground steadily throughout 15 July. Driving out of the Punchbowl, the I Corps cut the lateral Kansong-Hongch'on road and early on

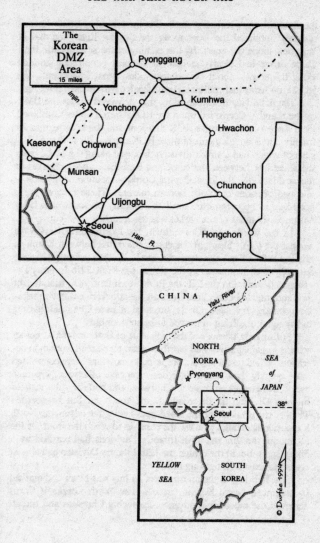

The
Korean
DMZ
Area

15 miles

Imjin R.

Pyonggang

Yonchon

Kumhwa

Hwachon

Kaesong

Chorwon

Munsan

Chunchon

Uijongbu

Seoul

Han R.

Hongchon

CHINA

Yalu River

NORTH
KOREA

SEA
of
JAPAN

Pyongyang

38°

Seoul

YELLOW
SEA

SOUTH
KOREA

© Durfee 1990

the sixteenth took Kansong itself. But the arrival of South Korean reserves stabilized the front along the Soyang River line and at Yangyang along the coast. By the evening of the seventeenth, the I Corps' drive had clearly stalled, its deepest penetration coming along the coast—about twenty-five miles. Most importantly, the ROK First Army had contained the offensive with its own resources.

The main North Korean blow, that delivered across the DMZ by the II and V Corps, fell upon the ROK-United States Combined Field Army (CFA)—twelve ROK divisions and the U.S. Army's 2d Infantry Division. Elements of three ROK corps—the I, V, and VI— each of which had a single division deployed along the DMZ, held the allied line between the coast and Kumhwa. Other reserves in the west included the ROK Capital Corps—a reinforced division— and two brigades of South Korean marines. These reserves were not likely to be committed until the security of Seoul, which lay within thirty miles of the DMZ, was assured.

In the words of LTG Freeman, the North Korean offensive against the CFA "blew out the entire allied line between Kumhwa and the Yellow Sea." On the right, the ROK 15th Infantry Division fell back from Kumhwa. In the center, the ROK 12th Infantry Division collapsed. On the left, the ROK 9th Infantry Division fought well and inflicted heavy casualties on the attackers but nevertheless lost ground everywhere. On the situation maps at CFA headquarters in Uijongbu, the front appeared to be in shambles.

Fortunately, because of the high state of alert, and the successes achieved against attempted North Korean rear-area commando operations, allied reserves were prepared to move and were committed more quickly than might have been the case otherwise. Freeman had ROK reserves en route to Chorwon, and had the American 2d Infantry Division on the road toward Yonch'on. But he doubted whether the units along the DMZ could delay the advancing North Koreans long enough to allow the reserves to reach the front. By the afternoon, the 9th and 15th Infantry Divisions had patched up a line of sorts. But in the center, the 12th Infantry Division had almost ceased to exist as a fighting unit.

The fighting on the afternoon of 15 July was bitter and marked by continued North Korean success. The North Korean V Corps achieved the most rapid advance, capturing Chorwon and threatening Yonch'on. The II Corps drove south as well, reaching the Imjin river line north of Munsan.

In the early evening of the fifteenth, MG Lorenzo Merriwether, commander of the United States 2d Infantry Division, pushed elements of his 1st Brigade up Route 33 and into action about three miles north of Yonch'on. The American counterattack, conducted by M-1A1 Abrams tanks of the 4/69 Armored Battalion, supported by the 3/5 Cavalry Mechanized Infantry Battalion, drove back a regiment of the North Korean 8th Infantry Division. "It isn't much of a success," Merriwether admitted, "but it's the only ground that we've managed to retake the whole goddamned day and that's good enough for me."

★ ★ ★

For LTG Freeman, the successful American riposte north of Yonch'on brought the first day's fighting to an upbeat conclusion. The American commander in South Korea confidently reported to CINCPAC: "ROK and US troops fighting well; NKs taking heavy losses and advancing slowly; air attrition rates heavily in US/ROK favor." Freeman passed to Hawaii reports from the South Korean Joint Chiefs of Staff that indicated that North Korean rear area raids had been contained and that ROK reserves would not be pinned down for more than a few days.

Nevertheless, Freeman noted that, however slowly, his forces were "yielding ground along entire front and cannot afford to continue such retrograde at present rate another forty-eight hours without losing Seoul." And while North Korean losses had been heavy, so too had South Korean casualties in the fighting along the DMZ. The ROK 12th Infantry Division had all but disintegrated. Freeman concluded: "Timely US reinforcement and resupply critical."

TWELVE

At 0130 on 15 July, Chief of Naval Operations ADM John H. "Jack" Cardswell sat exhausted in his chair in Flag Plot, sipping lukewarm coffee as aides reviewed the first day's operations. The CNO had just returned from a late-night JCS meeting with the president, the Secretary of Defense Walter Martin, Secretary of State Lyman Ritchie, and National Security Advisor Richard Zucker. The meeting, the fifth of the day for the Chiefs, had focused on Cuba. At the last minute, the president had cancelled planned air strikes against Cuban airbases and SAM installations. Cardswell had sweated the decision, agreeing with the president only at the last minute. The CNO had been somewhat surprised by his commander-in-chief's reluctance to launch a preemptive strike even in the midst of a global war. Yet the president had stated firmly that "Americans just do not attack first."

Cardswell considered such sentiments misplaced, given the circumstances. But the navy's senior admiral recognized the wisdom of the president's thinking. The Cubans had remained remarkably quiet during the fourteenth. At 2230 Cuban President Fidel Castro had issued a statement, obviously timed for maximum coverage on American late evening news, calling for all parties "to prevent the spread of war to the Americas." Was this a bluff by Castro? Or had the American warnings delivered to the Cubans earlier in the afternoon at their United Nations mission in New York paid dividends? A letter, signed by the American president, had warned that the United States was prepared to use its military power "to the maximum extent necessary" to ensure that shipping, critical to the war effort, not be subjected to attack by any forces operating from Cuba. Although the president had ruled out the use of nuclear weapons, he was prepared to use Strategic Air Command bombers to "bomb the hell out of that damned island." The president's determination to act ruthlessly had been purposefully leaked to the White House press corps and had been reported on the evening news.

Both the president and Secretary of State Ritchie were convinced that such threats were responsible for Castro's seemingly responsible attitude. Cardswell agreed, but suggested that Havana's restraint might not last once American forces presently deployed in the southeastern United States moved to reinforce the European,

Pacific, and Middle Eastern commands. "You don't really think we can trust Castro," he asked, "do you?" "Certainly not," the secretary of state replied, "but what options do we have?"

The existence of a potentially hostile Communist base astride the major Caribbean sea routes especially troubled Cardswell. The navy would be responsible for escorting past the island more than a score of convoys carrying troops, equipment, and supplies to Europe and the Middle East. As much as half of the army's heavy equipment, and 90 percent of petroleum-oil-lubricants that had to be moved overseas would be shipped from Gulf of Mexico ports and would have to pass Cuba. The three *Foxtrot* diesel submarines operating from Cienfuegos and over eighty torpedo- and missile-armed fast attack boats of the Cuban navy posed a significant threat to the SLOCs. Of the 20 squadrons of the Cuban air force, about 250 combat aircraft, at least a fifth—a dozen or so old MiG-17s armed with bombs and three dozen MiG-23BNs armed with AS-7 Kerry ASMs—were capable of strikes against American shipping. There were also Soviet forces in the Caribbean and in Cuba itself.

But as anxious as Cardswell and the other chiefs were to take out the island, no one was eager to see American assets earmarked for other theaters needlessly diverted and possibly tied down in a Caribbean campaign. The Cubans had not entered the war. "Why open up another theater of operations?" Zucker asked. "Its risky," Cardswell responded. "Sure," the NSC advisor replied, "but so are the alternatives; can you guarantee that Cuban air and naval forces can be eliminated quickly." No such assurance was forthcoming. "Then why stir up a hornets' nest?" Somewhat reluctantly, the chiefs had agreed to go along with the president and his advisors and to leave Castro's Cuba "armed and dangerous."

What American decision makers in Washington did not know on the evening of 14 July, was that Castro's apparent restraint was less the result of American warnings, than of a Soviet decision made weeks before to delay Cuban entry into the conflict. Soviet planners estimated that the important NATO-bound convoys would not be ready to leave Gulf of Mexico ports until the second week of the war. Cuban entry into the war on D day would provoke an immediate American response. In Moscow, the analysts of the general staff concluded that such attacks would destroy Cuban and Soviet Cuban-based air and naval assets within seventy-two hours. The planners recommended that the Cubans "play up their neutrality" until such time that convoys critical to the NATO effort were within striking distance. The Supreme High Command agreed, and instructed Soviet forces in Cuba to refrain from actions that might compromise Cuban neutrality. In a private meeting shortly before the war, the Soviet commander in Havana, GEN Mikhail Odintsov, told Castro: "we have no desire to spend our assets prematurely. We'll wait until we're ready, and by then, American forces in the region will be much weaker."

★ ★ ★

But not all Russian forces in the Caribbean were based in Cuba. At the outbreak of war, five Soviet submarines began operations against American and allied shipping in the region. At 1410 local time on the fourteenth, an American container ship was torpedoed and sunk fifty miles west of Providence Island, a small Columbian possession off the eastern coast of Nicaragua. About two hours later, a U.S. Navy P3-C patrol plane reported a submarine contact seventy-five miles north of Providence. Short of fuel, the Orion broke off an attempt to localize and attack.

At 1820 the American submarine *Bluefish* began a run at periscope depth for its scheduled communication period. With its radio antenna extended, the *Sturgeon*-class SSN established a downlink with a communications satellite and in short databursts received the messages relevant to its operations. Several coded dispatches involved the projected movement of the contacted Soviet submarine making its way north, perhaps toward the Yucatan Channel or the Cuban base at Cienfuegos. Southern Command (SOUTHCOM) instructed the *Bluefish*, then about a hundred miles southwest of Swan Island, to intercept and attack.

As the *Bluefish*'s commander, CAPT Jesse "Cat" Kraus, read the message, he felt a sudden sense of exhilaration. After years of training, real action seemed at hand. With his XO, CDR Thomas Donovan, Kraus made a quick study of the navigation charts and concluded that the Russian submarine, if it continued north, would probably pass between the Gorda and Rosalind Banks. Kraus made his decision. "Take her down to five hundred feet; come to course 135; crank her up."

For two hours the *Bluefish* ran at twenty-four knots, its depth reducing the cavitation noise produced by the high revolutions of the propeller. At 2030, in position midway between the two banks, Kraus brought his boat up to 315 feet and found a shadow, or blind sonar zone, under a thermal layer. Slowed to five knots, trailing its BQR-15 towed array sonar, the *Bluefish* headed SSW as sonarmen listened for the sounds a high speed submarine would make.

Patience was the essence of ASW operations. The minutes passed slowly for Kraus and his crew. Donovan paced restlessly.

"Contact!" The report from Pete Matthews, the *Bluefish*'s most experienced sonarman, startled Kraus. "Bearing 110." Kraus looked at his watch. It was 2110.

"Come to 090. Maintain depth and speed. Let's have some analysis."

Within minutes the contact had been classified. It was Soviet, an *Alfa*-class SSN, moving at 30 knots. *Alfas* were noisy and easy to distinguish, but they were fast, capable of speeds of up to forty-five knots, nearly twenty knots better than a *Sturgeon*. And the *Alfas* could dive deep, deeper than the *Bluefish*.

"OK, come to 045, at ten knots." The *Bluefish* turned slowly as the sonar module worked to improve its solution. By 2135, a clearer picture had developed. The *Alfa*, now bearing 080, was moving away at high speed. The distance separating the two SSNs was about ten miles, and growing. Tom Donovan looked at the plot and shook his head. "Can't catch this mouse, Cat." But 'Cat' Kraus had a trick up his sleeve. "Torpedo room, let's get a Sea Lance in tube four."

The Sea Lance was a stand-off ASW weapon still in development: a Mach 1 rocket with a thirty-mile range that propelled a Mk-50 Barracuda torpedo to the target. The *Bluefish* had been scheduled to take part in sea trials for Sea Lance off the eastern coast of Florida, but, because of the crisis with the Soviets, the navy cancelled the trials and ordered Kraus south into the Caribbean.

As the torpedomen rushed to unload tube four's Mk-48 and replace it with the Sea Lance, Kraus directed the work of his crew on the Mk 117 fire control console. "I want the shot about a third of a mile from the *Alfa*, to port, deep, with a starboard search pattern." Kraus knew that if the *Alfa*'s low frequency sonar detected the missile's launch, the Soviet commander would immediately take evasive action and turn. If he went left, the Sea Lance would land right on target, if he went right or straight, the Mk-50's pro-grammed search pattern would still have a good chance of homing in on the Russian.

In less than a minute, only Kraus's command was needed to initiate the attack. All eyes focused on the captain. "OK, fire." The *Bluefish*'s number-four tube ejected the Sea Lance capsule. Kraus immediately ordered a course change to 000 and his speed to fifteen to put distance between the *Bluefish* and the launch point in case the *Alfa*'s commander fired a blind shot along the bearing. Sixty seconds after launch, the missile ignited.

"He's turning, captain, to port!" Kraus restrained a smile, satisfying himself with his patented smirk. He dismissed the con-gratulations. "Just a lucky shot, a lucky guess." The Sea Lance was airborne for little more than a minute. "We've got splashdown," came the report from Matthews. Kraus watched the consoles of the computer which integrated the information from the *Bluefish*'s var-ious sensors. He saw the Barracuda diving deep, its active seeker searching for the Soviet submarine. The torpedo turned left, ob-viously homing. Suddenly, another blip appeared. "Noisemaker, sir." The *Alfa* kept turning left. "He decoyed our fish, sir."

Kraus could feel the disappointment growing among his crew, as well as a sense of foreboding. Would the hunter suddenly become the hunted? Kraus immediately sought to cut the tension. "Not so quick, guys, this fish has a bit more life to it."

The torpedo, momentarily confused, began to search as pro-grammed, to the right, bringing it directly into a stern chase of the Russian boat. The *Alfa* was at its apparent flank speed—forty-four-knots—diving deep, but the torpedo was pursuing at sixty knots. The Soviet commander released another noisemaker, but too late. The Barracuda found its prey. "Explosion, sir. We got her." Donovan slapped Kraus on the back. A cheer swept through the boat. But Matthews raised his hand, signalling for quiet. After a pause he looked up. "Machinery noise, sir. She's still moving."

"Damn those torpedoes!" Kraus was one of many naval offi-cers concerned about the small, "directed energy," fifty kilogram warhead of the Barracuda. The warhead of the old Mk 48 torpedo carried three hundred kgs of explosive. "Damn," Kraus repeated, "I'd like to direct some energy up the butts of whoever designed that shittin' warhead." The *Bluefish*'s commander just stared at the computer console. "Okay, we at least slowed her down, so now we can catch the bastard and kill her the old-fashioned way."

But just as Kraus started to give the order to increase speed, Matthews interrupted. "Sir, she's still going deeper." Donovan peered over the sonarman's shoulder. "She's out of control." "No, no," interjected Kraus. "It's her momentum. She was doing what, forty-five knots, diving when we hit her? How deep?" Matthews paused for a few seconds, "About 850 feet, maybe 900." Kraus just nodded. "She's in big trouble, big trouble." All who could watched as the contact continued on course, Matthews reading out new depth estimates. The *Bluefish* was quiet. Then Matthews turned to face his captain. "Explosion sir." "No, Matthews, that's *im*plosion," replied Kraus. "Take us up to fifty feet; we've got a message to send."

★ ★ ★

CNO Cardswell read the copy of the message an aide pressed into his hand as he entered the briefing room. He was unsure just what he enjoyed more, news of the *Bluefish*'s victory, or the opportunity to embarrass his briefers. "Your chart contains incorrect information, lieutenant."

The briefers, pointers in hand, just looked at each other. "Sir?"

"You've got five Russian subs in the Caribbean, they've only got four."

"Sir, intelligence . . ."

"That's old information lieutenant. Cat Kraus's *Bluefish* just sent an *Alfa* to the bottom, first successful use of Sea Lance. Let's change the numbers up there. And get on with this briefing. I'm an old man and I need some sleep."

"Yes sir."

As the two young lieutenants continued their briefing and the day's operations unfolded on a giant map of the world, Cardswell found himself growing increasingly enthusiastic about the president's decision regarding Cuba. As much as he regretted passing up an opportunity "to kick some Cuban butt," Jack Cardswell recognized that the war was not to be won in the Caribbean. The Cuban shit was a sideshow, and he knew it. The navy's job was to concentrate its greatest strength in the two most important theaters—the northeastern Atlantic and the northwestern Pacific. Not

125

having to deploy, at least for the time being, major forces in the Caribbean meant that additional assets were available for operations elsewhere.

Cardswell noted the positions of American naval forces. Ten of the U.S. Navy's fifteen carrier battlegroups (CVBGs) and two battleship battlegroups (BBBGs) were at sea. The CNO thought back to his innumerable appearances before Congressional committees. The navy's fifteen CVBGs, with their multi-billion dollar price tags, had been a constant target for budget cutters. There had been times when even Cardswell had thought that perhaps the navy could survive with fourteen, or thirteen, or twelve. But now, deployed around the globe, the carriers seemed terribly exposed and far too few to meet American commitments.

Fortunately, the navy had survived D day without losing a carrier, despite the fact that they had all begun operations independently. The various carrier task forces at sea in the North Atlantic, the Mediterranean, and the Pacific were just beginning to concentrate.

The optimal battlegroup included four carriers. Navy analysts had determined that a CVBG's power increased geometrically when carriers operated collectively. Two carriers operating together, for example, were far more than twice as effective as a single carrier. But with only ten carriers available for operations, the navy could hardly concentrate four-carrier groups in the four theaters in which it found itself engaged. Only VADM Emerson, Commander, Second Fleet, now designated NATO's Commander, Striking Fleet Atlantic (COMSTRIKFLTLANT), controlled four carriers, although they were spread across the North Atlantic. VADM Turner would have to get by with a pair of carriers in the Mediterranean, RADM Anthony Moore with the *Nimitz* in the Indian Ocean, and ADM Thomas Jernigan with three in WESTPAC. In the Atlantic base at Mayport, Florida, yard personnel were hard at work readying the *Saratoga* for sea. But Cardswell doubted that the carrier would be operational any time soon. Of the Pacific Fleet's additional carriers, the *Ranger* was getting SLEPed (sea life extension program) on the east coast, the *Enterprise* was in the yard for her planned, laborious, atomic refuelling, the *George Washington* had just completed trials, and the *Constellation* was refitting on the west coast.

The situation in the North Pacific especially concerned the CNO. Cardswell considered the Seventh Fleet too weak to undertake the operations envisioned for the command. But there was little that could be done until the *Vinson* completed its operations in the South China Sea or the *Nimitz* its role in the Indian Ocean. The carriers could then be shifted to the North Pacific.

That decision, of course, would not be Cardswell's. Despite his title, the Chief of Naval Operations had not controlled his service's operations since the 1950s. The CINCs directed operations, and the secretary of defense, or the president, who was *the* commander-in-chief, made the strategic decisions.

As the navy's senior uniformed officer, and a member of the Joint Chiefs of Staff, Cardswell did play an advisory role, an important one when it came to naval-related issues. It had been the CNO who had argued in the final days before the war that the *Abraham Lincoln* should be assigned to the Second, and not the Sixth Fleet. "I want at least one damned four-carrier battlegroup deployed somewhere," Cardswell argued. And it was the northeastern Atlantic theater that he considered "most critical." Secretary of Defense Martin wanted to send three carriers to the Mediterranean. But as war became imminent, and with the *Abraham Lincoln* two days out of Norfolk, Cardswell argued that the carrier would not reach the Mediterranean in time. "The situation in the Med," he assured Martin, "will work itself out so quickly that the campaign there will be decided before *Abe*'s arrival." The CNO's insistence on concentration won the day and the *Abraham Lincoln* was steaming northeast toward the Norwegian Sea.

As he looked at the slide showing a map of the world and the location of forces, Cardswell reviewed in his mind the grand strategy that guided deployments. For all its seeming complexity, allied strategy was actually pretty damned simple: defend on land, gain control of the sea, reinforce, and counterattack. That was it. The ground forces had to hold the line in Europe, the Middle East, and Asia. Allied navies had to clear and secure the sea lanes. Reinforcements would fly and steam across the oceans. And then the alliance would strike back.

The first two elements of the strategy were the most critical. Unless the ground forces could hold the line, there would be no one to reinforce. And unless the navies could gain command of the sea, the ground forces would be lost. That was true in Germany, Norway, southern Europe, and the Korean peninsula.

What always amazed Cardswell was how little the strategy had changed since the late 1940s. There had been innumerable strategic debates about this and that, but the basic outlines of allied strategy pre-dated the North Atlantic Treaty Organization.

This was especially true for the naval forces. In the late 1940s, planners considered it impossible to hold on the ground in Germany or in Korea. But from the start of the Cold War, the British and American navies expected to deploy their naval forces forward in the event of war. The allies planned to push powerful battlegroups consisting of three or four carriers and attack submarines right into the Soviet Union's northern Atlantic and northern Pacific approaches. Naval planners believed that threats to the sea lanes could best be countered at the source by an early offensive against the air and naval bases from which Soviet forces would sortie. Moreover, only successful forward, offensive naval operations could secure the SLOCs to Norway and Japan which, unlike Germany, were all but isolated within sea zones likely to be contested in wartime.

"Let's see the north flank map," Cardswell suddenly demanded, startling the briefers who had assumed that the CNO, who had not uttered a sound for some time, had fallen asleep. A lieutenant slid the world map to the right and pulled from behind it a more detailed map of the northeastern Atlantic. With a long pointer he began indicating the locations of the various American task forces while on an adjacent rear-projection screen flashed charts showing the latest CASREPs (casualty reports). Cardswell laughed when the briefer, summing up the situation on the northern flank, described it as "hairy." "Hairy indeed," said the CNO as he stood up. "Let's just hope that we're not too late getting up there."

THIRTEEN

While Norwegian naval and air units and NATO submarines bore the brunt of the fighting in the Norwegian Sea during the fourteenth of July, CINCLANT (Commander-in-Chief, Atlantic), American ADM Wayne Taylor, concentrated ADM Hugh Emerson's Second Fleet in the North Atlantic. Designated under NATO nomenclature Striking Fleet, Atlantic (STRIKFLTLANT), Emerson's powerful command included the carriers *Forrestal*, already in the Norwegian Sea, the *Dwight D. Eisenhower*, a day behind the *Forrestal*, the *America*, three days behind the *Ike*, and the *Abraham Lincoln*, a day behind the *America*. A major amphibious task group had reached Reykjavik, Iceland, positioned to reinforce the small island nation in the event of a sudden Soviet invasion, or to move northeast toward the Norwegian coast. RADM Raymond Hucks's Amphibious Striking Force (AMPHIBSTRIKFOR) included the amphibious assault ships *Wasp*, *Saipan*, *Iwo Jima*, *Inchon*, and *Guadalcanal*, and seven LPDs, LSDs, and LSTs. Embarked was LTG Jeffrey Campbell's Marine Striking Force (MARINESTRIKFOR)—over fifteen thousand marines of the 8th Marine Regiment, the 3d and 4th battalions of the 10th Marine Artillery Regiment, and support units.

Once ashore, "Bull" Campbell would control II Marine Expeditionary Force (MEF), which included the embarked amphibious forces—the 8th Marine Expeditionary Brigade (MEB)—as well as 4 MEB, the personnel of which were being air transported to Orland, near Trondheim, where they would marry up with their prepositioned equipment. The marines of Campbell's 6 MEB were in or on their way to the Mediterranean.

South of Iceland, four convoys transported the equipment and supplies for the marines and other NATO forces expected to be deployed in north Norway. Ten Canadian and American destroyers and frigates escorted the convoys.

In the eastern Atlantic, the warships of the Royal Navy's Second Task Group (NATO's ASW Strike Force), commanded by RADM Brian Hough, had left United Kingdom bases and were steaming for the Norwegian Sea. The British fleet operated in one amphibious and three formidable ASW task forces which together consisted of two light carriers, eighteen destroyers and frigates, six amphibious transports, and supporting vessels. Each of Hough's small carriers—*Illustrious* and *Invincible*—carried nine Sea King HAS 5 ASW helicopters, eight VTOL Sea Harriers, and three Westland Sea King AEW helicopters. Although effective ASW platforms, the British light carriers were far less capable than their American counterparts.

The amphibious task force transported the 4,000 men of the United Kingdom-Netherlands (UK-NL) amphibious force—the Royal Marine 3d Commando Brigade. With a nominal lift capacity of 2,700 men, the Royal Navy assault ships *Fearless* and *Intrepid*, and the Royal Fleet Auxiliary Service's 5 LSLs (logistic landing ships) were jammed with British and Dutch marines. Officially, the British described conditions as "hard lying," but the situation aboard the ships was more akin to standing room only. The situation was nearly unbearable.

In addition to the Royal Navy's Second Task Group, a pair of Royal Netherlands Navy ASW task forces raced north to support RADM Hough. CINCEASTLANT, ADM Hill-Norton, had requested that CINCHAN transfer the seven Dutch ships from the North Sea to the Norwegian Sea. "It came as no surprise to me," Hill-Norton told an aide, "that my call for assistance was so readily answered." The admiral, of course, served as both CINCEAST-LANT and CINCHAN.

About a dozen Soviet submarines of various types, both diesel and nuclear-powered, lay athwart the sea lanes leading to the Norwegian Sea. The Soviet Northern Fleet staff had charged its submarines with three tasks: reconnaissance for long-range SNA strikes, delaying the movement north of key American convoys and task forces, and attacking NATO ships and installations with torpedoes and missiles. The first Soviet strike came at 0101 Icelandic time (0301 in Germany) when a *Charlie I* class SSGN came to periscope depth just twenty-five miles off the southern coast of Iceland and fired eight SS-N-7 surface-to-surface missiles at the NATO airbase at Keflavik. The missiles narrowly missed critical runways and fuel storage tanks.

Such near misses occurred frequently during the course of the war and may have been related to the fact that the Soviets were slow to update terrain-matching guidance software in their SSMs. The shape of the earth changes constantly, and that process actually

shifts the latitude and longitude of locations. Although the differences were relatively minor, and of little importance to missiles with
atomic warheads, they were significant enough when combined with
the normal circular error probable to degrade the effectiveness of
missiles armed with conventional warheads. American cruise missile programs were subject to regular upgrades.

The Soviets had far better success with more traditional attacks. In the first twenty-four hours of the war, Soviet submarines
and strike aircraft sank nearly half of the twenty-five ships in the
four convoys steaming for north Norway. By the evening of the
fourteenth, one American destroyer, five frigates, and five freighters
were at the bottom of the North Atlantic.

★ ★ ★

CDR Walter Hemphill was the senior officer present afloat (SOPA)
of a four-ship convoy that included his own frigate *Gary*, the *Trippe*,
and the freighters *Banner* and *Cape Carthage*. The small American
convoy, about 650 miles southwest of Keflavik, had been shadowed
throughout the thirteenth by a Russian Bear reconnaissance aircraft. When Hemphill learned at 0100 local time that the war had
begun, he "expected to be attacked straight away."

Hemphill had adopted a column formation for his convoy, with
the *Gary* leading, trailing its SQR-19 towed array sonar, followed at
a distance of about a mile by the *Banner*, then at half-mile intervals
by the *Cape Carthage* and the *Trippe*. One of the *Gary*'s SH-60B
Seahawk helicopters flew about ten miles ahead of the ships.

Hemphill was eager to reach Keflavik. On the twelfth of July,
his second Seahawk had blown an engine and the replacement
would be choppered out to the *Gary* when she neared Iceland. In
the interim, the SOPA had to rely on his remaining Seahawk—an
up-to-date LAMPS III—and the *Trippe*'s old LAMPS I, an SH-2F
Seasprite. Island Commander, Iceland (ISOCOMICELAND) had
promised Hemphill support from Keflavik-based P-3Cs, but except
for a single appearance early on the thirteenth, no Orions had operated anywhere near the convoy.

For over three hours the convoy steamed unmolested on
course at a speed of ten knots. Then, suddenly, at 0405 Hemphill
heard an explosion and ran out onto the starboard bridge wing
of the *Gary* only to see the *Trippe* burning, already listing to port.

A Soviet *Foxtrot*-class diesel submarine had evaded the frigate's SQR-18A2 towed array, slipped into her baffles, and fired a spread of four wire guided torpedoes, all of which struck the *Trippe* in quick succession. Fire on the fantail of the stricken ship prevented her crew from launching her Seasprite before the frigate rolled over and sank.

Hemphill ordered his airborne Seahawk to search the area behind the convoy while the ships slowed to five knots as the *Gary*'s Raytheon SQS-56 sonar began an active search for submarines. The ASW helicopter searched for fifteen minutes before establishing contact. Unfortunately, the Seahawk had been airborne for a considerable time and was running low on fuel. At Hemphill's orders, the helicopter dropped a homing Mk-46 torpedo in the area of the contact then returned to the *Gary* to refuel. The attack failed.

The convoy continued on course, Hemphill watching the smoke from the burning *Trippe* grow smaller in the distance. Because of the proximity of an undetected enemy submarine, no effort, except an emergency call to Iceland for sea-air rescue (SAR), had been made to save the frigate's men in the water, all but a few of whom perished. Hemphill sullenly paced the bridge, occasionally stopping to watch the progress of the Seahawk's refuelling on the closed circuit TV mounted on a bulkhead behind the helmsman.

At 0520 the LAMPS III was again airborne. Hemphill stood on the port bridge wing to watch the helicopter as it made a banking turn to fly ahead of the convoy. But again the sound of an explosion reached the *Gary*. The *Banner* had been struck, starboard side, by multiple torpedoes. Hemphill was frustrated and irate. He stormed down to the combat information center and cursed everybody working the sonar equipment. "Where the hell are these damned submarines?" But acoustic conditions were abominable in the North Atlantic south of Iceland on the fourteenth. Contacts would be few throughout the day.

And Hemphill had additional problems. The *Banner*, a well compartmented ship, was still afloat and making five knots. Her captain requested that the convoy slow to allow the freighter to keep up. But the SOPA, wisely, decided to press on, increasing speed to sixteen knots. "At that speed my sonar will be virtually useless," Hemphill told his executive officer, "but it hasn't been much use up

THE WAR THAT NEVER WAS

to this point in any case." Worse still, his sole remaining helicopter blew an oil pump and was returning to the *Gary*.

Hemphill's plight had not gone unnoticed. A pair of Orions were on their way from Keflavik to assist the battered convoy. But the Northern Fleet KPF had also monitored the progress of the American convoy. Based on the reports of the Bear the previous day, the KPF had vectored a force of four submarines—two *Foxtrots*, an *Echo II*, and a *Charlie I*—into positions to intercept, track, and assail Hemphill's ships. Thus far, the Soviet commanders had executed a series of textbook attacks, one *Foxtrot* sinking the *Trippe*, another damaging the *Banner*. Hemphill's decision to increase speed had taken him away from the danger posed by the two old Russian diesel submarines which closed in on the *Banner* and at 1020 sent the freighter to the bottom. But the faster, nuclear-powered *Echo II* and *Charlie I* boats were still approaching the convoy from the north.

At 1100, Hemphill ordered the *Gary* slowed to five knots to allow its sonar a chance to sweep the area. At 1115, back on the bridge, the SOPA received a report: "Submerged contact, bearing 010." Hemphill raced down the ladder to the CIC where he found everything in order. The Mk-32 launchers were prepared and the Mk-46 Honeywell torpedoes were armed. The crew was angry and anxious to get some revenge. Unfortunately, the next report from sonar was not a firing solution, but a warning—"four high speed screws heading our way." Hemphill ordered full power and the two General Electric LM 2500 gas turbines soon had the ship moving at more than twenty knots. The *Gary*, trailing its Fanfare torpedo decoy, turned hard to port as all hands braced for what seemed the inevitable explosion. Then from the flight deck came the report. "Four wakes passing aft."

Hemphill cursed his lack of a single working helicopter. If he maintained high speed, he was sonar-deaf. If he slowed, he would probably be shot at before he could get off a shot himself. He needed "a damned helo to work that contact."

What Hemphill did not realize was that two submarines were stalking his frigate. He had evaded the torpedoes fired by the *Echo*, but the *Gary*'s evasive maneuvers had taken her right across the bow of the *Charlie I*, at a range of no more than three-quarters of a mile. It took just a minute for the three wire-guided torpedoes to reach the starboard side of the American frigate. It split in two and remained afloat long enough for its position to be marked by a passing Orion.

The arrival of the P-3C, and its subsequent attacks on two separate submerged contacts, saved the *Cape Carthage* and probably damaged or killed one of the *Foxtrots*. But the loss of two frigates and a freighter, laden with important supplies and equipment, was a major setback for NATO.

★ ★ ★

About two hundred miles southwest of Cape Farewell, Greenland, a second American convoy began its day of travail. CDR John L. Roenken commanded the *Perry*-class frigate *Rodney M. Davis* and was the SOPA for a convoy that included the frigate *Clark* and the freighters *Lake* and *Pride*. Like Hemphill's ships, Roenken's had been shadowed during the thirteenth by a Soviet Bear.

Roenken had his frigates deployed ahead and to either side of his two wards, the *Clark* to port, and the *Davis* to starboard. One of the *Davis*'s two Seahawks patrolled ahead. The frigates alternately sprinted and drifted, racing ahead at high speed, then slowing to five knots and listening passively on the SQS-56 sonar.

At 0420, the drifting *Clark*'s sonar detected a submarine bearing 340. Roenken ordered the frigate to launch a Seahawk and, in combination with one from the *Davis*, "to work over the Russian." Within ten minutes the Seahawk was airborne and dropping a pattern of sonobuoys. The sonobuoy splashes apparently alerted the commander of the Soviet submarine, a *Victor II*, that he had been detected. He fired four homing torpedoes at a range of about six miles along the bearing established for the *Clark*, and turned away at high speed.

The *Clark* increased speed and began a series of evasive maneuvers. The frigate avoided the first pair of torpedoes but the second struck her stern. Torn by violent explosions, the ship sank within thirty minutes.

The two Seahawks continued their hunt for the *Victor* and reported an explosion. But the Mk-46 torpedo failed to destroy the double-hulled Soviet submarine. Damaged, it limped toward the north away from the track of the American convoy. Three hours later it ran near the surface, extended its antenna, and radioed a report of its attack back to the Northern Fleet KPF.

The *Victor*'s message, although it contained information several hours old, allowed the Northern Fleet's staff to estimate the approximate position of the convoy. It took another hour to organize a SNA strike, and another two and one-half hours for the regiment of Backfires to reach the target area.

At 1945, local time, the *Davis*'s SPS-49 radar picked up a score or more of contacts bearing 010 at a range of 180 miles. They closed to within about ninety miles when suddenly the twenty or so contacts became sixty or more. The Backfires had released their air-to-surface AS-4 Kitchen missiles.

In the *Davis*'s combat information center (CIC) the radar plot displayed the obvious. Barring a miracle, the ships were "dead meat." The *Davis* only carried three-dozen Standard MR-SM1 surface-to-air missiles. The American SAMs, with a limited effective range of twenty-five miles—a distance the Mach 3.5 Kitchens would cover in about forty-five seconds—had to be guided to their targets by the *Perry*-class frigate's single Mk 13 fire control radar. In a pinch the *Davis* could use its 76mm guns' Mk 92 controller to illuminate a second target, but that still only allowed the crew us to work with two ASMs at a time.

Less than four minutes after the Backfires released their missiles, the *Davis* and the freighters *Lake* and *Pride* were burning hulks. CDR Roenken and 147 of his 198 officers and men were dead.

★ ★ ★

For NATO, the loss of six of ten escorts and five of fifteen freighters, was a major defeat. ADM Taylor considered the loss rate "atrocious and unsustainable." The convoys were still a day or more from effective air cover from Reykjavik, although Tomcats from the *Eisenhower* would be able to provide some degree of protection on the fifteenth. But the submarine threat remained. "We've lost eleven ships," Taylor informed SACEUR, "and we've cost the Russians only a single confirmed kill, and perhaps damaged another submarine or two. That sucks. Another day like this and we'll be in big trouble in Norway."

Fortunately, combat air patrols from the *Eisenhower* and Keflavik, ably directed by American AWACS aircraft, forced two Backfire strikes to abort before reaching their targets. Not a single ship was lost south of Iceland to SNA attack on the fifteenth.

But despite the assignment of continuous coverage by U.S. Navy Orions to the two remaining convoys, Soviet submarines, aggressively directed by the Northern Fleet KPF, pressed their attacks with success. During the course of the fifteenth, Soviet submarines sank the Canadian frigates *Ottawa* and *Saguenay*, and four more American cargo vessels, bringing the two-day total to eight escorts and nine freighters.

Only on the sixteenth did the Russian submarine offensive weaken south of the GIUK Gap. Increased effectiveness on the part of Canadian and American ASW operators certainly played a part, but so too did the profligate expenditure of torpedoes by Soviet submarines.

The nine submarines operating south of Iceland carried approximately 140 torpedoes, of which 25 were nuclear. Before they left their bases for their first patrols, many Soviet submarine commanders tried to unload their nuclear torpedoes and replace them with conventional ones. The general staff, fearing the possibility of nuclear escalation, refused.

By the morning of 16 July, Soviet submarines operating south of Iceland had expended over one hundred torpedoes. The typical successful Soviet submarine attack, of which there were seventeen south of Iceland on the fourteenth and fifteenth of July, expended four torpedoes. The average unsuccessful attack, of which there were at least twelve, expended a pair of torpedoes. Two Soviet submarines were known sunk, taking an average of eight conventionally armed torpedoes with them to the bottom. Thus the typical submarine had only two or three non-nuclear torpedoes remaining, torpedoes which most Russian commanders no doubt wished to retain for the long, dangerous return voyage to the Kola.

Although the allies had suffered heavy losses at sea, by the morning of 16 July the Soviet "happy time" in the waters south of Iceland was at an end. Similarly, the half-dozen Russian submarines that had begun the war off the eastern coasts of the United States and Canada had either been hunted down and destroyed or expended their torpedoes. Most of the remaining Russian submarines were heading north for the Kola. The few still at large were subjected to an increasingly effective ASW campaign.

SACLANT headquarters in Norfolk welcomed the respite from Soviet submarine attacks. But ADM Taylor and other NATO leaders wondered how long would it last. "Whether or not the Russians will be able to resume effective operations," Taylor pointed out to Secretary of Defense Martin, "depends on the extent of their success in the battle for the northern flank."

FOURTEEN

At Allied Forces, Northern Europe (AFNORTH) headquarters in Kolsaas, a small Norwegian town west of Oslo, reports of Soviet submarine successes in the North Atlantic, especially the loss of five of the fifteen American freighters bound for Norway, added to a growing sense of concern. CINCNORTH, British GEN Sir Owen Peirse, "found the logistical situation shaping up rather poorly on the northern flank." The Norwegian government had supported the prepositioning of equipment and supplies for its own forces and for the U.S. Marines' 4 MEB, enough to support operations for a month. Unfortunately, several storage sites had been overrun by Soviet paratroopers and marines, and the troops and air units in north Norway were expending ordnance at rates faster than anticipated. LTG Bjol, Commander, North Norway, reported that his remaining supplies would last no more than a fortnight. The successful defense of north Norway would necessitate timely and adequate resupply.

But the prospects of success for such a logistics effort were problematic. With the Russian 76th Guards Airborne at Bodo, the E6 was unlikely to remain open to traffic for long. The air transport picture was grim. Russian troops had captured the airfields at Bodo and Evenes and had cut the overland connection to Andoy Island and its airfield. Soviet bomb and cruise missile attacks during the fourteenth had reduced the capacity of Bardufoss, the only major airfield through which COMNON's forces could be reinforced and resupplied, by nearly 50 percent.

The Soviet supply situation, in contrast, appeared quite favorable. NATO strike aircraft were unable to interdict movement along the E6. Heavily escorted Russian air transport convoys moved troops, equipment, and supplies to airheads behind NATO lines at Bodo and Evenes. A large convoy of eight Soviet cargo vessels carrying supplies and equipment had rounded the North Cape and was making its way to Harstad. Attacking NATO aircraft were driven off by the *Tbilisi*'s Flankers and Forgers. The Soviet carrier had covered the landing of the Northern Fleet's marines at Harstad and seemed likely to safeguard the movement of the brigade's equipment and supplies to the newly established beachhead as well. Moreover, the carrier's fighters hindered movement by air of Norwegian reinforcements from the south to Bardufoss.

To Sir Owen, the continued presence of the *Tbilisi* in the Norwegian Sea ensured early defeat for NATO in north Norway. "I would never have believed before the war," he confided to his naval aide, "that one relatively small carrier could cause so many large problems." At 0430 on the fifteenth of July, a tired GEN Peirse called CINCEASTLANT Hill-Norton at his Northwood, Middlesex, headquarters and explained the situation. "Ben, your subs have got to get that Russian carrier out of there so my air can get to their cargo ships. Otherwise we're facing disaster up north. My Norwegian boats can't do it alone."

Hill-Norton was sympathetic. The ability of the *Tbilisi*'s air group to fend off attacks from NATO land-based air and the *Forrestal* had surprised the Royal Navy's CINC, upset a variety of plans, and led to the wholesale destruction of Norwegian surface forces. "Yes," Hill-Norton responded, "if we are going to get that carrier any time soon, our submarines will have to do the job. I'll talk to Dave."

Hill-Norton immediately made his way to the SUBEASTLANT headquarters, another resident of the British Northwood complex. He found RADM David Livesay sorting through position reports from his boats. The two admirals and their chiefs of staff held an impromptu conference.

"Dave, how soon can you get your boats concentrated on the

Tbilisi group?" Hill-Norton asked. Following the successful Soviet amphibious landing at Harstad, Livesay had directed his submarines to focus their efforts against the well-screened Soviet supply convoy making its way along the Norwegian coast. Many of his submarines had been drawn in toward the coast in an unsuccessful last-ditch attempt to prevent the amphibious landing on Hinnoy Island. Others had sparred, with some success, throughout D day with the Russian ASW group which screened the *Tbilisi* force further north. Later-arriving boats had been sent toward the North Cape, to loop around the rear of the powerful Russian task forces covering the approach of the supply convoy, and to get at the freighters, the sinking of which Hill-Norton himself had assigned top priority.

"*Tbilisi*'s here," said Livesay, pointing to a chart, "about 150 miles northwest of Tromso. I don't have a boat within 30 miles, been trying to avoid her to tell you the truth. Heavy ASW activity all about."

"How long?" repeated Hill-Norton.

"She's not moving, not coming further south, so we'll have to go in and get her. That ASW group screening her is keeping the boats down. They're not coming shallow for their communications periods, it's too dangerous."

"How long?"

"I really expected air to have taken her out by now."

"So had I, but they haven't. How long?"

"It could take at least four hours, maybe even ten. It depends on conditions and Russian vigilance. If we press it, we're likely to lose quite a few boats."

"I'm sorry Dave, but it's one of those situations. We've little choice. Issue the proper instructions. I'll get an official message over here shortly."

The two men shook hands, Hill-Norton wishing the younger Livesay luck.

By 0600 on the fifteenth, the British SSNs *Trafalgar*, *Superb*, and *Warspite*, and the American nuclear attack boats *Spadefish*, *Hammerhead*, and *Greenling*, had managed to make shallow runs and "pick up their mail," as one U.S. Navy submarine commander later put it. All six NATO SSNs promptly initiated a converging attack on the Russian carrier group.

★ ★ ★

The *Warspite* was the first NATO submarine to penetrate the Soviet ASW screen. At 0735, an irregular magnetic anomaly detector reading alerted a Ka-27 Helix A from the destroyer *Gremyashchy* to the presence of a probable enemy SSN that had worked its way between the ASW screen and the *Tbilisi*. The *Gremyashchy*'s Helix, aided by a trio of Helixes from the Soviet carrier, localized the contact by about 0815. While one of the ASW helicopters established active contact with its dipping sonar, others dropped homing torpedoes. At least one found its target. The *Warspite* sank, along with its crew of 115.

As the *Warspite* vainly maneuvered to evade its Russian hunters, the American SSN *Greenling* attempted to penetrate the Soviet ASW screen from the southeast. The *Sturgeon*-class boat had reached a position within fifteen miles of the *Tbilisi* when the destroyer *Osmotritelny*'s active sonar detected the slowly moving submarine. Both ships simultaneously fired homing torpedoes. As the pair of Mk-48s from the *Greenling* neared the Soviet *Sovremenny*-class destroyer, its commander fired off a barrage of his RBU 1000 ASW mortars. The explosions failed to destroy the approaching torpedoes, but the desperate and unusual effort saved the ship, apparently confusing the guidance systems of the torpedoes. The *Greenling*'s evasion effort met with less success. The *Osmotritelny*'s sonar detected a single explosion, followed seconds later by two more. A Soviet helicopter spotted surface wreckage, later identified as of American manufacture.

Royal Navy CAPT George Stanhope's nuclear attack boat *Superb* was proceeding at ten knots along a northeasterly course toward the reported position of the *Tbilisi* group. At 0735, the *Swiftsure*-class SSN's Ferranti type 2046 towed array sonar detected three surface contacts bearing between 035 and 055 degrees. Stanhope immediately ordered the boat slowed to four knots as his sonar operators worked to provide further data on the range, course, speed, and identification of the Soviet ships. The surface ducting was fair and it was not long before Stanhope had good target motion analysis on the lead ship—a *Udaloy*-class destroyer, coming along course 245, making about nineteen knots, at a range of a little over six nautical miles. *Udaloys* were effective, although rather noisy, ASW platforms, carrying a pair of Ka-27 Helix A helicopters.

Stanhope continued his silent approach. Periodically, the Soviet destroyer would drift, reducing its speed below five knots to improve its sonar picture. When the Russians slowed, the stress level in the British boat increased substantially, as contact would be lost momentarily. At 0800, the *Superb*'s sonar picked up a fourth contact—a submarine of undetermined nationality, bearing 100. Minutes later sonar reported distant splashes bearing 340, followed by the telltale emissions of active Soviet sonobuoys. Then at 0806, the *Udaloy* once again slowed.

Although there were as yet no indications that the Soviets had detected the *Superb*, Stanhope was concerned. "The Russians are certainly getting more active; the bastards are looking for someone off to port," he told his exec. The *Udaloy* continued on its course, directly for the *Superb*. The submarine contact to starboard, if it was Russian, was completing the circle of activity around the boat. Stanhope decided that when the *Udaloy* again sped up and he had a firm position on it, he would fire off a pair of Harpoons and disengage.

Stanhope gave the orders to prepare the UGM-84 Sub-Harpoons for launch. Minutes later, when sonar again detected the sound of the *Udaloy*'s screws at a range of 6.5 miles, Stanhope gave the appropriate orders. "Fire tube three." Stanhope paused five seconds. "Fire tube four. Course to 180; full revolutions; take her to 800."

In seconds the Harpoons broke the surface, revealing the NATO SSN's position, and sped at 560 knots toward the Soviet destroyer. The *Superb* turned to the south, increasing speed to over thirty knots, as it dove to eight hundred feet where the ocean's pressure would reduce propeller cavitation. With its own speed increasing, the *Superb* lost contact, but forty seconds after launch, sonar reported an explosion, followed seconds later by another.

The Soviet destroyer *Udaloy*, part of the *Tbilisi*'s ASW screen, was mortally wounded. Although the burning ship remained afloat for seven hours, she had suffered a mission kill and would play no further role in the evolving battle.

Seconds before the American-built Harpoons struck the *Uda-*

loy, the Russian destroyer fired a pair of homing torpedoes along the bearing of the attack. One torpedo missed, and the *Superb*, now moving at high speed, easily evaded the second that homed on her. But the trial of the British SSN had just begun. Ringed by sonobuoys, Stanhope's submarine twisted and turned, released noisemakers and decoys, reduced speed and accelerated, struggling for an hour to escape the Russian ASW helicopters that sought retribution for the strike against the *Udaloy*. At 0930, after ten quiet minutes had passed without an alarm, the ordeal ended. Stanhope looked about at his men: "tired-eyed and mostly wringing wet from perspiration, although the boat was actually rather cool."

The *Superb* had survived the attack unscathed, although Soviet defensive efforts had driven the British SSN to the southwest, well away from the *Tbilisi*. Other NATO submarines would now have to stalk the Russian carrier, its ASW screen weakened substantially by the loss of the destroyer.

The next allied SSN to contact the *Tbilisi* group was the *Hammerhead*. The *Sturgeon*-class attack boat approached from the southeast and, like the *Superb*, encountered the carrier's ASW screen.

When passive sensors detected the pinging of a sonobuoy line laid by some Russian helos, the *Hammerhead*'s commander gave the order to fire two Harpoons at the nearest contact—a destroyer bearing 340 at a range of fifteen miles—before beginning evasive maneuvers that took the submarine to safety, but out of position to resume the attack. Both Harpoons struck the *Sovremenny*-class destroyer *Osmotritelny*. The first missile hit forward, and the second hit just aft of the stack, into the helicopter hangar, where crewmen were refuelling a Ka-25 helo. Fuel from ruptured lines quickly ignited and a massive explosion tore apart the rear of the destroyer which sank in twenty minutes.

As Soviet ASW forces concentrated on driving the *Hammerhead* toward the southeast, a second American *Sturgeon*-class boat stalked the carrier from the west. CAPT Hugh McNamara's *Spadefish* picked up its first sonar contact at 1035—an unidentified, fast, large, loud contact. McNamara was a good friend of Jack Longacre, who had been the first American submarine commander to trail the new Soviet carrier and record acoustic data. Longacre had told his friend that "the *Tbilisi*'s a noisy son-of-a-bitch." McNamara assumed that he had located the Soviet navy's biggest asset.

Unfortunately, his boat was poorly positioned to press an effective attack. The *Spadefish* was about fifteen to sixteen miles from the *Tbilisi*, which was moving toward the southeast at about twenty knots. McNamara turned south to intercept, but the Russians went south themselves and were moving away. McNamara decided to head due east and move in behind the carrier's starboard screen, a *Sovremenny*-class destroyer, and then swing at high speed into the *Tbilisi*'s baffles for an attack.

At McNamara's order, the *Spadefish* went deep to eight hundred feet and closed the range at fifteen knots. A Russian destroyer was pinging, but it passed by the American submarine at a distance of about three miles. Increasing speed to nearly thirty knots, the *Spadefish* began its run into the Soviet formation's rear. To McNamara, everything was going beautifully, too beautifully.

Unknown to the *Spadefish*'s commanding officer, the commander of the Soviet carrier group, concerned by the continuous NATO submarine attacks and his weakened ASW screen, decided to reverse course and turn to the north. A pair of Il-38 May patrol aircraft, flying from the Kola, covered the course change, laying lines of sonobuoys to the rear of either side of the task force.

The fast-moving *Spadefish*'s sonar failed to detect the splashes made by the sonobuoys. Only when one of the Mays completed laying its pattern and turned on the sensors did McNamara and his crew become aware of the danger. The American commander immediately ordered the boat slowed to 4 knots as the *Sturgeon*-class SSN sought the safety of a thermal layer at 292 feet. But it was too late. McNamara's sonarman reported high-speed screws bearing directly for the *Spadefish*. The *Sovremenny*-class destroyer *Gremyashchy*, directed by the May, was heading toward the American boat at thirty-two knots.

McNamara had few good options. If he pressed the attack to achieve a better firing position, he and his crew would undoubtedly end up "dead in a hurry." McNamara decided to fire three Mk-48s at the *Tbilisi*, and the Harpoon in tube four at the destroyer, and then "to bug out."

The distance to the Soviet carrier was just short of seven miles,

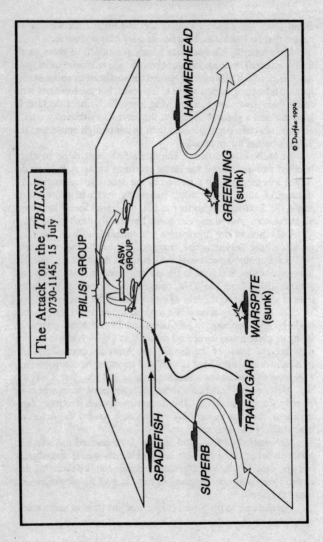

The Attack on the *TBILISI*
0730-1145, 15 July

TBILISI GROUP

ASW
GROUP

HAMMERHEAD

GREENLING (sunk)

WARSPITE (sunk)

SPADEFISH

SUPERB

TRAFALGAR

© Durfee 1994

a long shot, but one well within the range of the Mk-48 ADCAP torpedo. The *Spadefish*'s three unguided "fish" raced at 60 knots toward a preplanned activation point less than a mile from the position the Mk-117 fire-control system predicted the *Tbilisi* would occupy eight minutes after the torpedoes' launch. The Harpoon took less than ninety seconds to reach the *Gremyashchy*.

The destroyer's captain saw the American missile break the surface and skim across the ocean toward his destroyer. He ordered a hard turn to starboard to bring his defensive armament to bear and to use his chaff to best effect. But to no avail. The Harpoon climbed high and suddenly plunged down into the ship. Struck forward on the port side near its SA-N-7 mount, the *Gremyashchy*, still making over thirty knots, turned back toward the *Spadefish*'s bearing at the direction of its vengeful commander. But at high speed, the wind fanned the fire that had followed the ignition of the Harpoon's unspent fuel. The bridge was soon blanketed with smoke and reports indicated that the fire was spreading. The Soviet commander ordered his destroyer slowed to five knots.

As the crew began to fight the fire, lookouts reported three torpedoes approaching and then passing ahead of the *Gremyashchy*. The destroyer's crew breathed a collective sigh of relief. All assumed, incorrectly, that the torpedoes had been fired at their ship. No one noticed that the torpedoes were heading toward the *Tbilisi*.

The carrier's sonar only detected the approaching American torpedoes when they went active about a mile—sixty seconds—from their target. The sixty-thousand-ton vessel, which had slowed to twelve knots to allow escorts to come up to replace the *Gremyashchy* in the port screen, had little time to increase speed and change course. Its towed torpedo decoy attracted the lead Mk-48 which exploded nearby, destroying the device. The sonar on the second torpedo apparently failed to activate and the Mk-48 passed harmlessly across the *Tbilisi*'s wake. But the third torpedo detonated beneath the carrier's stern, causing extensive damage to all four shafts and jamming the rudders.

As McNamara's *Spadefish* effected a successful escape despite a dozen close calls, CAPT First-Class Yevgeny Sorokin of the *Tbilisi* struggled to control his damaged ship. He found the flooding manageable, as long as revolutions were reduced, but at speeds over ten knots, severe shaft vibration threatened the ship. Damage control also reported that the rudders were jammed in the position in which they had been when the American torpedo struck. Sorokin's *Tbilisi* was making a steady five-degree turn to starboard. The only way to counteract the effect was by decreasing the revolutions on the port shafts. The *Tbilisi* continued steaming north at eight knots, steering with its engines.

The Royal Navy SSN *Trafalgar*, commanded by CAPT Michael Leigh, was the unidentified submerged contact that had earlier troubled Captain Stanhope of the *Superb*. The sudden ASW activity to the north and northwest caused Leigh to alter course to starboard. The *Trafalgar*, lead ship of its attack submarine class, headed southeast for nearly an hour before Leigh again headed north. Frequent sonobuoy drops by ASW helicopters slowed Leigh's progress and continually forced him to adopt a more northeasterly course. The *Trafalgar*'s commander several times considered breaking off the approach, but nevertheless continued his attempts to work his way toward the Soviet carrier—"the big prize."

At 1145, again heading north, Leigh was rewarded for his persistence. Sonar reported four large contacts, bearing between 330 and 350, heading northeast. The ships were the battlecruiser *Frunze*, the carrier *Tbilisi*, and the cruisers *Kerch*, and *Kronshtadt*, steaming in column at eight knots, the best speed the wounded Russian carrier could manage.

Leigh continued on course 000 as his sonar solution gradually improved. The initial contact had occurred at a range of about twelve miles. Leigh thought about firing Harpoons at the *Tbilisi*. The standoff attack was safer, but he did not think that a single submarine could get enough Harpoons airborne to penetrate the close-in defenses of the carrier and the nearby *Frunze*. Leigh continued to close the range as his torpedomen worked to unload the Harpoons in tubes three and four. Leigh was "determined to go in with all five tubes loaded with Tigerfish." The *Trafalgar* continued its approach, alternating deep runs to reduce the cavitation from its seven-bladed propeller at fifteen knots to shorten the range, with shallower "drifts" at five knots during which the sonarmen would work to improve their solution. At 1245, the *Trafalgar* had completed a deep run and had come to 290 feet, just above the thermal layer. Leigh now had a very good picture of the situation. The range was down to five thousand yards and sonar reported strange swishing

146

and swirling sounds, caused by the *Spadefish*'s successful torpedo attack, coming from the *Tbilisi*.

Leigh decided to attack. He was well within range for his Tigerfish. At thirty-five knots, the wire guided torpedoes would cover the 5,000 yards to the *Tbilisi* in about four minutes. Leigh fired all five tubes, dove beneath the thermal layer, and altered course slightly to starboard. He chose not to make any dramatic course changes that might break the guidance wires, because he assumed that the Soviets would pick up the sounds of the launch and take evasive action. Leigh wanted to be able to correct the torpedoes' course if necessary.

As the *Trafalgar* fired the last torpedo, sonar picked up a transient contact, bearing 350, no doubt a torpedo launched by one of the carrier's escorts. The Russian torpedo snaked along its bearing at thirty knots looking for a contact—an effective search pattern, but one that wasted time. Leigh continued on course, knowing that his fish were going to get to their target first. As technicians stood ready to direct the Tigerfish toward the *Tbilisi*, Leigh waited for the Soviet carrier to begin evasive maneuvers. But the wounded ship, steering with its engines, was able to do little but begin a slow turn to starboard before it was struck in succession by all five British torpedoes. The sounds of the violent explosions that tore the *Tbilisi* apart for the next twenty minutes helped cover the *Trafalgar*'s escape.

✷ ✷ ✷

Although the *Tbilisi*'s sinking left Soviet naval forces in the Norwegian Sea without CAP protection, NATO remained unable to take immediate advantage of the situation. At 0815, GEN Peirse was shocked to learn that "we had lost track of the damned supply group as it rounded the North Cape." The eight Russian freighters and their escorts had disappeared in the early morning coastal fog. Soviet fighters shot down a Norwegian P-3 sent north to search for the ships. The Soviets were successfully jamming allied radar satellites and there would be no photo satellite surveillance for several hours. Peirse asked SACEUR for the services of a TR-1.

The high flying TR-1, an updated version of the Lockheed reconnaissance aircraft known as the U-2, failed to locate the missing Soviet task group, but it did return to its British base with photographs of an obviously damaged *Tbilisi* steaming in a circle. Peirse ordered an immediate strike on the Russian surface support group off Harstad to see how badly the damage to the carrier had affected its operational tempo.

The attack, coordinated through SACLANT with the *Forrestal*, met no opposition in the air. Unmolested, RAF Buccaneers from Orland and U.S. Navy Intruders from the *Forrestal* sank the destroyer *Stroyny*, the frigates *Gori* and *Orlovskiy*, and four LSTs, and heavily damaged the cruiser *Tula* and destroyer *Otchyanny*. An 1830 follow-up attack completed the destruction of the Soviet group. In all, NATO strike aircraft sank the cruisers *Tula* and *Sevastopol*, two destroyers, five frigates, and ten amphibious ships off Hinnoy Island. Although the resupply group escaped air attack, NATO had at least ended the threat of local amphibious operations in the vicinity of Narvik, the alliance's main supply port.

★ ★ ★

At his Severomorsk headquarters, reports of the loss of the *Tbilisi* shook ADM Boris Obnorsky. The Northern Fleet commander had grown concerned earlier in the morning when reports from KUG 1 indicated that NATO submarines were making a concerted effort to penetrate the carrier's ASW screen. Obnorsky had issued orders to move the *Tbilisi* north, away from the NATO SSNs, and where its weakened screen could be reinforced by escorts from KUG 2, which had moved into position to cover the approach of the supply convoy. But Northwest Front was slow to approve Obnorsky's plans. GEN Golikov's approval reached Severomorsk shortly after noon—1100 in the Norwegian Sea—too late to save the doomed *Tbilisi*.

As Obnorsky's task forces regrouped in mid-afternoon on the fifteenth, less the carrier and a pair of destroyers, the Northern Fleet commander faced the prospect of continuing without air cover the campaign in the Norwegian Sea in support of the advance of Northwest Front. His revised plan relied heavily on Soviet air assets in the Kola. Northwest Front assured Obnorsky that frontal aviation assets would complete the neutralization of Bardufoss by day's end. SNA Tu-16 Badgers and Tu-22M Backfires would concentrate their efforts against the *Forrestal* task group and either sink the American carrier or prevent its movement further north. Soviet patrol aircraft—Be-12 Mails and Il-38 Mays—would operate in advance of the Russian ASW and surface strike groups. Under cover of these operations, Obnorsky's escort group would shepherd the freighters south to Harstad.

But the Soviet plan quickly came unwound. E-2C Hawkeyes of VAW 122—the "Steeljaws"—vectored F-14s of VF 11's "Red Rippers" and VF 31's "Tomcatters" into a late-evening ambush of a thirty-six-plane strike of Badgers and Backfires, being escorted by a regiment of long-range Su-27s from the Archangelsk air defense sector. While the Tomcats engaged the Flankers, the "Scorpions"— EA-6B Prowlers of VAQ 132—jammed the Puff Ball, Short Horn, and Down Beat radars of the Badgers and Backfires that attempted to penetrate the *Forrestal*'s combat air patrols. The Soviet strike commander, unable to locate any of the ships of the American carrier group, all of which were operating under strict emissions control, aborted the strike when several Hornets, hastily refuelled and rearmed after their raid against the support group off Harstad, joined the battle and downed four Badgers.

The *Forrestal* continued to steam north and by midnight was two hundred miles west-south-west of Bardufoss. Its roaming combat air patrols began to assist Norwegian Falcons in their defense of the critical northern airbase. Most importantly, the carrier's Tomcats, guided in their operations by the ever-present Hawkeyes, downed six patrol aircraft, prompting ADM Obnorsky to order the immediate cessation of Kola-based ASW operations within three hundred miles of the *Forrestal*.

As air battles raged over the Norwegian Sea, under the surface British, American, and Norwegian submarines engaged in running battles with Soviet ASW forces. Between 2130 and midnight, four NATO boats penetrated the Russian ASW screen and located the supply group. The Norwegian submarine *Stord* was the first, and its commander, CAPT Horst Olafssen, got off a position report before he began his attack. Sending the radio message alerted the Soviets to the diesel submarine's presence and ASW helicopters forced down and drove off Olafssen's boat. But the information the Norwegian supplied revealed the position of the "lost" supply group. The air staff at AFNORTH headquarters began planning a coordinated strike from Orland and the *Forrestal*. "We're getting rather good at the drill after two days of this sort of thing," one RAF squadron commander remarked.

As NATO strike aircraft rearmed and refuelled, the SSNs *Whale*, *Superb*, and *Talent* contacted and attacked the supply convoy. NATO subsequently credited each of the allied boats with sinking a Russian freighter.

By 1130, Northern Fleet destroyers, frigates, and ASW helicopters had forced the attacking submarines away from the supply ships. At Severomorsk, reports of several kills of NATO SSNs raised the spirits of ADM Obnorsky and his staff, but the claims were exaggerated. Not one of the NATO submarines involved in the late-evening attack was lost. The defensive ASW effort had forced the dispersal of the Soviet formation. The ships were scattered, many of the escorts operating at a great distance from the freighters—too far to provide effective defensive AAW support.

The convoy was only ninety miles from Harstad when the NATO air assault began at 1145. American Hornets and Intruders from the *Forrestal*, Norwegian Falcons and RAF Buccaneers from Orland, and even a pair of Norwegian F-16s from Bardufoss, still operational despite several heavy Soviet bombing raids, struck the convoy. Armed with laser-guided "smart bombs," Norwegian-built Penguin ASMs, and American Harpoons, the NATO aircraft concentrated on the destruction of the freighters. All five were sunk, along with two escorting frigates. Allied losses were surprisingly light—four aircraft.

★ ★ ★

The loss of the Harstad-bound convoy and the sinking of the *Tbilisi* convinced ADM Obnorsky that Soviet surface forces had to be withdrawn, at least temporarily, from the Norwegian Sea. The Northern Fleet commander considered sending his surface strike vessels south to press a missile engagement on the American carrier task force. But many of the Russian ships were low on fuel, anti-air missiles, and antisubmarine munitions. The slow speed of the Soviet support vessels, and the prospect of at-sea replenishment while fending off NATO submarine and air attacks made such a course seem suicidal. The ships in the Norwegian Sea would retire northward to positions where Kola-based fighters from the Archangelsk air defense sector could provide CAP and Soviet submarines in the Barents Sea could establish an ASW screen. SNA assets—ASW-capable Mails and Mays, and Badger and Backfire strike aircraft—

would assume the burden of maintaining the initiative at sea off the Norwegian north coast.

FIFTEEN

Confirmation of the sinking of the *Tbilisi* and the destruction of the Harstad-bound Russian supply convoy instilled a new sense of confidence in the AFNORTH headquarters staff at Kolsaas. The improving situation in the Norwegian Sea and in the air over north Norway made a Soviet "blitz" victory on the Northern Flank unlikely. At 0130 on 16 July, after reviewing the reports, an exhausted Sir Owen Peirse retired to a cot in a small office and slept for the first time since the beginning of the war.

Three hours later, CINCNORTH was again awake. "The situation on my southern flank has taken a nasty turn for the worse," Peirse informed SACEUR. At 0415, Danish LTG Niels Thorsen, Commander, Baltic Approaches (COMBALTAP), reported that Warsaw Pact airmobile forces had landed on the small Danish island of Funen (Fyn) and were attacking the towns of Odense and Nyborg.

The sudden Pact assault on Funen surprised Thorsen. Thus far, the Soviet Baltic Front's operations had been deliberate and predictable, and had developed at a pace far slower than had been expected. On the fourteenth of July, Soviet airmobile forces had landed on Bornholm, a weakly defended Danish island outpost in the Baltic, while Polish and Soviet marines and amphibious ships remained at Gdansk and Baltiysk in the Gulf of Danzig. On the fifteenth, Pact airmobile forces extended their operations to Lolland and Falster, seizing intact the key road and rail bridges that connected the islands to each other and to the main Danish island of Sjaelland. Both COMBALTAP and CINCNORTH expected the Warsaw Pact to feed additional airmobile troops into this bridgehead and to support a direct drive on the Danish capital of Copenhagen with the airborne and amphibious landings that had been expected since D day.

The slow pace of Warsaw Pact operations against BALTAP during the first days of the war was attributable not to caution, but to a realistic appraisal by Soviet planners of the difficulties they faced in the Baltic. NATO speculation about the speed and ease with which the Pact would overrun Denmark failed to take into account geography and the true correlation of forces.

The Russian and Polish tank and motor rifle divisions earmarked for the campaign in Schleswig-Holstein and Denmark grossly outnumbered the Danish and West German forces of BALTAP. But these second-echelon Warsaw Pact formations could not begin their drive north until the Second Guards Army's first-echelon Soviet and East German divisions drove across West German Holstein to the North Sea. In the interim, Baltic Front had to rely on a handful of airmobile units, for the naval situation in the Baltic and a shortage of transport aircraft ruled out an immediate commitment of airborne and amphibious forces.

While the balance of naval power in the Baltic favored the Warsaw Pact, the Danish and West German navies were formidable and held the geographic advantage. The well equipped German navy took NATO's concept of maritime operations (CONMAROPS) seriously and believed that the interdiction of enemy naval forces should be effected immediately in front of their own bases. Quiet and efficient West German diesel submarines began the war off East German, Polish, and Soviet ports. Until the U-boats could be hunted down and eliminated, or at least located, the movement of slow amphibious transports through the Baltic was suicidal. Further west, the narrow passages around the Danish Islands channeled all movement and were expected to be heavily mined. Before Russian, Polish, and East German minesweepers could begin their work, the modern warships of the Danish navy and the Bundesmarine had to be eliminated.

While control of the skies over the Baltic was inextricably linked to the overall air picture on the central front, the aviation assets specifically attached to BALTAP and the Baltic Front were roughly balanced, the Pact holding a quantitative, and NATO a qualitative advantage.

The Royal Danish Air Force, while small, operated seventy American-built F-16 Falcons and forty-five Swedish-built Saab F-35 Drakens. A squadron of Norwegian F-16s flying from southern

Norway was also available to support operations in BALTAP. The Marineflieger, the Bundesmarine's naval air arm, posed the major threat to any premature Pact move in the Baltic. Marinefliegergeschwaders 1 and 2 operated 112 maritime-strike-capable Panavia Tornados armed with Kormoran anti-ship missiles.

The SNA assets attached to the Soviet Baltic fleet included 135 strike-capable aircraft—40 Tu-22M Backfires, 30 Tu-16C and D Badgers, 15 Tu-22 Blinders, 30 Su-17 Fitters, and 20 Su-24 Fencers. The Polish Navy's aviation assets were obsolescent—12 MiG-21s and 40 MiG-17s. The 225 MiG-21s, 23s, and 27s of the Baltic Military District, and the over 600 aircraft of the Polish Air Force, gave the Warsaw Pact a significant numerical advantage, although few of these aircraft were capable of anti-shipping strikes and most, based far to the east, were able to do little more than provide combat air patrols over the central and eastern Baltic.

Baltic Front success depended heavily on a rapid advance through Schleswig-Holstein by the 2d Guards Army, allowing second echelon forces to overrun the Bundesmarine's airfields and naval bases. Soviet planners believed that only after their tanks had driven through Jutland, crushed the enemy's aircraft on their runways, and flushed his ships from their hiding places, could the Warsaw Pact launch a major airborne operation against BALTAP, dispatch strike aircraft to destroy the German and Danish navies to clear the way for an amphibious assault, seize control of the Baltic exits, sweep them of mines, and prepare the Red Banner Fleet to sortie into the North Sea.

Shortage of air transports also made a large D day airborne operation impossible. Three thousand large aircraft were necessary to lift the army's seven airborne divisions simultaneously; Soviet military transport aviation (VTA) controlled only 600. Of the available air transports of all sizes, which numbered about 650, 100 were in the Far East. Nearly 400 supported the two regiment-sized drops in Norway and the landing of the 103d Guards Airborne Division east of Istanbul. Small company, battalion, Spetsnaz detachment, and emergency supply drops on the central front tied up another 50 aircraft. The VTA's commander considered the activation of most of the 1,600 aircraft augmentation fleet not worth the investment in crews other than in a replacement capacity.

Militarization of many of the 1,600 aircraft of the "civilian"

Aeroflot fleet began in the early morning hours of fourteen July. The VTA's commander had requested that the conversions begin earlier, but was told that sudden changes in Aeroflot schedules and the substitution of small planes for newer, larger types would alert NATO. Moreover, only 250 of the Aeroflot aircraft were large, capable Candids and Cubs.

Soviet planners estimated that it would take seventy-two hours to move sufficient numbers of activated reserve aircraft and militarized Aeroflot transports to airfields in the western Soviet Union and Poland to lift the Russian 7th Guards and the Polish 6th Airborne Divisions into Denmark. Given the balance of forces in the air over the Baltic, neither Nektari nor the general staff in Moscow considered the delay significant.

★ ★ ★

On the morning of the fourteenth of July, the right flank formations of the Second Guards Army—the Soviet 94th Motor Rifle Division and the East German 8th Motor Rifle Division—drove back West German border and reconnaissance troops and seized bridges across the Elbe-Lübeck Canal. In the afternoon, the two divisions sought the open country between the conurbations of Lübeck and Hamburg. Soviet plans called for a rapid advance and the avoidance of fighting in built-up areas. But urban sprawl had reduced the corridor between the West German cities to less than twenty miles, traversed by a single road. By the late evening hours of the fourteenth, a regiment-sized operational maneuver group (OMG) from the 94th driving north along this road had reached Bad Segeberg. The OMG then turned west and by dawn on the fifteenth had cut the A7 autobahn between Kiel and Hamburg.

Despite the rather dramatic Russian advance, West German units continued to hold firmly on the haunches of the salient. Rapidly mobilizing reserve formations controlled Hamburg and the 6th Panzergrenadier Division (PGD) had easily repulsed the few Pact probes made in the direction of Lübeck. Bundesheer MG Hans Wagner, Commander, Allied Forces Schleswig-Holstein and Jutland, believed a prompt counterattack could close the gap and isolate and destroy the Pact forces that had broken into the NATO rear. About noon, elements of the 6th Panzergrenadiers attacked southwest along the A1—the main autobahn from Lübeck to Hamburg. East

The Front in Germany

0 50 100
MILES

© Durfee 1994

DENMARK
Arhus
NORTH SEA
Copenhagen
BALTIC SEA
Flensburg
Kiel
Rugen Is.
Bremerhaven
Lübeck
Oder R.
Schwerin
Oldenburg
Hamburg
Wittenberge
Szczecin
Bremen
POLAND
Osnabrück
Hannover
Weser R.
Berlin
Münster
Magdeburg
Paderborn
Kassel
Elbe R.
Bonn
FEDERAL REPUBLIC of GERMANY
Erfurt
Leipzig
Dresden
DEMOCRATIC REPUBLIC of GERMANY
Rhine R.
Koblenz
Frankfurt
Hof
CZECHOSLOVAKIA
Mainz
Bamberg
Prague
Würzburg
Nuremberg
Karlsruhe
Regensburg
Passau
Strasbourg
Stuttgart
Ulm
Danube R.
Linz
FRANCE
Freiburg
Augsburg
Munich
AUSTRIA
SWITZERLAND

155

German troops held the attack throughout the afternoon and into the evening. During the night of the fifteenth-sixteenth July, the West German 11th PGD's 32d Panzergrenadier Brigade completed its movement from its barracks near Schwanawede through Hamburg to the northern bank of the Elbe. At dawn, the East Germans, struck on both flanks, at last fell back. Although the now isolated Soviet 94th Division proved too powerful to destroy, the West Germans had closed the gap between the Elbe and the Baltic.

On the morning of the seventeenth, the East Germans, reinforced by the Polish 12th MRD, again struck northwest, punching a hole through to the 94th MRD. Skirting the northern limits of Hamburg, Pact forces reached the lower Elbe, driving the 32d Panzergrenadier Brigade and the 6th Panzergrenadier Division north through Neumunster toward Kiel.

As the Warsaw Pact forces resumed their advance in Holstein, Soviet airmobile troops completed their capture of Odense after a day of heavy fighting. The spirited resistance of the Danish reservists in Odense, sparked by the senseless destruction by Russian soldiers of Hans Christian Andersen's birthplace, surprised GEN Nektari. But despite the delay, the E20—the road-ferry route running from the North Sea at Esbjerg to Copenhagen on the Baltic— had been cut. Sjaelland was isolated.

By the morning of seventeenth, Nektari's airborne and amphibious forces prepared to administer the coup de grace to BALTAP. For three days, Soviet, Polish, and East German air, surface, and subsurface ASW assets had hunted down and destroyed seven West German diesel submarines that Bundesmarine VADM Heinrich Bracher, Commander, Allied Naval Forces, Baltic Approaches had positioned off the Bay of Danzig. The U-boats' efforts had not been in vain. They had delayed the movement of Soviet and Polish amphibious forces for at least forty-eight hours and had torpedoed fifteen Warsaw Pact ships, sinking eleven.

Despite these losses, on the morning of 16 July Baltic Front began the concentration of a large landing force off the coast of Polish Pomerania. That night, over sixty Warsaw Pact amphibious ships passed north of the East German island of Rügen, heavily escorted and screened by Baltic Fleet submarines, a KUG, and a KPUG. Overhead, swarms of East German and Polish fighters provided continuous combat air patrols.

Alerted to the Pact concentration by a Bundesmarine Tornado flying a reconnaissance mission over the Baltic, COMNAVBALTAP correctly assumed that the amphibious force was headed for Sjaelland. Six West German and two Danish submarines were already positioned to intercept such a move. But Bracher knew that a handful of U-boats could not prevent the landing. He nevertheless decided to risk the surface engagement he had thus far sought to avoid. A Bundesmarine surface action group steamed from Kiel Bay. RADM Klaus Scholz commanded a nine-ship force that included his flagship, the destroyer *Mölders*, the four *Hamburg*-class destroyers of the 2d Destroyer Squadron, and four *Bremen*-class frigates of the 4th Frigate Squadron. Bracher intended to coordinate the attacks of his submarines, his surface forces, and his Marineflieger Tornados and destroy the Warsaw Pact amphibious task force before it could reach Sjaelland.

★ ★ ★

As the doors on the hardened aircraft shelter opened, LT Josef "Sepp" Schmitz slightly increased the throttle setting on his Panavia Tornado IDS. Reaching the runway, he took a quick glance over his right shoulder to make sure that his wingman was in position—behind and to the right, just out of the lead plane's jet exhaust. Cleared for take-off, the lead Tornado raced down the runway and as the airspeed hit 180 knots, Schmitz pulled back on the stick and gently coaxed the plane into the air. As the landing gear retracted, he banked right to course 040.

"Gerry, how's the computer?" Oberfeldwebel Gerhard "Gerry" Reich, the navigator of the lead Tornado, pushed the button to run a quick diagnosis on the aircraft's central digital computer. Schmitz and Reich had personally programmed the CDC before take-off with information on their projected flight path. Throughout the mission, the CDC would automatically update the plane's position, course, and speed and provide the information to the aircrew in a variety of digital, tabular, and map-like displays. "No problem, Sepp, AOK."

Schmitz's was one of four two-aircraft flights launched from Marinefliegergeschwader 2's base at Eggebeck, south of Flensberg. Their mission was to take out the ships of a Soviet ASW group screening the main Warsaw Pact amphibious force heading for Sjaelland's Fakse Bay. At the pre-mission briefing, their commander had made clear to Schmitz and his fellow pilots that the ships of the Russian ASW group "were in the way and had to go." The warships not only screened the enemy fleet from Danish and West German submarine attack, but also were positioned to interfere with Tornados making low-level approaches against the amphibious ships. Schmitz's Tornado, armed with four Kormoran II air-to-surface missiles and a pair of AIM-9L Sidewinders, was to sink or damage as many screening ships as possible.

"Feet wet," Schmitz called as his Tornado crossed the moonlit shoreline where the coast of Schleswig met Kiel Bay. Schmitz took a quick glance back over his right shoulder to ensure that his wingman was in position. He was. At 550 knots, the two Tornados streaked eastward over the water's black surface only 200 feet below. The planned flight path would take the Tornados from Eggebeck over Kiel Bay, the Danish islands south of Funen, and Sjaelland. The Bundesmarine Tornados would then turn east, and using a low-level, terrain-masking approach, recross the Baltic coast at Fakse Bay. There, the aircraft would split and approach the Russian ships along different tracks from the northwest. The entire approach to the target area would take less than fourteen minutes.

As Schmitz's Tornado streaked over Sjaelland, the aircraft's terrain-following radar allowed the crew to keep the plane below 250 feet, using the contours of the island to hide from Soviet radars looking for approaching attackers. In the backseat, Reich established contact with a NATO AWACS and began receiving data on the positions of Warsaw Pact ships and aircraft.

"Sepp, we've got tons of targets out there. Plenty of air activity, but they're high."

"Roger, Gerry. Keep your eyes on those fighters." The Tornado continued on course. Flight time over Sjaelland was less than four minutes.

"Sepp, final waypoint in fifteen seconds."

"OK, Gerry." Schmitz took a deep breath to release the stress that he could feel building.

"Sepp, come starboard to 135."

"Roger." Schmitz gently banked the Tornado, keeping his eye on the altimeter. It did not take long to lose two hundred feet in a turn. He blinked his lights, making the signal for his wingman to break off and make his own approach.

"Sepp, we're active." In the rear seat, Gerry Reich had turned on the Tornado's Decca Type-72 pulse-Doppler radar and had begun searching the horizon for targets. "Contacts, surface, bearing 140, range thirty-two nautical miles."

"OK, Gerry, taxi time. Tell the driver where you want to go." Attaining a radar lock on a surface contact and directing the approach to a release point was the navigator's job in the Tornado. Driving and dogfighting were the pilot's.

"Come to 140, Sepp."

Schmitz again banked the plane to starboard, as Reich continued to work the radar.

"I got a lock, bearing 139, range twenty-three nautical miles. Give us a little altitude."

Schmitz banked slightly to port and pulled back on the stick to bring the Tornado up to five hundred feet. The missile ejection system would push the Kormoran away from the aircraft and a missile launched from a plane flying too low could strike the surface before ignition.

"Firing in three. Three, two, one."

Schmitz immediately pushed the stick slightly forward as he felt the 630-kilogram missile drop off its rack.

"Firing in three," Reich again announced as he armed a second missile. "Three, two, one."

With the second missile airborne, Schmitz brought the Tornado back down below two hundred feet, and safety. But the launch had alerted the Russians.

"Sepp, their scanning us. Activating ECM." Reich turned on the Tornado's countermeasures, hoping to confuse the Soviet search radars long enough to complete the mission. He then quickly began lining up for a second Kormoran launch. "Come to 142. Back up to five hundred."

Schmitz banked right and pulled back the stick. In his headphones he could hear the warning sounds that indicated that the Tornado had been locked up by a Russian radar. "Let's go, Gerry, let's go."

"In three, Sepp," replied the navigator as he began the now

familiar countdown. As the fourth Kormoran sped toward its target, the Tornado banked to starboard and headed for home.

As the plane streaked west over the Baltic, Reich monitored the movement of Warsaw Pact interceptors on his display as the AWACS fed a steady stream of information into the Tornado's computer. But the Pact pilots, relying on air search radars with inferior or nonexistent look-down capability, failed to locate the escaping Marineflieger attackers. Ten minutes later, Schmitz's Tornado touched down at Eggebeck. Their four Kormorans had mortally wounded a pair of Soviet frigates.

★ ★ ★

The attack by the Tornados at 0220 on the seventeenth marked the beginning of the ten-hour-long battle of the Kodel Channel. In one of the most confusing naval actions of the Third World War, NATO forces sank thirty-three of the Warsaw Pact amphibious transports, as well as nine frigates and corvettes. But Soviet surface and air launched missiles sank all nine NATO ships. Three West German U-boats and one Danish submarine were lost, and the survivors withdrew in the late morning after having exhausted their supply of torpedoes. While Danish Falcons of Squadrons 723, 727, and 730 from Skrydstrup, and West German Tornados of MFG 1 flying from Jagel fought off Warsaw Pact combat air patrols, the Tornados from Eggebeck concentrated on strikes against enemy ships. Of those sunk by NATO forces, twenty-six, including seventeen amphibious vessels, fell victim to Kormoran ASMs. Seven Tornados and six Falcons were lost. Warsaw Pact air losses were estimated at over sixty aircraft.

Despite heavy losses, the Pact landing force reached Fakse Bay in the early morning hours of the seventeenth and, even as the Tornados pressed their attacks, began landing Russian, Polish, and East German marines on the Sjaelland shore. After linking up with Soviet airmobile formations operating from Falster, Pact forces began an advance northward along the E47 toward Copenhagen.

The third element of the Warsaw Pact plan for the conquest of Denmark involved landing two airborne divisions near Arhus along the E45 in central Jutland. From Arhus, Pact paratroopers could overrun NATO airfields in central and northern Jutland, move south along the E45 to prevent the withdrawal of LANDJUT's ground forces, seize advance bases for further operations to open the passages into the North Sea for the Baltic Fleet, and threaten southern Norway.

Although it had managed to concentrate the four hundred air transports needed for the initial lift at airfields in Poland and Western Russia before dawn on the seventeenth, the staff of the Baltic Front rescheduled the airdrop for 1400. "Until the amphibious operation against Sjaelland is completed," GEN Nektari informed his air deputy, "our fighters cannot give their full attention to the protection of our air transports." The Baltic Front commander also expected that the air battles over the beaches of Sjaelland would exhaust and weaken NATO air defenses and prepare the way for the airdrop.

American spy satellites already had detected the assembly of so many air transports. Shortly after noon on the seventeenth, NATO AWACS aircraft began to detect hundreds of aircraft making their way north and then west over the Baltic. The reports convinced GEN Peirse that "the Pact is about to make a massive airlanding somewhere in my command, probably against Sjaelland, although a drop elsewhere in Denmark or even around Oslo cannot be discounted." CINCNORTH, aware that his resources were inadequate to prevent such an attack, called SACEUR and requested the support of the Second Allied Tactical Air Force, the NATO air assets supporting NORTHAG operations along the central front.

SACEUR conferred by secure phone with his air deputy, Commander, Allied Air Forces, Central Front (COMAAFCE) at his headquarters at Ramstein airbase outside Frankfurt. SACEUR, who favored giving CINCNORTH "all the help we can muster," was somewhat surprised to find that COMAAFCE and his staff were actually eager to weigh in.

COMAAFCE'S reasoning was simple. "Hell," he told SACEUR, "there ain't no fixed boundaries up there in the wild blue yonder. What's the difference where we shoot down their aircraft?" Additionally, the AAFCE commander and his staff saw the projected battle as an opportunity to force Pact fighters into engagements at a disadvantage as they sought to protect slow flying transports. As one British squadron commander put it, "who can pass up an opportunity to put the Pact on the defensive in airspace where, for once, we don't have to worry about their bloody SAMs?"

For three hours on the afternoon of seventeen July, Norwegian, Danish, Belgian, Dutch, British, French, West German, and American squadrons battled East German, Polish, and Soviet air regiments in the skies over the western Baltic and Denmark. For the loss of 27 Allied interceptors, at least 130 Warsaw Pact fighters and as many as 100 air transports were shot down. Many other transport aircraft aborted before reaching their assigned drop zones.

Nevertheless, as many as five thousand men of the Soviet 7th Guards Airborne and the Polish 6th Airborne Divisions landed along the E45 between Randers and Horsens. Although the paratroopers frequently found themselves far from their planned drop zones, with units intermixed, and without heavy equipment and supplies, the elite Warsaw Pact troops soon secured an airhead and sent out columns toward the NATO airfields at Alborg, Karup, and Vandel, pushing aside Danish reservists. At Karup, the BALTAP staff began burning secret documents and preparing the headquarters for evacuation to Oslo. Rumors of a separate peace swept the Danish capital.

At his Brussels headquarters, SACEUR was keenly aware that the alliance had to provide the Danes with some assistance, if only token, to keep them in the war. GEN Robert Sexton decided to take advantage of the improving air picture over the Baltic and at 0130 on eighteen July, ordered that the aircraft of the Canadian air transport group, then midway across the Atlantic en route to Lahr, in Baden, divert to Vaerlose airbase outside the Danish capital. By the following morning, the men of the Canadian Airborne Regiment from Petawawa, Ontario, were taking up positions along the E47 south of Copenhagen.

On the morning of the eighteenth, the Second Guards Army resumed its drive west through Holstein, attempting to complete the encirclement of Hamburg. COMLANDJUT decided to seize the opportunity and to counterattack once again toward the south. MG Wagner ordered the lead elements of the Danish Jutland Division to move south and to cover the right flank of the West German advance. "The attack is risky," Wagner admitted, "but given the deteriorating situation in central Jutland we have little to lose." The offensive began at 1700. Surprised East German defenders quickly gave way but by 1930 the thrust south had stalled short of the A7.

At dawn on the nineteenth, the Second Guards Army struck north. Elements of three Polish divisions—the 8th and 12th MRDs and the 20th Tank—attacked Lübeck, defended by West German territorial troops of Heimatschützbrigade (HSB) 51. The Poles fought their way into the southern sections of the city located south of the Elbe-Lübeck Canal, but the Germans easily repulsed attempts to cross the thirty-meter-wide water barrier. Soviet officers attached to the Polish divisions reported that several regiments all but disintegrated in the face of heavy German defensive fire.

To the northwest of Lübeck, the West German 11th PGD's 32d Panzergrenadier Brigade held Neumunster against the attacks of East German motor rifle troops. But mixed tank and mechanized infantry teams from the Soviet 94th MRD drove north from Itsehoe toward the western end of the Kiel Canal. On the morning of the twentieth, lead elements of the Soviet division crossed the canal, driving back the defenders of the West German 61st HSB, and pushed through the town of Heide toward the Eider River line.

★ ★ ★

During the first week of the war, NATO forces in BALTAP had fared better than many pre-war analysts had expected. Danish and West German naval forces still controlled the heavily mined narrow exits from the Baltic straits and had prevented the Soviet Baltic Fleet from breaking out into the North Sea. The Danish army continued to fight in Jutland, in Schleswig-Holstein, and on Sjaelland. West German troops still controlled Hamburg, although Warsaw Pact forces had cut all roads into the city. Bundesheer regulars and territorials also held the eighty-mile-long Lübeck-Bad Segeberg-Neumunster-Rendsburg-Kiel Canal-Eider River line.

Nevertheless, the situation in BALTAP appeared bleak. "In many ways," GEN Peirse confided to his staff, "BALTAP is lucky to have survived a week, but I am afraid our good fortune is about to run out." In central Jutland, Danish reserve forces seemed incapable of checking the advance of Pact paratroopers operating from their Arhus airhead. The evacuation of the headquarters staff from Karup had begun. On Sjaelland, Russian, East German, and Polish marines, supported by airmobile troops, were closing their net around Copenhagen as Pact artillery began to bombard Vaerlose. In Schleswig-Holstein, the northward thrust of the Soviet 94th MRD across the Kiel Canal threatened to outflank the NATO defensive line and trap the 6th PGD, 32d PGB, two HSBs, and the Danish Jutland Division in a pocket centered on Kiel.

Although the deepening crisis in BALTAP was obvious to all senior NATO commanders once the Warsaw Pact had managed to land its marines on Sjaelland and its paratroopers in Jutland, there was little that could be done. CINCNORTH's Norwegian reserves could not be sent to Denmark. The decision to commit SACLANT's amphibious forces to the northern flank had already been made. SACEUR's major air transportable reserves—the ACE Mobile Force—had likewise been committed to north Norway. And with Vaerlose under artillery bombardment, the air transport of additional NATO forces to defend Copenhagen was impossible.

SIXTEEN

GEN Sir Owen Peirse recognized that his decision to allow the reinforcement of his northern Norwegian flank to proceed, despite the deteriorating situation in BALTAP, was a gamble. But it was a risk he took in full confidence, and in consultation with the major NATO commanders—SACLANT, SACEUR, CINCHAN, all of whom agreed that the situation in north Norway was both more promising and more crucial.

Peirse looked north with confidence. The destruction of the *Tbilisi*, the elimination of the supply convoy bound for Harstad, the arrival of the *Forrestal* task force in the central Norwegian Sea, and the movement of American and British air reinforcements to Norwegian airfields appeared to have shifted the balance of forces in NATO's favor. The presence of the *Forrestal* immediately took pressure off the alliance's battered northern airfields. On the morning of the sixteenth of July, reinforcements, both ground and air, began to reach north Norway. The *Forrestal*'s combat air patrols also complicated Soviet efforts to resupply and reinforce their airheads at Bodo and Evenes.

★ ★ ★

At 1045 on the morning of the sixteenth, U.S. Navy Tomcats and Hornets from the *Forrestal* "bounced" a dozen Soviet MiG-25 Foxbats attempting to clear the skies over Evenes before the arrival of air transports carrying the heavy equipment of the Leningrad Military District's air assault brigade. The resultant air-to-air battles were short and only three Russian fighters were shot down, but the reports from the surprised Soviet pilots prompted Northwest Front headquarters to abort the transport mission. The Russians expected to meet weak opposition in the air, maybe a pair or two of Norwegian F-16s, but instead they met a score of American naval fighters, ECM aircraft, and controllers.

Further south, Soviet MiG-31 Foxhounds found the sky over Bodo free of NATO interceptors. At 1240 sixteen transports that had overflown Finnish Lapland and northern Sweden reached Bodo where they began to unload the men of the 234th Regiment's 3d Battalion and the fifteen hundred men of the 237th Regiment of the 76th Guards Airborne Division.

About 1310, a pair of Norwegian Falcons from Orland attempted to penetrate the Soviet fighter screen. Both were shot down, but not before they had drawn the covering Foxhounds to the south. At 1330, a small strike force from the *Forrestal*—a dozen Hornets, Intruders, and Prowlers—flew undetected at low altitude down the valleys north of Bodo. Meeting virtually no SAM or air opposition, the American pilots quickly destroyed ten of the thirteen Candids still on the ground and badly cratered Bodo's runways. Before the MiG-31s could react, the strike was over and the Americans had disappeared back up the valleys.

The following morning, the Soviets again attempted to resupply and reinforce Evenes and Bodo. Regiment-sized escorting formations of Foxbats and Foxhounds attempted to screen the transports from the *Forrestal*'s Tomcats and Hornets over Evenes, and from USMC Hornets, RAF Phantoms, and Norwegian Falcons over Bodo. The fast but unmaneuverable MiGs were no match for the less numerous but more nimble NATO fighters which were soon in among the transports. A score of Cubs and Candids and eight MiGs were shot down for the loss of three NATO aircraft. Those transports that survived the attack aborted and returned to their bases in the Kola.

Northwest Front immediately cancelled all transport missions to Evenes and Bodo until the situation in the air over north Norway improved. The two airheads were isolated from both air and sea resupply, at least temporarily.

At Bodo, MG Dimitrii Malygin, commander of the 76th Guards, took the news philosophically and maintained an optimistic front for his troopers. "I told the men that we had already landed two full regiments and that three thousand paratroopers could certainly block a single mountain road for the week it would take the Sixth Army to reach us." But privately Malygin was worried. The lack of BMD personnel carriers for the men was of marginal significance in the mountainous terrain, but the almost total absence of mobile SAMs and antiaircraft guns and artillery larger than mortars could prove of critical importance when the expected NATO counterattack on Bodo began. Out of earshot of the division's political officer, Malygin told his chief of staff, "I think we may have jumped a fjord too far."

★ ★ ★

The increased tempo of NATO air operations over north Norway eased SACEUR's and CINCNORTH's effort to reinforce COMNON. Whereas on the fourteenth and fifteenth only a single battalion had reached north Norway by air, over the second forty-eight hours of the war, NATO transports flew five additional battalions into Bardufoss.

On the morning of the sixteenth, transports carrying the British 1st Battalion, Parachute Regiment, the lead unit of the ACE Mobile Force—West German LTG Uwe Gysae's Allied Command Europe, Mobile Force (land), began to arrive at Bardufoss. Throughout the day, Norwegian C-130s carrying the men of the 13th Brigade, whose equipment was prepositioned near the airbase, also landed at Bardufoss. The resultant congestion at an installation still recovering from heavy Soviet air attacks during the first forty-eight hours of the war delayed the movement of Gysae's other units from Germany to north Norway. The transports bearing the men of the Italian Susa

Alpini Battalion were held at airfields in southern Norway until the morning of the seventeenth. Days passed before Gysae had his entire command at hand.

Nevertheless, by the evening of the seventeenth, six of the eighteen NATO battalions in Fortress Norway had arrived by air.

Substantial reinforcements were on hand to meet the initial Soviet offensive against Fortress Norway.

Throughout the sixteenth and seventeenth of July, COMNON—Norwegian LTG Torbjorn Bjol—continued his planned withdrawal from Finnmark as reinforcing battalions took up defensive positions in Troms. There was no retreat. The men of the Porsanger and Alta battlegroups and the remnants of the Finnmark Brigade delayed the invader every step of his advance. The Norwegians mined roads, destroyed bridges and ferries, and ambushed Soviet columns. The occasional strike by Norwegian Falcons from Bardufoss also slowed the Soviet columns strung out along the E6. Four days into the war the Soviet 45th Motor Rifle Division had captured Alta and Kautakeino, but was still seventy miles, and nearly twice that distance by road, from the Norwegian main line of resistance.

The Soviet 54th MRD suffered similar delays in Finnish Lapland. The right flank column, moving along the E78, had reached the base of the Finnish Wedge by the late evening of the seventeenth, but still lay sixty miles, and a good day's march, from the Norwegian border.

The left flank column, after making fairly rapid progress on the fourteenth and fifteenth, found the bridges blown over the Kemijoki River at Rovaniemi. Under pressure from division headquarters to speed the advance, the commander of the 118th MRR ordered his leading troops to cross immediately, assuming that he faced just another Finnish delaying action. In fact, Rovaniemi was defended by the entrenched Lapland Jager Battalion.

At 0730, as the amphibious BMP-1's attempted to cross the river, several were destroyed by ATGMs. The survivors quickly retired. The Soviets bombarded suspected Finnish positions and at 1000 began a second assault. Fire from repositioned ATGMs and a platoon of dug-in Finnish T-54s again forced the attackers to withdraw.

The regimental commander decided to delay the next assault. A battalion of T-62s from the divisional tank regiment had crossed the Kemijoki upstream and in several hours would be positioned to strike the Finns' left flank. The third attack was planned to begin at 0400 on the seventeenth. Frontal aviation fighter-bombers would open the assault with bombing runs against suspected Finnish positions. At 0430, Soviet artillery would begin to lay smoke along the river. As the motorized infantry of the 118th MRR attacked frontally, the tank battalion would strike into the Finnish rear.

Nothing went according to plan. Two squadrons of Finnish J-35 Drakens surprised three regiments of Su-17 Fitter ground-attack aircraft as they began their approach. Caught at low level, the Soviet fighter-bombers were at a decided disadvantage and at least two dozen were destroyed. A stiff breeze quickly dissipated the smoke laid by the Russian gunners revealing the crossing effort of the BMPs to the Finns. As Soviet T-62s drove into the left flank of Rovaniemi's defenders, lead elements of the Finnish Pohjan Brigade, which had made an unobserved approach march, struck the Russians' flank. Caught without infantry support, the column of three-dozen tanks was soon stalled along a marsh road and destroyed. Although several companies of the 118th MRR managed to fight their way into Rovaniemi, Finnish reinforcements soon pushed them back out. With their backs to the river, the Soviet troops driven from the town were massacred. Finnish losses were heavy, but they held the critical road junction of Rovaniemi.

Although Soviet threats to open a drive toward Helsinki deterred the Finns from continuing their counteroffensive, the setback at Rovaniemi forced the 54th MRD to keep half its strength in Lapland to screen the Finnish forces that took up positions between the Kemijoki River and Aavasaka along the Swedish border. Only two, rather than three regiments of the 54th MRD would be available for the drive through the Finnish Wedge.

As the Soviet Sixth Army's CAD forces raced south through Norway, the airborne and amphibious RINOK units worked to consolidate their positions athwart critical NATO routes of advance and reinforcement.

On 16 July, lead elements of the 76th Guards Airborne's 234th

Regiment reached and cut the E6 at Fauske. In commandeered civilian transport, the paratroopers then raced south, taking Rognan in the late afternoon where they established a blocking position. The battalions of the 237th Regiment, which landed during the sixteenth, marched from Bodo and were stretched back along the connecting road from the airbase to the E6.

At 0230 on the seventeenth, an engineer detachment attached to the 234th regiment moved south from Rognan toward Pothus where the E6 crossed the Saltdal River. Malygin directed the engineers to prepare the town's bridges for demolition and blow them at the first sign of an enemy advance. At 0345, riding north of the town in a cavalcade of stolen automobiles, the Russian paratroopers stumbled into an ambush.

The 1st Battalion of the Norwegian 14th Brigade had reached Pothus several hours earlier. The battalion commander found the phone lines between Pothus and Rognan still working and was soon apprised of the strength and positions of the Soviet paratroopers in Rognan, as well as the movement south by the engineer detachment. The Norwegians established themselves on the high ground overlooking the E6 midway between the two towns and waited. Heavy machine guns made quick work of the Russians' automobiles. The Norwegians rounded up and interrogated the few survivors.

With two battalions on hand—nearly sixteen hundred men— COL Tomas Reike ordered his 14th Brigade to advance immediately on Rognan. At 0400, the 1st Battalion, supported by a company of M-48A5 tanks, attacked the town while the 2d Battalion bypassed the engagement and struck east, following the E6 north toward Finneid where the road crossed the upper Salt Fjord.

There were no more than three hundred Soviet paratroopers in Rognan but they held off attack after attack. The Norwegians at first fought cautiously, attempting to limit damage to the town hoping that the Soviets, who clearly had little hope of surviving, would surrender. But as the 76th Guards troopers continued to resist, and as Norwegian casualties mounted, the battalion commander at last decided to call in all available firepower. At 1400 the final assault began, supported by Norwegian 105mm howitzers as well as by a squadron of USMC F/A-18 Hornets. By 1545, the shattered town had been secured. The Norwegians took only twenty-five prisoners.

The advance of the 2d Battalion swept toward Finneid, meeting no opposition. But at 0630, as the M-113s of the reconnaissance company reached the high ground overlooking the town, the E6 bridge blew and dropped into the fjord blocking further advance north until bridging equipment arrived.

Further north, the LAAB pushed east to seize the Labergdal, the three-thousand-foot-high mountain that commanded the approaches to Evenes and from which the Soviets could sever the E6 and push either north toward Bardufoss or south toward Narvik. Norwegian reservists of the 15th Brigade halted the Russians' first dash toward the heights on the fifteenth. The next morning, the Soviet air assault troopers launched a set piece attack and, supported by heavy mortar fire, wrested control of the summit from troops of the 15th Brigade's 2d Battalion. But Norwegian counterattacks at Gratangen by the 1st/15th, led by Leopard Is, and at Bjerkvik by the 3d/15th, led by M-48A5s, drove back the flanks of the Russian advance. To cover the Evenes airhead, the Soviets fell back to a shorter, ten-mile-long line with its right flank resting on Bogen.

As the LAAB struggled with the Norwegian 15th Brigade, the marines of the 63d Kirkenes Brigade secured the Harstad port area and Hinnoy Island. At 2230 on the seventeenth, lead elements of the 1st Battalion captured intact the ferry operating between Hinnoy and Andoy Islands. BG Ganenko immediately reinforced the 1st Battalion and ordered his marines to cross the And Fjord and drive north to capture the NATO airfield at Andoya.

The threat to Andoya prompted COMNON to divert a Canadian company of the NATO Composite Force for Norway (NCFN) from a planned landing at Bardufoss to one at Andoya. Several air attacks had failed to destroy the ferry and its continued operation imperiled the important NATO airbase. At the request of the local Norwegian commander, the debarking Canadians marched south to reinforce the reservists covering the ferry crossing. But before the Canadians reached the ferry site, they found themselves caught up in a rout as retreating Norwegians fled north before advancing Soviet marines. The Canadians attempted to block the Russian advance at Dvarberg, but while one battalion engaged the NATO troops frontally, a second Soviet battalion conducted a flank march. The Canadians, heavily outnumbered and surrounded, were killed where they fought or surrendered. The Soviet advance continued throughout the eighteenth and at 1730 on 19 July Ganenko's marines overran Andoya.

As his marines began to ring Andoya on the afternoon of the nineteenth, Ganenko prepared to fly in a captured Norwegian civilian helicopter from Harstad to the headquarters of his 1st Battalion to coordinate the final assault. But at 1420 the Soviet marine commander received word that the Norwegians had recaptured the bridge at Skanland.

Ganenko and his staff had monitored the battle that had begun earlier in the day east of Evenes and the situation, while clearly tenuous, had appeared relatively stable. At 0300 NATO forces had hit the LAAB battalions hard and driven them back. Without heavy equipment, the Soviet troops had been unable to resist the advance of the 15th Brigade, led by Norwegian tanks and well supported by NATO ground-attack aircraft. At noon, the LAAB's commander, COL Mavericki Bazkhan, had informed Ganenko that the brigade could no longer hold and would have to withdraw over the Skanland bridge to Hinnoy Island, giving up the airfield at Evenes. The retreat had seemed to be proceeding as planned and Ganenko's major concern had become the success of the attack on Andoya, critical now that the surrender of Evenes was inevitable.

Until 1300, the Norwegian 15th Brigade's attacks had been confined to the coast roads and the Soviet center had been progressively stripped of troops as the LAAB's commander attempted to strengthen his flanks and prevent a breakthrough toward Evenes. But about 1310, West German mountain troops of the 233d Gebirgsjäger Battalion struck the center of the Soviet position and made rapid progress toward Skanland. The West German battalion, attached to the ACE Mobile Force, had landed at Bardufoss on the morning of 18 July and COMNON had sent it south toward Evenes, rather than north. The Bundesheer mountain troops had spent the morning of the nineteenth moving through the difficult terrain into their assigned assault positions north of Bogen. When they finally moved forward, they struck thin air. By 1330, the Gebirgsjägers were less than five miles from the bridge.

To stem the German drive on Skanland, COL Bazkhan hurried his reserve battalion into a blocking position to cover the retreat. The counterstroke managed to delay the Germans. But at 1400, as planned, the Norwegian 15th Brigade's 1st Battalion conducted a direct heliborne assault on the bridge. The handful of Soviet defenders and troops retreating over the span were surprised and quickly driven from the bridge.

As word of the Norwegian coup spread through the units now trapped between Skanland and Evenes, the exhausted men, many of whom had expended their ammunition, panicked. At 1445, a company of Norwegian Leopards reached the bridge. Five minutes later, the West Germans hustled across to support the Norwegians in a successful effort to seize the high ground overlooking the crossing. NATO forces captured over 750 Russians, including COL Bazkhan.

With only the remnants of the shattered LAAB and his own 3d Battalion remaining, Ganenko hastily organized the defense of Harstad. Only the exhaustion of the Norwegian 15th Brigade, heavy helicopter losses incurred during the assault on the bridge, and the absence of motorized transport for the Germans saved Harstad from immediate capture. Throughout the twentieth, NATO troops somewhat lethargically closed the ring around Harstad, beginning a long-range bombardment of Russian positions. Ganenko's well dug-in troops suffered little, but the Soviet marine commander knew that his men, dangerously low on ammunition, had little chance of repulsing a full-scale assault.

✯ ✯ ✯

Shortage of ammunition was also the major concern of MG Malygin at Bodo. Not a single transport reached the captured airhead on the eighteenth, nineteenth, or twentieth. Norwegian infantry of the 14th Brigade were moving overland in an attempt to outflank the 76th Guards' positions to the east of Finneid. The Norwegian 5th Brigade faced the Soviets at the site of the blown bridge and maintained a steady harassing fire, to which the Russian defenders, low on ammunition, could not reply. Malygin "prayed" that the Norwegians would attempt a crossing. But the 5th Brigade's commander held his position waiting for the arrival of engineers with bridging equipment and the marines and helicopters of the American 4 MEB, then racing north along the E6. There was little Malygin's paratroopers could do but dig in, wait, and hope for relief, or at least resupply.

★ ★ ★

Prospects of relief appeared bleak. The advance of the 45th MRD along the E6 continued slowly, harassed at every step by the retreating Norwegians. Not until the afternoon of the twentieth did the 45th MRD strike across the Lyngen Fjord, seizing the old ferry crossing at Lyngen. A well orchestrated amphibious-heliborne assault by the lead elements of the 253d MRR, supported by Soviet helicopter gunships and close support aircraft, drove back the weary men of the Norwegian Porsanger Battlegroup and the 3d Battalion of the Finnmark Brigade.

The advance of the 54th MRD also progressed more slowly than expected. Not until the late evening of 18 July did the 81st MRR reach the Finnish-Norwegian border. The regiment launched an immediate assault along the E78 with little preparation or reconnaissance. A Norwegian platoon was quickly driven from Kilpisjarvi, just inside the Finnish border, but as the Soviets continued their drive along the road, they came under heavy ATGM fire, losing a dozen BMPs. When the Russian infantry dismounted and began to advance on foot, the Norwegian defenders called in artillery fire from 105mm howitzers dug in near Helligskogen. Throughout the afternoon and evening, the Norwegian Chief of Defense (CHOD) Reserve Battalion and the 1st Battalion, Nordland Brigade, repulsed the 81st MRR's attacks. The Soviets suffered at least six hundred casualties. The CHOD Battalion, struck in the late evening by a heavy Russian air strike, lost over two hundred men.

At 2200, BG Mikhail Pisarev, commander of the 54th MRD, called off the attack. "There's no point in continuing the assaults," he told Northwest Front, "until an additional regiment and the division's heavy artillery reaches the front." By the following afternoon, the guns were in place. The 377th MRR had taken up positions on the 81st MRR's right flank. The infantry disembarked from their BMPs and began working their way through the mountainous terrain north of the E78.

At 1530 on the twentieth, with full artillery and air support, the 54th MRD struck again. The initial blow fell on the Italian Susa Alpini Battalion which earlier in the day had relieved the battered CHOD Battalion in line astride the E78. As had the Norwegians the day before, the Italians repulsed attack after attack as the Russians attempted to force their way northwest along the road to Skibotn. The Italians were dug in, their ATGMs were well sighted, and they were ably supported by the 105mm howitzers of the 40th Battery of the Pinerolo Mountain Artillery and the 1st Battalion of the Norwegian Nordland Brigade.

The battle appeared to be going well, despite constant Soviet air attacks against the Italian positions. But at 2215, Russian troops appeared before Helligskogen, deep in NATO's rear. A battalion of Soviet infantry had worked their way unseen around 3,700-foot-high Mt. Kapperusvaarat, passing through the Norwegian positions guarding the Italians' left flank. The Nordland Brigade's 1st Battalion promptly pulled back to defend the key town, and the bulk of Norwegian and Italian artillery. But this retrograde movement uncovered the flank of the Susa Alpini. A second Russian battalion hit the Italians' left and cut the road behind them. Trapped, the Italians struggled to break out to the northwest. The Soviets took over two hundred prisoners, although many of these men were wounded. Another two hundred were dead. In small groups, 113 Italians made their way back to NATO lines, but as a fighting force the battalion had ceased to exist.

The 54th MRD had taken Helligskogen, for the loss of another six hundred men. But the Norwegians still held the mountains north of the town and, well supported by the artillery that had been successfully evacuated to the west, barred the way to further movement.

★ ★ ★

Hoping to exploit success, Northwest Front ordered both the 45th and 54th MRDs to resume the advance the following morning. But the two division commanders, supported by Sixth Army commander LTG Aleksandr Berdiaev, who visited both headquarters on the evening of the twentieth, considered such an immediate renewal of the offensive impossible. BG Pisarev considered Northwest Front's orders "asinine." His two regiments in Norway had already lost a third of their rifle strength. "You talk about echeloned attack and the momentum of the advance," he protested to the front commander's chief of staff, "but I don't have a fucking second echelon. It's hundreds of kilometers away making sure the Finns don't fuck me up the ass!" BG Fedor Muratov, commander of the 45th MRD, considered talk about echeloned attack in Norway laughable. His staff advised him that it would take at least twenty-four hours to ferry the entire first echelon across the Lyngen Fjord. Neither division would be ready to attack until the early hours of 22 July. At Berdiaev's insistence, Northwest Front agreed to postpone the attack.

SEVENTEEN

On the morning of 16 July, aircraft from the *Forrestal*'s Carrier Air Wing 6 not only drove off the Soviet air transport armada headed for Evenes, but also supported strikes by RAF Buccaneers from Orland against Soviet surface forces retiring northwards. An unfortunate Soviet support group, caught off the North Cape, bore the brunt of day-long NATO air attacks.

RADM Georgi Kostyuk commanded the replenishment force which steamed from Pechenga on the fourteenth and reached the Norwegian Sea late in the afternoon of the fifteenth, just in time to begin retracing its wake. Kostyuk discovered that the surface forces he expected to replenish were racing north at full speed seeking the protection of Kola-based fighters. The support group's commander knew that his slow but irreplaceable ships were being left behind and that his force of two destroyers and a frigate was inadequate to screen the replenishment ship *Boris Chilikin*, two submarine depot ships, two missile support ships, and a pair of tankers. When Kostyuk requested assistance, Northern Fleet headquarters responded that all high value ships were needed for the defense of the Kola. "Things must being going pretty damned bad," Kostyuk confided in his chief of staff, "I thought I commanded high value ships."

To COMSTRIKFLTLANT, VADM Hugh Emerson, Kostyuk's replenishment ships were high value targets. Emerson's uncertainty about whether or not the lone *Forrestal* task force could sustain itself in the Norwegian Sea made him eager to destroy the Soviet support group. Emerson expected the Russians to throw everything at the *Forrestal* in an effort to knock it out before the *Eisenhower* reached the scene. If he had to withdraw from the Norwegian Sea under air pressure, the Russians would lack the means to pursue. "Here's our chance to cut the sea legs off the Russian fleet," Emerson told his staff. "If we can take out these ships, we'll shorten the leash on those mothers."

Strikes against Kostyuk's group continued into the late afternoon, by which time the entire force had been destroyed. The attacks on the sixteenth downgraded the Soviet Northern Fleet from a blue, to a green-water fleet. NATO losses totaled a single RAF Buccaneer.

Fortunately for NATO, Northern Fleet headquarters was in disarray after the debacles of the fourteenth and fifteenth and lacked firm intelligence on the positions of the American carriers. With the Soviet navy's stock so low, demands from the Sixth Army commander—LTG Berdiaev—that all air assets be directed against Bardufoss, led Northwest Front to order most SNA strike aircraft to support operations against NATO airfields in north Norway.

The situation over north Norway on the sixteenth remained precarious. Soviet strikes damaged Bardufoss and hampered reinforcement. But the airbase remained operational and throughout the day pairs of Norwegian F-16s arrived from the south to strengthen the defense. Aided by U.S. Navy aircraft from the *Forrestal*, the Norwegians repulsed most of the Soviet strikes.

Although Soviet air losses were significantly higher than NATO's, American and Norwegian aircrews were tiring. By the evening of the sixteenth, RADM Brian O'Bannion, commander of the *Forrestal* task force, was concerned that his exhausted air wing would be vulnerable should the Soviets suddenly turn their attentions against him. O'Bannion warned Emerson: "Consider current tempo flight ops unsustainable more than twenty-four hours."

The dangerous situation in the northern Norwegian Sea presented COMSTRIKFLTLANT with a dilemma. The *Eisenhower*, positioned midway between the NATO airbases at Keflavik and Orland, was still a full day's steaming—about seven hundred miles—from the *Forrestal*. Emerson, who had already shifted his flag from the 23-knot amphibious command ship *Mount Whitney* to the 33-knot *Eisenhower*, was "anxious as hell to steam at full speed to join O'Bannion up north." But the *Ike* was also shepherding RADM Raymond Huck's AMPHIBSTRIKFOR, the ships of which were about ten knots slower than those of the carrier task force. If Emerson raced north, the amphibious ships would fall behind and by afternoon would be outside the *Eisenhower*'s effective CAP umbrella.

Emerson and his chief of staff choppered to the *Mount Whitney* to confer with Hucks and LTG Jeffrey "Bull" Campbell, commander of II MEF. Emerson proposed that the amphibs head east for Orland, rather than north. According to the proposal worked out by STRIK-FLTLANT staff, they would be uncovered for only about twelve hours. Hucks believed that the risk was too great and recommended that if O'Bannion felt unable to maintain his position he ought to retire and to regroup with the main force as it proceeded north. The amphibious force commander also expressed concern about a Soviet submarine that only hours before had torpedoed the *Eisenhower* task force's replenishment ship—the *Camden*. Campbell's major worry was that the detour to the east would delay the arrival of the MEF off the Troms coast by about a day.

Emerson faced his first tough decision of the war. As he pondered his next move, an aide handed him a message: the submarine that had been stalking the task group had been located and destroyed by the *Conolly*'s LAMPS. "Scratch one sub," Emerson remarked to Hucks.

Although the amphibious force commander remained reluctant to see the task group divided, COMSTRIKFLTLANT had made his decision. "Ray, I'll leave you the [Aegis destroyer *Arleigh*] *Burke* for air defense; we're heading north." Emerson then turned to Campbell, who shrugged his shoulders and said "Go for it; they're your ships."

COMSTRIKFLTLANT immediately passed the order for the *Eisenhower* and the *America* task forces to "make all possible speed" to reinforce O'Bannion's lone carrier in the Norwegian Sea. CINCNORTH was given a heads up to prepare to cover the AMPHIBSTRIKFOR as it neared Trondheim.

Throughout the fifteenth of July, the Soviet Northern Fleet had vectored several submarines into positions to attack American carrier task forces as they steamed toward the Norwegian Sea. Late on the fifteenth, a *Sierra*-class SSN had scored a single hit on the fast combat support ship *Camden* before being sunk the following morning. Escorting destroyers and helicopters from the *America* task force turned the tables on the Russians and sank two submarines—a *Victor III* and a *Foxtrot*.

Soviet efforts to prevent the movement of other NATO surface forces into the Norwegian Sea fared better. SNA reconnaissance aircraft, working with a regiment of Backfires, located STANAV-FORLANT midway between Trondheim and Narvik, and in a well executed attack, sank the destroyers *Lütjens* and *Iroquois*, the frigate *Banckert*, and severely damaged the frigate *Phoebe*. The only surviving ship of the NATO force, the frigate *Knox*, took the stricken *Phoebe* in tow and proceeded slowly toward Trondheim. "That's it for 'Sniffle,'" Emerson remarked when he received the report of the successful Soviet strike.

Air and ASW engagements also took place around the Shetland Islands. Northern Fleet air assets struck repeatedly at British and Dutch forces moving north toward the Norwegian Sea, while patrols by RAF Nimrods and the active ASW efforts of Dutch and British helicopters kept Soviet submarines at a distance.

In the air, Royal Navy Harriers drew first blood, ambushing an early afternoon regiment-sized Backfire strike, shooting down at least a dozen of the Soviet aircraft. But in the evening the Backfires returned. Several of the SNA bombers, specially outfitted with air search radars and armed with AA-10 air-to-air missiles, downed seven surprised Harrier pilots. The remaining conventionally armed Backfires penetrated the British CAP screen and attacked a Dutch ASW group, sinking the destroyer *De Ruyter* and the frigates *Piet Hein* and *Van Galen*.

The battle of the Shetlands continued. Royal Navy and Dutch ASW ships and helicopters, ably supported by RAF Nimrods, sparred with Soviet diesel and nuclear submarines, destroying six. The Russian boats failed to execute a single successful attack on a NATO ship.

But British and Dutch ASW expertise was offset by the weakness of the Royal Navy's air defense system. Inadequate airborne early warning capability and insufficient fighter strength left NATO surface forces north of the Shetlands at risk. The British and Dutch task forces fortuitously avoided detection on the seventeenth, but the next day, Soviet reconnaissance aircraft located a Royal Navy amphibious task force. AAM-armed Backfires again took on the Harriers, each force losing five aircraft. But other Backfires pressed the attack and sank the logistic landing ship *Sir Tristam*, the tanker *Bayleaf*, and the replenishment ship *Fort Austin*. Although all but sixty of the five hundred Royal Marines aboard the *Sir Tristam* were rescued, sixteen APCs and twenty helicopters of the Royal Marine Brigade were lost.

With the air squadrons of the *Illustrious* and the *Invincible* nearly eliminated—only three Sea Harriers remained—CINC-EASTLANT ordered the Dutch and Royal Navy surface forces to race for Trondheim where Norwegian and RAF squadrons flying from Orland could provide air cover. Fortunately, the destruction of the Russian submarine force north of the Shetlands allowed the sprint to proceed unimpeded. By noon on the nineteenth, British and Dutch surface forces and the transports carrying the Royal Marine Brigade were nearing the Norwegian port as RAF Phantoms patrolled overhead.

★ ★ ★

As long-range SNA Backfires struck NATO naval forces in the Shetlands, older, shorter-ranged Badgers continued to operate against Bardufoss. NATO interceptors repeatedly drove off the bombers and ran up impressive kill ratios, but allied air defenses were weakening in what was becoming a war of attrition in the skies over north Norway, a war many senior NATO leaders feared the alliance was losing.

Fortunately, on the morning of the eighteenth, F-14 Tomcats from the carrier *Eisenhower* joined the fray over Bardufoss. The relief was immediate. After returning from a CAP mission, one Red Ripper pilot from the *Forrestal*'s VF 11 was overheard telling another aviator: "Hell, just seeing one of those Pukin' Dogs [Tomcats from the *Eisenhower*'s VF 143] gave me a big fucking lift. We're not alone anymore and there's gonna be hell to pay." Not a single Russian bomber got through to Bardufoss on the eighteenth.

Undisturbed, Norwegian engineers completed repairs to the runways and service facilities.

The next morning, the Soviets again launched a strike against Bardufoss, but American and Norwegian fighters controlled the skies. The attackers were decimated and driven off. Hawkeyes from the American carriers and NATO AWACS aircraft monitored Soviet air activity over the Kola, but no further strike materialized. Under the umbrella of the strengthened CAP screen, ground and air reinforcements continued to fly into Bardufoss.

On the twentieth, NATO fighters became more aggressive, conducting occasional offensive sweeps over the Barents Sea and Finnmark. Air reinforcements continued to arrive at northern airbases, including Evenes, the recapture of which, unfortunately, was offset by the loss of Andoya to Ganenko's Soviet marines.

While frontal aviation fighters and fighter-bombers supported the Sixth Army as it closed on the Lyngen position, SNA and AADS assets reduced their offensive operational tempo. Reports of severe aircrew fatigue and declining readiness led Northwest Front commander GEN Golikov to rest his principal air defense and strike forces. The Americans had two carriers in the Norwegian Sea and would soon be joined by a third. Major air battles would take place over north Norway as Soviet ground forces closed with NATO. Golikov wanted to have fresh air reserves on hand.

★ ★ ★

The first week of the war on the northern flank had been costly for both the Soviets and NATO. The allies had lost over 100 combat aircraft, 17 surface combatants, 12 Norwegian fast attack boats, 4 submarines, and 13 support ships—tankers, replenishment and supply vessels, and amphibious transports. Soviet losses were substantially higher: 276 combat aircraft, at least two score air transports, 20 surface combatants (including the carrier *Tbilisi*), 19 submarines, and 30 support vessels, including all of the Northern Fleet's amphibious ships.

Although the Northern Fleet remained an impressive surface force, the loss of its only carrier and its most modern replenishment and amphibious vessels limited its usefulness in any but defensive operations. The loss of over twenty submarines (another three were damaged)—nearly two-thirds of those directly engaged in the Norwegian Sea—had a crippling effect on subsequent operations. It was clear by the evening of the twentieth, that the Soviet navy had failed to prevent the concentration of NATO naval forces in the Norwegian Sea.

In the air, while operations had yet to reach a decisive point, heavy Soviet losses, the arrival of the *Forrestal* and *Eisenhower*, and the movement of significant reinforcements to north Norway began to shift the balance toward NATO's favor. Nevertheless, Golikov believed that the decision in the air would come when the ground offensive began. Both the Soviet Northwest Front commander and CINCNORTH expected that titanic attritional battles waged in the skies over north Norway would decide the ultimate outcome of the campaign. But VADM Emerson disliked "the idea of remaining tethered to Bardufoss in support of ground operations." In the early hours of 21 July, the STRIKFLTLANT strike ops staff was hard at work developing a plan that would meet Emerson's concept of operations. "I want a plan," he told his staff, "that will make the most of the mobility and offensive striking power of this carrier task group."

EIGHTEEN

One of the many factors that caused VADM Emerson to insist that his carriers concentrate in the Norwegian Sea as quickly as possible was the course of operations in the Mediterranean on 15 July. The position of the *Forrestal* in the northern Norwegian Sea was somewhat analogous to that of the *Roosevelt* in the eastern Mediterranean—out on a limb. On the fourteenth and fifteenth of July, the Soviets had thrown everything but the proverbial kitchen sink at the *Roosevelt* in an effort to sink the isolated carrier.

RADM Reece's CARSTRIKGRU 1 had barely survived D day as an intact fighting force. Reece attributed his survival to the close and efficient cooperation of the Israeli air force. After weathering the late-evening attack on the fourteenth in which the *Biddle* and

Semmes were sunk, Reece contentedly "tucked" his task group into what he believed to be a secure carrier haven off the Israeli coast.

But on the morning of 15 July, the Soviets struck again. Russian fighters and fighter-bombers penetrated Turkish air space, engaged NATO interceptors, and knocked out several NADGE sites in central Anatolia, punching additional holes through an already porous air defense system. Elements of two regiments of SNA Backfires and four of Badgers, escorted by a regiment of Flankers—a force of well over a hundred aircraft—swept through this gap and headed south. The longer-range, faster Backfires swung around the western tip of Cyprus and approached the American carrier group from the northwest. The slower Badgers flew over eastern Cyprus and headed south.

American AWACS and Hawkeyes had no trouble monitoring the massive attack. In the CIC of the *Roosevelt*, Reece watched the assault develop. It quickly became apparent that the scope of the strike would place a severe strain on Reece's CAP, so he put in a call to the Israelis.

But the Soviet Black Sea Fleet command had planned its attack well. As Crimean-based strike aircraft neared the American carrier group, Soviet and Arab fighter-bombers took off from Syrian airfields and headed not for the *Roosevelt*, as had been expected, but directly for Israel's urban centers. The Israeli air defense command reacted promptly, sending all available interceptors over Lebanon and the Golan. Initially, Reece was shocked when they turned down his request for assistance, but he could see the attacks shaping up over Syria and understood that the Israelis were more concerned about the safety of their own cities than they were of an American carrier. The *Roosevelt* was on its own.

At 0840, a dozen Tomcats of the *Roosevelt*'s Black Aces (VF 41) and Jolly Rogers (VF 84) engaged Russian Flankers over the southern coast of Cyprus. Although the American fighters were outnumbered nearly two-to-one, their long-range Phoenix AAMs gave them the upper hand. Nearly half of the Soviet fighters were destroyed before they were close enough to fire their own missiles. But in the ensuing dogfights, the agile Su-27s held their own with the Tomcats, downing four F-14s for the loss of another six Flankers.

Although the *Roosevelt*'s F-14s virtually destroyed an entire regiment of Su-27s, the Flankers succeeded in engaging the Tomcats

THE WAR THAT NEVER WAS

until the Soviet strike aircraft reached positions within range of their stand-off missiles. American aircraft control officers, airborne in a pair of E-2C Hawkeyes, attempted to get several of the Tomcats to disengage and to vector F/A-18 Hornets into intercept positions before the SNA bombers released their air-to-surface missiles. At least four Tomcats and a half-dozen Hornets attacked and destroyed several Backfires and Badgers, but not before the majority of the bombers were able to launch their ASMs. There were just too many Russians.

Estimates of the number of missiles actually released vary from sixty to a hundred. Many of the Soviet ASMs malfunctioned. The Aegis cruisers *Shiloh* and *San Jacinto* downed most of the missiles that penetrated the inner defense zone. Airborne and shipboard electronic countermeasures caused other missiles to miss. Point defense systems, such as Vulcan-Phalanx, destroyed many more. But seven ASMs found targets. Four struck the destroyer *Deyo* and two hit the already damaged *Detroit*. Both ships sank. At 0852, a single missile, believed by ordnance experts to have been an AS-4 Kitchen, struck the *Theodore Roosevelt* on the port side midway between deck elevator four and the outboard waist catapult. The explosion of the thousand-kilogram warhead disabled both the elevator and the catapult and started a fire, fed by jet fuel, on the hangar deck. Fortunately, damage control teams and the carrier's chemical washdown system contained the conflagration before it spread to nearby ordnance. Five aircraft were destroyed.

Despite the damage, the *Roosevelt* was soon launching aircraft from the two forward catapults. Reece sent his bingo (short of fuel) aircraft to Israeli fields and recovered them later. Within fifteen minutes of the attack three Israeli tankers were also airborne, re-fuelling the carrier's CAP aircraft. By 0925, the fire had been extinguished. At 0930, the *Roosevelt* began recovering its planes. The loss of elevator number four was minor since it was rarely used. The loss of catapults three and four was more serious and significantly reduced the carrier's tempo. But the *Roosevelt* was still operational.

The successful Soviet strikes on the fourteenth and fifteenth against CARSTRIKGRU 1 caused consternation at senior American and NATO commands in Europe and the United States and induced COMSTRIKFORSOUTH to order the withdrawal of the American task group to the central Mediterranean where the *Roosevelt* and the *Kennedy* could rendezvous and operate together.

RADM Reece disagreed with the decision and discovered myriad reasons to avoid its prompt execution. An immediate movement westward, Reece believed, would be taken by the Israelis as a sign that the Americans blamed the IDF for Soviet successes and that Israel, engaged in desperate fighting with the Syrian Army in Lebanon and on the Golan, was being abandoned. Reece also considered it safer to remain off the Israeli coast than to move west toward the *Kennedy*. After talking with the IDF, Reece agreed that the Soviets' heavy losses made further large-scale strikes unlikely.

Reece's assessment was accurate. American and Israeli interceptors had downed at least fifty Soviet and sixty Syrian aircraft during the morning raids. The Americans had lost six fighters and the Israelis four. After the fifteenth, the Soviets were unable to mount a raid of similar magnitude. The air battles of the morning of 15 July left the IAF with the initiative in the air, an initiative it never surrendered.

Indeed, in the early afternoon, Israeli aircraft, supported by small strikes from the *Roosevelt*, began to hit Syrian airfields. By that evening, the Syrian air force had lost at least a hundred planes in the air and on the ground.

★ ★ ★

In addition to the air threat to COMCARSTRIKGRU 1, powerful Soviet and Syrian surface forces remained at large in the eastern Mediterranean. The remnants of the *Slava* and *Minsk-Kirov* groups finally rendezvoused off Tartus and sought safety and replenishment in the harbor where they were soon joined by Syrian surface forces. The powerful concentration in the Syrian port included the cruiser *Slava*, flying the flag of RADM Penza, the destroyers *Ognevoy* and *Vitse-Admiral Kulakov*, two frigates, the tanker *Elnya*, the *Alligator*-class LST *Nikolay Vilkov*, the missile support ship *Voronezh*, the replenishment ship *Berezina*, two Syrian *Petya II*-class frigates, and ten Syrian *Osa I* and *II* missile boats.

Penza's combined Syrian-Soviet force clearly outgunned Reece's task group off the Israeli coast, but throughout the fifteenth made no move to the south to engage the Americans. Penza lost his nerve after the morning battles of D day when he suddenly found himself thrust into command following the death of VADM Gudkov on the *Kirov*. In his reports to the Crimea, Penza attributed the delays in getting his force back out to sea to the Syrian squadron commander. Penza directed the Syrians to replenish at Latakia because the facilities at Tartus could not service both groups simultaneously. But Latakia's port facilities were hit hard by an Israeli air strike on the fourteenth and the Syrian commander retired instead to Tartus. The overcrowded harbor facilities, a deteriorating relationship between the Russians and their Arab allies, frequent air raids against Tartus, and confused leadership kept Penza's ships immobile during the fifteenth.

For the Americans and the Israelis, the concentration of enemy surface forces at Tartus became a primary target for both air and surface strike operations. The distance from Haifa to Tartus was only 150 miles, a 4.5-hour sprint for 30-plus knot Israeli fast attack craft. Throughout the fifteenth, the IDF sent groups of frigates and missile boats north to positions twenty to thirty miles southwest of Tartus where they would fire off their missiles, then race back to Haifa to replenish. The Israeli air force covered these dashes and, in combined operations with American attack aircraft from the *Roosevelt,* also struck port facilities at Tartus. The Israeli-American attacks sank the destroyers *Vitse-Admiral Kulakov* and *Ognevoy* as well as eight Syrian missile boats.

Under such constant air and surface attacks, Penza's ships were not ready to sortie until the late afternoon of 17 July. A weakened Soviet-Syrian surface strike group left Tartus and steamed south. An Israeli surface force intercepted Penza's group at 0540 on the eighteenth. In a short battle, the Israelis sank the *Slava,* two Soviet and two Syrian frigates, four Syrian missile boats, and the replenishment ship *Berezina*. The Israeli's lost the *Saar 2* missile boats *Mivtach* and *Akko,* and the *Aliya*-class missile boat *Romat* was badly damaged. As the Russians and Syrians retired northwards, IDF strike aircraft completed the destruction of Penza's surface group. Not a single ship returned to Tartus.

The Israeli successes completed the allied naval victory in the eastern Mediterranean. By the evening of 18 July, the operations of the navies and air forces of the United States, Israel, Egypt, and

Turkey had succeeded in sinking or putting out of action every Soviet and Syrian surface warship and submarine in the eastern Mediterranean.

★ ★ ★

COMSTRIKFORSOUTH's desire to have the *Roosevelt* move west to rendezvous with the *Kennedy* was not based solely on concern for the damaged carrier's safety. Despite the successes of the fourteenth, VADM Turner had doubts about the ability of the *Kennedy* battlegroup to operate offensively against Libyan airbases in Cyrenaica and simultaneously to shield NATO surface forces in the central Mediterranean from SNA attacks originating in the Crimea. Turner advised CINCSOUTH, ADM McMichaels, that the situation in the central Mediterranean was precarious. STRIKFORSOUTH faced both Libyan and Russian surface forces, the greatest concentration of enemy submarines in the Mediterranean, Backfires coming out of the Crimea, and, simultaneously, was expected to take out the Libyan air force. In fact, Turner first questioned his staff about bringing the *Roosevelt* west late in the evening of the fourteenth, hours before the carrier was damaged.

Given the distance to be covered and RADM Reece's purposefully slow disengagement from Bagel Station, by the time the *Roosevelt* was in position on 16 July to join the *Kennedy* in air strikes against Libyan and Soviet forces and bases in Cyrenaica, the crisis in the central Mediterranean had passed. In a confusing combined operation, American, Italian, and French naval and air forces waged a successful three-dimensional campaign against enemy assets in Libya and the central Mediterranean.

On the fifteenth, Turner used the *Kennedy*, supported by the French carrier *Foch* and NATO land-based aircraft flying from Sicily and southern Italy, to continue the aerial offensive against enemy bases along the northern coast of Libya. Italian and American ASW groups, and French, Italian, and American submarines screened the carriers and allied amphibious task forces from Soviet and Libyan submarines.

A five-frigate American ASW task force screening the southern flank of the NATO forces bore the brunt of Libyan and Soviet attacks during the fifteenth. At 0840, LAMPS III helicopters from the task force, which included the frigates *Simpson*, *Boone*, *Doyle*,

Capodanno, and *Aylwin,* located and sank the submarine *Al Ahad,* which the previous day had announced Libya's entry into the war when it torpedoed an American tanker. About noon, the *Doyle* detected a second submarine but before its LAMPS reached the area, a Soviet *Tango* torpedoed the *Simpson* which lost all power two hundred miles northwest of Benghazi. American ASW helicopters promptly destroyed the *Tango* before it could finish off the stricken frigate.

The damaged *Simpson* now became the centerpiece of a developing battle. Qaddafi, obsessed by a determination to have his navy sink an American ship, ordered his surface forces to destroy the stricken *Simpson.* In a series of night engagements, Libyan frigates and fast attack craft sortied from bases in the Gulf of Sidra and Cyrenaica. In the ensuing engagement, the Libyans managed to sink the American frigates *Simpson, Aylwin,* and *Capodanno,* and to damage the *Boone* and *Doyle.* Libyan losses were also heavy. American forces sank the *Koni*-class frigate *Al Hani* and at least twenty missile boats, either by gunfire and missile attacks from frigates, or by SUCAP Hornets and Intruders operating from the *Kennedy.*

CAPT Abdullah Abu Khairallah, the commander of the Vosper Thornycraft Mark 7 frigate *Dat Assawari* and senior officer of the Libyan strike group, had all but eliminated the American task force. Based on intelligence provided by the Soviet command center at Benghazi, Abu Khairallah decided to follow up on his success and to continue north to attack an American amphibious task force.

The Libyan success stunned NATO commanders on the scene. Italian VADM Donello, in the carrier *Giuseppe Garibaldi,* was certain that the message reporting the American losses had been improperly decoded or mistranslated. VADM Turner could not believe that the lowly Libyans had wiped out one of his task forces. Turner now scrambled to scrape together forces to throw in the path of the attackers. He hastily concentrated destroyers and frigates from nearby American task forces and convoys into an ad hoc surface action group. He directed the amphibious task force to turn north and to disperse.

Turner's efforts might have come to naught had not the French nuclear submarine *Rubis* intercepted, torpedoed, and sunk the *Dat Assawari.* The French put a pair of ECAN F17 wire-guided torpedoes into the Libyan frigate which exploded in a massive fireball.

Leaderless, the Libyan force promptly turned to the south. But twenty minutes later, the Americans intercepted a clear, uncoded voice transmission from Qaddafi to his ships to continue the attack.

The Libyans turned about and steamed north, but their window of opportunity had closed. Two French and three Italian submarines, the scratch American SAG, six Italian Harriers from the *Garibaldi*, and eight hastily rearmed Intruders that had returned to the *Kennedy* after late night strikes against targets in Cyrenaica, lay in ambush. By 0700, a third Libyan frigate and sixteen missile boats had been sunk. The Libyans had failed to engage a single NATO surface vessel, nor had they managed to shoot down any of the attacking aircraft. "The Libyan navy," VADM Turner reported to CINCSOUTH, "has ceased to exist."

As a result of the night battles, Turner believed that a successful conclusion of the campaign in the central Mediterranean was within his grasp. The *Theodore Roosevelt* had reached a position 150 miles northeast of Matruh, well within range of Cyrenaica. With the *Kennedy* and *Foch* steaming east, three allied carriers were closing in on RADM Nikolai Chubinidze's small, exposed, Soviet surface task group off Tobruk. In a succession of strikes, American and French carrier aircraft destroyed the entire Soviet force, including the cruiser *Azov*, two frigates, four *Nanuchka*-class missile corvettes, a pair of freighters carrying SAMS for Libyan air defense sites, and the submarine depot ships *Dmitry Galkin* and *Tobol*.

With Soviet and Libyan naval and air power eliminated in the central Mediterranean, the only remaining threats to NATO's complete control of the central Mediterranean were the Russian and Libyan submarines still at large. The Black Sea Fleet KPF vectored its remaining naval assets into attack positions in an effort to destroy the three Allied carriers before they could concentrate for offensive operations in the Aegean.

These final Soviet subsurface operations in the central Mediterranean achieved mixed results. The Russians lost two submarines attempting to close to within torpedo range of the carrier *Kennedy*. A third Soviet SSN penetrated the ASW screen of the *Foch*. Detected and attacked at the last moment, the Russian SSN fired a four-torpedo spread at the carrier before beginning evasive maneuvering to avoid French homing torpedoes. Three of the hastily fired torpedoes missed; the fourth struck the port side of the *Foch* but failed to detonate. Minutes later, a massive underwater explosion indicated that the French counterattack had succeeded. The Black Sea Fleet headquarters vectored a pair of SSNs into position to attack the *Giuseppe Garibaldi*. Italian ASW helicopters detected, localized, attacked, and sank one of the submarines at 1725, but at 1740, a Soviet *Alfa*-class SSN fired four torpedoes at the *Garibaldi*. All struck the Italian carrier's starboard side. At 1800, the Italians were forced to abandon what had become a flaming wreck. At 2345, with all its Harriers still aboard, the *Garibaldi* rolled over and sank, joining its attacker—the *Alfa*—on the bottom where a counterattack at 2130 had sent her.

By the evening of 18 July, all Soviet and Libyan submarines in the central Mediterranean had been destroyed. Those few still operating in the western Mediterranean, devoid of support and air cover, would be killed off one by one. In six days of combat, Soviet submarine strength in the Mediterranean had gone from twenty-four to one, and that a lone submarine in the Atlantic approaches to Gibraltar, heading home with a single torpedo remaining. The allies, in contrast, had lost five submarines.

★ ★ ★

On the morning of 17 July, the carriers *Kennedy*, *Roosevelt*, and *Foch* rendevouzed off Crete and steamed into a position north and east of Cape Spatha, where combat air patrols could cover the movement of several convoys bound for Greek and Turkish Aegean ports. Soviet surface and submarine forces in the Aegean had already been eliminated in a series of air, surface, and subsurface engagements fought between 15 and 17 July.

Following the suicide of RADM Filiminov on the fifteenth, CAPT Petr Kamensky, commander of the *Moskva*, became senior officer of the Soviet surface group in the Aegean. KPUG 2 included the *Moskva*, the damaged cruiser *Ochakov*, the destroyers *Admiral Zakharov* (damaged), *Otlichnny*, and *Slavny*, and two frigates. Two submarines screened the group to the south. Four *Osa I*-class missile boats, the LSTs *Aleksandr Tortsev* and *Donetsky Shakhter*, and the cargo transport *Onda* remained at Lemnos.

Kamensky saw little purpose in remaining in the Aegean and believed that the best hope of the KPUG would be to break out into the eastern Mediterranean. But Kamensky had his orders to fight a

MICHAEL A. PALMER

delaying action in the central Aegean until the ground forces of
Southwest Front opened the straits.

The NATO forces closing in on Kamensky's group were powerful. Six NATO submarines were moving north. Turkish and Greek
surface task forces and NAVOCFORMED were in the southern
Aegean. Greek and Turkish air squadrons operated freely from their
bases around the Aegean periphery.

At 1300, Greek A-7H Corsairs of Moiras 340 and 345 from
Suda Bay, Crete, struck the Soviet force at Lemnos and sank the
LSTs *Aleksandr Tortsev* and *Donetsky Shakhter*, all four *Osas*, and
the *Onda*. The following morning, 16 July, the Corsairs struck the
main Soviet force, sinking the *Moskva*. Kamensky shifted his flag
to the *Ochakov*.

As KPUG 2 fended off the attacking A-7Hs, four German-built
Type 209 diesel submarines of the Greek Navy approached the
Soviet force from the west. The *Glavkos*, *Triton*, *Pontos*, and *Nereus*
stalked Kamensky's ships throughout the day. At 1147, the *Glavkos*
torpedoed and sank the *Admiral Zakharov*. At 1742, the *Triton* sank
the *Otlichnny*. At 1800, Kamensky decided to ignore the "unreal-
istic orders" of the Black Sea Fleet and to break out of the Aegean.
The only door that appeared to remain open was that between the
eastern end of Crete and Turkey.

Turkish reconnaissance aircraft monitored Kamensky's dash to
the south and RADM E. Gordon Smith-Humphreys's NAVOCFOR-
MED immediately began to steam eastward along the northern
shore of Crete, supported by Greek and Turkish squadrons. Since
the Greeks and Turks refused to cooperate with each other, Smith-
Humphreys allowed them to operate independently to either flank
and hoped that they would weigh in when the time came.

At 0055 on 17 July, NAVOCFORMED ran head-on into Kamensky's force about a hundred miles northeast of Iraklion. The
Greeks hit the Russians on the left, and the Turks hit them on the
right. The night action appeared to be a "classic" surface engagement, but the outcome was totally fortuitous and the plan of battle
serendipitous. Smith-Humphreys not only did not plan the battle as
it was fought, but he was unsure the Greeks and Turks would even
fight the Russians instead of each other. Nevertheless, NAVOCFOR-
MED totally destroyed Kamensky's force. NATO losses included

THE WAR THAT NEVER WAS

the American destroyer *Hayler*, the Greek destroyer *Kanaris* and the frigate *Limnos*, and the Turkish frigate *Yavuz*.

As KPUG 2 was being destroyed, NATO ASW forces concentrated on the destruction of the two Soviet submarines still operating in the Aegean. At 0940, a pair of Turkish S-2A/2E Trackers detected and sank a *Victor I*-class SSN north of Lesvos. At 2135, an *Alfa*-class SSN ambushed and destroyed the Greek submarine *Glavkos* west of Limnos. At 2340, the American SSN *Memphis* turned the tables on the Russian and destroyed the *Alfa*.

* * *

On the afternoon of 17 July, the American fast sealift ship *Algol* docked at Izmir, Turkey, carrying equipment and supplies for the air element supporting the U.S. Marine's 6 MEB. To ADM McMichaels at his CINCSOUTH headquarters in Naples, the safe arrival of the *Algol* symbolized NATO success at opening the SLOCs to the southern flank. Following the tragic loss of the *Guam*, carrying the marines of the 22d MEU on the morning of D day, the Soviets and their allies had failed to sink or severely damage a single amphibious vessel or any of the supply and support ships carrying the troops and equipment of the American, Italian, and French marine contingents bound for the Aegean. At 1130 on the eighteenth, the four vehicle cargo ships of MPS Squadron 1 reached Izmir. Over the next twenty-four hours, three auxiliary sealift ships anchored in the Turkish port. Izmir was soon one of the busiest ports in southern Europe.

On the morning of the eighteenth, with the *Roosevelt*, *Kennedy*, and *Foch* operating northeast of Cape Spatha, allied amphibious squadrons, covered by the carriers' combat air patrols, made their way into the central Aegean. Shortly before dawn on the nineteenth, the French amphibious ships *Foudre*, *Ouragan*, *Orage*, and *Bougainville*, carrying the lead regiment of the French 9th Marine Division, began to disembark their troops at Thessaloniki. A dozen transports carrying the division's heavy equipment arrived at the Greek port over the next three days. The troops of the remaining two regiments flew into Thessaloniki on the twentieth and twenty-first.

At noon on the nineteenth, the Italian LPD *San Giorgio* docked at Izmir and disembarked the 750 marines of the San Marco Battalion. By 1800, the Italian amphibious ship had left the harbor to make room for the American amphibious transports carrying the personnel of 6 MEB. Turkish trains, trucks, and air transports soon arrived to speed the movement of the Italian and American marines, their equipment, and their light amphibious craft to the southern shore of the Sea of Marmara.

In less than a week, NATO had won the naval war in the Mediterranean. By 19 July, except for a few small patrol boats, Soviet, Syrian, and Libyan naval forces had been completely eliminated from the Mediterranean. Allied forces had lost seventeen major combatants and a dozen fast attack craft; the Russians and their allies had lost fifty-four combatants and forty-eight fast attack craft. In the air the battle had gone decidedly in the allies' favor. Allied losses totalled ninety-four combat aircraft; the Soviets and their allies lost nearly four hundred. The Syrian and Libyan navies and air forces had effectively ceased to exist.

With allied carriers operating in the southern Aegean, with French, Italian, and American marines disembarking at Thessaloniki and Izmir, and with the SLOCs to Greece, Turkey, Israel, and Egypt now secured, CINCSOUTH set his staff to work developing plans in which allied naval power could be brought to bear to win the battle on the southern flank.

NINETEEN

To Turkish GEN Vural Ersari, Commander, Allied Land Forces, Southeastern Europe, the 17 July message from CINCSOUTH reporting the arrival of the *Algol* at Izmir was welcome news. Ersari faced an imminent Warsaw Pact offensive against Turkish positions around Istanbul, and the fact that the SLOCs were open permitted far greater flexibility in planning and operations. The Turks still faced pressing shortages of munitions, as did all of the belligerents, but at least they knew that critically important items would reach them eventually.

★ ★ ★

At 0430 on 18 July, Warsaw Pact units began their offensive against the Turkish Catalca line. The Romanian assault force consisted of two armored and four motor rifle divisions. Each of the two lead motor rifle divisions attacked on a five mile-long front. The second echelon consisted of another pair of motor rifle divisions. The two tank formations made up a third echelon.

Southwest Front at Vinnitsa expected this overwhelming concentration of force to smash through the Turkish defenses. Given the speed and ease of the Pact advance in Thrace, the planning staff saw no reason to believe that the Turks would be able to halt the fresh Romanian divisions.

But the Turkish defense line was short and heavily defended. The Turkish 3d Mechanized and 23d and 33d Infantry Divisions held the fifteen-mile-long line. The three divisions were bloodied enough to have become veterans, but not battered enough to have been significantly weakened. The Romanian divisions were as yet untested. Behind the front, the Turkish First Army's 2d Tank Brigade, with its sixty-two German-built Leopard I tanks, remained in reserve. Although much of the Turkish equipment was obsolescent, that of the Romanian divisions was obsolete. All but a handful of the attacking armored divisions' tanks were T-54s and T-55s. The tank battalion of one of the MRDs was actually equipped with World War II-vintage T-34s.

For seven hours, the Romanians attacked but failed to break through. "The ground in front of our positions," one Turkish officer with the 3d Mechanized Division reported, "is littered with burning tanks and APCs and cluttered with the bodies of Romanian dead."

At 1145, the Romanians committed their last intact armored regiment into an assault along Route 20. The exhausted infantrymen of the Turkish 23d Division were subjected to the heaviest air strikes of the day as Romanian air force MiG-17 ground attack aircraft pounded the defenders' positions. The Turks knocked out thirty-three Romanian T-55s before, at last, giving way. About sixty Romanian tanks, accompanied by a battalion of infantry, poured through the hole in the Catalca line.

The Turkish First Army command had placed battalions of Leopard Is in prepared positions astride each of the roads leading from the Catalca position to Istanbul—the E5N and Route 20. MAJ Orhun Ulusoy commanded the 2d Armored Brigade's 1st Battalion, the tanks of which lay in prepared hull-down positions on either side of Route 20.

A company of Romanian infantry in BTR carriers led the Pact attack. The Turks opened fire on the lead vehicles at a range of a thousand meters. Only three platoons of Ulusoy's beloved "Leos" fired, but in seconds five APCs were brewed up, along with their infantry. The surviving BTRs came to an abrupt halt and scurried about the open ground looking for cover. The Leopards finished them off one by one.

As Ulusoy's center company duelled with the APCs, a regiment of Romanian T-54s and T-55s advanced to within range, coming forward without firing, knowing that the Leopards had much greater range and accuracy. The Romanian regiment was arrayed in three battalion-lines, about two hundred meters apart.

At a range of twelve hundred meters, Ulusoy gave the order for his entire battalion to fire at will. The initial salvo destroyed four of the T-55s. The attackers, continuing to advance, spread out in an attempt to turn both of the Turks' flanks. In minutes Ulusoy's Leopards had knocked out another twenty tanks. Not a single Leopard had been hit.

Despite the effectiveness of Turkish defensive fire, Romanian tank companies began to work their way around Ulusoy's flanks. The Turkish battalion commander received reports that two Leopards of his right flank platoon had been destroyed. He was so busy directing the battle, that he could no longer keep track of the enemy's losses, but knew they were far greater than his own. Ulusoy told everyone to keep firing and to stay put.

With their positions outflanked, four more of Ulusoy's Leopards were destroyed over the next few minutes, but the Romanian attack had spent itself. The Turks had knocked out most of the Romanians' command tanks, and the survivors appeared to mill about aimlessly. Ulusoy personally led his center company, which had destroyed all of the tanks to its front, onto some high ground overlooking the Turkish left, where his flank company had lost three of its tanks but was still engaging the enemy. Ulusoy's counterattacking Leopards, firing their 105mm guns on the move, eliminated the six Romanian T-55s that had outflanked his line. The wrecks of over seventy Romanian tanks and APCs littered the battlefield.

With his remaining twenty-five Leopards, supported by some infantry, Ulusoy launched an immediate counterattack along Route 20 and plugged the gap in the line. The Leopards knocked out another two-dozen armored vehicles, including some antique T-34s. Many of the Romanian tanks were abandoned, undamaged, by their crews.

About 1300, the battle ended and a strange quiet descended over the Catalca line. The Romanian and Turkish troops were totally exhausted. With only a single battalion of the 2d Tank Brigade in reserve, the Turkish First Army commander rejected calls from his staff for an immediate counterattack. Despite the failure of the Turks to follow up their success, Warsaw Pact operations in the Southwestern TVD had suffered a major setback. The offensive against the Turkish Catalca position had failed and the six Romanian divisions involved in the assault were physically shattered, their morale broken.

At 0430, COL Villem Kirsanov's Black Sea Fleet marines and the paratroopers of the 103d Guards Airborne Division's 393d Regiment attacked toward Uskadar. "Three days of marching and fighting under the hot Turkish sun has exhausted my men," Kirsanov informed MG Panferov, the commander of the 103d Guard Airborne Division, "nevertheless, the promise of reaching the Bosporus keeps us going." Unfortunately for Kirsanov, Turkish resistance, which had increased as the Russians neared the strait, now solidified. The Turks stopped the Soviet marines in their tracks with heavy casualties.

When Panferov, to whom the marines were subordinated, learned that air missions planned to support the attack had been cancelled, he ordered Kirsanov to halt his offensive and to take up secure defensive positions. Southwest Front commander COL GEN Kambarov had diverted all available air assets to the support of the Romanian drive against the Catalca line.

At 1000 on the morning of the nineteenth, the Turkish 2d

Infantry Division, supported by the elite Turkish Airborne Brigade, struck eastward from Uskadar. Between the Black Sea and the Sea of Marmara the Turks drove back the Russian marines and paratroopers. By nightfall, elements of the 2d Infantry Division had retaken Gebze and Turkish paratroopers had stormed through Sile. Panferov hastily threw a battalion-sized force of paratroopers into a marching column and sent it west to stiffen Kirsanov's defenses.

Panferov's concern about the deteriorating situation on his right flank was matched by his fear that the Turkish Second Army was preparing a counterattack of its own. Reports from the front indicated that fresh Turkish units were taking up positions opposite the lines of the 103d Guards Airborne Division.

On the morning of 20 July, the Turkish Second Army attacked along the entire line from Izmit to the Black Sea. The 6th Infantry Division, 20th Mechanized, 5th Tank, and 70th Infantry Brigades spearheaded a drive that forced back the paratroopers of the 688th Guards Airborne Regiment, crossed the Sakarya River, and recaptured Karasu. By evening, American-built M-48s of the 5th Tank Brigade were fighting in the outskirts of Kandira.

At Southwest Front headquarters in Vinnitsa, the sudden turn of events between 17 and 20 July stunned Kambarov and his staff. With the Bulgarian army fully committed to the Greek front and the elimination of the remaining NATO pockets in Thrace, no fresh units were on hand to resume the drive on Istanbul. Reports from the front indicated that the Romanian divisions had nearly disintegrated during the final stages of their offensive and had only been saved by the exhaustion of the Turkish defenders. The offensive of the Turkish Second Army against the Russian paratroopers and marines holding Izmit and Kandira threatened to overrun Panferov's isolated force. The promising drive of a Soviet air assault brigade that had begun working its way down the Gallipoli peninsula on the eighteenth had likewise been checked on the twentieth when Turkish reserve infantry at Canakkale threw back a Russian heliborne assault across the Dardanelles.

Nevertheless, Kambarov remained optimistic. In a review of the situation prepared for the general staff late on the evening of 20 July, he focused on the early victories achieved by his Russian,

Bulgarian, and Romanian troops and concluded: "these successes, while they have failed to lead to the total defeat of the enemy, have shifted the correlation of forces from one that favored the enemy to one of balance." Istanbul remained isolated as long as Panferov's men continued to resist. The Greeks had yet to demonstrate any desire to conduct offensive operations. The Turks, who had suffered enormous losses in Thrace, were nearly exhausted. Final victory, Kambarov argued, would be won by the side that could first reinforce its position in Thrace. The Warsaw Pact, with its secure land communications, held a decided advantage.

TWENTY

For VADM Anokhin, the Soviet commander in the Indian Ocean, there could be no hopes for reinforcement. Deep in his heart, the admiral knew that his forces were on their own and were expendable.

Unfortunately for Anokhin, by the morning of 15 July the situation in the Indian Ocean theater had deteriorated markedly. American F-15s flying from Muharraq, together with the small air forces of Kuwait, Qatar, Bahrain, and Oman, gradually gained control of the air over the Persian Gulf and the North Arabian Sea in an effort to cover the movement of allied and neutral tankers. American and Bahraini fighters turned back several raids against Muharraq. Elsewhere in the Gulf, the Soviets lost over twenty planes, including six MiG-29 Fulcrums flying long-range patrol and escort missions, but sank only two small tankers.

As a result of the late night raid against Ras Kharmah, and the decision of Oman to actively support the United States, the allied air picture also improved over the Gulf of Aden. Omani Tornados and Jaguars patrolling the eastern Gulf downed a half-dozen Soviet reconnaissance aircraft during the fifteenth. French Mirage F1s, flying from Djibouti, challenged Yemeni and Ethiopian fighters—outclassed MiG-21s and MiG-23s—for control of the air over the western gulf. With the loss of a single Mirage, French pilots shot

197

down at least twenty enemy planes, including several Soviet Il-38 Mays.

French and Omani air activity, combined with American fighter patrols from the *Nimitz*, effectively blinded the Soviet fleet command post at Aden during most of 15 July. VADM Anokhin had only the most general idea of the location of the American carrier. The *Nimitz*'s late night strike against Ras Kharmah made it obvious that the carrier was within the attack radius of its F/A-18s, something under 450 miles. For Anokhin, that information was of little use since his air strike arm had been blunted. Moreover, calls for assistance failed to elicit support from Southern Front headquarters in Baku. Heavy D day losses and mounting Arab fighter activity over the Persian Gulf and the Gulf of Oman—operations controlled by Saudi Arabian AWACS aircraft—made long-range strikes from Caucasus bases unlikely to achieve surprise and, without fighter escort, too dangerous to risk.

VADM Anokhin had several options. First, he could continue to operate in the Gulf of Aden under the air umbrella provided by Socotra, although increasingly he viewed the central position in the Gulf as a trap. To the west, a French surface task force had left Djibouti; to the east, the *Nimitz* CVBG continued to close on Socotra; and to the northeast, an American surface action group had steamed from Raysut. At least four allied submarines were in the area. Moreover, Anokhin was uncertain how much longer his air cover at Ras Kharmah would survive. Second, the *Kiev* KUG could retire up the Gulf of Aden and attempt to destroy the French task force operating from Djibouti while the Yemeni and Ethiopian air forces provided cover, although such a course would take the KUG into narrow and shallow waters. The aircraft of Yemen and Ethiopia were mostly obsolete. Nor did Anokhin possess much faith in his allies. Moreover, such a westward movement would uncover Ras Kharmah and abandon the critical Socotra-bound convoy coming from Vladivostok. Third, the SOVINDRON could steam east in an effort to engage the *Nimitz* battlegroup in a surface action. This final course Anokhin considered extremely dangerous, since it could take the SOVINDRON well beyond the effective CAP range of Ras Kharmah's Flankers.

As Anokhin and his staff debated their next move, an aide appeared with a report that the *Kiev* KUG was under attack and that an allied SSN had torpedoed the destroyer *Simferopol*, part of the ASW screen off Abd al Kuri. No more than ten minutes later, further evidence of possible allied submarine activity reached Anokhin as the airbase at Ras Kharmah reported incoming cruise missiles. The Tomahawk strikes, conducted by the SSNs *Miami* and *Mendel Rivers*, inflicted additional damage to Soviet runways and depots, one of which, containing surface-to-surface missiles for the KUG, exploded in a massive pyrotechnic display. The American attacks convinced Anokhin that he had no choice but to adopt the most aggressive course. Only an offensive stroke could allow him to cover the convoy, relieve the pressure on Socotra, and offer any chance for victory.

Unchecked by Soviet air attacks, RADM Moore's carrier battle-group continued to steam toward Socotra, screened by one British and three American SSNs. Moore's staff was planning the next strike against Ras Kharmah when they received a report from the SSN *Albany* that the Russians had altered course and were steaming east at high speed. Moore's chief of staff considered the report indicative of a high-speed sprint to escape the *Albany*, but CJTFME "had a hunch that the Russian's coming out to attack, principally, because if I was in his shoes, that's what I would do."

Moore now faced a dilemma. The CVBG could continue the air offensive against Ras Kharmah or switch its focus to the Soviet KUG. Moore's staff favored another attack against Ras Kharmah, arguing that the follow-up strikes, if delayed, would allow the Russians to recover from the late night and early morning attacks. Moore knew that his aircraft had already been armed for such an attack and to "reweaponeer" the air wing for an anti-ship strike would take several hours. Nevertheless, Moore canceled the planned attack and ordered a course reversal. He told his staff, "look, the Russians can advance faster than we can retreat, saddled with the amphibious task force. So we're gonna conduct a fighting withdrawal, striking and slowing their ships as we retreat eastward."

About 1015, Harpoon-armed Hornets and Intruders from the *Nimitz*, covered by additional F/A-18s carrying air-to-air missiles, attacked the Soviet battlegroup. The plan was to attack first with stand-off weapons to knock-out the *Kiev* and to damage their most effective AAW capable ships. A second strike would then use more accurate and deadly laser-guided bombs to complete the destruction of the Soviet group. But, because of effective air defenses and electronic countermeasures, few Harpoons found their intended targets. A pair of missiles struck the *Kiev* which slowed temporarily while its crew fought the fires that threatened to engulf the superstructure. But the small carrier's VTOL aircraft remained operational and the Russians continued on course. The disappointing results forced Moore to reassess his plans and to cancel the planned bombing attack. With the *Kiev* still operational and Soviet air defenses intact, he could not risk sending his planes into what could prove to be a meat grinder. "I only have a single carrier," he reminded CINCCENT, "and I can't afford to bleed my air wing."

As aircraft from the *Nimitz* struck the Soviet battlegroup, other American forces, at Moore's direction, maintained whatever pressure they could against Ras Kharmah. U.S. Air Force B-52s from Diego Garcia launched a stand-off cruise missile attack against the airbase, as did the attack submarine *Albany*, inflicting significant damage. An *Akula*-class SSN, apparently alerted by the *Albany*'s Tomahawk launch, ambushed and sank the American submarine.

The successful strikes against Ras Kharmah again presented Moore with the opportunity to take out the battered airbase. He knew the Russians were hurting. The remnants of the Badger regiment had fled Ras Kharmah for Aden, but had been intercepted en route by four French Mirage F-1s from Djibouti which downed ten of the bombers. Moore also knew from TARPS reconnaissance overflights that the *Kiev* was again underway at over thirty knots and that the Soviets were continuing to close on the American carrier and amphibious task forces. He ordered the cruiser *Arkansas* and the destroyer *Hewitt* to launch their Tomahawk land attack missiles against the airfield while the air wing prepared for a second strike.

To cover his retrograde maneuver, Moore concentrated the attack submarines *Haddock* and *Mendel Rivers* in Anokhin's path. The British *Trafalgar*-class SSN *Turbulent* also moved into a position to support the Americans. About 1300, the *Haddock*, an old *Permit*-class boat, sank the *Udaloy*-class destroyer *Admiral Levchenko*. Twenty minutes later, the *Mendel Rivers*, a *Sturgeon*-class SSN, closed on the Soviet main body and torpedoed the *Slava*-class cruiser *Chervona Ukraina*. At 1435, the *Turbulent* tangled with Anokhin's ASW screen and sank the *Sovremenny*-class destroyer *Boyevoy*, and damaged her sister ship the *Okrylenny*.

Nevertheless, Anokhin directed the KUG commander to press his approach and by 1615 the weakened group was within range. Anokhin decided to delay the strike until a pair of SSNs were in position to launch a more effective coordinated attack. Unfortunately for the Soviets, American fixed-wing and helicopter ASW forces drove off both submarines, damaging a *Sierra*-class SSN. With two of Anokhin's seven ships sunk, and three others damaged, the attack lacked the intensity necessary to overwhelm American defenses. "We didn't take a single hit," Moore informed CINCCENT, "although we had a few nervous moments." Nevertheless, as the Americans concentrated on the attack, one of the Soviets SSNs finally managed to penetrate the ASW screen and torpedoed the LSD *Tortuga*.

The ineffective Soviet attack convinced Moore that the *Kiev* KUG no longer posed a threat to his operations. By early evening, CJTFME's major concern had become the steadily worsening weather. Pressed for time, Moore ordered the amphibious task force to continue steaming to the east while the *Nimitz* group turned back toward the west to maintain contact with Anokhin's group and to close on Socotra. At 1830, the Americans launched what Moore later admitted was "a rushed, premature SSM attack" against the Soviet surface striking force. "We fired off a hell of a lot of Harpoons," Moore told his staff, "but we only managed to sink a single vessel"—the damaged destroyer *Okrylenny*. Anokhin's ships struck back with a poorly executed SSM attack of their own that did nothing but exhaust their remaining supply of missiles.

Moore next sent his air wing's attack assets against the Soviet KUG. While a squadron of F/A-18s made quick work of the four Forgers that attempted to break up the American attack, A-6E Intruders, armed with laser-guided bombs instead of standoff missiles, further damaged the *Kiev* and sank a destroyer and the damaged cruiser *Chervona Ukraina*. Simultaneously, a second squadron of *Nimitz* Hornets led the way for a B-52 attack against Ras Kharmah. Only seven Su-27 Flankers rose from the airbase's damaged runways to intercept the strike. All were quickly downed, with the loss of only two F/A-18s. Shortly thereafter, the B-52s obliterated what remained of the base, destroying a score of aircraft on the ground.

The focus of the allied effort now switched to the two Soviet convoys in the Gulf of Aden. Earlier in the day, Omani Tornados struck a convoy bound for Socotra from Aden and sank a corvette and a minesweeper. In the evening, the French SSN *Casablanca* joined the attack and sank a frigate and a freighter. The American SSN *Haddock* attacked the southern convoy, sinking a corvette and another freighter.

★ ★ ★

The fifteenth had gone badly for the Soviets. Arab cooperation with the Americans was increasing. The Iranians were talking toughly about Soviet overflights. The evening of the fifteenth was notable for the nearly complete absence of offensive Russian air activity, although a few long-range aircraft dropped mines in the shipping channels of the Strait of Hormuz. For VADM Anokhin, the only positive development was the deteriorating weather in the Gulf of Aden. At his Aden headquarters, Anokhin hoped that this development might give his command a breather and allow him to get a handle on events that were getting out of control.

A breather was just what RADM Moore was determined not to give the Russians. He ordered an attack as soon as possible, despite the badly heaving deck of the *Nimitz*. Eleven Intruders, accompanied by a pair of Prowlers, struck the *Kiev* group at 0545. "There weren't any Russian fighters airborne," LCDR Evan Johns, an A-6 driver reported on his return from the mission, "and it looked like many of their ships had been hit topside." Damaged fire control radars and missile launchers, combined with the excellent ECM work of the Prowlers, handicapped Soviet defensive efforts. "They got one of our planes," Johns told the debriefers, "but we put quite a bit of ordnance into the *Kiev*, a destroyer and a *Kresta II*." TARPS reconnaissance reported all three ships "dead in the water." The *Kiev* remained afloat the longest, sinking about 1430.

Having destroyed the *Kiev* group and neutralized Ras Kharmah, Moore now adopted a new plan. Screened by allied SSNs, the *Nimitz* battlegroup would work its way up the Gulf of Aden, "taking out Yemeni and Ethiopian air along the way." The amphibious task force, which had resumed an eastward course at 0600, would land its marines on Soviet-controlled Perim Island in the Strait of Bab el Mandeb.

Anokhin's remaining naval assets—his SSNs—made no effort to challenge Moore's advance. Of the three Soviet submarines in the Gulf of Aden, one was badly damaged, another had expended all but a single torpedo, and a third—an *Akula*—had taken station off Aden to block passage through the Bab el Mandeb. Allied submarines, in the meantime, had located the two Russian convoys, sinking another frigate and six merchant ships.

Deteriorating weather in the Gulf forced Moore to cancel planned airstrikes from the *Nimitz* against Yemeni airfields. Fortunately, elements of the 3d Marine Aircraft Wing from El Toro, California, had reached Salalah, Oman, during the fifteenth. At 0430, two squadrons of marine F/A-18 Hornets, supported by EA-6B Prowlers, attacked and heavily damaged the Yemeni airbase complex at Al Mukalla. "We caught the Arabs with their pants down," a jubilant VMFA 314 pilot recalled after his return from the mission, "hell, we must have shot up at least two dozen MiGs on the ground." By day's end, the marines had finished off Al Mukalla as Moore's task group continued its movement up the gulf.

Elsewhere in the Indian Ocean, allied operations proceeded with a similar degree of success. Two Australian air force P3Cs flying from Singapore sank a Russian *Kilo*-class diesel submarine off Sumatra and a U.S. Navy Orion flying from Masirah, Oman, sank a *Sierra*-class SSN in the Gulf of Oman. American P-3Cs based at Diego Garcia detected, but failed to sink either of the two Russian diesel submarines—a *Tango* and a *Foxtrot*—cruising off the United States' only Indian Ocean base. Nevertheless, the patrols of the Orions of VP 19 covered the movement of two important convoys to Diego Garcia during the sixteenth. The frigate *Jarrett* and five container ships anchored safely in the morning. In the early evening, the destroyer *Hayler* and a seven-ship convoy appeared off Cust Point.

***

With his own SLOCs secure, Moore continued his movement up the Gulf of Aden on 17 July. The *Turbulent* and *Casablanca* led the way for the *Nimitz* battlegroup while the French surface task force closed on a large but weak Russian-Yemeni group off the Yemen coast that consisted of three frigates, a pair of corvettes, four Yemeni missile boats, two minesweepers, two stores ships, and eight freighters. Moore ordered the *Hue City* surface action group to escort the five ships of Maritime Prepositioning Ships Squadron 2, carrying the equipment for the 7th Marine Expeditionary Brigade, and a pair of tankers through the Strait of Hormuz to Bahrain as a sign of the American commitment to the security of the Persian Gulf. Moore had earlier directed the American attack submarine *Miami* to head for the Gulf of Oman where reports indicated that a Soviet *Victor II* was active.

In an attempt to escape the approaching French, the Soviet group off Yemen took shelter in Al Mukalla harbor. Informed of the move by the French task force commander—RADM Jacques Roignant—Moore decided "to dig the bastards out with air." The CJTFME staff quickly produced a plan for a coordinated strike that would include naval aircraft from the *Nimitz*, marine assets from Salalah, and U.S. Air Force B-52s from Diego Garcia.

About 1100, with the skies clearing, the attack began. B-52s struck the port facilities. Marine Hornets and Prowlers from Salalah suppressed the Soviet-manned SAM sites. Navy attack aircraft sank the combat stores ship *Dnestr*, four merchant vessels, and two Yemeni missile boats. Six American aircraft were lost, including two B-52s. The Russian SAM operators, after their experiences the previous day, were wide awake on the seventeenth.

The air strikes continued into the afternoon, further knocking out port and air-defense facilities and sinking a corvette, a minesweeper, two frigates, another replenishment ship, and four freighters. From his headquarters in Aden, Anokhin ordered the commander of the mixed surface group "to get out of the harbor before your force is completely destroyed."

Shortly before 1500, the Soviet ships upped anchor. At 1610, Roignant's French squadron—the destroyers *Jean Bart*, *Duquesne*, and *Duguay-Trouin*—intercepted the Russians racing westward along the Yemini coast. In a short, sharp surface engagement, Roignant's ships sent a Soviet frigate, a corvette, a minesweeper, and two Yemeni missile boats to the bottom.

Anokhin's three remaining SSNs operational in the Gulf of Aden fared little better. With its next to last Tigerfish torpedo, the British SSN *Turbulent* sank an *Akula* patrolling the approaches to the Bab el Mandeb. A second *Akula* repeatedly tried but failed to penetrate the *Nimitz*'s ASW screen. Later that evening, an *Oscar* reached Aden to replenish its spent torpedo supply. But as the SSN docked, a massive allied air strike began. U.S. Navy Hornets shot down the few Yemeni MiGs that attempted night intercepts. Attack aircraft from the *Nimitz* and U.S. Air Force B-52s gave Aden "the Al Mukalla treatment." At least a score of fighters were destroyed on the ground. Among the heavily damaged port facilities was the Russian torpedo storage depot. By midnight, the *Oscar* had put to sea, torpedoless, for a dangerous race against time up the Red Sea to Assab, Ethiopia, where a Russian store ship carrying a shipment of torpedoes lay at anchor. Early the next day, a French Atlantique from Djibouti caught and destroyed the *Oscar* in shallow water near Massawa.

As allied aircraft struck Aden, the American warships *Hayler* and *Jarrett* rendezvoused with the Australian task force escorting four American container ships to Diego Garcia. An Australian S-70B-2 Seahawk ASW helicopter flying from the frigate *Adelaide* sank a *Foxtrot*, one of two Soviet diesel submarines still at large in the area.

Based on the final position report from the *Foxtrot*, the Aden KPF directed a *Kilo*-class SS then operating about four hundred miles north of Diego Garcia to intercept the Allied convoy. The *Kilos* were the newest, and the quietest and most capable, of the Soviet diesel boats.

★ ★ ★

At Diego Garcia, CDR Paul "Standby" Ciani, commanding officer of VP 19, was trying to catch up on the squadron's paperwork when he received the alert call in his office. The tired squadron commander, who knew he should have been catching up on sleep, rather than doing paperwork, nonetheless was "happy as hell to get out from behind the desk."

Ciani's P-3C was the ready aircraft sitting on the runway, preflight checked, armed, and fuelled with a "ramp-load." Since the big Orions could not be left "on the deck" fully fuelled, a ready state meant a one to two-hour delay before takeoff. At the alert, the aircraft's non-tactical crew rushed to prepare the plane for the upcoming mission.

Ciani and his crew, who earlier in the afternoon had pre-flighted the aircraft and been pre-briefed on the general situation in the Indian Ocean, communication frequencies, and turnover procedures, now hurried to the ASW operations center for their final briefing. Based on "locating information," probably the triangulation of an enemy radio message, intelligence had concluded that a Soviet submarine, most likely a diesel boat, was about four hundred miles north of Diego Garcia. Late the previous day, another of the squadron's Orions had reported spotting what appeared to be a snorkeling submarine in that general area, but had been unable to prosecute the contact. The "intell weenies" estimated that this was the same sub, and that it had been directed eastward to attack the American convoy, the only target in vicinity. Since Russian diesel boats had speeds of between twelve and twenty knots, and since it would take Ciani two hours to get airborne and fly to a likely interception point, that could leave a rather large area to search.

The briefing continued and Ciani and his crew received updated acoustic and nonacoustic briefs on the target, local conditions, as well as a weather update. Ciani then gathered his crew for a "last-minute pep talk and a short, nondenominational prayer."

Twenty minutes later, Ciani's Orion was airborne, flying "full out" at 400 knots, rather than the usual cruising speed of 330 knots. "The quicker we get where we're headed," Ciani told his co-pilot, "the smaller the box we have to search."

An hour later, the aircraft reached the target area and Ciani set Condition 5, forcing his crew into their seats. With computer-supplied steering cues from his tactical coordination officer, Ciani took about thirty minutes to drop a wide area search pattern, with sixteen to twenty miles between each of the passive sonobuoys, across what the ASWOC staff had estimated to be the Soviet submarine's most likely course to intercept the convoy. The Orion then retraced its flightpath and replaced the five buoys that had failed.

As he completed the sonobuoy drop, Ciani found himself "reviewing all the things that could possibly screw up an attack." The enemy could detect the sonobuoy drop itself and an alerted submarine was infinitely more difficult to track and kill. Ciani also felt that his crew had gone stale and appeared somewhat fatigued. The long flight across the Pacific from Moffett Field and the heat at Diego Garcia had taken quite a bit out of the men. "Just flying in the Indian Ocean is hot work," Ciani had written his wife a few days before, "especially at low altitude, with the heat produced by the equipment and the Orion's stinking air conditioning." Even before the plane got down to low altitude for the attack, one of the crew had the vacuum cleaner on exhaust blowing air on the AQA-7 IPADS [improved processing-and-display system], the brains of the plane. Ciani wondered whether the plane was really all that hot, or was his crew simply getting nervous? Then there was the Mk-46 torpedo which, to quote the VP 19 commander, "sucked." The torpedo was accurate, but its forty-five-kilogram warhead was too small. Ciani had helped develop a two-torpedo attack doctrine, which made up for the lack of killing power. The tactic was a tricky procedure, since the Mk-46's active sonar could result in the torpedoes drawing each other away from the target, or even acquiring one another. Nevertheless, Ciani would have tried it if he had had four torpedoes, but since Orions were limited to two per mission until the convoy arrived with a large supply of torpedoes, he considered it too chancy. Ciani also had some doubts about his acoustic warfare operator. "They're usually prima donnas," he had told his exec earlier that day, "too damned smart for their own good—ours is prone to coast." Of course, that had been in peacetime. Ciani just hoped to hell that this guy, who was basically a good kid, got serious.

"Contact!" The TACCO's call made Ciani jump in his seat. As the men at the sensors began working the submarine, he addressed the crew.

"Make it good, fuck heads, first shot. If we alert him, we might not just miss him, he might get us. Remember, these guys carry SAMs. *Kilos* got 'em on their masts. I don't want you shitheads sitting around fat, dumb, and happy, eating your box lunches, while some Russian shoots a SAM up our ass."

There followed a short delay before the TACCO reported "direct path," then came a pause that seemed like an eternity. "Bearing 303, range eight miles, and 'Standby,' I think it's a *Kilo*."

"Shit," the co-pilot interjected, "autopilot's out." The Orion's ASW-31 had failed.

"No problem," Ciani responded. "Let's all standby, guys. This is it, mothers."

Now phase two of the hunt began as Ciani worked "to get

close enough for government work," within five hundred yards of the submarine. Ciani's crew had less than five minutes to get in, drop sonobuoys, and to get set up for the attack. Guided by his computer prompts, Ciani flew the Orion north to drop another six sonobuoys, a thousand yards apart, along a line through which the TACCO expected the submarine to pass. If the Kilo remained on course and drove through the sonobuoy line, Ciani would have automatic attack criteria.

As he completed the drop, Ciani brought the P-3C into a clockwise shallow banking turn, giving the submarine a wide berth to prevent its sensors from picking up the aircraft's engine noises, and coming up from behind the expected, "hoped and prayed for," track of the Kilo. Ciani let the Orion's altitude drop to two hundred feet and opened the weapons bay doors. He struggled to keep the plane as level and stable as possible, despite the increase in turbulence caused by the open bay. With his co-pilot, Ciani began the run-through of the weapons checklist. As the two pilots completed the list, Ciani kept up a steady conversation with the TACCO, and kept one eye on the scope for the appearance of the symbol and track of the submarine, and another on the on-top position indicator. The key for an Orion pilot was to time his arrival so that he reached the point at which the submarine hit the sonobuoy line just seconds after the submarine, the whole time monitoring the plane's airspeed and altitude. With the Orion now flying level on the same course as the Kilo, Ciani noted the usual onset of tunnel vision as his world seemed to narrow to the track along which he was flying. He sensed that he could be no more than seconds away from the submarine. The tension of the hunt and the heat of the aircraft, left him bathed in sweat. "Sensor three," he called over the intercom to the technician who monitored the magnetic anomaly detector display, "stand by, MAD." There was a short delay, during which Ciani felt his stomach muscles tense. He choked back the bug juice that kept trying for a second chance.

"Madman! Madman!" came the call from sensor three. Ciani saw the submarine's position marked on his scope and pressed the weapons release switch. As the Mk-46 hit the water and began its spiral turn in search for the Kilo, Ciani dropped a single sonobuoy in front of the Russian submarine, closed the weapons bay doors, and began a starboard turn to lay another line of sonobuoys across its path. If the *Kilo* survived the first attack, it would find itself trapped between two lines of sonobuoys.

As Ciani brought the plane onto the new course, the acoustics operators in the rear of the Orion reported over the intercom to the mission commander. They could hear the submarine, the Mk-46 making its run, the Russian's countermeasures, then after about two minutes, they heard an explosion. Ciani heard the cheers from his crew.

But then came the report—the *Kilo* was still alive, slower and noisier, but still alive. Ciani would have to set up and repeat the attack, this time against an alerted boat.

Minutes later, the Orion dropped a second torpedo, but it ran its programmed six minutes and failed to find a target. Then, after several more minutes, the TACCO reported an explosion. Damage from the first torpedo had evidently caused the submarine to lose depth control and to plummet into the depths of the Indian Ocean where it imploded.

★ ★ ★

After the disappointments of the first four days of the war, July 18 dawned somewhat better for the Soviets. A surviving *Akula* managed to achieve an attack position and at 0200 fired a pair of Type-65s in the direction of the *Nimitz*. One of the torpedoes blew the stern off the Aegis cruiser *Thomas S. Gates*. Heavily damaged, and left powerless, the ship fell out of formation and later sank

After launching its torpedoes, the *Akula* apparently broke off its approach and attempted to evade the expected counterattack. But the American task force's ASW warfare commander had launched a pair of ready-five S-3 Vikings from the *Nimitz* as soon as a sonar report from the destroyer *Hewitt* had warned of incoming torpedoes. The Vikings, working their way along the bearing of the torpedoes, detected, localized, attacked, and sank the *Akula* about forty miles from the *Nimitz*.

VADM Moore now slowed the task force to allow his smaller ships to replenish. His destroyers needed to be refuelled and the *Nimitz*'s air wing had expended the greater part of the carrier's ordnance.

By sundown, the task force had resumed a westerly course. At 2000, the *Nimitz* launched the first of eight air strikes against Perim

Island and nearby airfields in Ethiopia and Yemen. At 1330 on the nineteenth, American marines of the 11th MEU "hit the beach" on tiny Perim Island. The *Nimitz*'s attacks had softened up the island and destroyed scores of enemy aircraft at nearby bases. The heavy bombardment of the island had, in fact, induced the Yemenis on Perim to take to their boats in an attempt to escape. The Soviet defenders, about twelve hundred technicians and two companies of infantry, remained in their bunkers and offered minimal resistance as the marines came ashore. The Soviet garrison commander was so shaken by the Arab defections, that he considered an active defense pointless. At 1430, he surrendered the island to the 11th MEU's commander.

By the night of 20 July, the campaign in the Indian Ocean had concluded. Earlier in the day, the American SSN *Miami* had sunk the Soviet *Charlie II* SSGN in the Gulf of Oman. With Egyptian air and naval assistance, American, French, and Saudi forces had secured the Red Sea. All the nations bordering the Indian Ocean were either supporting the United States, had declared their neutrality, or had seen their air and naval forces destroyed by allied offensive action. Although the United States' National Command Authority decided, at RADM Moore's recommendation, to keep the *Nimitz* battlegroup in the Indian Ocean "for diplomatic reasons," the war in the Indian Ocean had ended. Fully loaded tankers were making their way out of the Persian Gulf carrying cargoes of fuel for allied warships in the western Pacific and Mediterranean. Allied access to the oil fields of the Middle East had been secured.

TWENTY-ONE

The entry of Japan and South Korea into the war had an immediate impact on the struggle for control of the air over the Sea of Japan and the southern Sea of Okhotsk. Throughout 15 July, American, Japanese, and South Korean fighters duelled with Soviet and North Korean aircraft. By noon it was clear that the allies held the upper hand in the air war and were achieving impressive kill ratios. As a result, Soviet aircraft were unable to conduct reconnaissance and ASW missions, while allied aircraft kept close tabs on Soviet surface forces. The time consuming prosecution of ASW contacts in the Sea of Japan remained difficult because of the threat of interception.

The Soviets' inability to conduct basic reconnaissance had a deleterious effect on their naval operations. Satellites could, at best, provide strategic intelligence, but for operational and tactical intelligence commanders needed more conventional platforms. For example, the destruction of four SNA Il-38 Mays over the Tsushima Strait in the late evening and early morning of 14-15 July left RADM Yevgeni Tarasov's KUG virtually blind as it raced north for Vladivostok and safety.

When Tarasov learned that the war had spread to the Korean peninsula, he decided to take the eastern passage through the Tsushima Strait—between Tsushima Island and Japan—rather than the western passage—between the island and South Korea—which might bring him into action with ROK naval forces operating from Pusan. Tarasov only discovered that Japan had allied itself to the United States as the Soviet KUG steamed between Tsushima island and Shimonoseki. He immediately ordered his ships, then under emissions control, to actively search the horizon with their radar. To his horror, Tarasov discovered that two separate groups, most likely Japanese warships, were closing on his KUG.

ADM Isamu Tazawa, Chief of Staff, Maritime Self-Defense Force (MSDF), had concentrated two major surface groups in the Tsushima Strait in an effort to intercept and destroy Tarasov's KUG. RADM Kiyoshi Matsunaga, with his flag in the destroyer *Kurama*, commanded the Sasebo-based, four-ship Escort Flotilla 2, that closed on Tarasov's KUG from the east, while RADM Seiji Kase, with his flag on the destroyer *Haruna*, commanded the five ships of Escort Flotilla 3 which had raced south from Maizuru and now was positioned northeast of the Soviets.

About 0500, Tarasov turned east to attack Matsunaga in an effort to prevent the concentration of the two Japanese forces. As the KUG completed its course change, sensors indicated that the Japanese had launched as many as two dozen Harpoons. Soviet SAMs and countermeasures downed or deflected most of the SSMs but several hit the cruiser *Admiral Yumashev* which caught fire and later sank. One struck the bridge of the flagship—the *Kresta II*-class cruiser *Admiral Makarov*—killing Tarasov.

The KUG commander's deputy, CAPT Second Class Vasily Klemkov, now faced a difficult situation. Matsunaga's group had itself altered course and headed southeast. The *Makarov*'s still functioning Top Sail air search radar revealed high-speed aircraft approaching at low altitude—an attack profile. Klemkov ordered an immediate course change to the north, fearing that to continue to the east would lead to an air attack and allow the enemy's northern group to block his escape route.

At 0535, Klemkov's three remaining ships, after successfully beating off an attack by four Japanese Mitsubishi F-1s, were making over thirty knots heading north when the commander of the KUG's westernmost ship—the cruiser *Admiral Oktyabrsky*—reported that his radar had detected a third large surface force, of at least a dozen vessels, to the northwest. Klemkov correctly assumed that the ships were South Korean, probably elements of the Third Fleet from Pusan. He decided to alter course and to engage the smaller Japanese force to the northeast. "The southern group reversed course when we closed with them," Klemkov told his chief of staff, "I just hope that the northern group reacts the same way and allows us to get out of this fucking strait."

But RADM Matsunaga's course change had not represented an unwillingness on the part of the Japanese to risk battle. ADM Tazawa hoped to lead Tarasov deeper into the trap set for him, whereas RADM Kase's Escort Flotilla 3 had orders to prevent the escape of the Soviet KUG from the Tsushima Strait.

Thus Klemkov found his way blocked and himself at a grave disadvantage. His two remaining cruisers were armed with SS-N-

14 missiles. The dual-capable Silex was principally an ASW weapon—a powerful missile designed to carry a homing torpedo to a range of thirty miles. But in its anti-ship mode, the Silex could only strike at targets closer than twenty miles. Only the destroyer *Gremyaschy* carried longer-ranged weapons—eight SS-N-22 Sunburn missiles with a range of about sixty miles. Klemkov knew that the Japanese ships carried American-made Harpoons, effective out to distances of seventy-five to eighty miles.

As expected, the Japanese launched first and about 0630 four Harpoons hit the cruiser *Admiral Oktyabrsky* which caught fire, lost power, and dropped out of formation. Seconds later, the *Gremyaschy* launched four Sunburns which hit and sank the *Hatsuyuki*-class destroyer *Setoyuki*. Under the cover of the attack, Klemkov rushed to close the range sufficiently for his cruiser to engage the Japanese. But RADM Kase launched the remainder of his Harpoons, sinking the *Admiral Makarov* and the *Gremyaschy*. About 0730, the South Koreans finished off the crippled *Admiral Oktyabrsky*.

The second battle of Tsushima stirred Japan's sense of national pride. Once again, Japan had begun a war with a smashing success at sea. Politicians and news commentators were quick to draw comparisons between the situation in northeast Asia and that during the 1904-1906 war with Russia. Japanese began speaking openly about the possible "liberation" of the Northern Territories—Kunashiri (Kunashir), Iturup (Etorofu), Shikotan, and the Habomai Islands—seized by the Soviets at the end of the Second World War.

For the Japanese Maritime Self-Defense Forces, Second Tsushima was a particularly important victory. It also demonstrated within the alliance that the Japanese navy was capable of performing more than just convoy escort and ASW missions. While it was true that the Japanese had some differences of opinion with the Americans over the latter's "Maritime Strategy," for the most part the problem was not one of concept, as much as it was a dislike of the rather limited role accorded to the Japanese within the American scheme. Most Japanese military leaders favored forward, offensive operations, but wanted to perform those missions themselves. They called their naval squadrons "escort flotillas," but armed their destroyers with Harpoon SSMs. Second Tsushima vindicated their judgment, and legitimized a broader role for the maritime self-defense force.

At Vladivostok, news of Tarasov's defeat shocked GEN Ilichev, but not ADM Ushakov. When he learned that the Japanese had entered the war, the POF commander knew that Tarasov was doomed. Despite his apparent sangfroid, Ushakov was deeply concerned about the situation in the southern Sea of Japan: with Tarasov's force destroyed, nothing remained to prevent a direct attack on Vladivostok except light forces and a half-dozen or so North Korean submarines. Ushakov had concentrated the bulk of his surface and subsurface forces in the north against the Americans. As a result, he knew that he had to win up north, and quickly.

No sooner had Ushakov digested the reports of the Soviet defeat in the Tsushima Strait than more disturbing information reached the Pacific Fleet headquarters. Shortly after 0700, American carrier-type aircraft struck at air and SAM installations around Petropavlovsk. "Initial reports indicate forces caught off guard," Ilichev informed Ushakov. "Damage to air defense installations heavy."

In the early hours of the fifteenth, RADM Carr's Carrier Task Group 33.4 had swept southwest between the Aleutians and the Komandorskies into attack position about 350 miles from Petropavlovsk. The Americans launched their surprise strike in a heavy overcast, "pea soup conditions," according to Carr's report. The *Kitty Hawk*'s aircraft, supported by a squadron each of marine and navy A-6Es from Adak in the Aleutians, pounded Soviet airfields, SAM sites, and command and control centers, and overwhelmed the dozen or so MiG-31 Foxhounds on CAP. Several A-6Es mined the harbor exits through which the submarines still in port would have to pass to get to sea.

Carr later attributed his success at Petropavlovsk to the element of surprise. At the strategic and operational levels, good planning and poor weather allowed the Americans to avoid detection by Soviet photographic and radar satellites as well as patrol aircraft. The achievement of tactical surprise depended principally on efforts by Carr's "Harbingers."

The "Harbinbgers" were a pair of U.S. Navy F/A-18s, piloted by specialists in extremely low-level approaches. The two Hornets, each armed with a pair of Sparrows and Sidewinders, led the attack against Petropavlovsk. Their mission was to launch about thirty minutes before the strike, to ingress on the deck, to penetrate the Soviet radar net, and to shoot down the AWACS presumed to be airborne over southern Kamchatka.

Both Hornets escaped detection and approached the Petropavlovsk area from different bearings. About 0700, the pilot of one of the Hornets detected the Mainstay on a passive sensor, turned on his radar, and minutes later downed the AWACS with a Sparrow. The second pilot, alerted to Logan's success by a coded signal, contributed to the attack's success when he "hosed a Foxhound" during his return flight to the carrier.

For the Soviets, Carr's surprise strike was a significant blow. Petropavlovsk, on the Pacific coast of the Kamchatka Peninsula, was the only major base from which Pacific Fleet forces could operate without having to pass through the barriers of the Kuriles or the Japanese home islands. It was a principal submarine base and several boats, both diesel and nuclear-powered, were still in port outfitting for a war patrol. Moreover, the destruction of air defense force interceptors based around Petropavlovsk left Soviet coastal shipping in the Bering Sea vulnerable to American attack from the Aleutians.

Although the attackers had initially focused their efforts against airfields and local air defenses, Ushakov knew that subsequent strikes would target navy installations and the dozen submarines still in port. The POF commander directed all the Petropavlovsk boats to put to sea before follow-up strikes materialized.

With his Kamchatka-based SNA Tu-26M Backfires and reconnaissance aircraft grounded because of damaged runways, Ushakov hoped that the three SSNs—a *Victor I* and a pair of *Victor IIIs*—then operating off Petropavlovsk would locate, attack, and destroy the suspected American carrier battlegroup. But the three attack submarines, having sunk the *Los Angeles*-class SSN *Omaha* on the fourteenth, had spent the early hours of the fifteenth attempting to catch the elusive *Pogy*. The American SSN, as planned, had worked its way to the south, drawing the Soviet *Victor*s away from the approaching *Kitty Hawk* CVBG as it swung south out of the Bering Sea.

As Ushakov feared, the attackers returned shortly after noon. American navy and marine aircraft flying from the *Kitty Hawk* and Adak devastated Soviet SNA and AAD air assets based in Kamchatka in strikes that continued for several hours. Carr's attack force destroyed nearly a hundred aircraft on the ground, including a score of SNA Backfires, and sank twelve submarines, including five SSNs at their moorings. The attackers also struck fuel and ordnance storage depots with great success. American losses were heavy—eighteen aircraft.

★★★

The successful American strikes against Soviet bases around Petropavlovsk forced ADM Ushakov to rethink his plans. As the result of the destruction of ordnance and supply depots throughout the peninsula and the high expenditure of SAMs, GEN Ilichev's logistics staff recommended a priority effort to resupply Kamchatka. But Ushakov's staff argued that the suppression of Soviet air defenses, with an American carrier battlegroup still at large, made the movement of surface forces toward Kamchatka too dangerous. With two convoys then underway in the Sea of Okhotsk, Ushakov decided to order the northernmost to continue on course for Oktyabr'skiy, a port on the southwestern coast of the peninsula, while the southernmost turned back toward Korsakov, a port at the head of Aniva Bay on the southern coast of Sakhalin Island where Soviet shipping had begun to concentrate.

The Petropavlovsk strike also convinced Ushakov of the need to concentrate his surface assets in the Kuriles as quickly as possible. The rendezvous of the *Novorossiysk* and *Baku* groups might lead to the destruction of the *Independence* battlegroup, and would certainly prevent the concentration of the two American carriers, allowing the Soviets to operate with support from land-based air power. By noon, the *Novorossiysk* group had rendezvoused with the *Tashkent* KUG and had steamed west to a position only 350 miles from the *Independence*. The *Baku* KUG had in the meantime neared the La Perouse Strait.

By the late morning of 15 July, the campaign in the North Pacific had become a race to see which side could first concentrate in the Kuriles, with the Americans moving from the north and south, and the Soviets from the east and west. Both deployed additional forces to hinder the other's movement. The American submarines *Flasher* and *New York City* raced eastward to intercept the *Novorossiysk* group. Japanese and American submarines moved to block La Perouse Strait. A Soviet *Victor I* and a *Victor III* attempted to attack the *Independence* but ran afoul a screening Japanese force. In a running battle, ASW helicopters from Escort Flotilla 4 damaged the *Victor I*, but the second Soviet SSN torpedoed the destroyer *Hiei*.

★ ★ ★

In both the CINCPAC and the CINCPACFLT operation plans, Admirals Cooper and Jernigan and their staffs had called for early strikes against Soviet airbases in the Kuriles before the two American CVBGs rendezvoused northeast of Hokkaido. The Americans expected the Russians to stage aircraft into their bases between Hokkaido and Kamchatka and wanted to prevent that by knocking these bases out as soon as possible. During the fourteenth, the American carriers had been out of range and U.S. Air Force squadrons based at Misawa in northern Honshu had been too hard pressed to conduct offensive operations. But in the early hours of the fifteenth, with the *Independence* group moving north, and with Japan now an ally, American planners adapted an existing contingency plan for a strike against the major Soviet base in the Kuriles—Yuzhno Kurilsk on Kunashir.

On paper, Soviet air strength in the southern Kuriles was impressive. The regiment of air defense force interceptors based at Kunashir had been reinforced during the fourteenth by a second regiment of MiG-23 Floggers. But of this force of nearly fifty fighters, no more than sixteen were available to meet an attack on the morning of 15 July. Over twenty Kunashir-based MiGs had either been shot down or badly damaged in air-to-air engagements against American and Japanese fighters during the fourteenth and early hours of the fifteenth of July. Nor were the Floggers qualitatively on par with the best of the attacking allied fighters—American-built Tomcats, Falcons, and Hornets. Moreover, the southern Kuriles were isolated, lying about 250 miles from Soviet airbases on southern Sakhalin Island, and too far forward for effective cover from Il-76 Mainstay AWACS.

About 1025, Soviet air defense radar in the Habomais detected a mixed force of sixty Japanese and American fighter, attack, and ESM aircraft approaching Kunashir from the south and east. The allied planes included U.S. Air Force F-16s, F-4G Wild Weasel jammers, and Japanese Mitsubishi F-1s from Misawa; and U.S. Navy Tomcats, Hornets, Prowlers, and Intruders of Carrier Air

Wing 2 from the carrier *Independence*. The local Soviet air defense commander vectored all available fighters into intercept positions, but the Russian pilots, handicapped by a cumbersome ground-controlled system, were swept from the skies. American and Japanese pilots claimed at least a dozen MiGs destroyed in the air and as many on the ground. The allies lost seven aircraft.

Despite this apparent success, reports from the strike leaders indicated that the main runways at Yuzhno Kurilsk had not been destroyed and that many hangars, depots, and command centers had escaped damage. Fifth Air Force planned a second strike for the afternoon without the participation of the *Independence*'s air wing. The follow-up attack failed to achieve decisive results, and at the cost of another half-dozen allied aircraft.

★ ★ ★

At 1105, Commander, Seventh Fleet—VADM Youmans—informed Fifth Air Force headquarters at Yokota, Japan, that the *Independence* could not support the second attack against Kunashir because of the critical situation in the North Pacific. A TARPS mission from the American carrier indicated that the *Novorossiysk* KUG had turned back west and Youmans recognized that the Russians had the inside track and, if not slowed down, would cut off the *Indy*'s move north. The Soviets would then be able to prevent the American carriers from concentrating and might well destroy them with naval and air power west of the Kuriles. Youmans had to slow the Russians down with air and submarine attacks, or else the *Independence* would have to turn back south to avoid a surface engagement.

About 1100, the American SSNs *Flasher* and *New York City* attempted to penetrate the Soviet screen, but good ASW work, especially by Soviet helicopters, kept the Americans at bay throughout the early afternoon, although the *Flasher* torpedoed and damaged the *Udaloy*-class destroyer *Admiral Tributs*.

At 1400, the *Independence* began launching its second air strike of the war. About 1515, a score of American F/A-18 Hornets engaged the *Novorossiysk*'s CAP of a dozen Yak-36 Forgers. The Soviet fighters were outclassed and destroyed in short order without loss to the Americans. About 1530, as the EA6-B Prowlers jammed Soviet sensors and communications, the "Swordsmen" of VA 145 began their attack. Sixteen A-6E Intruders, each armed with four

Harpoons, conducted low level runs against the Soviet carrier. Three Intruders were downed by SAMs, but the remaining thirteen released fifty-two missiles, at least nine of which struck the *Novorossiysk*.

Although the carrier was heavily damaged topside and incapable of further air operations, the crew managed to control the numerous fires that threatened to spread throughout the superstructure and the ship still made thirty-two knots.

Throughout the late afternoon and early evening, as the *Flasher* and *New York City* continued to harass the Soviet KUG, the COMSEVENTHFLT staff drew up a plan for a massive air effort against the *Novorossiysk*. The *Independence*'s CVW 2 launched fifty strike planes—Hornets and Intruders—as well several ESM aircraft. Since the Americans knew that they would not face any CAP, all of the attacking F/A-18 Hornets were armed with Harpoons, rather than air-to-air missiles. In fact, the second attack virtually exhausted the air group's supply of Harpoons. The evening strike also included Harpoon-armed U.S. Air Force B-52Gs flying from Andersen AFB on Guam.

Between 2200 and 2300, allied aircraft launched 178 Harpoons against the Soviet KUG in stand-off attacks. Many apparently malfunctioned; more were destroyed by SAMs or decoyed by effective countermeasures. But a dozen turned the cruiser *Vitse-Admiral Drozd* into a raging inferno that exploded and disappeared beneath the waves at 2315, and no fewer than a score struck the already badly damaged *Novorossiysk*.

The American strike left the carrier burning with virtually all of its missile launchers and sensors inoperable and its speed reduced to eight knots. RADM Leonid Valens, unwilling to place his entire group at risk to protect the battered hulk, ordered the captain of his flagship—the *Kirov*-class cruiser *Kalinin*—to destroy the *Novorossiysk* with 3.9-inch gunfire. By midnight, the carrier, too, had sunk.

Despite the much heralded sinking of the *Novorossiysk*, the results of the evening strike disappointed VADM Youmans and RADM Dennis Hammond, commander of the *Independence* group. Sinking the *Novorossiysk*, was not the same as taking out an American carrier. With three Russian SSNs stalking the *Independence*, and fearing a night surface action with the still powerful Soviet

KUG, Hammond ordered a course change to the south with the approval of Youmans who accompanied the *Independence* battle-group in his flagship—the *Blue Ridge*. Youmans relayed the decision back to Jernigan in Hawaii.

CINCPACFLT had his doubts about the wisdom of the move, but he refused to overrule his subordinate. Jernigan admitted to an aide: "I feel in my gut that we shouldn't turn back, but Bud and Denny are on the scene; it's their call."

When he learned of the American decision, RADM Michitaka Shimada, commander of Escort Flotilla 1, and the senior officer of the two flotillas screening the *Independence*, suggested to Hammond that the Japanese cover the southward movement of the American ships with a night surface action. Hammond agreed. As the Americans turned south, Shimada in the *Shirane* led ten Japanese destroyers at high speed to the northwest to engage the Soviets and, hopefully, to block their path to the west.

In a confused series of engagements fought in the early hours of 16 July, the Soviets sank the *Shirane*, killing Shimada, pushed their way through the two Japanese flotillas, and continued steaming toward the Kuriles. The Soviets lost two ships, the destroyer *Bezuprechny*, and the cruiser *Vladivostok*.

★ ★ ★

Throughout the fifteenth, six allied submarines—four Japanese and two American—fought desperately to prevent the movement of the *Baku* group, as well as several Soviet convoys, through La Perouse Strait. The Japanese *Yuushio*-class diesel submarine *Setoshio* torpedoed a frigate early in the morning, the first kill for the Japanese submarine force, but was shortly thereafter sunk herself in a counterattack. About noon, a second *Yuushio*—the *Mochishio*—sank a merchant ship from the same convoy. The American diesel boat *Blueback* expended its last torpedoes, sinking a merchant ship at 1400. But despite these successes, the allied submarines had thus far failed to locate the *Baku* group.

About 1615, the *Takashio* located the Soviet carrier and promptly got off a contact report. Although the diesel boat was promptly detected, attacked, and driven off as a result of the report, the American *Sturgeon*-class SSN *Puffer* and the Japanese *Uzushio*-class diesel submarine *Isoshio* moved to intercept the Soviet KUG before it reached La Perouse Strait. At 1720, the *Puffer* sank the destroyer *Marshal Shaposnikov* and penetrated the *Baku*'s ASW screen and, at 1755, put a pair of Mk 48 ADCAP torpedoes into the *Baku* itself. The *Puffer* was the object of an immediate and sharp, but fortunately not lethal, Soviet counterattack, and the American submarine's commander decided that he could push the attack no further. Amidst the confusion, the *Isoshio* attained an excellent attack position on the opposite beam of the *Baku* and fired a spread of six high-speed (seventy-knot) Type-98 torpedoes, four of which struck the carrier amidships, breaking its keel.

Despite these allied successes, the Soviets brought most of their ships through La Perouse Strait and concentrated a powerful force of two cruisers, five frigates, sixteen corvettes, fourteen missile boats, three support ships, and sixteen merchant ships in Aniva Bay, about 550 miles from the *Kalinin* KUG still racing west toward the Kuriles. With the *Independence* group steaming south, it appeared that ADM Ushakov had won the race and would concentrate his surface forces in the Kuriles during the sixteenth, leaving the American carriers *Kitty Hawk* and *Independence* divided and at risk.

By midnight on the fifteenth, RADM Carr's *Kitty Hawk* group, which had been "chopped" to Seventh Fleet as Carrier Task Group 77.4, was about five hundred miles southwest of Petropavlovsk. Carr faced a difficult choice: should he remain in the area and follow up his successful attacks around Petropavlovsk, or should he steam south to rendezvous with the *Independence* group? He chose to move south, and so informed Seventh Fleet.

Carr knew that he had not completely destroyed all the bases around Petropavlovsk, but he also understood that bases were never "permanently" destroyed. He had accomplished what he had set out to accomplish. That is, he had surprised the Soviets and "Pearl Harbored them at Petro." U.S. Navy strike aircraft sank six submarines in port, demonstrating that Intruders with smart bombs, given the proper circumstances, could be excellent ASW platforms. Carr's attacks destroyed over a hundred enemy aircraft in the air and on the ground, innumerable storage depots for POL and ordnance. Soviet defenses were so depleted that he believed that American land-based air at Adak could continue the work. With only three carriers in WESTPAC, Carr believed it to be foolish to keep one permanently off Kamchatka. He also wanted to keep moving, to prevent the Russians from concentrating their forces against a single carrier. "We have to keep moving, in and out operations," he told his staff planners, "mobility's the key. The Pacific's a big ocean and there are still lots of targets for us to hit elsewhere."

As Carr expected, the Soviets were, in fact, vectoring five SSNs into position to destroy the lone American CVBG. Carr's decision to halt his attacks somewhat prematurely and to sprint south allowed him to escape the trap before it closed. Thanks to excellent ASW work from the group's escorts, helicopters, and the SSN *Pogy*, which sank a *Victor III* that blocked the carrier's route, Carr's task group moved south unscathed.

As the *Kitty Hawk* steamed away from Petropavlovsk, one of its TARPS Tomcats conducting a reconnaissance mission over the northern Sea of Okhotsk, located the enemy convoy heading for Oktyabr'skiy. At 2140, Hornets and Intruders from the American carrier struck the convoy, sinking two merchant ships and a frigate, and heavily damaging two others. The raid cost Carr two Hornets and an Intruder, and brought the day's losses to thirteen. "That may not seem like a lot of aircraft," Carr chastised one young, overzealous lieutenant on his staff, "and given what we've accomplished, I guess it isn't, but it's about 15 percent of our strength and at that rate, we'll be out of planes before the end of the week!"

★ ★ ★

Elsewhere in the western Pacific on 15 July, there were few naval actions of note. With so many Soviet submarines engaged in direct action against allied naval forces, relatively few were available for action against the SLOCs. By the late evening of 15 July, the American frigate *Vandegrift*, leading a convoy that included three other frigates and six large container ships, was within three hundred miles of the Japanese coast and had yet to be attacked. Early on the fifteenth, the battleship *Missouri*, accompanied by the cruiser *Truxtun*, the *Arleigh Burke*-class destroyer *John Paul Jones*, and the oiler *Andrew J. Higgins* reached Guam safely.

Nevertheless, CINCPACFLT was aware that several Soviet and North Korean submarines, both diesel and nuclear, were active off

Guam, Okinawa, in the waters between Japan and the Philippines, and in the Sea of Japan. Until these submarines could be located and destroyed, ADM Jernigan was unwilling to risk his high value assets—most notably the amphibious transports concentrated at Okinawa, and at Guam the MPS ships with their irreplaceable cargoes of marine equipment.

Throughout 15 July, the allies worked to eliminate these threats. In the southern Sea of Japan, Japanese submarines attempted to prevent North Korean diesel boats from breaking out to the south and reaching the Tsushima Strait as the escort flotillas that had smashed Tarasov's KUG replenished at Sasebo. ADM Youmans ordered the commanding officer of the *Truxtun* to form an ASW task force with three frigates and to operate offensively from Guam to eliminate the Russian sub menace and to clear the way for the movement of the MPS squadron to the west. The ad hoc group achieved limited success, damaging a *Victor III* in the late evening of the fifteenth. At Okinawa, U.S. Navy P3s fared better and about 1900 caught a *Foxtrot* snorting near the surface and destroyed the submarine in a well executed attack. Further south, the over forty-year-old American-built destroyers of Taiwan's navy joined Japanese frigates escorting tankers and other shipping as they moved north from the South China Sea. While no Soviet submarines were sunk, several were attacked and no allied ships were lost.

In the South China Sea itself, the fifteenth passed quietly. Since the virtual elimination of Soviet forces in the area and Vietnam's expressed desire to avoid further hostilities with the United States provided few opportunities for action, ADM Jernigan ordered RADM Holmes to leave behind the damaged destroyer *Thorn* and the support ship *Roanoke* and to bring the *Vinson* CVBG, along with the SSNs *San Juan* and *Springfield*, north "with all possible speed." At the same time, CINCPAC directed the transfer of a squadron of Phantoms and one of FB-111s, as well as some EW aircraft, from Clark AFB in the Philippines to Misawa, Japan. That evening, ADM Cooper wrote in his diary:

> Our forces in the Philippines and the South China Sea have per-
> formed well. We have cleaned up the enemy quickly in the south. But
> the Soviets, by their deployment at Cam Ranh Bay, have nonetheless

forced us to deploy critical assets far from the area of decision. It will take Holmes four or five days to bring the *Vinson* north, and by then the war in the Pacific might well be decided.

TWENTY-TWO

But 16 July was not to be a day of decision in WESTPAC. Despite heavy and costly fighting, neither the allies nor the Soviets seized the initiative in the Far East.

In the North Pacific, Soviet forces were unable to prevent the rendezvous late on the sixteenth of the *Kitty Hawk* and *Independence* task groups four hundred miles east of Hokkaido. Because of the CAP operations by Japanese interceptors flying from bases in Hokkaido and northern Honshu, and American F-14 Tomcats flying from the *Kitty Hawk* and *Independence*, ADM Ushakov considered long-range SNA strikes by unescorted Badgers and Backfires too risky. Moreover, allied control of the air in the North Pacific complicated the coordination of Soviet submarine operations. Because of the activity of patrolling allied aircraft and the efforts of the Japanese escort flotillas, all too often Soviet submarines were unable to run near the surface during scheduled communications periods and, thus, efforts to vector boats into attack positions were unsuccessful.

Throughout the morning of 16 July, the Maritime Self-Defense Force's Escort Flotillas 1 and 4 continued to cover the *Independence* task group. About 0930, the destroyer *Hamayuki* caught and sank the slow, sixteen-knot Soviet *Dubna*-class replenishment tanker *Pechenga* which had fallen behind the Soviet *Kalinin* KUG as it sped westward. At 1105, ASW helicopters from the *Hiei* located and sank a Soviet *Victor III*, and in the early afternoon a Mitsubishi Sea King from the destroyer *Shimayuki* destroyed a *Victor I*. Late that evening the Japanese destroyers, low on fuel and with most of their Harpoons expended, were forced to make an untimely withdrawal to the south to replenish.

The American destroyers attached to the two carrier task groups operating in the North Pacific were also running low on fuel while the carriers themselves had expended a great deal of ordnance. The *Independence* had nearly exhausted her entire inventory of Harpoons, and the *Kitty Hawk* was running low of bombs, especially PGMs. While both task group commanders were able to keep their destroyers fuelled, neither felt secure enough from sudden air or submarine attack to risk the movement of ordnance from the replenishment ships to the carriers.

Nevertheless, the American flattops were able to conduct offensive operations during the sixteenth. Aircraft from the *Independence* joined U.S. Air Force F-16 Falcons from Misawa and Japanese F-4 Phantoms from Hyakuri in early morning strikes against Soviet bases on Kunashir and Iturup. Allied interceptors shot down another dozen fighters and the raids completed the destruction of Soviet air power in the southern Kuriles. Simultaneously, the *Kitty Hawk*'s air wing continued its efforts to destroy the Soviet Kamchatka-bound convoy, sinking the remaining three frigates and two merchant ships.

In the afternoon, aircraft from the two American carriers cooperated with Harpoon-armed B-52s from Guam in attacks against the *Kalinin* KUG as it raced for the safety of the Sea of Okhotsk. The Soviet ships, which had been fending off allied air attacks for two days, had nearly expended their supplies of surface-to-air missiles and were unable to put up as stiff a defense as they had on the fifteenth. A combination of standoff and bombing attacks succeeded in damaging the cruiser *Tashkent* and sinking the destroyer *Admiral Tributs* and the *Kirov*-class battlecruiser *Kalinin*.

ADM Ushakov, frustrated by his inability to engage the American carriers, decided that his SNA strike aircraft could be put to good use by attacking allied airbases in northern Japan. In a two-hour meeting with GEN Ilichev, the Pacific Fleet commander convinced his superior to order a joint operation employing SNA Badgers and Backfires, frontal aviation and air defense force fighters, and strategic forces Blackjacks. About 1400, Soviet interceptors conducted sweeps as a prelude to bombing attacks against Chitose (Hokkaido) and Misawa (northern Honshu). The Soviet attack caught the allies by surprise. The Japanese lost six F-15s in air-to-air combat, while Soviet losses totalled fifteen fighters and bombers. Misawa suffered light damage, due primarily to the ineffectiveness of SNA strike aircraft used in a ground-attack role, but the runways and facilities at Chitose were heavily damaged, along with seven F-15s, by an accurate raid by Soviet Blackjacks.

★ ★ ★

As the fighting raged throughout the day, CINCPACFLT rushed allied tankers, convoys, and amphibious assets toward Japan. By late evening, the *Vinson* CVBG was off the northeast coast of Taiwan, the American amphibious task force which had left Okinawa for Pusan, South Korea, was just south of the Tsushima Strait, while a six-ship American supply convoy, also bound for Pusan, was steaming north through the strait itself.

The Taiwanese and South Korean navies played critical roles in covering allied movements through the East China Sea. At 0945, the Taiwanese diesel submarine *Hai Lung* sank a Soviet *Tango*-class boat recharging its batteries in the Basil Channel. Taiwanese destroyers and frigates formed the southern screen covering the route along which the American amphibious squadron moved from Okinawa to Pusan, while the ROK 2d Fleet duelled with North Korean submarines in the Yellow Sea. While the South Koreans prevented the enemy's movement to the south, they did so at the cost of the destroyer *Jeon Ju*, and the corvette *Po Hang*, both of which were torpedoed by a North Korean *Romeo*-class diesel boat.

Not all allied convoys were making their way safely toward Korea. MPS Squadron 3 remained in the harbor at Guam. Despite the efforts of the *Truxtun* ASW task force, the allies had been unable to locate and destroy the Soviet submarines known to be operating in the Marianas. At 1330, ADM Jernigan ordered the *Truxtun* group to return to Guam to refuel and to prepare to escort MPS Squadron 3, the battleship *Missouri* and several support ships across the western Pacific. When CINCPAC questioned the decision, Jernigan told ADM Cooper: "I know the Russians are out there, but we can't keep the MPS squadron, carrying the equipment for an entire Marine brigade, idle forever; we just have to accept some risks."

The North Korean high command certainly proved itself willing to take risks. VADM Pang Chong-ho, the navy commander, pushed his submarines south in a desperate effort to sever the SLOCs to South Korea. During the morning and afternoon, the North Koreans fought their way through a screen of American and Japanese submarines. At least seven Communist diesel boats were sunk: two by the American SSN *Cavalla*, two each by the Japanese SSs *Mochishio* and *Takeshio*, and one by the *Nadashio*. The destroyers of Japan's Escort Flotillas 2 and 3, after refuelling and rearming at Sasebo, took up blocking positions behind the allied submarine screen to prevent a North Korean breakout into the Tsushima Strait. In the late evening, several enemy diesel boats announced their presence in the strait when they conducted several unsuccessful attacks against Japanese destroyers. The MSDF ships promptly counterattacked, but without success.

The North Koreans' effort to interdict allied use of the Tsushima Strait was central to their campaign strategy for a quick victory over South Korea. The Communists could not allow the United States to reinforce the ROK-US Combined Field Army and still hope to achieve a blitzkrieg in the south.

Moreover, it had become apparent in Pyongyang as early as the morning of 16 July that North Korean air and ground forces were suffering frightful losses and could not long maintain the tempo of the advance. On D day + 1, American and South Korean fighter-bombers were already striking North Korean airbases. In a series of day-long aerial engagements, the North Koreans lost heavily. By the late evening of the sixteenth, over 250 Communist aircraft, including 200 fighters, had been destroyed, at least 100 on the ground. American and ROK losses totalled about two dozen aircraft.

Allied supremacy in the air had a direct and significant impact on both the naval and ground campaigns. At 1730, U.S. Marine Corps A-6E Intruders and F/A-18 Hornets from Iwakuni, Japan, caught North Korean surface forces at anchor in Wonsan harbor and sank two frigates and fourteen fast attack boats. The Wonsan strike crippled the North Korean navy for the remainder of the war.

While most of the allied air activity on the sixteenth was directed against the North Korean air force, the absence of Communist ground attack aircraft over the front played a significant role in covering the rapid movement of American and ROK reinforcements toward the front and allowed the ROK-US high command to provide occasional, but often timely, ground support. On the morning of the sixteenth, the North Koreans continued their drive to the south along the entire front. The most notable advance occurred on their right flank where the 27th Infantry Division established a bridgehead across the Imjin River west of Munsan.

Around noon, the ROK 9th Infantry Division, supported by American A-10s, counterattacked the bridgehead and drove the Communists back across the river, taking several thousand prisoners. Elsewhere along the front, other allied units conducted local counterstrokes. South Korean reserve units advanced about a mile toward Chorwon, but suffered heavy casualties. Elements of the United States 2d Infantry Division engaged North Korean armored units along Route 33 and brought the Communist advance toward Yonch'on to a halt.

Late in the afternoon, the North Koreans fed additional reserves into action along the entire front in an effort to keep the advance going. The U.S. 2d Infantry Division's 4th Battalion, 69th Armored Regiment suffered debilitating losses in tough fighting north of Yonch'on, but prevented the Communists from pushing further south. To the west, the units of the ROK 9th Infantry Division smashed a North Korean tank attack along Route 1.

In the evening, fresh battalions of the ROK Capital Corps reinforced the tired 9th Infantry Division and led a counterattack toward Kaesong in an effort to seize the initiative and prevent the North Koreans from clearing the north bank of the Imjin.

In Pyongyang, the failure to achieve a decisive breakthrough caused deep apprehension. The loss of nearly 40 percent of the North Korean air force in only two days, and the presence of allied fighter-bombers north of the DMZ, boded ill for the future course of the war.

TWENTY-THREE

At dawn on the morning of the seventeenth, the North Korean army resumed its advance along the entire line. Once again, the numerically superior Communist troops drove south, raising hopes of victory in Pyongyang. An official government communique monitored at 1000 in Tokyo declared:

"Troops of the Democratic People's Republic have gained the upper hand in the fighting against imperialist Yankee forces and their lackeys, and will soon liberate the entire peninsula." But the North Korean pronouncement of victory was grossly premature, for, by noon, the tempo of the advance had been lost. Frontline North Korean units reported heavy losses, stiffening enemy resistance, and harassment by ever-present allied fighter-bombers.

American and South Korean ground units, while they gave way before the North Korean assault, continued to conduct spirited and often successful counterattacks. When the North Korean 3d Infantry Division's drive along Route 1 threatened to reach the bridge over the Imjin River at Changdan, a prompt, surprise counterstroke by the 26th Regiment of the ROK Capital Corps halted the Communist advance, shattered two enemy regiments, and regained over two miles of South Korean territory. North of Yonch'on along Route 33, elements of the 2d U.S. Infantry Division continued to hold the line, knocking out over ninety tanks. At 1045, South Korean troops, reinforced by lead elements of a brigade of ROK marines, counterattacked toward Chorwon and cut off a Communist regiment that had broken through to the south toward Route 8.

In the afternoon, while the North Koreans attempted to continue offensive operations in the center and the east, they went over to the defensive north of Seoul. Pyongyang rushed VIII Corps reserves forward to enable II Corps to resume the southward advance from the Kaesong area.

But LTG Freeman saw the enemy's pause as an opportunity to seize the initiative north of Seoul, and maybe along the entire line. With the concurrence of the South Korean JCS, the ROK-US Combined Field Army went over to the offensive in the Third Army sector. Troops of the 9th Division and the Capital Corps struck north against the North Korean II Corps and began to push the Communists back toward the DMZ in a slow, costly advance. Attacks by the 2d Infantry Division failed to gain much ground, despite substantial air support, but brought the enemy's advance toward Yonch'on to a halt. South of Chorwon, ROK marines led a relief drive that by nightfall had reached a position only three miles from the town.

From his Uijongbu headquarters, Freeman sent a late night message to CINCPAC—ADM Cooper in Hawaii—that allied forces in Korea had wrested the initiative from the Communists, but that losses and ordnance expenditures had exceeded expectations. Freeman, who had learned from his staff that several convoys bound for the major supply port at Pusan had been detoured elsewhere or otherwise delayed, requested "immediate info re situation at sea."

★ ★ ★

While the allies clearly had gained the upper hand at sea by 17 July, several challenges remained to be overcome. American, Japanese, and South Korean interceptors continued to demonstrate their superiority over Soviet and North Korean fighters, downing about one hundred aircraft during the day, for the loss of seventeen. Nevertheless, formidable SNA assets remained capable of effective action, and although the allies had contained the Soviet surface threat in the North Pacific, a score of enemy submarines were operational beyond the Sea of Okhotsk bastion.

Moreover, all three American CVBGs had to replenish. Their escorting cruisers and destroyers were running dangerously low on fuel and the carriers themselves were short of ordnance. For VADM Youmans, the morning of 17 July "was an unnerving period during which we hazarded losing the momentum that we had gained thus far, and ran substantial risks to our own forces." At their Hawaii headquarters, Admirals Cooper and Jernigan monitored the underway replenishment operations closely, knowing that the Soviets were being presented with perhaps their last opportunity to get the carriers. Because of the torpedoing of the fleet support ship *Towada* late on the evening of the sixteenth, the two Japanese ASW flotillas that had screened the American carriers had been forced to turn south toward Yokosuka to refuel. The Americans had the technical capability to replenish the Japanese destroyers, but Youmans only had three support ships to serve his CVBGs. As a result, he directed the *Kitty Hawk* and *Independence* groups to steam to the east, away from the Soviet submarines known to be operating off the Kuriles, and away from the Soviet group fleeing for its life toward Sakhalin.

Despite the American effort to avoid submarine attack, the Soviets vectored several Soviet SSNs into attack positions against the Seventh Fleet CVBGs. At 1207, a four-torpedo spread from an *Alfa*-class attack submarine blew the destroyer *Oldendorf* in half, killing 307 of the crew of 324 officers and men. About 1315, SA-3

Vikings from the *Kitty Hawk* detected the Soviet SSN, and after a nearly two-hour hunt, destroyed the *Alfa*. At 1548, the *Tautog* ambushed and sank an *Oscar*-class SSGN as it attempted to approach the carrier *Independence*. By 1630, both CVBGs had completed replenishing and had turned back to the west, armed and ready to resume offensive operations.

The Soviets gained somewhat better results in the southern Sea of Japan. Based on position reports from North Korean submarines, SNA aircraft from Olga and Ussuriysk struck Japanese surface forces operating in the approaches to the Tsushima Strait. The attacking Badgers and Backfires, screened by regiment-sized formations of MiG-25s, found the seam between South Korea and southern Honshu-based combat air patrols. Foxbats overwhelmed the handful of allied fighters that intercepted the Soviet strikes, downing seventeen American, Japanese, and South Korean fighters. The Soviets lost three Foxbats and two Badgers. Only the inaccuracy inherent in the long-range, standoff missile attacks preferred by the Soviets saved the two Japanese escort flotillas from complete destruction. Russian air-to-surface missiles sank the destroyers *Kurama*, *Yamagiri*, and *Yuugiri*.

The successful Soviet strikes shook an allied high command that had come to believe that it had just about mastered the situation in the Sea of Japan and East China Sea. Early on the seventeenth, destroyers of the Taiwanese navy had sunk a *Tango*-class diesel boat, the last Soviet submarine at large in the East China Sea. South Korean surface forces continued their running engagement with North Korean submarines, losing three more destroyers, but preventing Communist submarines from reaching the approaches to the Tsushima Strait. Japanese ASW forces had reportedly sunk two North Korean submarines in coastal waters east of Pohang. The Japanese had withdrawn several of their diesel boats to Sasebo, Maizuru, and Ominato to replenish spent torpedo supplies.

Soviet air operations in the Tsushima Strait immediately raised concerns for the safety of an American convoy then bound for Pusan as well as for the American amphibious task force from Okinawa. CINCPACFLT directed that the convoy continue toward Pusan but that the amphibious force remain off Tori-Shima, south of the strait.

"We can't afford not to send the convoy on to Pusan," ADM Jernigan stressed, "the supplies it carries are desperately needed by our air and ground forces in Korea." Nevertheless, Jernigan knew that the amphibs were too valuable to risk in the strait given the present circumstances, and, since the situation on the ground south of the DMZ appeared to be stabilizing, he believed the amphibious ships could be left behind for the time being.

In the interim, the Japanese Maritime Staff headquarters stepped up subsurface and aerial operations to eliminate the surviving North Korean submarines. During the afternoon and evening of the seventeenth, the Japanese diesel boat *Okishio* sank a North Korean submarine, the American SS *Barbel* sank a second, and Maritime Self-Defense Force Orions sank a third. The Japanese also withdrew Escort Flotillas 2 and 3 to Pusan where they regrouped, forming a single ASW task force consisting of the destroyers *Haruna*, *Asayuki*, *Mineyuki*, *Matsuyuki*, *Sawakaze*, and eight frigates pulled from convoy escort duty in the East China Sea. CINCPACFLT agreed to move the *Vinson* CVBG toward the strait to provide additional air cover for surface operations on the eighteenth.

★★★

The movement of MPS Squadron 3 from Guam to Pusan was potentially of critical importance to the campaign on the Korean peninsula. Until the four vehicle cargo ships reached South Korea with the equipment for I MEB, there was little point in airlifting the marines from Hawaii to Taegu, especially given the heavy demand on U.S. Air Force transport assets.

At 0230, a large American task force consisting of the battleship *Missouri*, the cruiser *Truxtun*, the Aegis-destroyer *John Paul Jones*, three frigates, three support ships, MPS Squadron 3, and two container ships left the anchorage at Guam for Pusan. A patrolling Soviet submarine apparently detected the departure, timed to avoid satellite surveillance, and relayed the information to Vladivostok. By late morning, three enemy SSNs converged on the *Missouri* group.

Alert American ASW forces drew first blood, sending a *Victor III* to the bottom about 1045. At 1230, a *Charlie I*, probably the same submarine that had detected the American task force, torpedoed the oiler *Andrew J. Higgins*. An *Alfa* also maneuvered into an attack position and torpedoed a container ship, one of which had been purposefully positioned on either side of the MPS vessels. Throughout the remainder of the afternoon and into the evening, the Soviets managed several other torpedo attacks, but sank no additional ships. Late in the evening the two submarines independently conducted SSM attacks, but the incoming missiles were easily destroyed by Standard MR-SM2 SAMs fired by the *John Paul Jones*. Thereafter, the attacks ceased.

Once again, the low torpedo load-outs of Russian submarines contributed to the Soviet failure. The *Charlie I* SSGN, for example, carried only fourteen tube-launched weapons, generally two surface-to-surface missiles, and two nuclear-tipped and eight conventionally armed torpedoes. Of the *Alfa*'s twenty weapons, only fourteen were conventional torpedoes. By contrast, World War II American fleet submarines designed to operate deep in the Pacific Ocean, far from friendly bases, carried two-dozen torpedoes. Even contemporary American submarines, which were able to operate from Japanese bases in close proximity to the Soviet Union, carried more weapons than most of their Russian counterparts. *Permit*-class SSNs carried sixteen weapons, *Sturgeon*-class SSNs twenty-three, *Los Angeles*-class twenty-six, and the improved *Los Angeles* boats thirty-eight. The typical Soviet SSN carried about eighteen weapons, Soviet SSGNs carried many more, but mostly missiles, rather than torpedoes. Thus in the Pacific, as in the Atlantic, aggressive Soviet submarine commanders firing three- and four-torpedo spreads, exhausted their torpedo supply after two, three, or at best four attacks. Whereas allied submarines operating in the Sea of Japan were rarely more than a day's run from a friendly port, Soviet submarines often found themselves as much as a week from home and facing a contested passage through narrow waters patrolled by allied ASW forces. As ADM Cooper liked to say, "the geography of war at sea is unforgiving."

And so it was for the Soviet navy. On the afternoon of the seventeenth, headquarters at Vladivostok received a congratulatory message from GEN Ilichev, praising the performance of the surface striking force that had at last reached Aniva Bay after "daringly successful operations in the North Pacific." Unfortunately, ADM

Ushakov viewed the effort as a marked failure. Several allied ships had been sunk on D day, but the American carriers had neither been destroyed nor prevented from concentrating. Moreover, the allies had annihilated Soviet air strength in Kamchatka and the Kuriles and had sunk half of the ten Soviet ships that had sortied, including the carrier *Novorossiysk* and the battlecruiser *Kalinin*.

The Pacific Fleet commander was relieved to learn that the Far Eastern High Command staff had dropped the plan for an airborne-amphibious assault of Hokkaido. From the naval point of view, Ushakov had considered the scheme suicidal. The Pacific Fleet controlled amphibious shipping capable of lifting only half of the 7,000 Soviet marines at Vladivostok. Soviet plans called for impressed civilian ships to make up the difference, but the history of amphibious operations demonstrated that such jury-rigged measures were typical of failed landings. The air force, which had initially supported the Hokkaido plan, had changed its mind given the situation in the air and commitments in Europe. And the army, which had been in the forefront of invasion planning, was suddenly loath to commit troops, especially its sole airborne division, against Japan as reports of the mobilization of the massive Chinese People's Liberation Army reached headquarters. Moreover, the Japanese Northern Army—three infantry and one armored division and supporting troops—had already been brought up to full strength. "Whatever chance we had of successfully invading Hokkaido," Ushakov warned Ilichev, "has long since passed."

The admiral nevertheless found himself in disagreement with his superior yet again. In the message, Ilichev directed Ushakov to keep his surface forces concentrated at Aniva Bay for possible defensive operations in the Kuriles or for an ASW effort against allied submarines that might threaten the Soviet SSBN bastion in the Sea of Okhotsk.

While he shared Ilichev's concerns, Ushakov considered Aniva Bay exposed. The anchorage was too close to allied land-based air in Japan and Russian air strength in Sakhalin had fallen sharply during the first days of the war. The Soviets had already lost over half of the four hundred fighters deployed within operating range of the Pacific approaches, and with the Chinese mobilizing an air force that included over 4,000 fighter types, frontal aviation and air defense forces headquarters were understandably reluctant to transfer additional planes from the interior to the coast. Despite Ilichev's promise to transfer at least fifty interceptors to Sakhalin as soon as possible, Ushakov argued that his ships should make an immediate run south to Vladivostok before the Allies turned their attention against Korsakov. "I've simply lost faith in the ability of our air to protect my ships," an enraged Ushakov told Ilichev, "Cam Ranh, Petropavlovsk, the Kuriles—time and time again our air defenses have failed."

As the two Soviet commanders argued throughout the afternoon, allied naval and air units completed their concentration in the north. For days, U.S. Air Force F-4s and FB-111s had been flying into Misawa from the Philippines and at 1800 on the seventeenth, CINCPACAF declared the three fresh squadrons fully operational. The *Kitty Hawk* and *Independence* had also completed replenishing, had steamed back west and were within striking range of Aniva Bay, the last two Soviet submarines stalking the American carriers having been sunk by the SSNs *Bremerton* and *Tautog*.

At 2030 Japanese and American planes initiated a series of attacks against Soviet air defenses in southern Sakhalin. The initial strikes involved over seventy-five allied aircraft, including U.S. Air Force F-117A stealth fighters now flying from bases in Japan. The Soviets lost over twenty interceptors in air-to-air combat, principally to U.S. Air Force F-16 Falcons flying from Misawa. Other air force, navy, and a handful of Japanese aircraft then hit airfields, SAM installations, and command and control facilities.

The late evening strikes preempted Soviet efforts to reinforce Sakhalin. As a result, the following morning allied aircraft met markedly less resistance and achieved near complete success. American and Japanese fighters downed another score of Soviet interceptors. Attack aircraft plastered airfields, destroying about forty SNA aircraft on the ground at Yuzhno Sakhalinsk. The attackers knocked out innumerable SAM sites around Korsakov and, in the early afternoon, struck Soviet ships as they fled Aniva Bay, sinking the cruisers *Vasily Chapayev*, *Tashkent*, and *Admiral Fokin* and two container ships.

"By the time I managed to convince General Ilichev to allow me to order the fleet south, we were about twelve hours too late," Ushakov lamented, "and now my ships have to run a gauntlet of mines and missiles in La Perouse Strait, and air and submarine attacks in the Sea of Japan."

Despite Ushakov's fears, the Soviets passed through the strait with only inconsequential loss. By the eighteenth, Soviet bombing raids had knocked out all but a few of the Japanese surface-to-surface missiles emplacements along the coast and effective countermeasures protected the vast armada as it made its way through La Perouse. The Japanese managed to sink only a single frigate. Nor had the allies, who wanted to keep the strait unobstructed to allow the passage of their submarines into the Sea of Okhotsk, mined La Perouse as Ushakov had feared. A new sense of optimism swept through headquarters as reports of the safe passage of the strait reached Vladivostok.

But the new mood was short-lived. Shortly after 0630 on 18 July, the Soviet surface force came under heavy air attack, the first of a series of strikes that would continue into the morning of the nineteenth. The Russian ships had only ineffective and occasional air cover from air defense force interceptors based 250 miles to the northwest around Sovetskaya Gavan. In bombing and standoff attacks, allied aircraft sank five frigates, eight corvettes, fourteen missile boats, two support vessels, and fourteen merchant ships.

In the midst of the airstrikes, allied submarines operating in the northern Sea of Japan closed in on the Soviet force. For the Japanese and American skippers, the running battle, which lasted for thirty hours, was a "shooting gallery, a submariner's dream come true." Allied submarines racked up impressive scores: the *Narushio* sank a destroyer and a corvette; the *Takashio*, a destroyer and a corvette; the *Isoshio*, a frigate and two corvettes; the *Blueback*, a frigate and a corvette; the *Puffer*, a destroyer and three corvettes; and the *Cavalla*, a cruiser, two corvettes, and a replenishment ship.

The allies had virtually destroyed Soviet naval power in the Pacific. Not a single ship reached Vladivostok from Aniva Bay. Ushakov's once proud Red Banner Pacific Fleet now consisted of the old *Sverdlov*-class cruiser *Admiral Senyavin*, a destroyer, a half-dozen obsolescent frigates, and two score of small missile boats. Fewer than five-dozen SNA Backfires and Badgers remained operational. "We've lost the initiative in the Pacific," Ushakov informed Ilichev, "Now the question we need to ask is what will our enemies do with it?"

By 19 July, that consideration had become a major source of Soviet concern, for the situation in the south had taken a disastrous turn. The eighteenth had begun well enough for the Soviets. SNA strike aircraft continued to dispatch Japanese surface ships to the bottom of the Tsushima Strait. An early morning attack sank the destroyers *Haruna* and *Sawakaze* and four frigates, but the Soviets' successful strike proved to be their last hurrah. The commitment of American fighters based in South Korea to air superiority missions over the Tsushima Strait and the arrival of the *Vinson* finally closed the door to "the alley." American F-15 Eagles intercepted an afternoon strike, drove off the attackers, and downed ten Soviet aircraft. At sea, the four American frigates that had escorted the convoy to Pusan formed an ASW task force and began operations in support of the Japanese, sinking a Soviet and a North Korean submarine, the last Communist boats in the vicinity of the Tsushima Strait. Allied air attacks completed the destruction of North Korean navy.

The North Korean army fared little better on the eighteenth. For the first time since the war began, the allies began the day on the offensive and conducted a series of attacks along the front from the Imjin to Chorwon. The North Koreans threw their reserves into action piecemeal, and far from reversing the tide of the campaign, they were swept up in what became a rout. By nightfall, ROK troops had reached the DMZ along much of the Imjin front. The U.S. 2d Infantry Division had driven to within five miles of Sananyong. ROK marines were fighting in the streets of Chorwon.

At 0415 on 19 July, the North Korean general staff directed the II, V, and I Army Corps to conduct "retrograde movements," even if such operations "required temporary shifts north of the 38th parallel." At 0710, the Central People's Committee requested "armed assistance" from Soviet ground forces. A protracted, broader Asian war appeared likely.

But the Chinese communists had no desire to see a Korean conflict again carried north toward the Yalu. Nor were the Chinese eager to see Soviet forces move into North Korea, win the campaign, and extend Moscow's political dominance. In rather complex diplomatic maneuvering, the Chinese presented separate ultimata to the governments of the United States, North Korea, and the Soviet Union. Beijing warned that if the troops of the United States, or of its South Korean ally, crossed the DMZ, Chinese troops of the

Moreover, despite the end of the immediate crisis over Korea, the PLA continued to mobilize. Border incidents and overflights by Chinese aircraft were daily occurrences.

The Chinese did not want a war with their Russians neighbors, but they were determined to do what they could to prevent the Soviets from winning the war, in Asia or elsewhere. A victory for Moscow posed far greater dangers for Beijing than a victory for the Americans. The Chinese did not want to allow the Soviets a free hand to move their forces toward the coast against the Americans and Japanese, or toward the west to Europe. They managed to achieve those aims through the cautious use of military resources. They allowed "controlled skirmishes" to develop along the border, "incidents" that had the desired impact and paralyzed the Russians into inaction.

The threat of Chinese intervention, the loss of hundreds of aircraft, and the destruction of the Soviet Pacific fleet left Moscow with few options in the Far East. In less than a week, the Soviets had lost over a hundred ships, including three small carriers and a battlecruiser, and over a thousand aircraft in the Indian Ocean and the Pacific. They had lost the initiative and had been thrown onto the defensive. A depressed ADM Ushakov waded through intelligence reports, attempting to divine where the allies would strike next—directly at Vladivostok with air and sea forces, at the Kuriles, or at the Soviet SSBN bastion in the Sea of Okhotsk? "Our problem," Ushakov admitted to his staff, "is that we're virtually powerless to contest whatever option the enemy chooses to pursue."

In allied headquarters in Japan and Hawaii, the victory in WESTPAC led not only to a debate over alternative courses of action in the theater, but also to a spirited defense against those in Washington who wished to "swing" American forces from the Pacific to the Atlantic. Admirals Cooper, Jernigan, and Tazawa were aghast at the idea of stripping WESTPAC of mobile offensive forces. ADM Cardswell, the CNO, supported his Pacific commanders. When confronted with the request by the secretary of defense, the CNO pointed out that such a transfer would take between thirty-three and thirty-eight days, depending on whether or not the ships used the Suez Canal, by which time the crisis the alliance faced in the North Atlantic would have long since passed.

TWENTY-FOUR

In Moscow, the results of the
first week's campaigning had tempered the optimism that had pre-
vailed on 14 July. As Chief of the General Staff Marshal Aleksei
Posokhov reviewed the initial operations, he could not help but note
the Soviet Union's numerous setbacks. The naval war in the North
Atlantic had not gone well. The Soviet Mediterranean fleet and the
naval and air forces of Libya and Syria had been all but eliminated.
Posokhov's staff considered the Southwest Front's repulse before
Istanbul and the near collapse of the Romanian army a major setback and a debacle. The Soviet Indian Ocean squadron had been
annihilated. The Pacific Ocean Fleet had been effectively destroyed.

Nevertheless, senior Soviet military leaders in Moscow remained convinced that victory lay within their grasp. COL Kaganovich was present at a high level conference—attended by Kubitskii, Posokhov, and Minister of Defense Marshal Durostnik—held
in the early morning hours of 22 July. There was no sense of pessi-
mism; no real sense of concern about what was taking place on the
flanks or in the Far East, Kaganovich noted. He concluded that on
the army-dominated staffs at the highest levels of the Soviet military,
the flanks were too often considered a distraction. The German
front was the decisive front. When Durostnik noted the apparent
failure of the Northern Fleet to threaten NATO's North Atlantic
SLOCs, Posokhov brushed aside the minister of defense's concerns.

"Certainly, we must smash NATO before the Americans resupply and reinforce their units in Germany," Posokhov retorted, "but,
as you know comrade, our plans have always called for as rapid a
victory as possible."

Kaganovich was somewhat dismayed by the chief of the general
staff's apparent lack of concern. Posokhov assured Durostnik that
it would be a week, and perhaps two, before American reinforcements could make themselves felt.

"By then," Posokhov asserted, "we will have crushed the enemy
in Germany and have won the decisive battle."

Posokhov then reviewed the situation on the German front.
"Our operations are going well and our senior Soviet and Warsaw
Pact officers remain confident of swift victory." When Durostnik
questioned the reliability of the non-Soviet Warsaw Pact troops,

noting the shakiness displayed by the Poles before Lübeck, Kubitskii acknowledged the weakness of the Polish formations but assured the minister of defense: "We will be sending the Poles into Jutland, mostly against the Danes and some West Germans isolated in Lübeck and Kiel, while our East German and Czechoslovakian troops, who are fighting well, will continue to be employed on the main front. I would point out, comrade minister of defense, that not all of the NATO troops are fighting that well either."

"That's true," Posokhov interjected, "the Greeks and Danes are fighting poorly, and the Dutch and Belgians have shown signs of cracking."

Posokhov then outlined Soviet plans for the central front. Russian and Polish marines would continue their operations to encircle, besiege, and assault Copenhagen, while Warsaw Pact airborne and airmobile troops expanded the Arhus and Odense airheads. The Polish army would take over the drive up the Jutland peninsula, allowing the Soviet and East German divisions of the Second Guards Tank Army to concentrate on their westward push.

The quite obvious lessened emphasis on operations against the Danish peninsula brought Durostnik's bushy eyebrows to attention. "What of our plans for Denmark and the Baltic Fleet?" the Soviet minister of defense inquired.

"My staff," Posokhov responded, "considers it highly unlikely that the Northern Fleet, given its defeats of the past few days, will be able to conduct effective operations against the North Atlantic SLOCs, therefore, we see little use in continuing operations to secure the Baltic exits and have assigned a lower priority to the campaign in Denmark."

"Besides," Kubitskii added, "the Baltic Fleet is itself badly battered, the Danes have heavily mined the exits, NATO submarines and missile and torpedo boats continue to operate from bases in Jutland and Schleswig-Holstein, and the air situation is becoming problematic. We are having some problems supplying the airborne and marines."

Posokhov continued outlining his strategy. The Poles would carry the offensive north, taking Lübeck, Kiel, and then driving toward a junction with the paratroopers at Arhus. The Second Guards Tank Army would complete the capture of Hamburg and then drive west, breaking the Weser River line between Bremen and

Bremerhaven. The Third Shock Army, assisted by the second-echelon Fourth Tank and Ninth Armies, would exploit its small bridgehead over the Weser between Bremen and Hannover and "pinch off" the Hannover-Braunschweig bulge. The Twentieth Guards Army would continue its westward drive toward the Ruhr. The Eighth Guards Tank Army would break the American-West German line between Kassel and Bamberg. The First Guards Tank Army would drive through Nuremburg. The Twenty-Eighth Army would continue its drive through Augsburg to a position west of Munich, while the Forty-First Army pushed westward south of the Bavarian capital to meet the thrust of the Twenty-Eighth Army.

Durostnik, who had been examining the situation map as he listened to the briefing, looked up as Posokhov finished. "Your forces are concentrating on the wings, Aleksei Alekseievich."

"Yes, comrade minister of defense, we are advancing more rapidly in the north and in Bavaria and we are reinforcing our successes. Nevertheless, our divisions in the center will continue to push west. We expect hard fighting, but if we maintain pressure along the entire front, NATO forces will crack."

"And how long will that take?" Durostnik asked.

"According to the calculations of my staff," Posokhov responded, "seven to ten days. Within a fortnight, the campaign in Germany will have been decided."

★ ★ ★

The success of the Baltic Front's operations on the twenty-first of July seemed to vindicate Posokhov's faith both in the reliability of the Soviet Union's allies and the ultimate victory of the Warsaw Pact. Polish and Soviet marines completed the encirclement of Copenhagen and its Danish and Canadian defenders. Other Pact airmobile forces expanded their areas of control on Fyn and around Arhus. Further south, elements of five Polish divisions struck German defenses south and west of Lübeck. By noon, the Poles were fighting in the city and by nightfall had secured the old town. In the darkness, Polish mechanized forces raced north, taking Oldenburg and Plon on the twenty-second. The left wing of the Polish advance swept into Schleswig the next day, completing the encirclement of Kiel.

COL Vladimir Chernaev, a Soviet liaison officer attached to the

Polish army staff, believed that had the Poles followed up their success at Lübeck with a continuous advance, Kiel, too, might have fallen. But the Poles halted a few miles from the town to bring up their artillery and to reorganize units that had become disorganized during the attack and subsequent pursuit. At 1100 on 24 July the Poles began their assault against Kiel. T-62s and T-72s of the 20th Polish Tank Division supported the attack of three motor rifle divisions. According to Chernaev, the Poles, elated by their victory at Lübeck, went into battle expecting minimal resistance from the Germans—elements of the 6th and 11th Panzergrenadier Divisions and some territorial formations. But the Bundesheer defenders, commanded by Generalmajor Ludwig Hesse, were determined to avenge their defeat at Lübeck and had no intention of "surrendering to Poles." Only minutes after the attack had begun, Polish army headquarters began to receive reports from the front indicating that the Germans were attacking. The counterstrokes threw the Polish offensive into disarray. Entire formations disintegrated over the course of the next few hours. Only with difficulty was the situation stabilized in the late afternoon when Soviet fighter-bombers appeared over a battlefield devoid of NATO fighters.

★★★

As the Poles began their offensive toward Lübeck on the twenty-first, assault elements and engineers of the Soviet Second Guards Tank Army opened their attack on Hamburg. West German resistance proved surprisingly light and the Russian troops advanced rapidly. The heavily outnumbered and isolated German defenders, many of them territorial troops with families trapped in the city, quickly gave way. By noon on the twenty-second, Hamburg had been secured except for a few snipers and die-hard defenders at large in the subway system.

The divisions of the Third Shock Army, positioned along the Weser and the outskirts of Bremen, received their first day of rest on 21 July. Northern Front headquarters ordered the army to halt its forward advance pending the completion of the Second Guards Army's operations in Hamburg and along the lower Weser. The army spent the day sighting artillery batteries and bringing up bridging equipment.

Further south, forward elements of the Fourth Guards Tank

Army, the first second-echelon formation to reach the front, stormed into Braunschweig. The divisions of the First Guards Tank Army and the Twentieth Guards Army continued their drives between Kassel and Bielefeld but made little progress, meeting exceedingly stiff resistance.

The armies controlled by the Soviet Central Front headquarters, operating between Kassel and the Austrian border, made little headway during the twenty-first. Between Kassel and Bamberg, West German and American divisions repelled attack after attack and held a line along the A7 autobahn. South of Nuremberg, Warsaw Pact units made better, but nevertheless insignificant progress.

Along the entire front, NATO resistance stiffened, especially around the bulge where the First Guards Tank and Twentieth Guards Armies had broken across the Weser River. During the nineteenth and twentieth, NORTHAG—British General Sir Ian Carton de Wiart—had assembled considerable forces around the Pact penetration. When it became evident that the Soviet westward drive had lost much of its momentum, thanks to the sharp counterattack delivered by the Dutch at Paderborn, Carton de Wiart planned a counterstroke to seal off the penetration at its base.

At 1330 on 22 July, while Dutch divisions maintained pressure along the periphery of the bulge, British and West German divisions attacked south from Hannover while American and West German divisions struck north from Kassel. The counterstroke, well supported by NATO ground attack aircraft, smashed through weakened, overstretched Soviet divisions and by noon on the twenty-third the NATO pincers had met at Hoxter, a small town along the Weser. The allied attackers overran three Soviet divisions and pocketed another eight Russian and East German divisions and supporting troops—nearly 150,000 men.

The NATO counteroffensive caught the Soviets by surprise. Northern Front headquarters ordered the First Guards Tank and Twentieth Guards Armies to continue their attack westward without concern for flanks, fine tactics as long as the front was still mobile, but by the twenty-first things were starting to gum up and one had to become concerned about flanks.

At Northern Front headquarters, GEN Roman Gribachev, alarmed by the NATO success, ordered his staff to draw up a plan for the two entrapped armies to immediately break out to the east and for the Fourth Guards Tank and Ninth Armies to launch a simultaneous relief attack to the west. Before his orders could be executed, they were countermanded by Moscow. At Marshal Posokhov's personal direction, the isolated divisions were ordered to continue to strike westward while an offensive mounted by the remaining armies of the Front—the Second Guards, Third Shock, Fourth Guards Tank, and Ninth Armies—broke through to the entrapped troops and completed the destruction of NORTHAG. The chief of the general staff saw the NATO counterattack as an opportunity, rather than an extremely dangerous development.

The Pact attack, which began at 0545 on the morning of 24 July, achieved only mixed success. The Second Guards Tank Army's mobile formations faltered in difficult street fighting in Bremen. The lead divisions of the Third Shock Army forced their way over the Weser at Nienburg and drove toward Onasbruck, pushed elements of the West German 7th Panzer Division back to Diepholz, creating a second bulge in NORTHAG's already overstretched lines, but failed to reestablish contact with the two isolated Warsaw Pact armies. The West German 5th Panzergrenadier Division repulsed numerous Soviet attacks across the Weser north of Kassel, holding the critical haunches of the pocket.

Undeterred by the mounting pressure on his left flank, General Carton de Wiart continued his counterattack in an effort to seize the initiative on the northern part of the front. On 26 and 27 July, NORTHAG threw everything he had at the existing Soviet pocket as well as the new penetration over the Weser. The British 1st Armored Division, attacking south along the Weser, caught the Soviet 7th Guards Tank Division in the flank. At 1340 on the twenty-seventh, Challenger tanks of the 22d Brigade, 14th/20th King's Hussars, retook Nienburg, and isolated the Third Shock Army's advance divisions.

While NORTHAG's attacks failed to eliminate the Warsaw Pact divisions encircled between Kassel and Hannover, NATO forces cut the pocket in two and inflicted heavy losses on the defenders. The attacking forces also suffered heavily. The Belgian 16th Motorized Infantry Division and the French 10th Armored Division were, to quote a NORTHAG report, "considerably shot up and too weak to conduct further sustained operations."

In Bavaria, NATO counterattacks also checked the Warsaw

Pact advance. The armies of the Soviet Central Front resumed their drive on Munich on the twenty-first. Strong Soviet and East German forces of the Eighth Guards Tank Army drove back the West German 4th Panzergrenadier Division to Weissenburg, while Russian and Czech forces advancing south of Munich crossed the A95 and threatened to encircle the Bavarian capital. But on the twenty-fifth, NATO forces launched a three-pronged counterattack—American forces from the north, West German divisions from the south, and fresh French divisions from the west—against the advancing Warsaw Pact formations. During forty-eight hours of bitter fighting, two Soviet tank and a pair of motor rifle divisions disintegrated. Victorious CENTAG units drove the surviving Pact forces eastward across the A9 autobahn that connected Nuremburg and Munich.

Despite extremely heavy losses of men and material, the battles fought along the German front between 21 and 28 July were indecisive. At SACEUR's headquarters in Belgium, officers began to compare the on-going operations to those conducted on the Western Front during the First World War. SACEUR made such an analogy at a 27 July conference held at Casteau attended by both NORTHAG and CENTAG. "We've had all kinds of mobile operations, movement backwards and forwards, but when you look at the situation maps," GEN Sexton stressed as he gestured toward a pair of maps showing the front lines on 21 and 27 July, "after a week of heavy fighting, you can't help but notice that the Pact hasn't been going anywhere." After recovering from the initial Soviet blow, prompt NATO counterattacks, delivered by reserves moving toward the front, had checked successive Soviet advances. Warsaw Pact ripostes likewise had halted the NATO drives. "Now the obvious question is," Sexton continued, "whose reserves are going to run out first?" After a pause, Sexton fielded his own question. "Unfortunately, gentlemen, the answer is not quite so obvious."

Ironically, Soviet officers were drawing similar comparisons in Warsaw Pact headquarters, although such talk was often muted. "No one wants to confront what's quickly becoming an obvious reality," COL Kaganovich advised Marshal Kubitskii, "that our offensive has stalled along the Weser, much like the German offensive of 1914 ran out of steam on the Marne." Most senior Soviet commanders insisted that the Pact possessed superior reserves close at hand and that continued attacks would wear NATO down. Unfortunately for Kaganovich, high ranking officers such as Kubitskii disliked First World War analogies and preferred to draw parallels between the situation along the front and the Kursk battle of 1943 in which Soviet forces had engaged in over a week of bitter and costly fighting before the Fascist forces finally broke under the pressure and were forced to conduct a head-long retreat to the Dnieper.

There were many younger officers, including Kaganovich, who were uncomfortable with the analogy, believing that the Warsaw Pact forces, which had initiated the offensive, were this time cast in the role of the Germans. "Moreover," Kaganovich recognized, "unlike the situation in 1943 when we were gaining aerial supremacy along the front, the current situation in the air is deteriorating daily." Soviet sortie rates dropped as losses mounted. The Pact air forces were proving extremely brittle and, except for a handful of East German squadrons equipped with MiG-29s, were next to useless. NATO fighter-bombers struck more often and deeper into the Warsaw Pact rear. Strikes against airfields, supply depots, transportation lines, communications facilities, and headquarters increased in intensity.

As the result of such attacks, by the end of the second week of the war chaos reigned in the Warsaw Pact rear and frontline formations began to run short of ammunition, spare parts, and POL. Marshal Kubitskii, who returned to Moscow late on the evening of 27 July after a tour of the front with Kaganovich, warned Marshal Posokhov that "if the rear area situation is not quickly cleaned up, and movement toward the front of reinforcements and supplies accelerated, further advance westward will be impossible and our troops will be forced to adopt the defensive."

In front of his staff, Posokhov dismissed Kubitskii's report as overly pessimistic. "What you saw at the front, Comrade Marshal, was the real face of war. Those of us with service in Afghanistan know that combat operations do not look as neat and orderly as do those of the maneuver ground."

But after the briefing ended, Posokhov took Kubitskii aside and apologized. "We have to keep a good front on things for the staff, my friend."

In fact, Kubitskii's report had deeply troubled the Soviet chief of the general staff. "Everywhere," Posokhov lamented to the Warsaw Pact commander, "we are losing the tempo of operations, I'm afraid we face some tough campaigning, my old friend, and the outcome will depend on our resilience. Will our army and people show the stamina that they displayed during the Great Fatherland War, or the weaknesses that spelled the end of tsarist rule in 1917?"

TWENTY-FIVE

July 21st passed quietly along the front in Fortress Norway. Sixth Army directed the concentration of the 45th and 54th Motor Rifle Divisions abreast the Lyngen position preparatory to the planned resumption of the offensive to the south. But behind the front lines, battles raged at Bodo, Andoya, Harstad, and at COMNON headquarters at Bardufoss.

After meeting with the officers of the shattered Susa Alpini, West German LTG Uwe Gysae, Commander, ACE Mobile Force, drove to Bardufoss for a meeting with COMNON, Norwegian LTG Torbjorn Bjol. Gysae wanted the non-Norwegian troops of the ACE Mobile Force and the NATO composite force for Norway concentrated under his control. He had acquiesced only reluctantly with the initial dispersal of his units because he recognized that reserves were few and it was natural to see the NATO forces thrown into the breach where they were needed. Gysae wanted to use the operational pause that began in the evening of 20 July to concentrate the ACE Mobile Force and the NATO Composite Force for Norway, the remaining units of which reached northern airfields on the morning of 21 July, as a reserve force centrally positioned around Bardufoss. "From such a location," Gysae told Bjol, "I can reinforce the Norwegian units holding the Lyngen line should they be driven back, and be in an excellent position to counterattack and to seize the initiative should the Soviet drive falter." Gysae considered further operations against the encircled Soviet forces at Andoya and Harstad a waste of time. He argued that the Russians could be contained easily by a few Norwegian battalions. The burden of continued attacks against the dug-in defenders would undoubtedly fall to the fresh NATO units, the strength of which would be expended to little advantage. Gysae's Italian and Canadian units had already been destroyed as effective fighting forces; he was afraid that within another twenty-four hours, his British, German, and Belgian units would be likewise burned out.

Gysae had learned that Bjol intended to further disperse the NATO troops. The British Parachute Battalion was moving into defensive frontline positions astride the E6 north of Skibotn. The West German Gebirgsjägers were continuing the advance on Harstad. The Belgian 3rd Light Infantry Battalion of the NCFN, which had flown into the newly recaptured airbase at Evenes, was being trucked to Andoy to reinforce the Norwegian assault on the airfield at Andoya. The only units under Gysae's command were the small Luxembourgeois Battalion of the ACE Mobile Force and Company C of the U.S. Army's 94th Engineer Battalion, attached to the NCFN.

The meeting between the two NATO lieutenant generals was hardly harmonious. Bjol had been angered by SACEUR's decision to subordinate the NCFN to Gysae, considering the move "a demonstration of a lack of confidence in the Norwegian command," an opinion shared by CINCNORTH, GEN Sir Owen Peirse, who considered the decision a political error. While Bjol agreed with Gysae that NATO forces would be most effective if concentrated, the Norwegian considered continued dispersal a practical and political necessity. The demands of the campaign had made such dispositions imperative. Moreover, Bjol argued that was it critical to the morale of the Norwegian units that they see allied forces at the front bearing the burden of Soviet assaults, and not just "sitting about in the rear waiting to clean up any breakthroughs or mopping up the enemy and gathering all of the laurels after the Norwegians had done the difficult work and halted the advance." Bjol also considered it essential that the Soviet pockets at Andoya and Harstad be cleaned up. The prospects of a sudden shift in the air picture, that would allow the Soviets to reinforce their isolated units and threaten COMNON's rear, concerned Bjol. He also believed that the recapture of the two towns and the elimination of the elite Soviet units would boost the morale of the Norwegian forces.

After an hour-and-a-half of acrimonious debate, Bjol agreed to concentrate the ACE Mobile Force and NCFN under Gysae's command as soon as the operations against Andoya and Harstad ended, operations Bjol now placed under the control of Gysae's headquarters, despite the fact that most of the troops involved were Norwegian. The two men parted with a handshake, but those present knew that major differences remained unresolved.

★ ★ ★

Earlier in the day, at 0630, Bjol had subordinated the Norwegian battalions of the 5th and 14th Brigades, operating against the Soviet 76th Guards Airborne at Bodo, to the headquarters of 4 MEB, commanded by U.S. Marine Corps BG Thomas Watson. Communication and effective control by COMNON of the two Norwegian brigades engaged around Bodo had proven difficult. Bjol, who recognized that the marine air-ground task force would carry the burden of the drive to reopen the E6 and to recapture Bodo, considered it sensible to allow Watson to coordinate the operations. Moreover, freed from the immediate responsibility to direct the battles at Bodo, Andoya, and Harstad, Bjol would be free to focus his attentions on the imminent battle for the Lyngen position.

During the nineteenth and twentieth, infantry of the Norwegian 5th and 14th Brigades passed around the upper Saltfjord between the fjord and the Blaamannsis glacier and worked their way into positions east of the E6, on the left flank of the two battalions of the 237th Guards Airborne Regiment, now numbering less than 1,000 men, which held the line at Fauske and Finneid north of the fjord. At 1330 on 21 July, the Norwegians struck west, while the three battalions of 4 MEB, using their amphibious and heliborne mobility to cross the Saltfjord, attacked north from Rognan under the cover of Cobra attack helicopters of HML/A 269 and A-6E Intruders of VMA 229. By 1700, both Fauske and Finneid were in American hands and the Norwegians had cleared a fifteen-mile stretch of the E6 north of the fjord. Soviet resistance quickly collapsed. About midnight, lead elements of the 1/2 Marine Regiment, entered Hopen, less than ten miles from Bodo. Two Russian battalions had been destroyed and 647 paratroopers had been taken prisoner. Two other battalions had been pushed north, where they continued to block the E6, but were unable to come to the assistance of the remnants of the 76th Guards. No more than 1,500 Soviet paratroopers, with little heavy equipment and dwindling supplies, remained to defend Bodo.

From his forward headquarters established at Evenes, LTG Gysae directed operations against Andoya and Harstad. At 1530, the Belgian 3d Light Infantry and the Norwegian 1/15 struck north against the Soviet marines holding Andoya. With NATO air support provided by RAF Harriers of 1 Squadron, the attack achieved complete and rapid success. By 1830 the town and airfield had been secured and over 600 Norwegian and Canadian prisoners had been released.

The attack on Harstad, held by Ganenko's marines and the remnants of the Soviet air assault brigade that had landed at Evenes on D day, fared less well. The NATO assault force, the Norwegian 3/15 and the West German Gebirgsjägers, encountered stiff resistance. A planned preliminary air strike by Norwegian Falcons failed to materialize. Gysae ordered the attack to proceed anyway and the Gebirgsjägers stormed the forward Soviet positions and took over three hundred prisoners.

As the Germans and Norwegians prepared to press on toward Harstad, RNAF F-16s suddenly appeared overhead. Bundesheer LT Hans Müller assumed the planes were going to strike the Soviet positions on the next ridgeline north, but to his surprise and horror he saw the aircraft bank into attack runs that paralleled the original front. Müller immediately ordered his men to find cover. For five minutes, Norwegian planes bombed and strafed NATO troops. The amicidal strike cost the lives of sixty-three Germans and forty-two Norwegians, while one enraged German downed a Falcon with a hand-held SAM. Ganenko, who watched the attack from a forward observation post, personally led a prompt battalion-sized counterattack that drove the shaken NATO units back to their original start line.

Bjol and Gysae blamed each other's headquarters for the failure to coordinate air and ground operations during the fighting for Harstad. Gysae believed that the strike had been cancelled, not just delayed. Bjol contended that his headquarters had not been informed that the attack had nevertheless begun. Obviously, the hard feelings that existed between the two generals did little to ensure smooth coordination between their respective commands.

* * *

At a 2230 staff meeting held at COMNON's Bardufoss headquarters on 21 July, Bjol's chief of staff reviewed the day's operations and the current situation in north Norway. Intelligence indicated that the Soviet Sixth Army would resume offensive operations within hours. Unfortunately, the failure to retake Harstad and to clear the E6 left COMNON's major overland supply and reinforcement routes blocked, with significant reserves still tied down clearing up the rear. NATO's Lyngen position was strong, but supplies were low and no additional reinforcements were scheduled to arrive by air. "The well at both SACEUR and AFNORTH has run dry," Bjol noted. The Soviet pockets at Bodo and Harstad had to be eliminated to free up additional forces for the front. COMNON's naval deputy reminded Bjol of the transports carrying the six American, British, and Dutch marine battalions and the resupply vessels then approaching the coast. The Soviet Northern Fleet's aviation assets had lately been relatively inactive and he believed that the troops would be ashore within seventy-two hours. Bjol disagreed. Throughout the day, he had tried but failed to get a commitment from COMSTRIKFLTLANT regarding the probable time and place of a marine landing. "According to the Striking Fleet staff," Bjol informed his assembled officers, "the air picture remains clouded and an increase in SNA activity is expected as the transports near our coast." When the deputy insisted that the marines would come ashore, Bjol just nodded. "Yes, captain, they will come ashore, the marines always come ashore, of that I am certain; but will they come ashore in time?"

* * *

The Soviet Sixth Army's plan of attack for 22 July was simple and direct. The surviving amphibious and airborne forces at Harstad and Bodo would defend their positions as long as possible to block reinforcement routes and to tie down potential NATO reserves, while BG Muratov's 45th MRD and BG Pisarev's 54th MRD launched concentric attacks toward Skibotn.

LTG Berdiaev, the Sixth Army commander, informed MGs Malygin and Ganenko that they could expect relief within forty-eight hours. Ganenko considered a breakthrough probable and believed that a relief column, even if it did not reach him in forty-eight hours, would at least force the NATO units surrounding Harstad to break off their attack. Malygin, defending Bodo nearly four hundred kilometers to the south, considered the army commander's expectations grossly optimistic and a psychological ploy rather than a realistic operational assessment. He recognized by the morning of 22 July that even if Sixth Army broke through at Skibotn, which he did not consider unlikely, advance elements could not possibly fight their way to Bodo in time to save the remnants of the 76th Guards Airborne Division. Nevertheless, the Soviet commander responded to his predicament philosophically.

At 0945, 22 July, the Soviet offensive began. The virtual absence of air support hampered the drive, although attack helicopter units provided excellent close support for the advance and artillery formations performed superbly despite the constant necessity to shift locations to avoid NATO air attacks. Thus supported, elements of the 54th MRD struck northwest toward Skibotn along the E78 in an effort to break the front of the first battalion of the Norwegian army's Brigade North. The 45th MRD, at last concentrated on either side of the Lyngenfjord, launched a two-pronged drive toward Skibotn. The 61st MRR conducted a feint attack along the E6 in an attempt to engage the British paras and prevent their movement toward either of the flanks. The main drive of the 45th MRD hit COMNON's left flank. The 253d MRR, supported by the bulk of the division's tank and artillery assets, drove south from the bridgehead at the Lyngenfjord ferry site seized two days earlier.

Nowhere along the roughly forty-mile-long front were the Soviets able to penetrate NATO positions. Well-sited ATGMs, effective Norwegian artillery fire, and repeated strikes by fighter-bombers blunted successive attacks by both the 45th and 54th MRDs. By noon, scores of burning Russian tanks and APCs marked the limits of the Sixth Army's advance.

The assault continued into the afternoon. While the Russians suffered heavy losses, so, too, did NATO. At 1420, the commander of Brigade North's first battalion, fighting astride the E78, informed COMNON headquarters that unless promptly reinforced, he would have to pull back. An air strike by Norwegian F-5s caught the Russian 2/54 tank battalion forming up along the E78 and destroyed twenty-one of the unit's twenty-seven remaining T-64s.

Nevertheless, the 54th MRD began to drive slowly toward Skibotn advancing eight kilometers by midnight.

To the west, along the E6, the British paras and the Norwegian Alta Battlegroup easily repulsed the 45th MRD's tentative advance. Given the tenacity of the Russian attacks elsewhere, the COMNON staff believed that the drive along the E6 was a feint. But Bjol felt compelled to keep his most effective frontline battalion in place. Of the three Russian drives, he felt that he had to block the direct route down the E6.

On the west side of the Lyngenfjord, two battalions of the 253d MRR, supported by artillery, tanks, and helicopters, launched the 45th MRD's primary drive south from the ferry crossing. Two Norwegian battalions—3/FM and the Porsanger Battlegroup—beat back repeated attacks throughout the morning, but began to yield ground slowly about 1500. "It was like the First World War," one Soviet battalion commander reported, "we measure our successes in meters." By day's end, the 45th MRD had gained no more than four kilometers.

At 2300, Bjol visited the front of the Finnmark Brigade's 3d Battalion during one of its many short retreats. The men looked tired, though certainly not defeated, and Bjol was surprised to learn that what he thought to be a platoon passing before him was, in fact, the remnant of a company. With his binoculars, COMNON could see first-hand the carnage inflicted upon the 45th MRD by the Norwegian defenders. Still, the Russians' losses seemed to have had little effect on their continued assaults and the NATO units were being bled white. "Despite our near-total control of the air," Bjol radioed Peirse, "my frontline battalions are being forced back. I have few reserves to plug the gaps that sooner or later are bound to be torn open in the front."

At Sixth Army headquarters in Kautokeino, the slow rate of advance troubled LTG Berdiaev and his staff. The army commander was frank in his assessment of the assault: "We expected to break through and we haven't, principally owing to our difficulties in the air." The frontal aviation assets under Berdiaev's control were too weak to operate effectively in the face of NATO's quantitatively and qualitatively superior Norwegian, Dutch, British, and American marine and air force squadrons operating over north Norway. Unfortunately, from Berdiaev's point of view, Northwest Front provided nothing but directives to keep attacking, and unwanted advice. From Murmansk came reports that mighty air battles were raging over the Kola and that all SNA and AADS assets were fully committed.

At 2330 on the twenty-second, Northwest Front did provide Berdiaev with a relatively detailed intelligence assessment concerning the state of the forces opposite the Sixth Army. The report indicated that severe casualties and constant Soviet pressure had induced a state of alarm at COMNON and that, because of inadequate reserves, Bjol's staff had begun to draw up a plan for a retreat on Narvik.

After receiving the intelligence summary, Berdiaev immediately flew to meet with his division commanders. He found the commander of the 54th MRD at his forward headquarters at Helligskogen. Pisarev was convinced that his troops were about to break through the Norwegian defenses and the new intelligence assessment reinforced his intention to continue the attack. The Sixth Army commander then flew to Lyngseidet to meet with Muratov. Berdiaev found the commander of the 45th MRD rather pessimistic and convinced that the report was grossly over-optimistic, perhaps even a fabrication by Northwest Front to keep the troops fighting. Berdiaev assured his subordinate that intelligence available at Sixth Army headquarters supported many of the conclusions of the Northwest Front assessment. Muratov appeared unconvinced, until an aide entered the room and handed the division commander an urgent dispatch from the front. Muratov read the message and smiled broadly as he handed it to Berdiaev. The commander of the 61st MRR had reported that the British paras had begun to pull back.

Despite heavy casualties, the Soviets had begun to crack the Fortress Norway position. Berdiaev believed that continued pressure would force COMNON into a headlong retreat, and perhaps a rout. The battle for north Norway had reached a critical moment. The Soviet Sixth Army still controlled fresh reserves immediately behind the front. Other than the Luxembourgeois and a company of American combat engineers, no NATO reserves were on hand. The only unbloodied battalions were over a hundred kilometers away, at sea, under the control of COMSTRIKFLTLANT.

TWENTY-SIX

VADM Emerson's STRIK-FLTLANT began to concentrate in the southern Barents Sea on the morning of 21 July. The *Forrestal* and *Eisenhower* task forces, designated Carrier Strike Group 1, at last rendezvoused about 250 miles north-northwest of Tromso. The two British carriers were located somewhat to the south, a position from which they could provide CAP for the amphibious task forces—one American and the other British-Dutch—which continued to steam north and were about a hundred miles west of Bardufoss. The *America* and *Abraham Lincoln* task forces were 250 and 600 miles, respectively, to the southwest of the *Forrestal-Eisenhower* CVBG.

The Soviet Northern Fleet could do little to prevent this concentration. ADM Obnorsky's surface and subsurface forces had been driven from the Norwegian and southern Barents Seas. The fleet's SNA assets were busily conducting ASW patrols off the northern Barents and Arctic Seas, assisting frontal aviation forces supporting the Sixth Army, or sitting in hardened aircraft shelters or on runways at Kola airfields.

Obnorsky considered Golikov's decision to restrict the SNA to operations against ground targets in north Norway and ASW patrols off the Kola to be asinine. "If we have a chance to prevent a NATO carrier concentration," Obnorsky argued, "we have to strike before they form their battlegroups." The Northern Fleet commander considered the assignment of his SNA Backfire and Badger crews to static bombing missions against Norwegian targets a waste of effort. "My men," he told Golikov, "are not trained for such missions and they'll perform poorly." And they did, at the same time suffering an attrition rate nearly as high as it had been when conducting strike operations against NATO naval forces.

Golikov viewed the situation somewhat differently. "The navy's had its chance," the Northwest Front commander responded, "you've failed to sink or to damage a single carrier, not even a British carrier. Yet you want to be 'unleashed' against the Americans, provided, of course, that the air defense forces supply interceptors to escort your bombers." Increasing NATO land-based and naval fighter strength had already led Golikov to insist that the Archangelsk air defense sector commit more and more of its fighters to the air battle raging over north Norway. Golikov's air staff and the air defense commander felt that the latter's forces were spread too thinly and that aircraft could not be made available to conduct offensive operations against NATO naval forces in the Barents Sea. "It's more prudent," Golikov suggested, "to concentrate our offensive air assets in support of the decisive battle for Skibotn. I think it's easier to deal with American naval aircraft in the skies, than on the decks of their carriers."

Col Dimitrii Malenkin, who headed the Northwest Front's air staff, agreed. A 20 July memorandum prepared by Malenkin for Golikov termed the American carriers "incredibly well defended, mobile airbases, complete with their own airborne warning and control aircraft, protected by the finest air defense interceptor in the world [the F-14 Tomcat], and escorted by surface platforms mounting SAM systems and integrated phased array radars. No NATO or Soviet land airbase possesses such impressive defenses." As long as the Striking Fleet restricted itself to the support of ground operations in north Norway, Malenkin considered it uneconomical to attempt to locate and destroy the carriers.

The debate that raged throughout the morning and early afternoon of 21 July concerning the proper use of SNA assets ended abruptly at 1705 when reports that the Americans were coming swept through the various Soviet staffs headquartered in the Kola. Satellite reconnaissance indicated that two American carriers were nearly a hundred miles further north than they had been at the time of the previous overflight. ADM Obnorsky immediately assumed that NATO's Striking Fleet was moving into position to attack bases in the Kola and the Northern Fleet commander requested permission to initiate SNA operations against the American carrier battlegroup. GEN Golikov hesitated, although he did order all SNA assets withdrawn from ground support missions over north Norway and readied for possible anti-carrier operations in the Barents Sea. At 1740, the Northwest Front intelligence staff informed Golikov that radio traffic and partially decoded intercepts indicated that COM-STRIKFLTLANT had received authorization from SACLANT to move north and attack the Kola. At 1745, the front commander ordered Obnorsky to initiate offensive operations against the American carriers before they could launch their own attacks. But Goli-kov did not change the air defense sector's priorities, which re-mained: first, the air defense of the Kola; second, flying air superiority missions over north Norway in support of the Sixth Army's planned offensive; and now third, the provision of escort for SNA strike aircraft operating within range of American carrier-based interceptors.

★ ★ ★

For VADM Emerson, the offensive against the Kola was the logical progression of what had thus far been a successful series of opera-tions conducted in the face of Soviet naval and air power. "We've weathered their attacks," Emerson told his staff, "now it's time to take the fight to the Russians, to strike them at their bases, and to finish them off."

Emerson was uncomfortable having the Striking Fleet tethered to Fortress Norway, although he acknowledged the wisdom of sup-porting COMNON. His primary mission was to support the land battle in north Norway. When the *Forrestal* was the only American carrier in the Norwegian Sea, Emerson had few offensive options. But with two carriers on hand on the morning of the twenty-first, and with the air picture over north Norway improving, Emerson immediately began to call for offensive operations against the Kola. "The best way to shape the air situation over north Norway," he reasoned, "isn't by sitting off Tromso and sending our planes over the beach." The air-space management problem over COMNON was horrendous. There simply was not sufficient room over a thirty to forty-mile front for several hundred planes. As NATO land-based reinforcements reached north Norway, the Striking Fleet increasingly found itself assigned packages behind Russian lines where its aircraft bombed and strafed roads and shot up trucks. Emerson's staff wanted to move north where it could gain a little elbow room.

LTG "Bull" Campbell, commander of the Striking Fleet's MARINESTRIKFOR/II MEF, also advised Emerson to move against the Kola. "If we don't go further north," Campbell warned Emerson, "my marines are going to get sent ashore behind NATO lines." While that would ensure an easy, uncontested administrative landing, it also meant to Campbell that his men would be wasted plugging gaps in the line or taking on the Russians in frontal attacks. The II MEF commander, who had choppered ashore to Bardufoss in the evening of 20 July to meet Bjol, considered COMNON "an able commander, but a guy who's all but drooling over the idea of getting his hands on my marines." Campbell wanted his troops "deposited on a beach, any goddamned beach, *behind* the Soviet front. If we aren't going to land on an enemy shore, why have we spent so much money building up our amphibious capability?" Nor did COMMARINSTRIKFOR demonstrate any concern about the dangers of the Soviets driving the Norwegians from their Fortress Norway positions. "The further south the sons-of-bitches drive," Campbell told Bjol, "the deeper shit they'll be in when I come ashore."

Campbell and his staff had drawn up a plan that called for landings in the Altafjord and the Porsangenfjord. To cover such an amphibious operation, Emerson's Striking Fleet would have to round the North Cape.

Emerson's strike ops staff had been developing their attack scheme for the Kola since the afternoon of 19 July. As directed by COMSTRIKFLTLANT, the objectives of the operation were "to destroy Soviet naval and air power at its bases and to shift the focus of the air war from north Norway to the Kola." While Carrier Air Wings 6 and 7 from the *Forrestal* and *Eisenhower* would bear the main burden of the attack, the Striking Fleet's cruise missile-armed cruisers and destroyers, American Tomahawk-armed SSNs, and land-based air assets would also support the offensive.

By the morning of the twenty-first, the strike ops staffers had completed their planning. The British and American attack submarines were already in position, having spent the last several days working their way north into the Barents Sea, clearing a path for the carriers. Off Tromso, the American carriers were already within range of the Kola. But Emerson wanted to get closer: "It's just a matter of moving a bit to the north and east as we swing on an arc around the North Cape," he noted. At 1120, Emerson ordered the shift north to begin. In the meantime, he set to work to get the OK from SACLANT, and support from COMSUBEASTLANT and COMNON for the operation.

The early afternoon hours passed slowly for Emerson as he nervously awaited SACLANT's response. At 1345 a helicopter arrived from Bardufoss carrying Bjol's air deputy. COMNON was less than enthusiastic about the plan. He wanted to know why Emerson wanted "to rock the boat and run additional risks" when things seemed to be going NATO's way. Despite Emerson's best efforts, and those of his staff, he could not convince the Norwegian of the wisdom of the operation. But that became academic at 1415 when a message arrived from Norfolk: SACLANT, after conferring with SACEUR and CINCHAN, signaled that the major NATO commanders supported the operation.

Emerson knew that he was running risks and that after the war there would be a great deal of debate about his decision to attack the Kola. "You know," he confided to his chief of staff, "I'm not gonna be able to win on this one no matter what happens." If the plan failed, and the Soviets sank several American carriers, Emerson would become the scapegoat for a failed campaign, or, worse yet, a lost war. Historians would portray the operation as unnecessarily risky and a potentially escalatory step. "I can see it all now. I'll be at some conference, assuming I survive, and some armchair strategist will be up at the podium telling us all that my move was a foolhardy gamble with irreplaceable forces, undertaken to prove some point about what had always been a foolish and incredible risky pseudo-strategy—the U.S. Navy's so-called Maritime Strategy of the 1980s."

Whatever the ultimate outcome, Emerson and the major NATO commanders knew that the decision to strike the Kola represented the logical continuation of the campaign on the northern flank. When asked by the secretary of defense about the plan, ADM Taylor responded: "Going north against the Kola has been part of our concept of operations for that flank for nearly fifty years." ADM Hill-Norton considered Emerson's plan "perfectly in step with NATO's long-standing, decades-old concept of maritime operations." As for SACEUR, GEN Sexton trusted "the judgment of Taylor and Hill-Norton, and when they say that in their professional opinion the attack on the Kola is the best way, even if seemingly indirect, to positively influence the air and ground battles for north Norway, that's good enough for me." Codenamed "Rampant Weevil," the attack on the Kola was to begin at 2200, by which time the *America* task force would be within range of most of the Soviet airfields in the western half of the Kola.

★ ★ ★

At 2110, as STRIKFLTLANT prepared for offensive action, NATO AWACS detected large flights of Soviet aircraft leaving their bases at Olenegorsk and Schagui in the Kola. The airfields, with their 4,600 meter runways, were the two main bases from which the SNA's Tu-22M Backfires flew. "To my mind," VADM Emerson told his staff, "the reports from the AWACS indicate that the Russians are getting ready to strike our carriers."

By the time the Hawkeyes of VAQ 132 and VAQ 140 picked up the Soviet bombers at 2130, Emerson had reinforced his CAP with substantial numbers of Tomcats and Hornets from his two carriers. Emerson had over fifty fighters and four Prowlers airborne and considered it "a pleasure to see the Russians paying some attention to us again."

Six ECM-equipped Tu-16 Badgers, but no fighters, accompanied the thirty-eight Backfires that streaked toward the Striking Fleet. A Hawkeye detected the Soviets about 350 miles from the carriers and vectored the Tomcats to the intercept. The resultant air battle developed over northern Norway. The aerial engagement was confusing at times, but before long it was clear that the Russians were taking a beating. Phoenix-armed Tomcats downed fifteen Soviet bombers during the initial intercept. Six Backfires penetrated the outer air battle ring but quickly fell victim to a score of Sparrow- and Sidewinder-armed Hornets. The remaining attackers aborted and returned to their bases in the Kola. "We didn't lose a plane," Emerson radioed Taylor, "not a single goddamned plane, not a one." Undeterred, the Striking Fleet continued steaming on a northeasterly course.

The failed Soviet attack marked the successful conclusion of the initial stage of "Rampant Weevil." The operation plan had several phases. The first was essentially a passive, defensive phase, one of movement to contact. Emerson and his staff expected that the Striking Fleet's shift north would be detected and would provoke a Soviet response. "We want their attention fixed on our carriers and on the threat from the west," Emerson explained to the staff, "because we intend to hit them next from the south with land-based air and really stretch their defenses and their control system." Moreover, an early strike conducted by the Soviets before the carriers moved too deeply into the Barents Sea would allow COMSTRIK-FLTLANT "to get a good feel for what the Russians could throw at us up there." If the pressure proved to be too great, Emerson was prepared to "head back south with our tails between our legs and run for cover." Emerson's staff prepared a contingency plan that called for the establishment of a carrier haven in the Westfjord. He was prepared "to put two carriers in there, mine them in to protect them from Russian subs, and line the fjord walls with SAMs."

The second phase called for the participation of land-based air assets flying from bases in north Norway. Again, the plans were tentative. AWACS would monitor the Soviet response and if Soviet air defense forces responded quickly and in strength, the raiders would abort. If the defense proved hesitant or weak, the attacking squadrons would strike SAM installations and airbases in the southwestern Kola.

Shortly after the commencement of the second phase of the operation, the American SSNs *San Juan*, *Groton*, and *Newport News*, operating in the Barents Sea, would conduct Tomahawk cruise missile strikes against critical Kola airbases, such as the Backfire and Blackjack airfields at Olenegorsk and Schagui. As the ground-hugging Tomahawks raced for their targets, pairs of low-flying strike aircraft—A-6E Intruders and F/A-18 Hornets—would begin making their way toward the Kola, some overflying north Norway, others coming in from the sea. CARSTRIKGRU 1's additional air assets—Hawkeyes, Prowlers, Hornets armed with HARM anti-radar missiles, Tomcats, and tankers—would support the attack by flying control, jamming, suppression, and interception missions.

"The general thrust of 'Rampant Weevil'" Emerson explained to his staff, "is to work our way across the Kola from west to east, taking out SAM sites and airfields as we go." Critical installations and assets, such as the few runways capable of handling Backfires and Blackjacks, phased array radar sites, and airborne warning and control aircraft, were targeted for specialized attack.

How long the air offensive against the Kola would last depended on how well its initial phases succeeded. If loss rates were high, the attack would have to be halted and the carriers would steam back south. But as long as the attacks yielded substantial results, results that offset the rate of loss, Emerson intended to continue the strikes until the Northwest Front's air assets and command and control structure had been destroyed. "Then," he told his staff, "I'll drop Bull Campbell's marines ashore and support his ass all the way to Archangelsk."

At the minimum, Emerson believed that his offensive would force the Soviets to concentrate their air assets defensively over the Kola. "As long as I keep the battle going up there," Emerson told COMNON, "our land-based air will have the skies to itself over north Norway, just as the expected Russian ground offensive's about to begin, so that even if I retire, I'll have secured you at least temporary air superiority."

★★★

Effective preliminary attacks against the major Soviet strike aircraft bases at Olenegorsk and Schagui were critical to the success of "Rampant Weevil." "We want to neutralize the airfields where the Russians Backfires are based," Emerson had directed his staff early in the planning stage, "That won't guarantee the success of our attacks, but it'll limit what the Soviets can do against the battle-group while we're up north in the Barents Sea."

The initial plan assigned this neutralization task to the American SSNs operating off the Kola coast. The cruise missile-armed submarines would launch TLAM-C BGM-109D and F Tomahawks against Olenegorsk and Schagui. The "D" version of the Tomahawk carried submunitions that were effective against unprotected targets, such as aircraft on runways. The "F" version was designed to destroy the runways themselves.

At 1830 on the twenty-first, LTG Elwood "Bud" Harter, commanding all U.S. Air Force assets in north Norway, learned of the navy's plan to take out the Soviets' major bomber bases in the Kola. Harter immediately contacted Emerson and offered COMSTRIK-FLTLANT the services of two of his F-117A Stealth Fighters. Armed with a pair of French-made Matra Durandals—retarded bombs fitted with rockets that drove the hard steel-jacketed warhead deep into a target before detonation—the F-117As were perfectly suited to the mission as conceived.

Emerson gratefully accepted Harter's offer. COMSTRIKFLT-LANT assumed that the offer was political and that the air force did not want to get left out of the big show in the event that it proved to be a success. As for Emerson, his primary concerns were for the success of the mission and he was "damned glad to have the services of a weapons system that they had and we didn't."

On 20 July, a pair of the F-117As had flown from CONUS to Evenes. Harter's and Emerson's staffs worked the two aircraft into the plan, assigning a plane each against Olenegorsk and Schagui. "I knew that they were the only two F-117As I was likely to get for the whole war," Harter recognized, "but I felt that this was it, that we were reaching the moment of decision in the air and that the Stealth fighters weren't doing anyone any good on the ground." With the Soviets' attention probably focused on the navy's carriers operating to the west of the Kola, the F-117A Nighthawks striking from the south could expect "the element of surprise to reinforce their stealthiness."

At 2205 on the twenty-first, the F-117As took off from Evenes and flew east. MAJ Thomas S. Rikers flew the northernmost F-117A: objective Olenegorsk. West of the Soviet air defense force base at Alakurti, Rikers ran into problems: three patrolling fighters— Su-27s—directed by a Mainstay. Rikers's efforts to evade detection failed. The Mainstay picked him up and directed the Sukhois to intercept. Rikers knew that he would never make it to Olenegorsk. He dove for the hard deck but failed to elude his pursuers. A near miss jarred the craft badly and smoke began to fill the cockpit. Rikers knew he could not make it back to friendly lines, so he turned to port to head for Sweden. As the damaged Nighthawk struggled south, the starboard engine exploded. There was nothing Rikers could do but bail out. Both pilot and the remnants of the plane fell into Soviet hands.

CAPT John Lansing, piloting the southern F-117A, fared better, possibly because Rikers's travails to the north kept the Russians busy. The second Nighthawk streaked toward Schagui over the Gulf of Kandalaska. The plane came out of nowhere and before the alarm had sounded, ground personnel could see parachutes descending toward the runway. Once the bombs hung vertically, their rocket motors fired and the Durandals drove themselves through the runway. A tremendous explosion lifted great sections of concrete and several planes into the air. Lansing had executed his mission well, dropping his Durandals at two different points during a vertical run along the runway. He escaped unscathed and landed at Evenes an hour-and-a-half later.

While the two Nighthawks kept the Soviet air defense off balance, a lone U.S. Air Force interceptor, reportedly a F-15C Eagle, swept over the Kola. Department of Defense officials and those involved with the mission refused either to identify the aircraft and pilot or to comment on reports that the plane overflew northern Sweden. "We flew over Lapland, that's all I can say," Harter told a reporter. Apparently entering Soviet air space from the east, the American fighter managed to get within Sparrow range of the southern Mainstay and downed the Soviet AWACS.

Soviet air defenses were still recovering from these shocks when a second full-scale strike developed from the south. Thirty-three U.S. Air Force F-16 Falcons and RAF Buccaneers streaked toward the Kola. With the Soviet's southern Mainstay a pile of wreckage on the tundra, the air defense effort in the southern Kola was rather feeble. Within minutes the NATO strike aircraft had hit forward frontal aviation airfields, nearby mobile and fixed SAM batteries in Finnish Lapland at Rovaniemi and Vuojarvi, and the air defense force base at Alakurti. Two Falcons and two Buccaneers failed to return from the mission; nine Soviet interceptors were shot down and at least a dozen aircraft of various types were destroyed on the ground.

As the Soviets reacted to the raids from the south, Emerson's carriers launched their preliminary strikes from the northwest. Two pairs of F/A-18 Hornets, one each from the *Forrestal* and *Eisenhower*, dashed east. Their job was to penetrate the Kola's air defenses and to go all out for the two AWACS the Soviets kept airborne over the Kola, and to down them with Sparrows. Emerson advised the pilots involved, all volunteers, that there was a good chance "these will be, pretty much, one-way missions."

Emerson had long believed that the Russian's centralized ground control system was their Achilles heel. In his view, the Russians suffered from doctrinal, qualitative, and quantitative weaknesses. He told his staff planners, "KAL-007, that West German kid who landed his Cessna in Red Square, these incidents convince me that Soviet air defenses are grossly overrated. We and the Israelis have flown against Russian IADS [integrated air defense systems] in Vietnam and the Middle East, and, while such defenses raised the attrition rate for the attacker, I can't think of a single instance where we were prevented from doing a job that could be considered critical, and frequently we were able to get in and get out without too much trouble, as we did in Libya in 1986."

One of the Soviet Union's greatest weaknesses was its lack of airborne warning and control aircraft (AWACS). The production of the Soviet Mainstay AWACS version of their Il-76 had progressed slowly throughout the 1980s. The aircraft was also markedly inferior to the American E-3C Sentry AWACS, at best being on par with the U.S. Navy's E-2C Hawkeye. Moreover, the Soviets had only twenty Mainstays, of which at the start of the war, four each were deployed in the far north, the German front, the Southwest Front, the Far East, and around Moscow as a reserve. During the first week of the war, two Mainstays had been lost over Germany, two had been destroyed in the Far East, and a third had crashed because of pilot error.

By comparison, the U.S. Navy deployed sixty Hawkeyes with the fleet, the U.S. Air Force controlled thirty-four Sentrys, and the NATO nations, collectively and individually, maintained another twenty. With five Sentrys controlled by Saudi Arabia in the Middle East, and ten Hawkeyes in the hands of the Japanese, the allies had a total of 129 AWACS aircraft—six times the force of the Soviet Union. On the northern flank, the Russians' four Mainstays faced eighteen Hawkeyes, four U.S. Air Force Sentrys, and four NATO AWACS.

Emerson hoped to capitalize on this alliance advantage. "Some people might think I'm nuts," Emerson admitted, "but I'm sure that if we can drive his Mainstays from the sky and keep him off balance by launching raids from all directions and all altitudes, that we'll wipe up the Kola."

With one of the four Soviet Mainstays downed as the offensive began, and with the weak response to COMNON's opening raid from the south, COMSTRIKFLTLANT's expectations began to look "well nigh reasonable." By 2315 both Mainstays had been destroyed. Of the four naval aviators who flew the anti-AWACS missions, one was killed when his Hornet exploded during a dogfight as he attempted to penetrate the Kola IADS. Another was shot down and captured near Murmansk. The third destroyed the southernmost Il-76 just as it became airborne to replace the one downed earlier by the U.S. Air Force F-15. The navy pilot, his Hornet badly damaged in an aerial engagement in which he also destroyed a

Su-27 Flanker, crash landed in Sweden where he was interned. The fourth aviator downed the northern Mainstay and returned safely to the *Forrestal*. All four pilots received the Navy Cross.

★ ★ ★

As the final minutes of 21 July ticked off, the air defense system in the Kola was in total disarray. Confusion and chaos reigned at air defense headquarters at Archangelsk. The integrity of the Soviet air defenses had been lost and the allied air offensive was only just beginning. By 2340, Soviet controllers knew that the Kola was under both air and cruise missile attack.

The American SSNs *San Juan*, *Groton*, and *Newport News*, launched over a score of Tomahawks against key Soviet airbases and installations. The *Groton* fired four TLAM Tomahawks, and the *San Juan* and *Newport News* fired twelve each from their vertical launch tubes. Eight each were targeted against Schagui and Olenegorsk, while four each went after Northwest Front headquarters at Murmansk, fleet headquarters at Severomorsk, and the phased array radar site at Kirovsk.

Many prewar critics had termed American cruise missile attacks against the Kola, that is, against Soviet territory, a dangerous escalatory step. As one civilian defense analyst wrote, "what if the Soviets assume that the Tomahawks are the nuclear version and launch their own atomic arsenal in response?"

Emerson dismissed such concerns, raised by one of his staff during the planning. It was true that the Soviets could not be certain what kind of warheads the Tomahawks carried, but, Emerson argued, "how the hell are they going to know what kind of bombs I've strapped on my Intruders? How the hell do I know what kind of warheads are on their air-to-surface missiles when they fire them at my carriers?" "You judge an attack within a context," Emerson pointed out, "and our attack on the Kola won't have any of the marks of an atomic strike; it'll look like a conventional attack and I doubt that any of the Russians sitting up there in the Kola will think that it's anything but a conventional attack."

About the only certainty Soviet air defense controllers had as "Rampant Weevil" began, was that the NATO attack was clearly conventional. As to the operation's scope and intensity, the Russians were quickly succumbing to confusion. Soviet air and ground defense forces responded poorly to the strikes and although several Tomahawks were either downed, successfully countered electronically, or simply malfunctioned, a least a single missile struck all the targets. At Severomorsk and Murmansk, damage was superficial, but nevertheless added to the confusion. All eight Tomahawks hit the airbase at Schagui. Two hit Olenegorsk causing substantial, but repairable damage to the runways. Five Tomahawks caused extensive damage to the radar facility at Kirovsk. Thus, as the major attack of the day began, both major SNA airbases, a critically important phased array radar site, and three of the AADS's four Mainstays were out of operation. As the offensive developed, the Soviets in the Kola were blinded and unable to strike back with anything other than their old Badgers.

No sooner had reports estimating the damage done by the Tomahawk strikes begun to reach the air defense sector headquarters at Archangelsk, than strike aircraft from the *Forrestal* and *Eisenhower* were over the Kola. MAJ Vladimir Krivonogov hurriedly sorted through messages. "It's clear we're getting hit by a big attack; some of the aircraft are coming in from the sea, others from the mountain passes of north Norway." The area between the Norwegian-Soviet border and the Tuloma River bore the brunt of the initial strikes. Frontal aviation, naval aviation, and air defense force airfields and nearby SAM installations at Pechenga, Salmiyaur, Koshkayaur, Murmashi, Murmansk, and Severomorsk were hit hard and many aircraft were caught and destroyed on the ground.

Throughout the twenty-second of July, the raids continued without cease. COMNON, despite the massive Sixth Army offensive that began during the course of the day, made a handful of NATO fighters and strike aircraft available for raids on the Kola to keep some pressure on Soviet defenses from the south. At 1000, aircraft from the *America*'s air wing joined in as the offensive spread over the entire peninsula. COMSTRIKFLTLANT's official reports for 21-23 July indicate that attacking aircraft hit runways, hardened aircraft shelters, fuel and ammunition dumps, SAM and radar sites, naval facilities, rail yards, bridges, command posts, and myriad targets.

About 1700, Emerson and his strike ops staff reviewed reports from attacking aircraft, photo-reconnaissance flights, and scattered intelligence intercepts. NATO losses had been relatively light. CAR-

STRIKGRU 1's two air wings had lost only sixteen aircraft; COM-NON's squadrons had lost seven. The allied strikes seemed to have heavily damaged and nearly disintegrated the Soviet's integrated air defense system. Nevertheless, Emerson's staff considered the reports from attack pilots over-optimistic. Post-strike F-14 TARPS photo-recon missions indicated that while the attacks had clearly been effective, they had not been decisive. "You rarely permanently destroy a SAM site or one of those double-thick Russian runways with a single strike," Emerson admitted, "and results, even when good, are frequently incomplete." The TARPS photos revealed a rather uniform picture of "targets hit hard, 80 percent destroyed, but still requiring a return mission to finish off." Nevertheless, COMSTRIKFLTLANT signalled SACLANT: "'Rampant Weevil' unqualified success: continued offensive operations likely to yield decisive results."

Eager to complete the offensive as quickly as possible, Emerson ordered that the number of Hornets allocated to interception missions over the Kola be reduced and the dual-role aircraft instead be assigned strike tasks. "CARSTRIKGRU 1's casualties have been comparatively light," Emerson reasoned, "but they've lost nearly 20 percent of their Intruders and Hornets thus far in the campaign." With the *America*'s air wing joining the offensive and with a higher proportion of the *Forrestal*'s and *Eisenhower*'s F/A-18s flying ground-attack missions, Emerson hoped to generate the striking power to "wrap things up." To replace the Hornets that had been flying fighter missions as "guardian angels" over the Kola, Emerson ordered COMCARSTRIKGRU 1 to shift Tomcats from combat air patrols over the carriers to an air superiority role over the Kola. The decision, Emerson readily admitted, was a gamble. By the evening of 22 July, Emerson was not playing the Soviets honest.

As Emerson well knew from fragmentary but "near conclusive" evidence, the Russians were growing desperate. At 0540 on the morning of 22 July, GEN Golikov, stung by the scope and effectiveness of the NATO attacks, as well as by "near hysterical communications from Moscow," ordered ADM Obnorsky "to use all resources—air, surface, and subsurface—to destroy attacking American carrier groups."

By 0900, the Northern Fleet KPF had vectored three Soviet SSNs and three diesel boats toward the American carriers. But the

Striking Fleet was well screened. COMSUBEASTLANT had deployed eight SSNs—*La Jolla*, *Phoenix*, *Conqueror*, *Spartan*, *Whale*, *San Juan*, *Newport News*, and *Groton*—into the Barents Sea. Four Norwegian Type-207s—*Ula*, *Stord*, *Sklinna*, and *Stadt*—patrolled the coast. In a duel off the Kola, a Soviet SSN sank the American submarine *Phoenix*. But by 1400, the *San Juan*, *Whale*, *Groton*, and *Ula* had each torpedoed and destroyed a Soviet submarine; the *Spartan* had sunk two.

The failure of the Northern Fleet's submarines to penetrate the allied SSN and diesel boat patrol line off the Kola was for ADM Obnorsky a double blow. Not only had his vaunted subsurface arm again proved unable to engage and destroy an American carrier, but their inability to at least weaken the enemy screening forces meant that Soviet surface strike groups now had to run a gauntlet of enemy submarines before reaching attack positions from which they could conduct operations against the Americans.

At GEN Golikov's insistence, Obnorsky ordered all of his remaining surface combatants to sea. The Northwest Front commander brushed aside a hesitant Obnorsky's remonstrances concerning the deterrent value of a fleet in being. "Deterrent?" an enraged Golikov responded, "they're sitting right out there off the Kola and they just bombed the shit out of my headquarters. Get your ships to sea or I'll order your men to the front in Norway."

By noon, two Northern Fleet surface strike groups, an ASW group, and a handful of support ships had sortied from Pechenga fjord. The still somewhat impressive force included the battlecruiser *Frunze*, eight cruisers, four destroyers, seven frigates, a tanker and a replenishment ship.

About 1730 the lead Soviet ASW group began a running battle with screening NATO submarines off the Varangerfjord. Within thirty minutes, three *Kashin*-class destroyers had been torpedoed: the *Obraztsovy* sunk by the *Spartan*; the *Smetlivy* torpedoed and damaged by the *Whale*; and the *Krasny Krim* left dead in the water after a Harpoon attack by the *Newport News*. Nevertheless, the Soviet ASW group succeeded where the submarines had failed. Two powerful surface strike groups penetrated COMSUBEASTLANT's patrol line and steamed at high speed toward CARSTRIKGRU 1.

The presence of the NATO submarine screen so far north had nevertheless retarded the movement of the Soviet surface striking groups. By 1800 it became clear at Northern Fleet headquarters in Severomorsk that it would be midnight or perhaps early on the twenty-third before a surface engagement developed. Obnorsky had planned to commit his SNA assets simultaneously with the surface attack, but his staff now advised him that "in a few more hours there will be no air striking force remaining to conduct such an attack." The SNA strikes would have to be mounted in isolation.

Obnorsky's staff labored throughout the afternoon to formulate a coherent plan in the midst of a rapidly deteriorating situation. The staff planners would draw up a scheme of attack that included bombers from a base only to learn minutes later that the base had been struck and the runway cratered or the planes destroyed on the ground. Nonetheless, by scraping up all the remaining Badgers at operational Kola airfields as well as some Backfires and Blackjacks that had been airborne at the time of the initial attacks and had been diverted to alternate bases east of Archangelsk, the Northern Fleet staff was able to put together a sizable force of over forty strike aircraft. At Golikov's direction, the Archangelsk air defense sector promised to support the strike by providing escorts for the bombers as they made their way west toward the American carriers.

The hastily drafted and often amended plan quickly came unraveled. Only a handful of air defense force fighters were able to disengage from the battle raging over the Kola and join the bombers. Many of the SNA bombers fell victim to American Hornets and Tomcats over the Kola. The few planes that escaped the raging aerial inferno over the peninsula were downed by F-14s flying combat air patrols in the outer air battle zone around the American carriers.

One group of subsonic Tu-16G Badgers flying from Ostrov Kilden got lucky, avoided interception over the Kola, and flew north toward the Arctic before swinging west and then south, making its approach toward the American carriers from the northwest. MAJ Maxim "Mad Max" Kotovodov led the remnant of an Soviet SNA regiment—thirteen Badgers flying just above the crest of the waves, a flight profile "atypical" for the thirty-year-old strike planes. The demands on the pilots during such a long mission were tremendous. One of the Badgers struck the surface and exploded.

Kotovodov's good fortune held. As the Soviet strike aircraft came within four hundred miles of the American carriers, one of the patrolling Hawkeyes suffered an engine loss and was forced to return to the *Eisenhower* before a replacement aircraft arrived. COMCARSTRIKGRU 1 shifted his remaining airborne E-2Cs to cover the now vacant patrol area looking east along the most probable threat axis, leaving the approaches from the northwest momentarily unpatrolled. Undetected, the Badgers continued on their way.

The task before Kotovodov remained daunting. The AS-6 Kingfish anti-ship missiles had an impressive range of over 150 miles when released from low altitude, but the Soviets' Short Horn radar could pick out large targets at no more than 60 miles, and then only under ideal conditions. With no Bear patrol aircraft or surface ships to guide him to the target, Kotovodov had no choice but to do his own searching, no picnic in a high-threat environment.

As the Badgers neared the area where pre-mission briefings had indicated the American carriers ought to be, Kotovodov led his regiment into a shallow climb to get a better view. The Soviets immediately found that they had popped up right into the missile envelope of the *Ticonderoga*-class Aegis cruiser *Leyte Gulf*. The American ship's SPY-1A air search radar detected the Badgers at a range of forty miles and within seconds SM2MR missiles were leaving the tubes of the cruiser's two Mk 41 vertical launchers. Kotovodov ignored the threat and continued south. He reasoned that an Aegis cruiser had to be protecting a carrier. Over the next minute, American missiles destroyed five of the Badgers despite evasive maneuvers and extensive electronic countermeasures. Then suddenly Kotovodov's radar operator reported a large contact due south. Kotovodov, "smelling a carrier," gave his final order without hesitation, directing all surviving Badgers to fire both their Kingfish missiles at the target. "There's no time to spare," Kotovodov told his co-pilot. Ten AS-6 air-to-surface missiles streaked toward the "large contact"—the carrier *Forrestal*. The carrier's point defense systems and SAMS fired by the *Leyte Gulf* downed six, but four Kingfish ASMs struck the *Forrestal*'s port side. From his perch in primary flight control, one sailor saw the flight deck lift up and peel back as the Soviet 10,800 pound warheads detonated. Seconds later, a series of explosions ripped through the *Forrestal*'s hangar deck as fuel and ordnance ignited. Damage control parties struggled heroically to control the fires but, despite their efforts, the *Forrestal*'s commanding officer had no choice but to report to COMCARSTRIKGRU 1 that his carrier was "out of action foreseeable future." With all its boilers flooded, the crippled ship remained dead in the water until 2300 when it was taken under tow by the destroyer *Richard E. Byrd*.

Eleven Soviet airmen were rescued, including Kotovodov. As the ranking officer, he was subjected to some rather pointed interrogation. The Americans seemed certain that the Russians had come from somewhere other than the Kola. In fact, the surprise attack from the northwest led to speculation by Emerson's staff that the Soviets had lengthened the runway at Longyearbyen on Spitsbergen Island, which had been seized by a Spetsnaz detachment landed from a diesel submarine on 15 July. Kotovodov sensed the Americans bewilderment and saw no reason to lessen their uncertainty. When the interrogators continued to press him, he feigned exhaustion and finally answered, "We came from Shangri-la."

★ ★ ★

For VADM Emerson, the operational loss of the *Forrestal* came at an inopportune moment in the battle. The presence of the two Soviet surface strike groups rounding the North Cape could no longer be ignored and only minutes before he received word of the *Forrestal*'s demise, Emerson ordered his entire air effort shifted from the Kola to anti-ship missions against the developing surface threat. Suddenly, Emerson's entire concept of operation was coming undone. COMSTRIKFLTLANT ordered his task forces to retrace their steps to the south. At 0030, he ordered the *Forrestal* "cut loose" by the *Richard E. Byrd*. Abandoned, the burning hulk was left for the Russians; in a way, a fiery monument to their success. During the Second World War, torpedoes launched from escorting destroyers had usually been necessary to dispatch heavily damaged Japanese or American carriers to the bottom. "But we don't have any destroyers with anti-surface torpedo capability," Emerson lamented, "and we can't afford to waste surface-to-surface missiles on the hulk. We'll have to leave the wreck behind." The burning carrier was, in fact, spotted by a Soviet destroyer in the early hours of 23 July and the report of the sighting sent a cheer through the Northern Fleet's striking force.

The euphoria was short-lived. At 0245, NATO aircraft turned their attention to the approaching Soviet surface groups. Land-based U.S. Air Force B-52Gs (armed with Harpoon anti-ship mis-

siles) flying from Loring Air Force Base in Maine, and RAF Buccaneers and Norwegian Falcons from Bardufoss, supported the efforts of Emerson's naval air wings in the developing battle off the
Norwegian coast. At 0300, Intruders and Hornets from the carrier
Abraham Lincoln, which, though still out of range of the Kola, had
reached a position three hundred miles southwest of the North
Cape, joined those from the *Eisenhower* and *America* in an effort
to destroy Obnorsky's surface strike groups before they could engage the NATO Striking Fleet.

By 0400, for the loss of eight aircraft, including a pair of
B-52s, seven Soviet cruisers, three destroyers, three frigates, and
two replenishment ships had been sunk. The *Kirov*-class battlecruiser *Frunze* had exploded following an attack with Harpoons
and laser-guided bombs by A-6E Intruders from the *America*. Only
the cruiser *Kursk*, the destroyer *Burny*, and four frigates escaped
destruction and continued south.

About 0415, a thirty-minute-long surface action began. The
Soviets struck first, mortally wounding the cruiser *South Carolina*
and sinking the destroyer *Richard E. Byrd* in a well executed attack.
The American riposte proved equally effective. Harpoons and Tomahawks completed the destruction of the Northern Fleet and ended
whatever hopes Obnorsky and Golikov had of destroying the Striking Fleet or driving it from the Barents Sea. "The Russians have
come out and fought," Emerson noted in a report to SACLANT,
"they have been engaged by the entire gamut of NATO air and naval
assets and have been destroyed." For all intents and purposes, the
battle for sea control in the North Atlantic was over. The Soviet
Northern Fleet, except for its SSBNs, had ceased to exist as a fighting force.

★ ★ ★

Having disposed of the Northern Fleet's surface striking groups,
Emerson directed COMCARSTRIKGRUs 1, the *Eisenhower*, and 2,
the *America* and *Abraham Lincoln*, to resume operations against
Soviet bases in the Kola. With three carriers again in hand, COM-
STRIKFLTLANT was determined to "complete our victory up north
and revenge the loss of the *Forrestal*." Intelligence reports seemed
to indicate that the Soviets had moved some additional aircraft to
bases on the peninsula and there was some concern on the Striking

Fleet staff that the pause in operations might have allowed the Soviets to overcome many of the losses of the twenty-first and twenty-second. But Emerson was insistent. The offensive would resume.

The raids began about 0730 and continued throughout the day. Soviet air defenses remained porous. By mid-afternoon NATO aircraft roamed freely over the Kola and completed the destruction of the peninsula's air defense system, while bombing communication and transportation sites. Some aircraft were even assigned targets of opportunity. By the twilight that passed for evening in the far north, Soviet opposition had become negligible. "Rampant Weevil" was over, judged by Emerson in his report to SACLANT: "an unqualified and complete success."

The Striking Fleet's Kola offensive, while successful, had nevertheless been costly. The *Forrestal* had sunk, and by the evening of 23 July, NATO had 91 fewer aircraft (including the 70 planes and helicopters that went down with the carrier). But the Soviets had lost another half-dozen submarines, the remainder of their surface fleet, and well over 350 aircraft. More than 250 planes had been destroyed on the ground. The few aircraft that survived withdrew to airfields east of Archangelsk.

Although these Soviet aircraft continued to fly CAP and interception missions over the Kola in an attempt to protect vital strategic bases (which for the most part had purposefully escaped NATO attack) and the rear areas of the Sixth Army operating in north Norway, VADM Emerson considered his operational goals achieved. "The Kola basing infrastructure," he informed SACLANT, "will not, for at least a fortnight, be able to support offensive operations in the North Atlantic or northern Norway. I've ordered the Striking Fleet to steam south and to provide direct support to COMNON."

TWENTY-SEVEN

As the surface battle raged off the North Cape in the early morning hours of 23 July, the Soviet Sixth Army resumed its offensive to the south. LTG Berdiaev demanded of his troops their "last ounce of strength for a final effort to crush the enemy." Reports of NATO withdrawals along the front convinced the Sixth Army commander that the Fortress Norway position was about to give way.

Indeed, LTG Bjol ordered a "tactical retrograde" movement along the entire line. His troops were exhausted; his reserves were few; his supplies were dwindling. Bjol believed that if he did not pull back his battered battalions, the Soviets would eventually punch a hole through the front and push a mechanized column south. Fortunately, complete control of the air enabled Bjol to disengage his forces, to slow the Soviet pursuit, and to prevent the retreat of his tired troops from becoming a rout.

As Bjol's forces fell back, COMNON himself scrambled to free reserves for the front. He called on LTG Gysae to speed the recapture of Harstad and BG Watson to complete the elimination of the 76th Guards Airborne Division at Bodo and to reopen the E6 northward.

But the principal object of Bjol's search for reinforcements was COMSTRIKFLT's American, British, and Dutch marines—nine fresh battalions, an entire division-equivalent. At 0940, COMNON requested that LTG Campbell fly to Bardufoss to discuss the commitment of 8 MEB and the UK-NL amphibious force.

Campbell, at VADM Emerson's direction, promptly departed the *Mount Whitney* and at 1105 arrived at COMNON's headquarters. To Campbell, the haggard Bjol had the "look of a defeated man, a man grasping for straws, a man looking for some way to get his hands on my people." The Norwegian commander wanted Campbell's marines to land at Tromso where they could secure the important harbor and airfield and also threaten the right flank of the Soviet advance along the E6. Campbell dismissed such a scheme out of hand. "No, no, that's too close to the front; there's no room there for maneuver. Sorry, no go."

Pushing several Norwegian officers out of the way, Campbell took command of the situation map and proceeded to give COM-

NON an ad hoc briefing. "We're coming ashore here, tomorrow morning," Campbell informed Bjol, pointing to Alta and Banak, "deep in the Russian rear." As he completed his briefing, he gestured with a pointer: "We're gonna stick it up his ass!"

Bjol just shook his head. "The threat's too remote from the front to provide immediate assistance. By the time you're ashore I'll have been forced back beyond Bardufoss."

All eyes were fixed on Campbell, who just shrugged, and in his worst French remarked, "C'est la guerre." Bjol stood drop-jawed, astonished by the comment, unable to speak.

Finally, Campbell turned to the Norwegian captain who served as translator. "Look, tell your general that when my people go ashore up north, the Russian drive is going to stop dead in its tracks; so all he's got to do is to hold on for twenty-four hours." As the captain completed the translation, Campbell again turned toward the map. "Can't you hold here," he asked, slamming his fist on the junction where the road from Tromso intersected with the E6, "just for a day?" Bjol studied the map for a while, nodded, turned toward Campbell, and offered his hand to the American, The two men shook hands, and five minutes later the II MEF commander was airborne.

* * *

Throughout the day, Bjol's men continued their retreat while Muratov's 45th and Pisarev's 54th MRDs launched concentric attacks toward Skibotn. At 1230, Norwegians of the Alta Battlegroup pulled out of the key road junction where the E78 and E6 met and about thirty minutes later advance elements of the two Soviet divisions made contact with each other in the town.

The capture of Skibotn convinced Berdiaev that victory was at hand. "Collapse of enemy front imminent," the Sixth Army commander signaled Northwest Front headquarters. At Murmansk, such reports renewed hopes for success. "The navy's performed poorly and the air forces have taken a beating," a cheered GEN Golikov told his staff, "but our army's undefeated, and it seems unstoppable."

Despite NATO's total command of the air, the Soviet advance continued. Norwegian rear guard detachments were routinely swept aside and at times the retreat nearly became a rout. At 2230 elements of the 45th MRD entered Kvesmenes at the head of the Lyngenfjord. By midnight, the 54th MRD's lead battalion had taken 1,596 meter-high Mt. Rostaf, while Muratov's advance elements had reached the Balsfjord and cut the road to Tromso.

The relentless Sixth Army advance gave new heart to the defenders of Harstad to whom relief began to appear increasingly likely. Throughout the twenty-third, intense fighting continued as two battalions of the Norwegian 15th Brigade and the West German Gebirgsjägers attempted to wrest the port town from its marine and airmobile brigade defenders. Ganenko was everywhere, rallying the men and leading counterattacks. Despite LTG Gysae's best efforts, and the support provided by NATO attack aircraft which continually bombed and strafed the defenders' positions, Harstad remained in Soviet hands at day's end.

Further south at Bodo, reports of the Sixth Army advance did little to cheer the remnants of the 76th Guards Airborne Division. With fewer than 1,500 men remaining to hold the airfield, MG Malygin recognized that he could do no more than delay the NATO forces now surrounding his command until his engineers had completed the destruction of the base's facilities and runways. When Front denied Malygin permission to carry out the demolitions, he was dumbfounded. He assumed that the order was expected to boost his morale and keep alive hopes for resupply and reinforcement. But the veteran paratrooper had no time for such games. Nor did he intend to allow the enemy to capture an intact airbase. He ignored the order.

At 0730 U.S. Marine Corps Intruders and Harriers struck Soviet positions around Bodo. At 0800 the artillery of the 10th Marines continued the barrage for another thirty minutes. Promptly at 0830 the main attack began with the 2d Battalion, 2d Marines, supported by M-60A3s of Company A, 2d Tank Battalion, driving directly along the road to Bodo. The 2d and 3d Battalions of the Norwegian 14th Brigade struck westward on the northern and southern flanks of the American assault. At 0900, the 10th Marines began firing smoke into the Soviet pocket. At 0910, the 3/2 Marines opened a direct assault on the airfield itself. LTG Watson reported: "Able Company came in from the south, amphibiously, across the Saltfjord, while Charlie Company moved by helicopter into positions to the west and north of Bodo."

Surrounded and pressed on all sides, Malygin's men put up a spirited, but short-lived resistance. They were short of everything except small arms ammunition, especially anti-tank rockets, and reports indicated that enemy heavy tanks had smashed their way through defensive positions and were nearing the airfield. Malygin, whose men had been fighting unsupported for ten days, decided that further resistance had become pointless. When his engineers confirmed that all demolitions had been completed, he sent two aides to the front of the 237th Regiment, to approach the Americans under a white flag to ask for a cease fire, pending an official surrender.

At 1210, Malygin met BG Watson at the latter's forward headquarters at Hopen. The Soviet division commander looked exhausted and Watson offered him some coffee. The two men then began to negotiate terms. Malygin wished only to surrender those troops actually fighting at Bodo, while Watson demanded that the entire 76th Guards Division surrender. Throughout the morning, the 1/2 Marines and the Norwegian 5th Brigade had struggled, with less than complete success, to clear the E6 of the remnants of the 234th and 239th Regiments which continued to block the road to the north of Bodo. Confronted by Watson's intransigence, and aware that further resistance by his exhausted men would prolong their suffering for little gain, Malygin felt he had no choice but to yield to the demands. At 1230, Malygin, with a marine escort, returned to his headquarters and ordered his entire division to lay down its arms.

The ten-day-long battle for Bodo had ended and the heavily damaged airbase was once again in NATO hands. By 1400, Norwegian troops of the 5th and 14th Brigades and American marines of 4 MEB were on the move, heading north along the E6 toward Fortress Norway. Alongside the road, tired, sullen Russian paratroopers, now prisoners of war, watched silently. Malygin himself was out amongst his men, cheering them up. "I know that for us the battle is over," he told his paratroopers, "but I believe that our sacrifices have not been in vain. The delays we've imposed on the enemy will cost them the campaign up north."

★ ★ ★

Indeed, the situation on the ground in COMNON in the early hours of 24 July appeared grave. Ammunition, especially for the Norwegian artillery batteries, was running short. At midnight, Bjol had been forced to commit his last reserve, the Luxembourgeois, to the front in an effort to hold the line. At Harstad, Ganenko's marines continued to resist Gysae's attacks. Watson's 4 MEB was still over a hundred kilometers south of Narvik, jamming the E6, along which the Norwegian resupply convoys were attempting to move. Aware of the increasingly desperate situation in COMNON, and concerned about the state of mind of its commander, GEN Peirse offered to fly to Bardufoss. Bjol, despite his near desperation earlier in the day, recommended that CINCNORTH remain at Kolsaas.

Bjol, surprisingly, had grown increasingly confident during the twenty-third. The roots of his optimism lay in the improved situation at sea. The Soviets could no longer prevent COMNON's resupply or reinforcement. "The SLOCs are open, wide open," he cheerfully told his staff. Three American ships, carrying supplies for II MEF, had reached Narvik late on the twenty-third. Small Norwegian freighters, loaded with ammunition, were already making their way north along the coast. The Striking Fleet's successes during the Kola offensive, and the return of the three American carriers to the support of operations in north Norway, had guaranteed COMNON complete mastery in the air. Moreover, Bjol was now convinced that Campbell's planned amphibious stroke deep in the Soviet rear would produce the results the American marine had projected.

Using amphibious and airmobile transport, Bull Campbell's marines began landing at the heads of the Altafjord and Porsangenfjord at 0230 on 24 July. Elements of the Dutch marines and Britain's 42 Commando went ashore at Alta, while 45 Commando conducted an airmobile assault on nearby Talvik. Harriers from the British carriers *Illustrious* and *Invincible* struck suspected Soviet positions ashore. Resistance was light, each locale being defended by a small, battalion-sized garrison of reservists from Murmansk. By 0500, both towns and the airfield at Alta were secure. The American marines of 8 MEB met even less resistance at Lakselv and in ninety minutes had captured the town and the nearby airfield at Banak.

At Northwest Front, the NATO amphibious landings came as a surprise, but not a shock. Given NATO's complete superiority in the air and at sea, Golikov had expected an amphibious landing but had concluded that the Sixth Army's successes at Skibotn would force the enemy's marines to come ashore as reinforcements at Narvik or perhaps in the Ullsfjord or Lyngenfjord flank where a landing could provide COMNON with immediate relief. To meet an amphibious assault deeper in the Sixth Army's rear, Golikov had moved the 111th MRD, a category-B division that had just completed its mobilization, to the Pechenga-Kirkenes area the previous evening. Northwest Front, which retained direct command of the division, ordered the 111th, commanded by LTG Nikolai Cherdantsev, to move into Norway in two columns—one south along the E6, and another along the axis Ivalo-Karasjok-Lakselv. Once reports of the NATO landings reached Golikov, he directed Cherdantsev to hasten his movements and to reopen communications with the Sixth Army.

Confident that the 111th was fully capable of sweeping aside the light amphibious forces that had landed at Alta and Lakselv, Golikov ordered Berdiaev to continue his offensive southward. Throughout the twenty-fourth, the 54th MRD advanced slowly through the mountainous terrain between the E6 and the Swedish border. In extremely heavy fighting, the Soviets, operating without their heavy equipment, drove the Norwegian CHOD battalion back to the Rosta River. To the northwest, the 45th MRD, after shifting two battalions back over the Lyngenfjord to screen Sixth Army's rear, continued its drive along the E6. The Soviets, under constant air attack, fought hard to capture Nordkjosbotn from its Norwegian, British, and Luxembourgeois defenders. The shattered town changed hands several times during the day, but at 2145, counterattacking British paras, well supported by Norwegian artillery and M-48A5 tanks, recaptured Nordkjosbotn and nearly cracked open the Soviet front. "Had my men not been so utterly exhausted, and the Norwegian tanks low on fuel and ammunition," MAJ Ian Dowling, commander of the paras told Bjol, "I think we could have advanced right up the E6 and broken the enemy."

Dowling blamed Bjol for the failure to follow up the paras' defensive success. Early on the twenty-fourth, Bjol withdrew three battle-weary Norwegian battalions from the front into reserve in

COMNON's rear, three battalions that he refused to commit to the battle at Nordkjosbotn. Instead, COMNON sent his Norwegians north by sea, to aid Campbell who, shortly before noon, requested that Bjol move the units into the "fjordheads" at Alta and Lakselv to guard prisoners of war and garrison ports and airfields. COM-NON now viewed Campbell's amphibious landing as the decisive stroke of the ground campaign and decided that it would be best if Norwegian units took part. Less these reserves, Bjol warned Campbell, COMNON's planned counteroffensive would be delayed at least twenty-four hours, nor were there troops on hand to take advantage of the Soviet repulse before Nordkjosbotn.

The II MEF's commander, no doubt more concerned about the expected attack of the 111th MRD than he admitted, recommended that the transfer begin. "No need to hasten movement north of Sixth Army, especially 45th MRD," read Campbell's signal to Bjol, "not yet time to flush game." So, over the next forty-eight hours, two under-strength Norwegian battalions of Brigade North moved by ship and helicopter to Alta. Bjol, having committed his few reserves to Campbell's support, now resigned himself to the necessity of waging a strictly defensive battle in Fortress Norway until the forces at Harstad and Bodo could move north.

At Harstad, a combined Norwegian, German, Belgian, Canadian assault at last recaptured the town. Gysae characterized the fighting as "the most difficult and bloody of the entire campaign in Norway." Despite the seeming pointlessness of continued resistance, the entrapped Soviet marines and airmobile troops refused to surrender. In the early hours of 25 July, a hundred or so survivors, led by "Vlad" Ganenko, still held out in the steel works overlooking the harbor. Gysae ordered a napalm strike against the Russians' final redoubt, over the objections of the Norwegians who believed that the resultant fire might well consume the entire town. The air strike did, in fact, cause a massive fire in Harstad, but it also brought to an end Soviet resistance as Ganenko and his men perished in the conflagration. As the battle for Harstad concluded, American and Norwegian troops raced north from Bodo by road, ship, and helicopter. By the evening of 25 July, 4 MEB's leading elements had reached Narvik.

For Bull Campbell, the twenty-fourth and twenty-fifth of July were days of consolidation, expansion, and extreme tension. The II MEF commander raced to push his beachhead inland both to prevent the movement south of the 111th MRD, to sever the communications of the Sixth Army, and to block the retreat of the 45th MRD. Campbell moved two battalions of the 8th Marines north to block the E6 and the road that ran along the Tana River from Nyborg to Karasjok. The 2/8 Marines entered Karasjok itself late on the twenty-fifth, just beating a battalion of the 111th MRD's 468th MRR to the Tana River bridge. Campbell moved his single battalion of Dutch marines south along the E6 to block any move north by the 45th MRD. Britain's 42 and 45 Commandos moved east in a series of ground and heliborne movements to threaten Kautokeino, where the Sixth Army's headquarters was located.

Campbell attributed his ability to expand his bridgehead and seize strong blocking positions before the arrival of the Soviet 111th MRD "to the fine work of the MAGTF's [marine air-ground task force] air contingent as well as that supplied by the Striking Fleet."

American marine and naval aviators made Soviet use of the few roads in Finnmark dangerous and slow work. Russian columns were subjected to constant attacks by enemy fighter-bombers in a theater where there was never any darkness to cover movements, secondary roads were non-existent or useless, and off-road movement generally left one bogged down in mud. Soviet mobile SAMs and anti-aircraft detachments, although they downed or damaged a score of attacking aircraft, provided only limited protection. In the forty-eight hours following the NATO amphibious landings, the lead elements of the 111th MRD had moved forward only 150 miles—an average of about three miles per hour. LTG Cherdantsev had intended to launch a coordinated three-pronged assault along the E6 by the 339th MRR, the Tana River road, by the 532d MRR, and the Ivalo-Karasjok road, by the 468th MRR. At 0200, less than an hour before the scheduled opening of the offensive, he learned that only the 532d MRR had concentrated sufficiently. Under pressure from Northwest Front headquarters, Cherdantsev nevertheless ordered the regiment to attack.

At 0250, the 532d MRR, supported by a battalion of T-62 tanks, hit the front of the 3/8 Marines at Mt. Rastegaisse north of Laevvajok. The American marines, dug in and supported by Harriers of VMA 542 flying from Banak, Intruders of VMA 533 flying from Evenes, Navy A-6Es and Hornets from the Striking Fleet, and Harriers from the British carriers, slaughtered the attacking reservists who fell back in disarray. Well over eight hundred Russians were killed or wounded and in a sharp counterattack the marines took another thousand men prisoners.

While Campbell held his left wing with the 8th Marines, he continued to drive on Kautokeino with the UK-NL amphibious force. The advance southward from Alta not only menaced the Sixth Army's headquarters, but also threatened the rear of the 54th MRD. The road south from Kautokeino led to the base of the Finnish Wedge and if Campbell's men could get that far, they would cut off both Russian divisions in Norway. When Bjol's Norwegian units reached Alta on the morning of 26 July, Campbell moved them down the E6 to relieve the Dutch who were then shifted south by helicopter to rejoin their brigade, commanded by BG James Duncan, Royal Marines.

Duncan's drive, after making rapid progress, had stalled late on the twenty-fifth south of Masi. Berdiaev had thrown every unit available into Duncan's path in an effort to buy time for Northwest Front to rush reinforcements to assist Sixth Army. Two battalions of the 76th Guards Airborne Division's 239th Regiment that had never reached Bodo, were now lifted to captured Finnish airfields and trucked toward Kautokeino.

At 1430 on the twenty-seventh, Duncan, now reinforced by his airmobilized Dutch battalion, resumed the advance south, using the Dutch to strike into the rear of the Soviet blocking force. "The Russians gave way," Duncan radioed Campbell, "we bounced them out of position after position until we entered Kautokeino about 1830." The Soviet paratroopers, delayed by NATO air attacks, arrived too late to prevent the loss of the town. Nevertheless, they prevented Duncan's forces from advancing further to the south, stalling the NATO drive at Oskal.

★ ★ ★

Despite the obviously deteriorating situation in the rear of the Sixth Army, Golikov refused to allow Berdiaev to order the 45th MRD to attempt to break out to the north along the E6, or even to permit the army to go over to the defensive. Reports that two Norwegian battalions had moved from the main front to the amphibious bridge-head led the Northwest Front commander to order Berdiaev "to maintain offensive momentum and maximize pressure on COM-NON until second echelon has dealt with enemy amphibious forces." Berdiaev, busily directing the defense of his own headquarters, believed that "only immediate retreat could preserve my command," but nonetheless felt compelled to follow orders and directed the 45th and 54th MRDs to launch a combined attack at noon on 26 July.

The Sixth Army's final offensive was, to quote COMNON, "over before it started." NATO aircraft attacked both Soviet divisions throughout the morning. The response to these strikes by Russian SAM batteries noticeably slackened, often the result of exhausted supplies. In fact, with all the roads in Sixth Army's rear either blocked or interdicted, all types of materiel, including food and fuel, were running short. The artillery barrage that was to herald the assault consisted of a few rounds fired into NATO's front line positions. A handful of small, mixed groups of tanks, APCs and infantry on foot then attempted to advance. Nowhere was COM-NON's front breached. Bjol, observing the Russian offensive from a forward observation post, saw entire units of company strength just throw down their weapons and raise their hands, all the while walking toward NATO lines. By 1330, the attack had ended. Allied losses had been extremely light, no more than thirty, according to official reports. Soviet casualties had been heavy, although the disaster overtaking the Sixth Army's two divisions precluded accurate record keeping. NATO units took 756 prisoners along the Fortress Norway front on the twenty-sixth.

Bjol sensed that the moment for a counteroffensive had come. With the troops moving up from Harstad and Bodo reaching the front, he ordered his staff to draw up plans for an early morning counterstroke. COMNON promptly informed Campbell of his intentions.

Reinforced by three Norwegian brigades, 4 MEB, and the remainder of Gysae's ACE Mobile Force and the NCFN, Bjol's front line units went over to the offensive at 0700. Although many of the allied battalions were understrength and battle-weary, a new sense of enthusiasm sparked the tempo of the advance. At 1430, the paras retook Skibotn. By midnight, the left wing of Bjol's advance had reached the Lyngenfjord at the ferry site. Both the 45th and 54th MRDs were being steadily driven back.

At 0230 on the twenty-eighth, Northwest Front, at Berdiaev's request, finally ordered the Sixth Army to retreat. Golikov directed the 45th MRD to fight its way north along the E6; the 54th MRD to pull back through the Finnish Wedge and Lapland; and the 111th MRD to continue to try to break through to the south.

At 0500, supported by two battalions of T-62s, the 532d MRR again struck the 8th Marines at Mt. Rastegaisse. The regiment's third battalion, which had stopped the Soviets' previous attack dead in its tracks, found itself under increasing pressure. A morning fog lingered along the river, and while the marines held fast up in the mountains, the Russian armored columned pushed through along the river road. Only the gallant defense of the regimental anti-tank platoon at Laevvajok and the effective support rendered by the Harriers of VMA 542 brought the Soviet attack to a halt. The Soviets, their advance stalled before the town as the fog finally lifted, were caught in the open and torn to shreds. Nevertheless, the 8th Marine's 3d Battalion had been shattered.

As the 111th MRD attacked south, the 45th MRD staged a two-battalion assault north along the E6. Again, early morning fog limited NATO air support. But the battered Soviet battalions retained little offensive punch and Norwegian infantry of Brigade North halted the drive after it had advanced less than two kilometers. As the attack faltered, small groups of enemy troops wandered toward the Norwegians' lines without weapons, some with their arms in the air, others waving white rags tied to sticks. By noon, nearly five hundred Russian prisoners had been taken.

Nevertheless, the unsuccessful, but determined and coordinated Russian attacks concerned Campbell. "I don't like the situation along the Tana River," he told BG Duncan, "and I know that the Norwegians holding south of Alta are pretty tired." At 0930 Campbell ordered Duncan to halt his drive toward the Finnish Wedge, to leave the Dutch in Kautokeino, and to shift 42 and 45 Commandos north toward Karasjok to relieve the 2/8 Marines.

Throughout the twenty-ninth, the 8th Marines, now concentrated between the E6 and the Tana River, repulsed numerous Soviet attacks. "The 8th's holding firm on my left flank," Campbell informed a concerned VADM Emerson, "the Brits and Dutch in the center, the Norwegians detached from COMNON on the southern flank, and my whole command's gonna serve as the anvil for COM-NON's hammer."

Bjol's offensive, begun the previous day, rapidly gained momentum. At 1030, elements of the Norwegian 15th Brigade reached the Finnish border near the E78. The U.S. Marine Corps' 4 MEB conducted a near-perfect heliborne-amphibious assault across the Lyngenfjord and turned the right flank of the 45th MRD. Hundreds of prisoners were falling into NATO hands. It was clear by the morning of the twenty-ninth that the now completely surrounded 45th Motor Rifle Division was near collapse.

★ ★ ★

Shortly after noon, an aide handed COMNON a message from CINCNORTH that left the Norwegian general speechless. It read:

> Advise that following information received via Swedish ambassador Oslo. At 1300 your time elements Swedish 22 Lapplands Jagarregimente plus supporting troops will enter Finland near Tornio at request Finnish government. Swedish government shortly will issue demand to both NATO and Soviet Union that all belligerent troops withdraw ASAP Finland. NATO council considering response. In interim, refrain from all movement into, or air action over Finland.

At Lakselv, the same message reached Bull Campbell. "Shit," the American marine responded, "the goddamned Swedes sit there and watch their neighbor get overrun by the Russians, and now, when they're running with their tails between their legs, the Swedes decide to do their thing for their neutral neighbor. This sucks. Where were the fucking Swedes on D day?"

Stockholm had, in fact, considered, but rejected, intervention on 14 July as "an act contrary to Swedish national interests." The Swedes did not favor "a forceful great power reorientation of their neighbors," but were unwilling to risk war to prevent it.

The situation changed dramatically by 29 July. It was not allied victory that the Swedes now feared, but the prospect of conventional or nuclear escalation. The defeat of the Sixth Army led Northwest Front to move six divisions into positions along the Soviet-Finnish border. Swedish intelligence believed, correctly, that the Russians were prepared to invade central and southern Finland to ensure their communications in Lapland. Moreover, the Swedes were concerned that if NATO attempted to pursue the beaten Russians into the Kola, the conflict could go nuclear.

With the Finns continually begging for help, the Swedes decided that only intervention could prevent a potential Scandinavian holocaust. By interposing their troops between the belligerents in Lapland, the Swedes hoped to prevent the populated areas of Finland from becoming a battleground. They assumed that given the precarious balance of forces in the Baltic and in Norway, neither NATO nor the Soviet Union would risk provoking Swedish entry into the war. Moreover, by restricting operations to the small Soviet-Norwegian border area, Stockholm believed that neither of the belligerents would be able to successfully conclude the campaign. There remained the risk of nuclear escalation, but the Swedes believed that their gambit would even lessen that risk.

At 1300, the Soviets, eager to avoid the total destruction of the Sixth Army, agreed to the Swedish demand, pending allied acceptance. In Brussels, the NATO council met in an emergency session that lasted until 1530.

The NATO meeting was tumultuous. Unlike the Warsaw Pact, which was a body totally subservient to Soviet wishes, both political and military, NATO was a true multinational alliance, in which all members were free to voice their opinions and pursue often differing national objectives. NATO's various political and military committees were just that: committees, with all of their inherent strengths and, especially, weaknesses.

None of the allies wished to chance Swedish intervention, despite communications from VADM Emerson and LTG Campbell that they believed that as long as NATO forces remained in contact with retreating Soviet units in Finland, "actual combat with Swedish Army remains unlikely." But the most important voice in Brussels was that of the Norwegians, who were adamantly opposed to risking a possible conflict with Sweden and had no wish to continue their pursuit of the Russians into either Finland or the Soviet Union.

The Norwegians certainly did not look at the Swedes as "Nordic brothers." The Swedish failure to come to Norway's aid on 14 July angered Norwegians, who remembered the Swedes' passivity in 1940 when the Germans invaded. There were many Norwegians who relished the thought of seeing the horrors of war visited on the Swedes for once. But the Norwegians were at the end of their rope. "Our army is victorious, but exhausted," a Norwegian diplomat argued, "and we seek nothing more than the expulsion of Russian forces from our country."

Only the United States' representatives appeared to be interested in the continuation of the campaign into the Kola. A communication from CINCNORTH indicated that he viewed the Swedish offer as an opportunity to concentrate his forces further south, in COMSONOR and BALTAP. He also cautioned that the loss of so many ships in the North Atlantic in the first days of the war had left his forces in north Norway short on supplies. In fact, Bull Campbell, for all his bluster about being "halted in my tracks by the striped-pants boys," knew that his deteriorating logistical situation would not have permitted operations to continue for more than a few days, at best another week. The Danes, their country nearly overrun, were understandably eager to see AFNORTH's assets shifted south. So, too, were the West Germans. The British, concerned about the tenuous situation in the Baltic, were likewise enthusiastic about any proposal that allowed them to concentrate their naval forces in the North Sea. The Belgians, Dutch, Greeks, and Turks were all willing to accept the Swedish offer, expecting that the non-Norwegian forces deployed in AFNORTH, such as the ACE Mobile Force, would become available to support operations in northern Germany or the eastern Mediterranean.

GEN Sexton, while clearly outvoted, nevertheless raised what he called the mega-question. "Okay, we don't want to seek a complete military victory on the northern flank. Fine, but how do we end the war along one part of the front? How do we pull out our troops if we can't be sure that the Soviets won't reinforce and hit Norway again? Do we keep our forces, our non-Norwegian forces, up there sitting on their hands when we could be using them elsewhere? We have a problem here—a conflict termination problem. We have a war on our hands and we have to start asking ourselves: How are we going to end it?"

The debate continued until about 1500 when Sexton suggested a counterproposal to the Swedish offer. NATO would agree not to pursue the 54th MRD into Finland and to advance no farther within Norway than the Tana River, *if* the Soviets agreed to withdraw immediately from both Finland and Norway, and the Swedes agreed to move their forces not only into Finnish Lapland, but also into the resultant no-man's land between the Tana and the Soviet-Norwegian border. "If the Soviets try to launch a second offensive," Sexton reasoned, "they will have to go through the Swedes to get to us." As for the timing of the truce, such as it was, Sexton, who "wanted to give COMNON and II MEF time to finish off the 45th MRD," suggested that it to go into effect at noon on the thirtieth.

The council readily accepted SACEUR's proposal and at 1530 communicated it officially to the Swedish government. The Swedes agreed, pending Soviet approval. The Kremlin, hoping to save the 45th MRD, demanded "immediate implementation" and threatened "dire consequences" if the terms of its ultimatum were not met. "Of course," a British NATO official sarcastically noted, "given the nature of the NATO alliance, responses to such communications inevitably require lengthy discourse and consideration."

As the NATO council stalled, Bjol and Campbell worked to complete the destruction of the remaining Soviet forces in Norway. Unable to move into Finland, or even to conduct air operations against Soviet communications in Lapland, both COMNON and II MEF concentrated all their efforts on the destruction of the 45th MRD. At 2315 on 29 July, BG Muratov, his once proud division pounded on three sides and trapped against the Norwegian coast, chose to surrender, despite appeals from Northwest Front that he continue to resist. "Our defense has collapsed," Muratov radioed Berdiaev, "my men are being slaughtered. We've run out of everything."

At 0100, NATO, assured of the 45th MRD's demise, "yielded" to the Soviet Union's demands. Within forty-eight hours, all Russian forces had withdrawn from both Norway and Finland. Swedish mechanized infantry units moved into Kirkenes. The most battered Norwegian army units deployed along the Tana River while the brigades still judged combat ready jammed the E6, moving south. American, British, and Dutch marines marched toward northern Norwegian ports, to reembark. Other non-Norwegian units moved toward airfields where air transports waited to ferry them to other fronts.

At Brussels, NATO officials argued about where these new reserves—ground, air, and naval—could best be employed. And argued, and argued. . . .

★ ★ ★

For NATO, victory on the northern flank—the retention of Norwegian airbases and the elimination of the Soviet Northern Fleet's air, surface, and subsurface assets—safeguarded the alliance's SLOCs and, in combination with allied naval successes in the Mediterranean, assured SACEUR of secure flanks and access to reinforcement and resupply from the United States. American naval forces in the North Atlantic had not, it is true, embarked on an extended strategic ASW campaign against Soviet ballistic missile submarines, nor had the Striking Fleet's amphibious element thrust into the Kola. Given the existing circumstances, NATO, as an alliance, chose not to push the Russians in the far north. NATO had gained its major objectives. The alliance had removed the threats to the SLOCs and defeated Soviet attempts to overrun north Norway. To VADM Emerson, as well as other senior American and NATO naval officers, the more dramatic aspects of the Maritime Strategy, such as an anti-SSBN campaign, were what they always had been: not ends in themselves, but means to an end. By 30 July the NATO alliance had achieved that end.

The cost of the campaign had been high. While the sinking of the *Forrestal* shocked many Americans, senior U.S. Navy commanders considered losses in the North Atlantic relatively light—one carrier, two destroyers, seven frigates, and a pair of SSNs. The British, West German, Dutch, Canadian, and Norwegian navies combined lost another three destroyers, seven frigates, fifteen fast attack boats, and three submarines. A score of allied ships were also damaged.

For the Soviet navy, the defeat on the northern flank was the greatest debacle since Tsushima. The Russians' only operational carrier—the *Tbilisi*—had been sunk along with a dozen cruisers, fourteen destroyers, twelve frigates, and twenty-five submarines of various types. The Northern Fleet had been totally destroyed.

In the air war, Soviet naval aviation, air defense forces, and frontal aviation units lost somewhere between six hundred and seven hundred aircraft, at least half of which were destroyed on the ground. NATO losses totalled 157, including the planes that went down with the *Forrestal*. Many of the NATO commanders considered the four-to-one kill ratio disappointing. Emerson, for example, liked to point out that the Israelis achieved ratios of sixty and seventy-to-one against the Arabs. Flying against the much better Soviets, the admiral had hoped for a fifteen-to-one ratio.

On the ground, NATO lost about 12,000 men. Several Norwegian battalions, the Italian Susa Alpini of ACE Mobile Force, and the Canadian company attached to the NCFN suffered horrendous losses. Soviet losses totalled over 37,000, including 20,000 POWs. The 76th Guards Airborne and the 45th Motor Rifle Divisions, and the Northwest Front's marine and airmobile brigades were virtually eliminated. Only the two battalions of paratroopers that had been unable to reach Bodo and a single airmobile battalion escaped the catastrophe in Norway. The 54th and 111th MRDs, although they avoided encirclement and destruction, nevertheless suffered heavily and were judged unfit for combat at the end of the campaign.

TWENTY-EIGHT

In the late morning of 30 July, ADM Jack Cardswell, the American Chief of Naval Operations, flew by helicopter to Norfolk, Virginia. A waiting car whisked the admiral to CINCLANT headquarters.

"Gentlemen, the CNO," announced an aide as Cardswell bounded into the CINCLANT briefing room, his hands raised in apology for an arrival delayed by more than twenty-fives minutes. "Sorry I'm late, sorry I'm late, gentlemen," Cardswell remarked, "but I was called away at the last minute by the president. And let me tell you, he sends you all, and the men and women out there on the ships, in the subs, and flying the planes, the marines, and our NATO allies, a BRAVO ZULU, especially Vice Admiral Emerson and," turning to CINCLANT himself, "you, Wayne."

Admiral Wayne Taylor was a busy man, and a double-hatted man. Taylor was both CINCLANT, that is the unified commander for all American forces in the Atlantic Command; and SACLANT, that is the NATO Supreme Allied Commander, Atlantic. In neither position was he subordinate to the chief of naval operations, who was not even in the American chain of command, which ran directly from the president, to the secretary of defense, to CINCLANT.

When the hand-shaking and back-slapping showed no signs of ending, Cardswell himself called the room to order. "Alright, now, we're all busy people and I didn't fly all this way to press the flesh. Wayne, what are you going to do next? And how can I help?"

While Cardswell was not in the chain of command, he nevertheless ran the navy and provided the ships and people that CINCLANT/SACLANT needed to run his war. Taylor knew that Cardswell had come to Norfolk to get an appreciation of future operations, so that he would not be taken by surprise by subsequent requests.

Taylor grabbed a pointer and began his briefing. He stated that the campaign on the northern flank was over. Desultory air and ASW operations would undoubtedly continue. Patrol squadrons, submarines, and ASW groups would have to remain in the northeastern Atlantic to ensure that the Soviets did not attempt to sneak any SSNs south to attack the SLOCs. "I think," Taylor suggested, "that it would be a good idea to leak to the press that most of our SSNs will remain up north, just to keep the Russians on their toes and on the defensive. It can't hurt." As for the bulk of the Striking Fleet's surface and amphibious assets, Taylor recommended that they be shifted to the eastern Mediterranean. "The naval battle's over down there," he admitted, "but the situation in Libya, the Levant, and the Aegean is precarious enough that we might find the arrival of another carrier group and two MEBs rather timely."

"What about Cuba?" Cardswell asked.

"Well," Taylor continued, "I assume you've seen the same intelligence that I have, the stuff from the Spanish, and in my opinion it looks like we're going to get away unscathed down there. Our successes in the Med have given them pause, and our victory up north, I think, has made them consider very carefully the question of their entry. I think they're going to adopt a real low profile for a while."

"Where's the *Midway*?" Cardswell asked.

"In the Florida Strait," Taylor replied.

The *Midway*, which had been slated for decommissioning and was without an air group, had been hastily outfitted with reserve marine and navy F/A-18 squadrons and sent out from Pensacola to cruise off the Cuban coast. Armed, combat-ready F-16 Falcons of

MICHAEL A. PALMER

the air force's 56th Tactical Training Wing at McDill Air Force Base also patrolled the waters off northern Cuba. To these powerful demonstrations of force, the president had added repeated and continuous threats, both through private and open channels, meant to convince the Cubans to remain on the sidelines.

Initially, Castro's protestations of neutrality had been a ploy, intended to lull the United States into a sense of complacency in advance of a Cuban intervention timed to coincide with the dispatch of critical convoys from Gulf coast ports to Europe. But the threats, shows of force, and, most importantly, allied victories at sea in the Mediterranean, the North Atlantic, the Indian Ocean, and the Pacific had convinced the Cuban leader that his country's policy ought actually to become neutrality. A Spanish diplomat who met with Castro often during the course of the war reported the content of his conversations back to Madrid, from whence they were passed to Washington. At one meeting, Castro had asked about the Spanish government's assessment of the military situation. The diplomat showed the Cuban president a top secret dispatch that stated unequivocally that the war, especially at sea, was going decidedly in NATO's favor. Castro scanned the message, nodded, and stated that he had determined that there was a good chance that the Russians were losing the war and that it would be suicide for Cuba to risk American retaliation. He intended to remain neutral and he chose to make his intentions known, through Spain, to the United States.

"Do you think he's sincere?" Cardswell asked.

"Yes, I do," Taylor replied, "as long as we keep winning."

"I'll buy that," came the CNO's reply. "So we go to the Med."

"Right. The only redeployment we can make in time to have some impact on the fighting is in the Med. Two air wings can make a difference in the air, and two MEBs and the amphibious shipping can do a lot, again, in Libya, off the Levant, or in the Aegean. It will also make a good show of force to keep the Jugs out."

Yugoslavian neutrality was becoming a question of some importance. The Yugoslavs had begun mobilizing on 15 July and at first had toyed apparently with the idea of entering the war alongside the Warsaw Pact. Now they were appearing very neutral.

"They're like windmills," Cardswell commented, "they spin whichever way the wind blows. But the wind's blowing our way."

294

"Yes, they are," Taylor added, "and a CVBG just might make the Jugs spin faster in our direction."

"Sounds good," Cardswell spoke as he rose from his chair. "If I were you Wayne, I'd get the ships moving south now."

"That's already been done, Jack."

"Good. And I'll give the chiefs a heads up."

"How do you think it will go?" Taylor asked.

"Well, the army and air force like a Denmark operation. So do the Brits. We can do that one in a couple of days. It's a logical follow-on. But I think the situation's already stabilized there."

"I'm not so sure about that, Jack. In my view BALTAP's just about shot. But, so what? Given the situation in the Atlantic, even if the Russians break out, where in the hell are they going to go?"

"I agree, Jack, but in the Med, as you say, the situation's still up in the air. How many days will it take to redeploy?"

"Nine, maybe ten days. We'll need air transport for 4 MEB."

"I'll talk to the air force. What about their equipment?"

"By ship, maybe as many as twenty days. They'll have to go light."

"Okay. I'll back you on this. Our stock is rather high right now, so I think the president will go along with us. As for NATO, they'll have the Brits and Dutch marines and the ACE Mobile Force for AFNORTH. That'll have to do."

TWENTY-NINE

At 1345 on the afternoon of 20 July, Muhammad Abu Ghasan, representative of the Arab League to the United Nations, requested a meeting with Theodore Parkinson, the American UN ambassador. At 1430 in Parkinson's office, Ghasan informed the American that the Syrians sought a cease-fire. In a week of heavy fighting, Israeli Defense Force units had advanced into Beirut and were driving toward the outskirts of Damascus. With the defeat of the Soviet Mediterranean squadron, the Romanian failure before Istanbul, and the crushing of Soviet forces in the Indian Ocean, the Syrians recognized that further resistance was pointless. In fact, by the end of the first week of the war, the bulk of the Arab states were siding with the United States, not the Soviet Union.

Late that evening, with the Arab League serving as a go-between, the Israelis, Americans, Turks, and Syrians agreed to an in-place ceasefire. All remaining Soviet forces in Syria were to be immediately interned.

During the course of these talks, Parkinson sought the good offices of the Arab League in an effort to work out comparable arrangements with the other Moslem nations at war with the United States—Yemen and Libya. At 0540 on the morning of the twenty-first, Parkinson met with representatives of Yemen and Ethiopia and reached an accord similar to that agreed to by the Syrians. But despite the annihilation of Soviet and Libyan naval and air forces in the central Mediterranean, and the general trend of events in the Middle East, Libya's Qaddafi rejected the Arab League overture and continued to exhort his army and his people to resist "American, traitor-Egyptian, and Zionist aggression."

"Did you make clear to him that we will not make another such offer?" Parkinson asked Ghasan when he learned of the Libyan refusal to stop fighting.

"Certainly."

"I don't understand."

"He is a madman," Ghasan told Parkinson. "He is crazy."

"In that case, Mr. Ambassador, I'm afraid my country must continue the campaign until the colonel is no longer in power."

"I understand."

After thanking Ghasan for his constructive assistance, the meeting ended. And the allied campaign against Libya continued.

★ ★ ★

Egyptian forces facing the Libyans along the Cyrenaican front remained in place on 21 July. The bitter Libyan defense of Tobruq left many Egyptian units disorganized and low on ammunition and supplies. The Egyptian air force attempted to maintain the pressure on the enemy and launched repeated and effective air strikes against retreating Libyan columns. At 1430, under the cover of these air operations, elements of the Egyptian 150th Airborne Brigade landed at Qaryat Az Zuwaytinah, a small town with an airstrip located along the coast road about a hundred miles south of Benghazi. If the Egyptians could maintain their airhead and keep the road severed, Cyrenaica would be isolated.

American marine and army units west of Tripoli spent the day regrouping after the difficult fighting of the preceding days. U.S. Air Force B-52s repeatedly struck the Libyan forces concentrating to defend the capital, including the Benghazi division which reached Al Buyrat, about two hundred miles from Tripoli.

The continued approach of the Libyan mechanized division, despite the best efforts of the Egyptian and American air forces, concerned GEN Gilchrist at his Cairo headquarters. "We simply can't let another division get into position around Tripoli," Gilchrist told his staff. With the fighting in the Persian Gulf and Gulf of Aden over, he decided to interpose a blocking force along the Libyan line of march.

At 0800 on 22 July, U.S. Army Rangers of the 1st Battalion, 75th Infantry, and the 5th Special Forces Group landed by air and sea at Homs, about sixty miles east of Tripoli. As the rangers came ashore, U.S. Air Force B-52Hs of the 5th Bombardment Wing hit the Benghazi division in an attempt to retard and disrupt its westward movement to give the rangers time to consolidate a defensive position.

As the Americans were seizing Homs, the Egyptians transported elements of their 182d Airborne Brigade to Qaryat Az Zuwaytinah. By noon, lead elements of the two Egyptian brigades were advancing both north and northeast. Simultaneously, Egyptian forces around Tobruq resumed their advance, with those units on the southern flank reaching out toward the paratroopers moving northeast in an effort to complete the encirclement of all Libyan forces in Cyrenaica. Overhead, Egyptian fighter-bombers continued their attacks against exposed Libyan columns that betrayed their positions by kicking up huge clouds of dust.

Similar air attacks hindered the movement of the Benghazi division. The air strikes increased in frequency and intensity as the Libyans neared Tripoli and came closer to American bases in Sicily. Late on the twenty-third, advance elements of the Benghazi division reached Zlitan, still forty miles east of Homs. In Tripoli itself, Qaddafi waited impatiently as his hoped-for relief force only slowly neared the Libyan capital.

On the morning of 24 July, Gilchrist directed what he expected would be the final moves against the Libyans, whose collapse seemed imminent. The 82d Airborne Division's 1st Brigade landed at Homs to reinforce the heavily outnumbered rangers and special forces. The Benghazi division, although it moved toward the American positions before Homs, was unable to undertake any type of offensive action and the 1st Brigade's landing proceeded like a peacetime exercise. Despite a furious Qaddafi's calls for an immediate attack, LTG Abdul Hussein, the division commander, reported to Tripoli: "My division totally disorganized by long and rapid march under constant air attack; unable to attack before 0900 25 July."

Throughout the twenty-fourth, Qaddafi grew increasingly desperate as reports reached his command center of the American offensive that began at 0700. The 82d Airborne's 2d Brigade and LTC Mike Harris's 26th MEU, well supported by marine Harriers and Hornets, drove on Tripoli from the west. The Libyans continued to put up a good fight. But by nightfall American paratroopers had taken Idris airbase south of the capital, although they had failed to reach their planned objective—the Mediterranean coast east of Tripoli.

The Egyptians fared somewhat better on the twenty-fourth. Armored and mechanized forces cut off and destroyed two retreating Libyan brigades about ninety miles south of Derna. South of Benghazi, the Egyptian paratroopers continued their advance on the Libyan city and they took over five thousand prisoners on 24 July. Obviously, the Libyans were much more inclined to surrender to their fellow Arabs than they were to the Americans.

The following day, Egyptian paratroopers stormed Benghazi, defended by a brigade of the Pan African Legion. By nightfall troops of the Egyptian 6th Mechanized Infantry Brigade had secured the city. Organized enemy resistance ended with the fall of Benghazi and over the next several days the remnants of Libyan forces between Tobruq and Benghazi surrendered. The campaign in Cyrenaica had ended.

But not so the fighting around Tripoli. On the morning of the twenty-fifth, the Benghazi division was still unprepared to begin its attack toward Homs. LTG Hussein requested an additional delay until 1500 that afternoon. Unfortunately, Qaddafi directed Hussein, under penalty of death, to order an immediate attack. The general complied and the assault began at 0930. Despite his men's best efforts, the division was unable to drive the Americans from Homs. Exhausted, the Libyans fell back on Zlitan.

As reports of the successful defense of Homs reached Cairo, Gilchrist adopted a plan he considered daring, but which LTG John Ferguson, the commander of the 82d, thought harebrained. Leaving the two ranger battalions to hold the battered Libyans at Homs, CINCCENT ordered the 82d Airborne's 1st Brigade to pull out of line and march west to join what would become a concentric attack against an isolated Tripoli.

The attack began at 1330 the following day. By 1645 elements of the 1st Brigade had linked up with the 2d Brigade, completing the encirclement of Qaddafi's capital. But the Libyans continued to resist, launching several armored counterattacks during the course of the battle. Marine and army units reported heavy fighting all along the line. The exhausted men of the 1st Brigade, who had marched nearly twenty-five miles before they even began the engagement, drove the Libyans back into the outskirts of the city but were unable to advance further. The offensive, to Gilchrist's chagrin, stalled.

Hussein promptly seized his opportunity. He worked ceaselessly throughout the night of the twenty-sixth to rally his division. By dawn the following morning, all was ready. Led by his last fresh battalion of T-62 tanks, the Benghazi division struck west in a surprise assault. By noon, the Libyans had retaken Homs. As night fell, the American rangers, heavily supported by marine and air force ground-attack aircraft, were fighting desperately to prevent the Libyans from driving into the rear of the 82d Airborne. In a late-evening report to the JCS, Gilchrist considered the situation "dicey," a judgment the 82d's commander considered a gross understatement.

THIRTY

At 0900 on the morning of
21 July, COL GEN Kambarov met with his staff at Southwest Front
headquarters in Vinnitsa. Despite the near disastrous repulse of the
Romanians before Istanbul on 18 July, Kambarov remained confident that the arrival of Soviet forces from the Kiev military district
would shortly allow him to regain the initiative. In the interim,
Kambarov directed his staff to concentrate their efforts on the elimination, within forty-eight hours, of the remaining Greek and Turkish pockets in Thrace, the recovery of the Romanian units that had
broken during the Catalca fighting, and the provision of maximum
air and sea support for MG Panferov's isolated airborne-marine
force in Anatolia.

In the late afternoon of 21 July, Romanian and Bulgarian divisions began their offensive against the Greek and Turkish units cut
off along the Meric. The Bulgarians made slow but steady progress
in their drives from the west and north. But to the east the Romanians demonstrated a noticeable lack of offensive spirit. A sharp
counterattack by elements of the Turkish 8th Infantry Division on
the night of 22 July routed the Romanian 81st MRD.

Alarmed by reports from the front of the continued uselessness
of the Romanians, Kambarov ordered that they be assigned a
strictly defensive role—containing the pocket—while the Bulgarians carried the entire offensive burden. As a result, an operation
planned to last for two days continued for five. Not until the evening
of 25 July were the last of the NATO defenders forced to surrender.
"We have taken tens of thousands of prisoners," Kambarov reported
to Moscow as the exhausted Turkish and Greek divisions laid down
their arms.

The prolonged resistance of the NATO troops along the Meric
caused great consternation at Vinnitsa. Kambarov's insistence on
wrapping up the operation within forty-eight hours was based on a
Southwest Front intelligence staff assessment that the Turkish First
Army would be prepared to attack from its Catalca position by the
twenty-third or twenty-fourth. Kambarov knew that he had to eliminate the remaining pockets and free up his reserves before the
Turks resumed the offensive. Fortunately for Kambarov, the Turkish
attack failed to develop. By the twenty-fifth, the last of the pockets

had surrendered and reports from the front indicated that most of the Romanian formations had recovered sufficiently to be considered battleworthy. Had the Turks attacked before the twenty-fifth, they might have driven Pact forces from Thrace.

Indeed, LTG Niyazi Erol, commander of the Turkish First Army, requested permission to launch an attack in an effort to relieve the encircled troops along the Meric. MAJ Ulusoy, who had taken over command of the 2d Armored Brigade after the death of its commander, believed that he could have driven all the way to Bucharest before the Romanians could have stopped him.

But after visiting the front, GEN Ersari forbade any offensive move from Catalca. Ersari was shaken by the extremely heavy losses suffered by First Army in Thrace and judged Erol's remaining units too exhausted to undertake a major operation. Ersari was also convinced that the Greeks could not be depended upon to pin the Bulgarians along the front in Thrace, especially since most of the encircled troops were Turkish. Logistical considerations also helped to shape Ersari's decision. Since the First Army's supply and ammunition stocks were extremely low, Ersari considered an offensive out of the question until Second Army had cleared the Russian paratroopers from Izmit and opened the road to Uskudar.

* * *

The morning of 21 July found the paratroopers of the 103d Guards Airborne Division and the marines of the Black Sea Fleet marine brigade clinging tenaciously to their Anatolian bridgehead. Kambarov, in a personal communication, ordered MG Panferov, the senior officer in the bridgehead that had become a pocket, to hold out as long as possible.

The fighting on the twenty-first centered around Kandira, defended by paratroopers of the 688th Airborne Regiment. The Turkish 6th Infantry Division, supported by tanks of the 5th Armored Brigade, launched repeated attacks against the town. One early evening assault actually carried into Kandira before being driven back by a timely counterstroke. As darkness fell, the town remained in Soviet hands.

The following morning, the Turks, well supported by heavy artillery, resumed their attack but succeeded only in turning Kandira into defensible heaps of rubble. The most notable success came north of the town where the Turkish 70th Infantry Brigade drove along the coast and reached Kefken, the only remaining port in Russian hands. The Turks found several small lighters in the harbor, sank three and drove off the others. Meanwhile, to the west, the paratroopers of the Turkish airborne brigade continued their drive along Route 25, pushing the Soviet marines before them. Kirsanov's marines, nearly out of ammunition, fell back hastily on Kandira, allowing the Turks to link up with the 70th Infantry Brigade along the coast.

That night, Ersari arrived at Second Army headquarters in Adapazari. Unhappy with the existing plan drawn up by the army's staff, the commanding general immediately ordered a halt to all attacks against Kandira and hastily sketched a new plan. Second Army would cut the Russian pocket in two by driving a wedge between Kandira and Izmit.

At 0930 on the twenty-third, two regiments of the Turkish 2d Infantry Division attacked Soviet positions north of Izmit. Simultaneously, twenty miles to the east, the 5th Tank, and 16th and 20th Mechanized Brigades drove west. By noon, the Turks had gained the high ground overlooking the connecting road between Izmit and Kandira. Panferov had no choice but to order the marines and paratroopers of the 688th Regiment to evacuate Kandira and retreat south. Throughout the afternoon and into the evening, the fighting continued, but despite their best efforts, the Turks were unable to cut the connecting road until 2200. Fewer than a hundred Russians were taken prisoner.

The struggle now centered on Izmit. From his headquarters in the Saray Palas Hotel, Panferov ably directed the defense. But surrounded by a force nearly five times as large as his own, he knew that he could do little more than delay the inevitable. The only successful resupply drop into Izmit consisted of rations—the one item, food, which the Russians had plenty of in the city—and not what they really needed, ammunition, especially anti-tank rockets. According to a Southwest Front report: "All but one attempt to resupply 103d Division by air forced to abort as result of NATO air activity or failed to deliver canisters vicinity friendly positions."

Nevertheless, Turkish efforts to recapture Izmit proceeded slowly. The well-trained, elite Russian paratroopers and marines excelled in house to house fighting. Ersari had no intention of seeing his Turkish divisions burned out in a fight for the city. He directed Second Army to rely on firepower, not manpower. Under a Turkish barrage that literally destroyed Izmit, the Russians were driven back block by city block into an ever smaller pocket. At 1630 on the afternoon of 26 July, Panferov surrendered. He had less than six hundred men under his personal control, almost all of them wounded.

As Turkish engineers worked during the twenty-seventh to clear the roads through Izmit, and to repair or establish detours around the damaged and destroyed overpasses of the E5, Ersari returned to his headquarters in Izmir. His staff, as directed, was already at work preparing plans for a counteroffensive. The units of the Turkish Second Army would reinforce those of the First, a move that would take several days given the state of the roads, the difficulty of moving over 60,000 men across the Bosporus, and the need to rest exhausted troops. What the COMLANDSOUTHEAST staff did not yet know was how Ersari intended to employ the NATO reinforcements that had arrived in Greece and Turkey. Advance elements of the French Force Action Rapide (FAR)—the 11th Airborne Division from Toulouse, and the 9th Marine Division—had completed their movement by air and sea to Thessaloniki. American marines of 6 MEB and the Italian San Marco regiment, after landing at Izmir on the nineteenth, had moved to positions along the southern shore of the Sea of Marmara. The opportunity for a counteroffensive existed; the big question was whether or not the Greeks would cooperate.

THIRTY-ONE

The final days of July found the political and military leadership of the Soviet Union beset by doubt and concern. On the streets of the capital, Muscovites appeared sullen. The excitement that had greeted the news from the front in the first days of the war had given way to visible disquiet as official silence about the course of the conflict was taken as evidence that things were not going well. Russians waited expectantly for word that their troops had reached the Rhine. But when no such communique was released after a week, and then after ten days, and then after a fortnight, people began to worry about their sons or husbands, and about the consequences of defeat.

In the Kremlin and the various military headquarters in Moscow, the deteriorating military situation was slowly being recognized. "We can no longer dismiss our defeats as marginal," COL Kaganovich warned Marshall Kubitskii, "our failures in the Arctic and the Far East, and the developing stalemates in Germany and Thrace bode ill for our efforts." Moreover, as July came to an end, a vociferous strategic debate divided the Soviet Union's military leadership. The subject was Yugoslavia.

On the afternoon of 14 July, the Yugoslavian government, surprised by the outbreak of war, issued a statement of neutrality. Nevertheless, the Yugoslavs remained in contact with both NATO and the Warsaw Pact and were perfectly willing to discuss the prospects of their entry as a belligerent. The American Ambassador in Belgrade reported to Washington that "the Yugoslavs keep a finger in the wind, their ears to the ground, and their hands outstretched in a simple gesture—make us an offer we can't refuse."

Initially, the Yugoslavs leaned toward entry alongside the Warsaw Pact. On 16 July, the Soviet ambassador in Belgrade found the "Yugos willing to enter the war as soon as they are fully mobilized." But three days later, the Yugoslavs informed the Soviets that their military high command had decided that they could not fight a two-front war against both the Italians and the Greeks. Until the Greeks were eliminated, and the Yugoslavian army could be concentrated against the Italians, Yugoslavia would remain neutral. Moscow recognized that no Yugoslavian help could soon be expected, since Soviet strategy for the Southwestern TVD envisioned an initial focus on knocking the Turks, not the Greeks, out of the war.

The subsequent inability of the Southwest Front to capture Istanbul, the annihilation of the Soviet Mediterranean squadron, and the apparent stalemate in Germany, caused the Yugoslavs to reconsider their decision to align themselves with the Warsaw Pact. At a 25 July meeting, the American ambassador noted the change of mood among the Yugoslavs who suddenly seemed serious about entering the war alongside NATO. He sent a coded message to Washington: "Yugoslavians may come in if enticed. Immediate and strong Italian military support key."

In Washington, Brussels, and Rome, the prospect of Italian assistance for Yugoslavia posed no problem. CINCSOUTH ADM McMichaels was eagerly searching for some way to get the Italian army into the war. Other than a marine regiment in Turkey, Italian ground forces had been left on the sidelines because the Russians had not invaded Austria.

The Soviet failure to strike through Austria on D day surprised many NATO analysts. McMichaels had always been advised by the experts that the Russians would shoot through Austria to take the Germans in Bavaria in the flank.

The Soviet general staff rejected an Austrian invasion for several reasons. Troops driving through the Austrian plain between the Alps and the Danube would issue into Germany to the east, not to the west of Munich. Russian planners calculated that their troops could reach this same area just as quickly and more easily from the Czech border. Most of Austria consisted of mountainous terrain that offered little prospect of rapid advance for the heavily mechanized Warsaw Pact troops. Moreover, the planners knew that by not invading Austria, a centrally placed neutral, the Italians would not be able to move their sizable army north of the Alps to assist the Germans in Bavaria.

To the NATO council, which had been painfully debating the possibility of invading neutral Austria itself, the prospect of Yugoslavian entry provided an easy way to get the Italians into the fight. Accordingly, NATO undertook a herculean effort to convince the Yugoslavs to enter the war. On 26 July, McMichaels secretly flew to Zagreb for a meeting with the Yugoslavs. He was empowered to promise them just about anything they demanded, and he did just that. CINCSOUTH was nevertheless disappointed to learn that the Yugoslavs would not enter the war for another two weeks, on or about 10 August. They refused to begin operations until their army had concentrated along their eastern border and the Italian army, which had moved into positions along the Alpine front, had redeployed to the Yugoslavian border.

Reports of McMichaels's "secret" meeting in Zagreb reached

the Kremlin on the morning of the twenty-seventh. The impending Yugoslav entry into the war caused little consternation in Moscow. For the past fortnight, Southwest Front had been concentrating three armies—the Tenth, Sixteenth, and Twenty-first—along the Yugoslavian-Hungarian border. These troops were positioned to go to Yugoslavia's assistance should it enter the war alongside the Soviet Union, but they were equally well placed to counter any sudden shift of direction in Belgrade.

Nevertheless, the apparent change of Yugoslavian heart prompted an immediate debate in Moscow between two factions that COL Kaganovich and other staff officers labelled "westerners" and "southerners." At an 1830 STAVKA meeting, the westerners— for the most part commanders responsible for operations in Germany—argued that the Yugoslavs posed little threat and, fur-thermore, that additional offensives in the Balkans against Turkey and Greece would yield no meaningful results. All reserve forces and the bulk of the remaining frontal aviation assets, the westerners proposed, ought to be concentrated in Germany for a decisive battle against NATO's principal forces—the West Germans, Americans, and British. The southerners—led by Kambarov, the Southwest Front commander who had flown to Moscow for the meeting— maintained that the Warsaw Pact had already "missed the boat" on the German front. While Yugoslavian entry itself posed little danger, Kambarov emphasized the possibility that the Italian army would march through Slovenia—northern Yugoslavia—and attack Hun-gary. Kambarov also reported that the Romanians and Bulgarians had been forced to redeploy several divisions to cover their respec-tive borders with Yugoslavia, detracting from the Southwest Front's effort in Thrace. A foreign ministry representative seconded Kam-barov's concerns, informing those present that the Hungarian and Romanian governments had expressed deep concern about possible Yugoslavian entry.

"All the more reason to refrain from any additional effort in the southwestern TVD," Marshal Kubitskii added, a sentiment with which Marshal Posokhov agreed.

But Kambarov persisted. "We already have three armies in place and they must remain there, and additional Soviet forces must reinforce the Romanians and Bulgarians whether they remain on the defensive or go over to the attack." Kambarov paused. "Look, let's be honest; we're in trouble. We're going nowhere in Germany. Why not shift the focus of our effort to the south?"

The conference room erupted in chaos until Minister of Defense Durostnik intervened. "What have you in mind, General Kambarov?"

"We already have three armies in place. The Bulgarians and Romanians are also moving units to the border. The troops moving from the Kiev military district toward my front—the Nineteenth and the Third and Sixth Tank Armies—I send instead against Yugoslavia. With such a force I could crush Yugoslavia, bottle up the Italians before they could get past Zagreb, and then wheel my tank armies south through Macedonia, hitting the Greeks in their left flank, isolating their forces in Thrace, and driving on to Athens. In a week, we knock both Yugoslavia and Greece out of the war, and perhaps drive into northern Italy."

"And what then?" Kubitskii asked.

"Then we use our air power to force the NATO navies out of the Aegean, isolate the Turks, and knock them out of the war."

"And then, Comrade General, and then?"

"And then we transfer our effort back to Germany and, I would recommend, we negotiate our way out of this war."

The conference room became eerily silent. The Soviet president stood and walked about. After several minutes he returned to his chair.

"Marshal Durostnik, Marshal Posokhov, you will see that Kambarov receives all the assistance he needs."

Posokhov and Kubitskii jumped from their seats, both shouting simultaneously.

The president pounded both fists into the table.

"Silence! You," he gestured threateningly at his two senior marshals, "you were the men who assured me of victory in a fortnight. And where is that victory? Now you say give us additional resources. No more! We'll shift our efforts to the south and," he turned to the foreign ministry representative, "we begin to sound out NATO on possible terms to end this war. How soon can you attack, Kambarov?"

"All will be in place by 4 August, comrade president."

"Until then we must keep up our efforts along the German front. And if, by chance," the president turned to Kubitskii, "you appear on the verge of achieving your long-promised breakthrough to the Rhine, be assured, Marshal, that you will be supported fully."

★ ★ ★

In the final days of July, Warsaw Pact forces in Germany struggled desperately to regain the momentum they had lost. Pact first-line troops were spent, and second echelon units reached the front weakened and exhausted as the result of continuous NATO air attacks. The rear area was a disaster. Supplies were running short at the front. Air support had become a rarity. But the Warsaw Pact commanders in Germany assumed, correctly, that NATO units were similarly weakened. Kubitskii, safe in his headquarters in Moscow, issued an order of the day to all units fighting in Germany: "Shake off the fatigue that has overcome you and make one final effort. Our destiny, that of our Motherland, and that of Socialism itself is to be found along the Rhine."

Despite such exhortations, Soviet and East German attacks launched along the northern and central sectors of the German front gained little ground. Pact forces made substantial advances only in Bavaria. Elements of the Twenty-Eighth Army shattered the French 1st Tank Division in a day-long engagement north of Augsburg. French resistance collapsed and Soviet armored forces drove west and south, lead elements reaching the outskirts of Augsburg. The only reserve units available to plug the gap was the West German 25th Airborne Brigade, but the lightly armed paratroopers were swept aside and the city fell on the evening of 28 July.

South of Munich, the Forty-First Army swung north from its drive along the Austrian border and took Schongau, fifty kilometers southwest of the Bavarian capital. Pact forces then hooked north in an effort to isolate Munich. At 1045 on 31 July, after three days of heavy fighting, the two Pact armies joined hands in Landsberg, west of the city.

The first of August was a relatively quiet day along the entire front. Both sides had grown weary of the fighting, and some soldiers thought, naively, that perhaps that was it, that the war would never get going again. In fact, overhead, the battle had continued unabated as the NATO air forces struggled to gain air supremacy and to exercise their control by striking at the Pact's rear areas, especially reinforcing units heading toward the front.

SACEUR believed that air superiority provided him with just the edge he needed in the reinforcement race. At GEN Sexton's direction, at 0400 on 2 August, COMNORTHAG—GEN Sir Ian Carton de Wiart—began a series of offensives designed to shorten his line by eliminating the Pact forces encircled west of the Weser. At noon the following day, Carton de Wiart reported complete success: "Resistance surprisingly light. Four Pact divisions bagged."

In Bavaria, COMCENTAG—GEN Brad McGinty—directed the effort to relieve Munich. Under the watchful eye of CINCENT, Munich-born German GEN Otto Kamper, McGinty's polyglot assault force, which consisted of American, French, West German, and Canadian units, hit a brick wall west of Augsburg. McGinty continued his assault, feeding in fresh forces throughout the second, while NATO strike aircraft interdicted Pact columns working their way along the roads south of Munich. By the morning of 3 August, the Forty-First Army's Czech and Soviet divisions were reporting major supply shortages. That afternoon, first one, then a second Czech division disintegrated during fighting west of Landsberg. Soviet units continued to hold Augsburg but, by evening, a West German mechanized column had forced its way through to the Bavarian capital.

The battle for Landsberg marked the beginning of the end for the Czech army. Like the Poles and the Romanians, the Czechs had failed to stand up to the rigors of the modern battlefield. The Czech government suggested that its army be withdrawn from the front and returned to its homeland "until such time that the units can recover their strength."

The Czech collapse, and the subsequent request from Prague, caused consternation in Moscow. The campaign had become a reinforcement race. Unfortunately, the arrival of additional Pact formations at the front was offset by the withdrawal of Polish and Czech divisions. The East Germans had fought well, but they had been bled white and had suffered disproportionate casualties. In a 4 August report to Durostnik, Kubitskii admitted frankly: "Burden of future operations along German front will rest squarely on shoulders of Soviet units. Pact formations reliable only for rear area duties. Hereafter front line use must be considered last resort."

THIRTY-TWO

On his return to Vinnitsa late on 27 July, Colonel General Kambarov directed his staff to complete the drafting of Plan "Suvorov"—the offensive against Yugoslavia. The following morning he flew to Plovdiv, headquarters of the Bulgarian forces facing the Greeks in eastern Macedonia.

As Kambarov had directed before his trip to Moscow, the Bulgarians had prepared a plan for an offensive against the Greeks. The Bulgarian commander considered the result a sensible plan that called for simultaneous offensives against Greek positions along the Nestos River and in the Sturma valley. The planned attacks, from both the east and the north, were designed to overpower the Greeks and drive them behind the Sturma. The offensive was scheduled to begin at 0300 on the twenty-ninth.

At a late morning conference on the twenty-eighth, Kambarov directed the Bulgarian commander to cancel the projected attack down the Sturma valley and to strike only with his left wing. The Bulgarian general, whose poor hearing was often a staple of headquarters humor, assumed that he had misheard the front commander. He had not. Kambarov insisted that only the Nestos offensive begin the following morning. Additionally, the Soviet commander personally assumed control of all Bulgarian reserve formations. The Bulgarians, unaware of the impending strike against the Yugoslavs, were understandably confused by the decision. "My men are being sent into a meat-grinder," he argued, "with little, if any, chance of success." Kambarov remained unmoved. "I am sorry general, but my decision stands. Execute it."

Kambarov's reasoning was, in fact, sound. While the Romanians remained on the defensive before Istanbul, the Bulgarians would attack the Greeks. Kambarov did not want the Greeks driven back. He hoped that they would reinforce their exposed positions east of the Axios before he struck through Yugoslavia into the Greek rear in Macedonia. For reasons of security, the Bulgarians could not be informed until the last moment.

At 0300 on the twenty-ninth, three Bulgarian divisions, supported by an independent tank brigade, attacked the Greek 10th Infantry Division along the Nestos River. By nightfall, the Bulgarians had driven the Greeks back through Kavala. The following

morning, reinforced by the 22d Armored Brigade, the Greeks counterattacked and retook the town. The Bulgarian commander requested permission to reinforce his front-line units in an effort to
regain the momentum of the advance, but Kambarov refused. Desultory fighting continued throughout the day before it tapered off
in the evening with both armies exhausted.

At a late night staff conference, Kambarov ordered the attack
halted and directed the Bulgarians to launch their assault down the
Sturma valley at 0600. As they had along the Nestos, the Bulgarians
broke through the Greek defenses and by noon had taken Sidirokastro. The advance continued the next day—1 August—with the
Bulgarians advancing into Seres. But there the Bulgarian offensive
thrust, again denied reinforcements by Kambarov, stalled. A late
afternoon counterattack spearheaded by the Greek 20th Armored
Division retook the town and carried north to the outskirts of
Sidirokastro.

At a conference convened at Plovdiv at 0830 on 2 August,
Kambarov at last informed the Bulgarians of the planned Yugoslavian operation scheduled to begin at 0500 on the fourth. The two
generals were discussing how best the Bulgarians could pin the
Greeks along the Macedonian front when an aide entered the room
and called the Southwest Front commander aside. At 0730, according to the report, NATO paratroopers had begun landing near Saray
in the rear of the Romanians. As he unleashed a string of expletives,
Kambarov passed the message to the Bulgarian commander, whose
only response was to shake his head and mumble something about
"the Romanians, again the Romanians!" "Yes, the Romanians,"
Kambarov replied, "they're useless, totally useless."

The allied airborne landing at Saray on the morning of 2 August
marked the beginning of a broader operation designed to destroy
Romanian forces in Thrace. The offensive, codenamed "Plevna",
was the brainchild of Turkish GEN Ersari. Assured of at least temporary air superiority by the presence of two American carrier battlegroups in the southern Aegean and the three F-16 squadrons of
the 401st Tactical Fighter Wing that had moved forward from Comiso to Turkish bases, Ersari devised a scheme that combined an

airdrop and an amphibious landing in the Romanian rear with a frontal assault from the Catalca position.

At 0730, Turkish, American, and French air transport assets had begun dropping elements of the French 11th Airborne Division and the Turkish airborne brigade around Saray. About 0745, American and Turkish amphibious craft began landing assault elements of the American 6th Marine Expeditionary Brigade and the Italian San Marco marine regiment at Tekirdag on the north-central coast of the Sea of Marmara. At 0800, the Turkish First Army struck westward from Catalca.

About noon, the paratroopers and marines joined hands along the E5N ten miles west of Corlu. BG Edwin Whelen, commander of 6 MEB, reported: "estimate elements five Rom divisions trapped." As Whelen's marines and the French paratroopers formed a line facing west to block any attempts to break into the pocket, the Turkish airborne and Italian marines formed an inner barrier to prevent the Romanians from escaping.

Meanwhile, the First Army struck westward, driving the Romanians before them. For MAJ Ulusoy, whose 2d Armored Brigade spearheaded the Turkish attack, the offensive was much like a Mongol hunt. The Turks drove their prey—the Romanians—into the waiting arms of the blocking force. By the evening, organized resistance had ended. It took NATO units an entire day to round up and disarm all of the enemy troops. Ersari's men captured over sixty thousand Romanians during the second and third of August. Ersari was surprised, pleasantly, by the speed and extent of the disintegration of the Romanian units.

Nor was the collapse confined to the pocket. At noon on 2 August, Kambarov ordered a pair of Romanian motor rifle divisions near Kirklareli to launch an immediate relief attack. Driving southeast along Route 20, the Romanians found their way blocked by French paratroopers at Vize. Shortly after a half-hearted attack began, Turkish F-4 Phantom II fighter-bombers struck the Romanians. The French watched as the Romanians abandoned their tanks and APCs and fled from the battlefield. The next day, the Romanian 4th Tank Division disintegrated in a short engagement with a French airborne battalion at Luleburgaz.

Operation "Plevna" had succeeded beyond Ersari's expectations: the Turks had virtually knocked Romania out of the war. COL

GEN Kambarov ordered all Romanian units withdrawn from operations and delegated to duties north of the Danube. Fearful of a Romanian mutiny, he felt compelled to keep Soviet units then transiting the country in place to secure rear-area communications. Moreover, Kambarov faced the problem of plugging a hundred-mile-wide hole in his front that reached from the Black Sea to the base of the Gallipoli Peninsula at the worst possible moment—on the eve of his long-awaited offensive against Yugoslavia.

THIRTY-THREE

In an early morning 28 July staff meeting, the usually overconfident GEN Gilchrist surprised his staff when he acknowledged that "we're in some deep shit around Tripoli." Gilchrist had overestimated the impact of air power on ground forces and underestimated the extent of Libyan tenacity. "I guess deep down," Gilchrist confided in an aide, "I really expected the Libyans to pack it up and go home once they saw our troops come ashore. Hell, they never fought that hard at sea, in the air, or against the Egyptians!"

Gilchrist sent calls for help to Cairo and Washington. The Egyptians responded within an hour, agreeing to push their units in Cyrenaica westward as quickly as possible. Unfortunately, because of the logistic restraints on an advance confined to a single coastal road, and the great distance to be traversed—nearly five hundred miles from Ajdabiyah to Homs—such assistance was likely to arrive too little and too late. That afternoon, the JCS agreed to release the 3d Brigade of the 82d Airborne Division to CENTCOM. The chiefs had intended to use the brigade to reinforce the Turkish offensive in Thrace but Gilchrist, unfortunately, had "screwed it all up."

Until reinforcements arrived, Gilchrist had no choice but to halt all offensive operations against the Libyan capital and to reinforce the hard-pressed rangers at Homs. But LTG Ferguson, commander of the 82d, exploded when he received orders to march the 1st Brigade back to Homs. "Shit, general, in forty-eight hours my men walked from Homs to Tripoli and fought a battle; now they're being ordered to reverse that march, and fight another battle, in twenty-four hours."

Gilchrist had few options. Throughout the twenty-eighth, the Libyans kept up the pressure at Homs and by evening, when the advance elements of the 1st Brigade began to arrive, fortunately via helicopter, the rangers had just about reached the end of their resistance. Only nightfall, continuous air attacks, and the arrival of the advance airmobile elements of the 82d saved the day.

The following morning, the Libyans attempted to resume their advance but now faced stiffened American resistance. By noon, all offensive action had come to a halt. The attack had failed, but the counterattack had forced Gilchrist to stop his assault against Tripoli.

On the morning of the thirtieth, the 3d Brigade from Fort Bragg began to arrive at airfields and airstrips between Zuwarah and Okbah ibn Nafi. Gilchrist, believing that his line at Homs, now reinforced by the 1st Brigade, was secure and with the Egyptians at Sirte, little more than 150 miles from Homs, decided to resume the attack against Tripoli at 1300.

At noon, the Benghazi division struck westward once again, taking the Americans by surprise. Forty-five minutes after the assault began, Libyan tanks, supported by infantry, had entered Homs. The Americans had intercepted messages from Tripoli ordering the division to attack, but other intercepts indicated that the Libyan commander had refused to send his men to their deaths. What the Americans had not intercepted were the threats Qaddafi's "commissars" had made against Hussein and his family. Forced to attack, but convinced that any attempt to concentrate his units for an assault would be detected immediately by the Americans, Hussein launched his offensive from his defensive positions without any preliminary artillery barrage.

Although caught off guard, the men of the 82d quickly regained their balance and shortly after 1400 launched a counterattack that retook Homs. The Libyans, suffering heavily from air attack, could not maintain the momentum of their attack. By 1700, quiet had returned to the front.

LTG Hussein's ill-fated offensive had again forced Gilchrist to cancel his planned attack against Tripoli and had convinced CINCCENT that the Benghazi division had to be eliminated before a final assault could be launched against the Libyan capital. During the

evening of 31 July, the battalions of the 3d Brigade moved by helicopter into positions on the flank and in the rear of Hussein's
division. At 0400, Ferguson's 1st and 2d Brigades, supported by
the rangers, began an enveloping attack against the already battered
Libyans. By the afternoon of 2 August, "the division that wouldn't
die," as Hussein's command had become known to the men of the
82d, ceased to exist. Ferguson, who later drove to Zlitan where
Hussein had been taken prisoner, described the battlefield as an
"abattoir."

That evening, the Arab League called for Qaddafi "to give up
the pointless and uneven fight" and to spare his people and his
capital additional suffering. The Libyan leader vowed "to fight to
the death and to accept martyrdom gladly." Worse yet, interrogations of the few Libyan soldiers who were making their way to
American lines and surrendering indicated that Qaddafi had ordered his special units to ready Libya's chemical arsenal, reports
confirmed by intelligence intercepts.

At a late night staff meeting, Ferguson noticed that "Gilchrist
was under a lot of heat." His questionable handling of the campaign
thus far, the chemical warfare threat, and the pressure from the JCS
and CINCSOUTH, who wanted the 82d Airborne Division freed
for redeployment as soon and as unbloodied as possible to take
advantage of the Turkish victories in Thrace, compelled CINCCENT
to seek some quick way to end the campaign. "If they want speed,"
Gilchrist remonstrated to his staff, "well, damn, I'll give it to them."

At midnight, at Gilchrist's orders, a dozen B-52s bombed Tripoli. At 0700 the next morning, the bombers returned and repeated
their attack. At 0800, the final assault on Tripoli commenced. After
thirty-four hours of bloody fighting, resistance ended when a small
East German security detachment surrendered the presidential palace. Qaddafi had escaped.

At 2230 on the night of 3 August, Gilchrist received word
from Cairo that a pair of Libyan officers had appeared at the headquarters of the Egyptian 1st Armored Brigade in Misurata and had
delivered, quite literally, Qaddafi's head. "I guess there's some sat-
isfaction knowing that Qaddafi's lost his head," Gilchrist told his
assembled staff, "unfortunately, this has all come to pass too late
in the campaign to save my ass." At 2400, the American secretary
of defense relieved Gilchrist of his command.

THIRTY-FOUR

The evening of 3 August found Colonel General Kambarov, the Southwest Front commander, at his forward headquarters in Timosoara, Romania, preparing to oversee the offensive against Yugoslavia scheduled to begin at 0200 the following morning. The tired CINC was reviewing last-minute changes to the plan when an aide called Kambarov to the phone.

"This is the president, comrade general, good evening."

"Good evening, comrade president."

"I've just come from a general staff meeting, and I must tell you that there are some cold feet in the Kremlin tonight. There's some real concern about the situation in Thrace."

"There is concern with that situation here, as well, sir."

"Well, there have been suggestions made that the offensive be cancelled."

"Sir?"

"I said cancelled, or at least postponed until the situation is stabilized."

"I think that's a poor idea, comrade president, a very poor idea."

"But the Romanians . . ."

"They're collapsing, I know, but the Turks aren't going any-where."

"There are reports they are near Varna!"

"Those reports are false, comrade president, utterly false, and even if they were true, I would still recommend that the offensive proceed. We must gain successes somewhere, even if we have to take risks."

"Yes, I agree. And you are confident of our chances?"

"Yes, sir, I am. If you'd like, I could fly up to Moscow?"

"No, you must remain at the front. I imagine this is a critical time. I'll support you from here. Don't worry."

"We'll succeed, comrade president, let me assure you that we'll succeed."

"You must understand, comrade general, I have heard many such assurances these last few weeks."

"Yes, sir, I know you have. But we'll succeed. Yugoslavian resistance will be crushed in less than a week! If not . . ."

"If not, what?"

"If not I will resign my command, comrade president, and fight at the front as a common soldier."

"Ah! Now that is an assurance I haven't heard before! Kambarov, I respect you for that, but I may also hold you to your word."

"Yes, comrade president."

"Good night, then, and good luck."

"Good night, sir."

Kambarov hung up the phone, feeling anything but confident. Several aspects of the impending offensive worried him. Had NATO or the Yugoslavs detected the preparations for the attack? How could they have missed the concentration of a half dozen armies in western Hungary and Romania? Were they likely to buy the deception plan—that the troops were in position to pressure the Yugoslavs into an alliance and to provide assistance? And what of the situation in the air? Despite some last minute reinforcements from the Soviet Union and transfers from Germany, NATO would still probably hold the upper hand. Kambarov imagined himself carrying a rifle, leaping from a BMP to join an assault. Then he looked at his pot belly and laughed loudly.

"Is there something wrong, sir?" A young aide had just handed Kambarov a folder and had assumed that the colonel general's outburst had been prompted by the enclosed memo.

"No, Yuri, there's nothing wrong. Tell me. How long until we take Belgrade?"

"Three days, sir. It's in the plan."

"But how long do you think it will take?"

"Sir?"

"How long Yuri?"

"Four days, no more."

"Yuri, I pray . . . I hope you're right."

★ ★ ★

At 0300 on the 4th of August, "Suvorov" began. The Southwest Front's plan involved simultaneous offensive operations by several armies composed of Soviet, Hungarian, and Bulgarian units. The Tenth Army formed the northern, and the Sixteenth Army the southern pincer of the Warsaw Pact drive against Zagreb. Following the capture of the city, the two armies were to continue their advances to the line Ljubljana-Rijeka to prevent the movement of the Italian army into Yugoslavia. The Twenty-first Army drove south along the M22 for Novi Sad, an important road junction and crossing point along the Danube north of Belgrade. The Sixth Guards Tank Army, concentrated in southern Hungary and Romania (Timosoara), struck at Belgrade from the north, while the Third Guards Tank Army drove on the Yugoslav capital from the south. The Nineteenth Army, from its jumping off positions in northwestern Bulgaria, began its push over difficult mountainous terrain to capture Nis and cut the main north-south road—the M1. The army would then drive south on Skopje in Yugoslavian Macedonia. The Bulgarians were assigned the demanding tasks of containing the Greeks in Macedonia while simultaneously swinging their left flank back to halt, or at least to delay the advance of the Turks in Thrace until the arrival of the Soviet Thirty-Eighth Army, then hurrying south through Romania.

D day went well for Kambarov's forces. Elements of the Twenty-first Army captured Novi Sad while the Third Guards Tank Army's 14th Tank Division seized a bridgehead over the Danube just south of its confluence with the Tisa. The Nineteenth Army made good progress in the south and captured Nis before noon.

On the fifth, the Tenth Army's Hungarian 2d Tank Division achieved a coup de main, capturing Ljubljana, while elements of the Sixteenth Army, which had also bypassed Zagreb, stormed Rijeka. As the Soviet ring around Belgrade closed in the center, the Nineteenth Army's 92d MRD entered Skopje while the Bulgarians seized the border passes to the east.

The Warsaw Pact assault had achieved complete tactical and operational surprise. Various NATO intelligence assets, both technical and human, had detected the concentration of forces along the Yugoslavian borders. The reports had troubled ADM McMichaels, but the analysts had insisted that the units identified were too weak to take on the Yugoslavs. But the analysts had underestimated the strength of the forces deployed along the border by fifty percent. The estimates of Soviet intentions were also flawed. McMichaels had been led to believe that the concentration of sufficient strength to knock out Yugoslavia would force the Russians to shift their center of gravity from Germany to the Balkans, a development that would never occur.

It had occurred and the resultant confusion in NATO's higher echelons caused the alliance to respond slowly to Yugoslav calls for assistance. NATO aircraft were in action over the beleaguered country before the end of D day, but not until the morning of 6 August did the Italians begin to move into Yugoslavia. And only late that evening, at LANDSOUTHEAST headquarters in Izmir, did the Greeks and Turks finally agree to coordinate their operations in Macedonia and Thrace in an effort to take some pressure off the Yugoslavs. It was already too late.

On the morning of 7 August, elements of the Tenth and Sixteenth Armies struck the Italians in Slovenija and drove them back toward the border, almost storming Trieste. To the east, the Twenty-first Army completed the capture of Zagreb, clearing the rear of the northernmost Warsaw Pact advance. The Third and Sixth Guard Tank Armies likewise completed the conquest of Belgrade. The advance elements of the Third Guards Tank Army smashed through Yugoslav resistance west of the capital and drove along the M19, seizing a bridgehead across the Drina and threatening Sarajevo. To the south, the Nineteenth Army struck the front of the Greek 15th Reserve Infantry Division and captured Niki, a small post along the Greek-Yugoslav frontier. By the evening of the eighth, it had become apparent to Kambarov at his forward headquarters in Timosoara that Yugoslavia was in the initial stage of collapse. Entire formations were beginning to surrender. Many advancing Soviet units reported little or no opposition as they swept through the countryside. The commander of a Hungarian division fighting in the north had to intervene to halt a firefight between Croatian and Serbian units more interested in destroying each other than in stopping the Pact advance.

Not all of the news was so favorable. NATO clearly held the initiative in the air and Warsaw Pact units moving in daylight along the roads in Yugoslavia suffered heavily. The Italians dug in their heels in the mountainous terrain of western Slovenia as reinforcements, including the American 101st Air-Assault Division, reached the front. On the ninth, a Turkish counterattack checked a Bulgarian armored drive into the left flank of the NATO advance in Thrace. A subsequent Italian-French amphibious and airmobile assault threw back the Bulgarians, destroyed two tank brigades, and reached the Meric River.

On the morning of 11 August, the Soviet-Hungarian Sixteenth Army launched an offensive toward Trieste. Soviet troops took Postonja, northeast of the city, but a counterattack by the Italian Ariete Armored Division, supported by Italian Tornado fighter-bombers, routed the Hungarian 4th MRD along the M12. By evening, the Pact offensive had ground to a halt.

As a result of the repulse before Trieste, Kambarov ordered his staff to draw up plans for the immediate transfer of forces from northern Yugoslavia to the south. The following morning Southwest Front began the movement of the Twenty-first and Sixth Guards Tank Armies to Thrace. Kambarov had wished to move the entire Third Guards Tank Army to Macedonia, but most of the formations were still bogged down in difficult fighting for Sarajevo which lasted until the final Yugoslavian surrender on 14 August.

Both NATO and the Warsaw Pact used the lull in the fighting to reinforce and regroup in the south. NATO's near total control of the air slowed Pact movements and hindered the buildup of supplies, while alliance forces arrived continuously by air and sea.

As a result, NATO struck first. On 16 August, with the American 10th Mountain Division reinforcing the lines north of Thessaloniki, the Greek command launched a surprise counterstroke from Florina. Spearheaded by the French 6th Light Armored Division of the FAR, the attack retook Niki and carried across the Yugoslav border as far as Bitola. The following morning, the Franco-Greek force resumed the advance along the M26 and reached Prilep before the Nineteenth Army recovered its balance and halted the NATO drive.

In Thrace on the morning of the sixteenth, a combined Italian-French-American-Turkish force smashed the Bulgarian front along the Meric at Ipsala and drove as far as Alexandroupoli. The following morning, the lead battalion of the American 6 MEB repulsed a counterattack that almost broke through the marines' lines. Prisoner interrogations revealed that the troops involved belonged to the Soviet 6th Guards Tank Division of the Sixth Guards Tank Army.

Alarmed by the report, COMLANDSOUTHEAST decided to halt his counteroffensive and withdraw to a shorter, more defensible line running from Tekirdag through Saray to the Black Sea coast. By the seventeenth, Ersari recognized that despite his successes, he had failed to gain the initiative and was about to get hit by a massive Soviet offensive along a front running from Albania to the Black Sea.

THIRTY-FIVE

Despite the shift in strategic emphasis from the Western to the Southwestern TVD adopted at the 27 July Kremlin meeting, the Soviet commanders responsible for the direction of operations along the front in Germany refused to adopt a defensive posture and continued their efforts to regain lost momentum and resume the drive toward the Rhine. The Soviet army was ill-suited to defensive operations and its senior leadership simply was not comfortable with anything but the offensive. Marshal Kubitskii was also concerned about the state of the Soviet Union's allies. The Warsaw Pact CINC believed that "if NATO gained the initiative it would focus its efforts on the destruction of the weak links in our line—the Poles, Czechs, and even the East Germans whose divisions, although they had fought well thus far, were beginning to show signs of exhaustion."

★ ★ ★

At 0500 on the morning of 4 August, for the second time in the war, Pact forces breached the Weser line at Nienburg, north of Hannover. But as lead elements of the Fifth Guards Tank Army pushed westward toward Diepholz, they were struck in the left flank by the British 3d Armored Division. By evening, the British had regained the river bank and destroyed the forces that had crossed the Weser.

In the south, Warsaw Pact forces sought to pinch off the NATO corridor to Munich. The main blow fell upon the already battered French 1st Armored Division near Landsberg. In the heavy fighting for the town, the old fortress, in which Adolf Hitler had dictated *Mein Kampf*, was destroyed. By the afternoon of the fifth, Landsberg was in Soviet hands and the Bavarian capital was again isolated.

Further north on 5 August, Soviet forces attempted to cross the Weser south of Hannover at Hoxter. Airmobile forces successfully seized several crossing sites but prompt counterattacks by the U.S. 4th Mechanized Infantry Division eliminated these bridgeheads before main force units could cross.

The front remained stable throughout the sixth, but the next day Warsaw Pact forces attacked both ends of the NATO line. In the north, Polish troops launched a desultory offensive against West German forces pocketed in Kiel. The attack foundered almost as soon as it began. In Bavaria, two Czech divisions, pulled from the line near Landsberg, attacked the encircled NATO troops defending Munich. Fighting in the eastern outskirts of the city continued into the afternoon of 8 August but came to a halt when Soviet advisors noted that the Czech formations were beginning to give way once again.

At 0430 on 9 August, NORTHAG forces under British GEN Carton de Wiart struck from their salient in Hannover, working their way northward with their left along the Weser. British Army of the Rhine (BAOR) troops led the offensive. The Pact Fourth Guards Tank Army threw its only fresh reserve formation—the Polish 16th MRD—into a counterattack about noon. The Poles suffered heavily from NATO ground attack aircraft during their approach and retreated shortly after establishing contact with British forces. A RAF liaison officer attached to the BAOR surveyed the scene and relayed his impression back to headquarters.

> It's like Dante's inferno. Everywhere one sees the charred remains of tanks, trucks, BMPs, assault guns, and other vehicles. Bodies are strewn about, burned and often hideously mangled. Everywhere there are weapons—rifles and the like—that had obviously been thrown aside in great haste. Then there are the odds and ends: a shoe, a pair of trousers, a fishing rod, a golf club, a pair of women's panties. How some of these things end up on a battlefield remains a mystery to me. When we resumed the advance, we came across groups of unarmed Poles. They came out of hiding with their arms raised and surrendered.

South of Kassel, CENTAG forces also went over to the offensive. Units of the III German and the V U.S. Corps struck eastward on either side of the A4. By nightfall, lead elements of V Corps had actually crossed the East German border.

In Bavaria, West German, French, and American units fought throughout the ninth to reopen a supply route into Munich. Warsaw Pact forces repulsed several attacks during the morning, but in the afternoon the East German 25th Tank Division, which had endured twenty-seven days of near continuous combat, disintegrated. By evening, the road through Landsberg had again been cleared.

The collapse of the 25th Tank Division on 9 August marked the beginning of the end for the East Germans. On the morning of the tenth, reports began to reach SACEUR that other East German formations were beginning to go the way of the Poles and the Czechs.

The NORTHAG offensive east of the Weser continued to gain ground, principally at the expense of the East German 21st MRD which broke when attacked by West German troops near Verden. The V Corps troops that had advanced into East Germany itself, found themselves greeted by the populace. Americans were shocked to discover that the people had come out of their homes to greet them as liberators. Communist officials had all fled east. The U.S. VII Corps, which launched a counteroffensive on the tenth that retook Bamberg, also encountered East German forces—the 79th Tank Division—that seemed happy enough to pull out of line and to "retreat like hell."

Along the front from the North Sea to the Austrian border, many NATO commanders sensed that the momentum of the war had swung decisively to their advantage. But in the rear, at the army group and at SACEUR headquarters, the growing sense of optimism remained tempered by caution.

In the far south, after relieving Munich, LTG Hans Wunsch, the commander of the II West German Corps, sent the 10th Panzer Division through the city in a daring drive to the east along the A92. Initially, COMCENTAG wanted Wunsch to widen the perimeter around the city, but he saw an opportunity to hit the Czechs who held the line to the east and expected to unhinge the entire Pact position in southern Bavaria. By late evening, the lead elements of the 10th Panzer had reached Landshut along the Isar. "Our attack is being slowed," Wunsch reported, "principally by the columns of Czech prisoners who are blocking the roads in the division's rear."

For the Soviet Union, the tenth of August marked the beginning of the end. The Warsaw Pact had lost the initiative in Germany. The front was beginning to crack.

★ ★ ★

Reports from the Far East were similarly depressing. On 7 August, allied aircraft operating from Japan, South Korea, and from the carrier *Carl Vinson*, struck at Soviet bases around Vladivostok. On the eighth, under the cover of these operations, a Japanese strike group moved to within Harpoon range of Vladivostok and attacked Soviet surface forces in port, heavily damaging the cruiser *Admiral Senyavin*, and sinking an oiler and five fast attack boats. GEN Ilichev responded promptly and concentrated several regiments of interceptors to defend what remained of the Pacific Ocean Fleet.

The Vladivostok strikes were a feint; allied objectives lay further north. At a high-level American-Japanese meeting held in Tokyo on 29 July, ADM Cooper (CINCPAC), pending the approval of the National Command Authority, had accepted a Japanese plan for a combined assault to liberate the Northern Territories—the disputed islands in the southern Kuriles. Japanese support for American efforts in WESTPAC during the first week of the war had been critical and the admiral believed that the requests from Tokyo for assistance in retaking the islands was justified and deserved U.S. support. The NCA agreed on 31 July, and the operation, codenamed "Crane," was scheduled to begin on the morning of 9 August, the anniversary of the Soviet Union's attack on Japan in 1945.

At 0130 on the ninth, allied aircraft, including planes from the carriers *Kitty Hawk* and *Independence*, and warships, including the battleship *Missouri*, opened the bombardment of Iturup (Etorofu). At 0515, American marines of 9 MEB began landing south of Hitokappu Bay (from which the Japanese carrier striking force had sailed in November 1941 en route to Pearl Harbor), as Japanese paratroopers of the 1st Airborne Brigade dropped inland. Simultaneously, elements of the Japanese 2d Division landed in the Hobomais.

The Soviet defenders, elements of an understrength division which had been isolated from supply for nearly a month and subjected to regular air attack, offered minimal resistance. By nightfall, the Communist defense had collapsed and allied troops were being ferried to Kunashir (Kunashiri) to complete the conquest of the disputed islands.

★ ★ ★

As a result of the setbacks in Europe and the Far East, Marshal Posokhov offered to resign at a tumultuous general staff meeting held on the morning of 11 August. "Resign!" the president thundered in response, "certainly not. No, comrade marshal, you are dismissed. And," he added as he gestured to an aide who opened the conference room door for entering security men, "placed under arrest." The president then ordered Marshal Durostnik, the minister of defense, to take over Marshal Posokhov's responsibilities.

★★★

Forced to adopt a defensive strategy along the Central Front, Durostnik struggled desperately to contain the NATO counteroffensive. He was one of the few men who actually recognized the magnitude of the dangers the Soviets faced in Germany.

The NATO offensive consisted of four major drives, the northernmost of which consisted of NORTHAG's push through Niedersachsen toward the lower Elbe. On 12 August, Russian troops, threatened with encirclement, evacuated Bremerhaven. On the sixteenth, the West German 3d Panzer Division routed the 7th East German MRD in a short engagement near Bremervorde. By the following evening, Dutch, West German, and British units had reached the line Cuxhaven-Luneburg and in several places were abreast the Elbe River.

CENTAG's three offensives made similar progress. The III West German and V American Corps continued their two-pronged advance on Erfurt. By the seventeenth, the advance elements of the III Corps had reached Eisleben, just west of Halle, while the American 3d Armored Division entered Saalfeld, southeast of Erfurt. The American VII Corps retook Nuremburg on 16 August, while the Franco-German advance east of Munich led to the near-total disintegration of the Forty-First Army and the capture of Wasserburg and Landau on the seventeenth by the 10th Panzer Division. Thousands of Czech troops, their retreat cut off by NATO forces, began to surrender or to seek internment by crossing the border into neutral Austria. "Czech units," Wunsch reported, "no longer capable of resistance."

After five bitter weeks of fighting along the Central Front, the Soviets, effectively abandoned by their allies, now faced aggressive NATO armies intent on advancing eastward. In an assessment for Marshal Kubitskii, Col Kaganovich concluded:

Our enemies have seized the initiative and are unlikely to lose it. Soviet reinforcements generally arrive at the front exhausted and battered after difficult approach marches interrupted by constant NATO air attack. Our supply system, geared to a short war, has all but collapsed under the pressures of an extended campaign and the allied air interdiction effort. We know that supplies and fresh American troops are reaching the front from across the Atlantic, unhindered by our navy. The situation is, in a word, bleak.

On 16 August, transports carrying the first major American unit shipped entirely by sea from the United States arrived in Dutch and Belgian ports. The Texas 49th National Guard Armored Division had departed Gulf coast ports in July and passed safely into the Atlantic through the Florida Strait. Not a single vessel had been lost and the troops were soon on their way to the front.

THIRTY-SIX

At 0630 on 18 August, three Russian armored divisions of the Sixth Guards Tank Army, supported by numerous Bulgarian formations, struck the fronts of the Greek 8th and 11th Infantry Divisions along the Sturma line. The Greeks, well supported by fighter-bombers, fought well throughout the morning, but in the afternoon the heavily outnumbered and outgunned defenders began to fall back toward Thessaloniki.

The Greeks only now began to transfer troops from the Aegean islands to the mainland. While the deployment of the Aegean command made some sense during the initial days of the war when Soviet naval and amphibious forces were at large in the Aegean, the troops could have been better employed in Macedonia after the elimination of the SOVMEDRON. On 22 July, CINCSOUTH had recommended the movement of three brigades to the mainland and had offered the services of American amphibious transports to assist such a transfer. But the Greeks had declined the offer, claiming that the formations were ill-suited to mobile operations. "My guess is," ADM McMichaels informed the Pentagon, "that even in the midst of this struggle, the Greeks are keeping one eye on the Turks." But now, five weeks later, facing disaster in Macedonia, the Greeks suddenly discovered a pressing need for such light formations in the mountainous northern regions of their country.

Unfortunately, the Greek decision came too late to save their armies in the north. In the afternoon of 19 August, Soviet forces entered the northern outskirts of Thessaloniki and after thirty-six hours of difficult and destructive fighting, secured the historic city.

With the bulk of the 8th Infantry Division consumed in the fighting for Thessaloniki, Greek resistance weakened. The battered 11th Infantry Division attempted to stem the Warsaw Pact advance along the Axios, but by the late morning of 21 August, Russian troops had forced the river. Their line broken, the Greeks began to move south along the Larissa-Thessaloniki road. While the direction of the retreat covered the direct route to the south and Athens, it uncovered the lateral roads that led into the rear of the NATO forces in western Macedonia and Yugoslavia. Seizing the opportunity, MG Mikhail Smirnov, commander of the Sixth Guards Tank Army, pushed one of his divisions westward. By evening, elements of the 20th Guards Tank Division had taken both Gianitsa and Alexandria.

The Pact forces continued their western drive throughout the night. While the 20th Guards pushed directly west towards Edessa, the Bulgarian 2d MRD and 5th Tank Brigade conducted a rapid advance to the southwest. By noon on the twenty-second, the Bulgarians had driven as far as Kozani—the hub of western Macedonia—where they met the Greek 96th Infantry Brigade, hastily transferred from the Aegean. In a short engagement, the Bulgarians swept the Greeks aside and continued their drive, reaching Grevena by nightfall, trapping several NATO divisions then fighting for survival further north.

At 0700 on 22 August, elements of the Soviet Nineteenth and Third Guard Tank Armies attacked the French and Greek forces that had pushed into southern Yugoslavia. In heavy fighting west of Prilep, the Russian 14th and 42d Guards Tank Divisions had destroyed the Greek 20th Armored Division and reached the M26, blocking the retreat of the remaining French and Greek divisions which were forced to conduct an overland withdrawal toward Edessa. Soviets armored columns were able to advance rapidly along the road and by nightfall had reached Ptolemaida and Kastoria. Combined with the successes of the Sixth Guards Tank Army and the Bulgarians, an elated Kambarov was able that night to report to Moscow that the American 10th Mountain Division, the French 9th Marine and 6th Light Armored Divisions, and the Greek 2d Mechanized, and 6th and 15th Reserve Infantry Divisions—about 60,000 men—were pocketed in the area around Edessa. "NATO resistance in Macedonia," Kambarov informed the general staff, "has been broken."

★ ★ ★

The fiasco in Macedonia on the twenty-second caused panic in Athens. Hordes of frightened civilians took to the roads in Thessaly, racing south for the safety of the Peloponnese. Greek political and military leaders, who had stood by silently while the Turks had borne the brunt of the war in July and early August, now appealed to Ankara for help. "WHERE ARE THE TURKS?" ran one headline in an Athens newspaper on the morning of 23 August.

"And where were the Greeks?" came the reply from the Turks. GEN Ersari, far from launching an offensive in Thrace, continued to withdraw into the shorter and more defensible Catalca position. The Turkish First Army, facing five fresh Soviet divisions of the Thirty-Eighth Army as well as another six divisions transferred from the Yugoslavian front, was incapable of taking any offensive action in Thrace to relieve the pressure on the Greeks. Nevertheless, Ersari did commit Turkish-based air assets to support the front in Macedonia and also agreed to transfer to Greece the American, French, and Italian units then fighting with the First Army.

Additional NATO reinforcements were also arriving in Greece. On the morning of 23 August, lead elements of the American 4 and 8 MEBs, fresh from their Norwegian triumphs, began landing along the Boeotian coast. "Bull" Campbell, the II MEF commander, was one of the first marines ashore. Shortly after his arrival he was driving up the coast road to Lamia when one of his aides pointed out that they were in *the* pass—Thermopylae. The poor man, new to Campbell's staff, began reciting Lacedaemonian poems about heroism and plunged into a discourse about the gallant stand of Leonidas and his three hundred Spartans.

"Just think," he told Campbell, "2,500 years after that stand, perhaps we can repeat history."

"Jesus Christ," Campbell interrupted, "stop this fucking hummer."

When the open-topped humvee came to a halt, Campbell stood up and looked around.

"Hey, Jack, I don't give a fuck about the . . . the . . . Lackeys, or whosomevertheywere. Get this straight, shithead, I saw that movie and the Spartans got slaughtered. Hell, I didn't come to Greece to repeat history, I came here to make it. Got that straight? And the answer's yes: you can have that transfer to a frontline unit."

Further south, the near panic that had gripped the Greek capital ended suddenly when transports began unloading the men and equipment of the American 35th National Guard Mechanized Division and the 107th National Guard Armored Cavalry Regiment. The American ambassador in Athens later attributed the shift in national mood to the mistaken belief that the "guard" designation signified "some kind of elite status, because Greeks I knew kept shaking my hand and kissing me, repeating over and over that the 'guards' had arrived and would save the country."

Until the American formations could get their equipment ashore and move north along roads jammed with civilians fleeing south, the Greek army continued to bear the brunt of the Warsaw Pact offensive. Unfortunately, the Greek forces that had survived the Macedonian debacle were few. Only the 98th Infantry Brigade, recently transferred from the Aegean island of Lesvos, blocked the advance of the Bulgarians to the south at Meteora in the Pindus River valley. To the east, the remnants of the 11th Infantry Division held the Aliakmonas River.

Throughout the twenty-third, Soviet and Bulgarian forces struggled to resume their heretofore rapid advance to the south. Along the coast, units of the Sixth Guards Tank Army broke through the Aliakmonas line. The Greeks, heavily supported by NATO fighter-bombers (including the air wings of three American carriers operating in the southern Aegean) and the sixteen-inch guns of the battleship *New Jersey*, gave ground slowly. By day's end, the Soviets had covered only half of the twenty miles to their objective—Katerini—and had suffered heavily. To the west, the 98th Infantry Brigade held Meteora against repeated Bulgarian attacks. During the morning, from atop almost inaccessible and impregnable monastery-topped pinnacles, the Greeks took a heavy toll on Bulgarian tanks and APCs that attempted to bypass the 98th's defenses. In the afternoon, the Bulgarians stormed the natural fortresses with infantry, but again without success. A late-afternoon helicopter assault against six of the pinnacles secured the Aghios Stephanos monastery, but failed elsewhere.

★★★

At noon on 23 August, LTG Campbell, USMC, commander of II MEF, donned a second hat as Commander, Allied Forces, Greece (COMALFORGRK). CINCSOUTH, ADM McMichaels, had suggested the establishment of the ad hoc command. The Greek army had been all but destroyed in the disasters in Thrace and Macedonia and McMichaels recognized that the defense of the country would increasingly be borne by NATO formations, principally American. Given the Greek track record thus far in the war, he was unwilling to place those units under Greek command. Since Athens refused to yield control of its army in Thrace to the Turkish GEN Ersari, COMLANDSOUTHEAST, McMichaels devised a scheme under which Campbell would assume temporary command of all NATO troops in Greece. "I am convinced," McMichaels reported to the NATO council, "that we need a commander on the scene, in Greece, because both Izmir and Naples are too remote."

Campbell greeted his new responsibility with mixed feelings. He asked McMichaels just where his Greek troops were, only to learn that most of them were in Bulgarian POW camps or cut off in the north. NATO forces? Two French divisions were pocketed at Edessa, and the Italian marines and French paratroopers were on their way, but were still in Turkey. Where were the other American units? The 10th Mountain Division was cut off up north and the others were still unloading in Athens. As a result, "Camelforce," as Campbell's marines started calling COMALFORGRK, initially consisted of American marines. "Hell," Campbell told McMichaels during a conversation on the twenty-third, "I don't need more responsibility, I need time: time to move my men north before the Pact breaks through the passes into Thessaly." Fortunately, thanks to the spirited resistance of the Greeks at Meteora and Katerini and the hard-pressed NATO forces surrounded near Edessa, Campbell gained the time to move his marines north.

Anxious to check out the ground himself, on the afternoon of the twenty-third, Campbell choppered to Trikala and drove from there to Meteora. He drove through orchards and a village with quaint little houses all painted white, pink, blue. When the humvee went around a bend, Campbell saw the rock formations that gave Meteora its name. Gigantic rock needles rose into the sky. Campbell's interpreter explained that the ancient Greeks believed that the rocks were meteors hurled at the Earth by an angry god. Campbell was impressed.

"Natural fortresses!"

"That's just what the Greeks used them for in the old days," the interpreter replied.

In fact, Campbell could see that the Greeks were still using the formations for defense. Greek flags were flying from most of the tops and down below there were scores of burning Russian-made Bulgarian tanks and APCs, and bodies everywhere. Several hundred had been taken prisoner. Campbell got out of the humvee and walked over to have a look at his opponents. They appeared to be totally defeated, exhausted, and filthy. They were begging for food, they were so hungry. Campbell thought to himself: "Hell, why not attack? These guys are ready to fold."

After completing his reconnaissance, Campbell rushed back to his headquarters at Lamia. From there he hurried his marines and the 107th Armored Cavalry Regiment towards Meteora and ordered them to attack northwards the next morning. Campbell also directed MG Constantine Triandos, commander of the Greek 2d Mechanized Division and senior officer in the Edessa pocket, to launch a breakout attack to the southwest the following afternoon—at 1400 on 24 August.

At 1030 on the twenty-fourth, the lead elements of the 107th ACR and the 4th and 8th MEBs passed through Meteora and surprised a Bulgarian MRR preparing to launch its own attack against the pinnacles. "We passed through those Bulgarians quicker than bad chili," Campbell radioed McMichaels. By 1400 the Americans had reached Grevena, thirty miles into the rear of the now shattered Bulgarian 2d MRD. At 1430, marine helicopters lifted a battalion of 4 MEB to Kozani. The Bulgarians fled as the Americans approached. Marines examined seventeen T-62s, all that remained of the 5th Bulgarian Tank Brigade, that had been abandoned by their crews outside Kozani.

The attack from the Edessa pocket also caught the Warsaw Pact forces off guard. The spearhead of the Greek 2d Mechanized Division broke through Bulgarian positions south of Lake Vegoritas and by sunset had captured Ptolemaida. Later that evening, Greeks and American marines met north of Kozani.

★ ★ ★

Campbell had punched a corridor through to the pocket, but the NATO divisions around Edessa were unable to withdraw. At 1500, Kambarov ordered the divisions of the Third Guards, the Nineteenth, and the Sixth Guards Tank Armies "to initiate offensive operations against Edessa pocket to prevent disengagement and withdrawal." The morning of the twenty-fifth found the weakened Greek 2d Mechanized Division overextended along twenty miles of bad road. "I'm not entirely satisfied with the results," Campbell informed CINCSOUTH, "but our troops, especially the National Guard guys, have fought well and the Bulgarians are at the end of their rope." The arrival of fresh American forces had shifted the momentum of the campaign. To Campbell the dynamic was simple: the Greeks and Bulgarians had been at each others' throats for six weeks, exhausting themselves in their struggles with obsolescent equipment, and then suddenly, fresh, full-strength American units arrived, armed with top-of-the-line equipment, putting new heart into the Greeks, and tearing the hearts out of the Bulgarians.

The impact was marked. Reports from the front indicated that enemy troops were eager to surrender, at least to Americans. The Bulgarians were afraid that if they fell into Greek hands they would be killed on the spot. Americans at the front considered such fears not entirely groundless.

Unfortunately, in the Edessa pocket the shift in NATO morale proved short-lived. It became clear during the twenty-fifth that a successful withdrawal was unlikely because the pressure along the perimeter was too great. The Greek 2d Mechanized Infantry Division reported grave difficulties holding open the corridor. Kambarov, eager to clear the lateral roads that connected his coastal and inland drives and to free up his Soviet formations for a drive to the south, ordered the Pact forces around Edessa to accelerate their assaults in an effort to complete the destruction of the pocket.

On the twenty-sixth, MG Triandos called his fellow division

commanders to a meeting in his headquarters in Edessa's Olympion Hotel. MG David Manchester, commander of the American 10th Mountain Division, found Triandos despondent following the receipt of reports that earlier that morning Soviet troops had broken through the 2d Mechanized Division's front in four places and that the commanders of the 6th and 15th Greek Divisions were being heavily pressed and were on the point of collapse. Triandos had decided that the time had come to surrender. The American and French commanders of the pocketed NATO divisions were aghast. Manchester had to physically restrain MG Jean Baptiste Desaix, the commander of the French marines, who appeared ready to assault Triandos. Desaix, the senior of the two French division commanders, stated that the French had no intention of surrendering. Manchester, likewise, refused to yield and told Triandos that the decision was premature. Triandos appeared shaken but, nevertheless, refused to change his mind and told his French and American colleagues that he could no longer accept responsibility for the defense and that he was resigning his command.

Since French forces predominated in the pocket, Manchester agreed to place the American 10th Mountain Division under Desaix's command. Together, the two men worked out plans for the continued defense of Edessa without overreliance on the Greeks. "As we had feared," Manchester recalled, "by the end of the day, as word of Triandos's resignation made the rounds, the Greek units at the front began to give up the fight and surrender."

The fight for Edessa continued throughout the twenty-seventh. At Meteora, Bull Campbell pushed the 107th NG ACR as far as Ptolemeida, but there strong Soviet mechanized forces blocked the American relief attempt, and the Americans were forced to withdraw. "Without a complementary drive from inside the pocket," Campbell reported to McMichaels, "break-in unlikely to succeed." Meanwhile, Kambarov had concentrated mobile SAM batteries around the ever-shrinking Edessa perimeter, raising the cost of the airdrops that had kept the pocket supplied, and prompting McMichaels at 1730 on the twenty-seventh to cancel all subsequent efforts. At 1345 the next day—28 August—Soviet forces stormed the Olympion Hotel, Desaix dying amongst his marines in the fighting. By late afternoon, the Americans, fighting north of Edessa, and the remnants of the French 6th Light Armored Division, fighting to the west of the town, had also surrendered. In the fighting for Edessa, the Warsaw Pact took over 50,000 NATO soldiers—Greeks, French, and American—prisoner.

★ ★ ★

Whether or not the decision to surrender was justified, the pocket's two days of resistance pinned down at least a half-dozen Soviet divisions, further exhausted the Bulgarians, and bought time for Campbell to assemble additional NATO forces in Thessaly. After the short surrender ceremony in Edessa, GEN Manchester noticed that the Russian troops present looked more like defeated than victorious soldiers.

Indeed, the commander of the Sixth Guards Tank Army was worried about the morale of his men. They had been in combat for nearly a month, fighting from Belgrade to Macedonia, always pushing to maintain the tempo of the advance, with scores of tanks and vehicles broken down along hundreds of miles of inhospitable mountain roads. Soviet casualties had also been heavy, and the troops had suffered especially from NATO air attack during the siege. Edessa was in retrospect a pyrrhic victory.

During 29 and 30 August, Southwest Front remained on the defensive—exhausted, reorganizing, regrouping, and attempting to bring up supplies to a front all but isolated by NATO air power. NATO used the pause to assemble its forces in Thessaly. By the thirtieth, 6 MEB had arrived from Turkey and for the first time in the war Campbell's II MEF was concentrated north of Meteora, along with the National Guard 107th Armored Cavalry Regiment. LTG Walter Whitecomb, the commander of the American XVIII Airborne Corps headquarters from Fort Bragg, North Carolina, set up shop in Larissa, superseding Campbell in the command of NATO forces in Greece. Whitecomb concentrated the newly arrived 40th NG Mechanized Infantry Division with the 50th NG Armored Division for a drive along the coast.

At 0400 on 31 August, NATO counterattacked. Campbell's II MEF, supported by the 107th ACR, drove north from Grevena and Kozani. To the east, Whitecomb's two National Guard divisions struck northwards along the Larissa-Thessaloniki coastal road. Simultaneously, the marines of the Italian San Marco and the Greek 32d Regiments landed at the head of the Thermaikos Gulf, between the mouths of the Alaikmonas and Axios Rivers. Air transports dropped the Greek 2d Airborne Regiment and two battalions of the 1st Brigade of the 82d Airborne Division around Gianitsa and Alexandria. Inland, the 2d Marine Aircraft Wing supported II MEF's offensive. Whitecomb's coastal operations received massive support from Greek, Turkish, French, and American fighter-bombers, including aircraft from the carriers *Foch, Kennedy, Roosevelt, Eisenhower,* and *America,* and the guns of the battleship *New Jersey.*

The few Bulgarian units still in the line quickly disintegrated. By noon, even the Soviet formations began to give way. By late evening, lead elements of the National Guard 50th Armored Division had reached the Axios. LT James Dooley, a Cherry Hill, New Jersey, pharmacist, led a platoon of M-60A3 tanks of the 2d Battalion, 102d Armored Regiment, in a night assault that carried through Soviet lines and established contact with the Italians at the Axios bridge. Campbell's drive met with similar success. At 1300, the 107th ACR secured Kastoria. At 2230, elements of 4 MEB had reached Florina and were poised to cross the border into Yugoslavia. "We've turned the tables on the Russians," Campbell informed Whitecomb. Camelforce had trapped elements of nine divisions around Edessa, with all the roads cut and the only way out over the mountains to the north.

At 2300, Campbell choppered to Katerini to discuss further operations with Whitecomb. The II MEF commander was outlining his plans to bag the Russians—about 100,000 men—when an aide handed Whitecomb a message.

"Shit," he said, and handed the flimsy to Campbell.

Campbell read the message, the gist of which was that he was to cease all offensive operations and abide by a ceasefire along the entire front as of 0200, his time, 1 September. Additional instructions would follow.

"Damn, another twenty-four hours and we'd have finished the Russians down here. We would have mopped them up just like we did up in Norway. What the hell's going on?"

THIRTY-SEVEN

As Kambarov's Southwest
Front began its 18 August offensive against Greece, Warsaw Pact
forces of the Baltic, Northern, and Central Fronts struggled desperately in Germany to halt NORTHAG's and CENTAG's counter-
offensives. Kaganovich, sent forward on 19 August to get a first-
hand appreciation of the situation at the front, found that he had
great difficulty moving by road and near Potsdam barely escaped
death at the hands of a West German Tornado conducting a low-
altitude attack. His report to Marshall Kubitskii stressed the impact
of the Pact's failure to control the air.

> I very quickly gained an appreciation of the difficulties our troops
> are laboring under at the front. NATO fighter-bombers are ever pre-
> sent and the roads are jammed by vehicles, some burned out, others
> locked in massive traffic jams. I was told that NATO airstrikes had
> initially focused on key bottlenecks—bridges and road junctions—
> but were now striking throughout our rear as our SAM batteries ran
> short of missiles. I asked why reloads had not reached the front, and
> was told that the truck convoys had either been destroyed or were
> stuck in traffic somewhere in the rear. All kinds of supplies—tank
> rounds, fuel, everything—is in short supply. NATO holds complete
> control of the air. The troops are nonetheless doing their best.

Along the front from Kiel to Austria, Pact troops fought to hold
their positions and to escape encirclement. On the afternoon of 18
August, in an effort to avoid being trapped against the Austrian
border by the West German 10th Panzer Division's drive to the Inn
River, four Soviet divisions struck north into the German rear. Their
advance reached Rosenheim where American A-10 tank busters
destroyed the leading armored battalion. On the nineteenth, American troops recaptured Braunschweig when the 16th Polish Tank
Division, after undergoing repeated air attacks, took to its heels at
the first sign of advancing American M-1A1 Abrams tanks.

The Braunschweig debacle led to the Wolfsburg Incident: the
commander of a Soviet motor rifle battalion ordered his men to
open fire on fleeing Poles when they refused to halt. When word of
the massacre reached Warsaw, a political crisis ensued. Late that
evening, both the president and Communist party chief resigned

and were replaced by a new provisional government led by leaders of the Solidarity trade union. At 0900 on the twentieth, the provisional government ordered all Polish military forces "to withdraw immediately, in an orderly fashion maintaining arms and equipment, to Polish national territory."

The Polish decision caught Moscow by surprise. The Kremlin directed Marshal Durostnik to disarm any Polish formation unwilling to continue the fight and to seize Warsaw. But Durostnik's staff, after making a quick study of the problem, concluded that Soviet forces in Germany "were incapable of taking action against the Poles concurrent with operations against NATO." Durostnik agreed to use reserve divisions then moving through Poland toward the front to secure key communication facilities should the Poles declare their neutrality or take some other action against the Soviet Union. "Until we are able to stabilize the situation along the front," Durostnik told the Soviet president, "we must, unfortunately, humor the Poles."

Throughout the twentieth and twenty-first, the Soviets juggled their forces in an effort to fend off NATO and to fill the gaps left in the line as the Polish divisions marched east. At least the transition was orderly. The Poles, in general, did not abandon their positions but waited until they were relieved. Nevertheless, the loss of nearly a dozen divisions from the orders of battle of the Baltic and Northern Fronts greatly increased the prospects for success of NORTHAG's counteroffensive.

COL Kaganovich considered it a miracle that no immediate collapse occurred in the north. Soviet troops, supported by the few remaining combat-worthy East German formations, kept at bay the British, Dutch, West German, French, and Belgian divisions. NORTHAG reported only minor gains on the twenty-second and twenty-third.

In the center and south, NATO made somewhat greater progress. A concentric Franco-American attack destroyed two Soviet MRDs trapped near Erfurt. Late in the evening of the twenty-third, the American 1st Cavalry Division liberated Erfurt. The U.S. 3d Mechanized Division crossed the Saale and advanced to the outskirts of Gera. The American 2d Armored Division drove through the Hof Gap along the E441 for Karl Marx Stadt, while the 1st and 8th Mechanized Divisions pushed into Czechoslovakia along the

Nuremburg-Pilsen road, encircling three Soviet divisions in the triangle formed by the East German, Czechoslovakian, and West German borders. To the south, French forces drove the remnants of a Czech tank division from Regensburg and trapped four Soviet divisions against the Austrian border. By the evening of the twenty-fourth, all eight of these divisions had surrendered.

At 0900 Moscow time on 25 August, the general staff ordered Warsaw Pact forces deployed along the central front to conduct a strategic withdrawal to the line of the Elbe, Magdeburg, Leipzig, Dresden, Prague, and thence along the Vltava River. Durostnik, alarmed by reports from the front, and from Kaganovich who had returned to Moscow, hoped to shorten and stabilize the line and to accumulate reserves. Significantly, while Durostnik's directive spoke of the need for local counterattacks, it made no mention of seizing the initiative or regaining the momentum of the advance. In a meeting with Durostnik, Kaganovich warned that "too many formations have been isolated and destroyed attempting to continue the advance or to hold onto ground as enemy forces swept around the flanks. Many soldiers at the front, and officers too, feel they are being needlessly sacrificed." Durostnik sat silently, impassively. "I was often asked," Kaganovich continued, "'why do they send a colonel to the front; why don't the generals and marshals come themselves?' Even the front commanders feel abandoned."

Durostnik's strategic withdrawal came too late. Soviet Front commanders continued to face crisis after crisis because NATO had not only seized the initiative, but had also destroyed the Warsaw Pact's equilibrium. Occasionally, Soviet units were able to slow, and occasionally to stem, NATO's advance. In heavy fighting in the Luneburger Heath area between 26 and 28 August, Warsaw Pact forces brought NORTHAG's heretofore rapid advance to a crawl. But in Hesse and Bavaria, NATO units continued to push eastward, leaving those Pact units that held their ground as isolated islands of resistance to be cleared up by rear echelon forces.

In Bavaria, those rear echelon forces were increasingly West German. On 26 August, the NATO Council decided that, for political reasons, American and French forces should lead the advance into Czechoslovakia, while the West German II Corps, which had spearheaded the advance in the south, concentrated on the elimination of encircled Soviet units. "Frankly, we aren't sure," GEN

Sexton advised the council, "whether the Czechs will consider the arrival of West German troops 'liberation,' whereas we've been led to believe, and we've had some indirect contacts through the Swiss with certain Czech government officials, that American or French troops will be greeted with open arms." On 29 August, when the American 8th Mechanized Division entered Pilsen without a fight, hordes of civilians took to the streets. Ben Wiley, a DOD pool reporter attached to the 8th Mechanized Infantry Division, compared the scene to the pictures he had seen of the liberation of Paris in 1944. To the south, the units of the French II Corps crossed the Danube and advanced through the Bohmerwald into Czechoslovakia and received a similar reception in every village, town, and city they liberated. "You might have thought from the outpouring of emotion we witnessed," a French officer informed his government, "that the Czechs had been our allies, and not our enemies."

In an effort to maintain the momentum of the advance in the south, at 0900 on 29 August CENTAG conducted a daylight drop of the 25th West German Fallschirmjäger Brigade near the intersection of the E55 and E40 north of Dresden. Simultaneously, the American 2d Armored Division conducted a direct drive along the E441 and E40 in an effort to link up with the Germans and to capture Dresden. The advance, supported by elements of the U.S. 3d Mechanized, 3d Armored, and 1st Cavalry Divisions, swept all before it. Heavy fighting on the twenty-ninth destroyed two Soviet MRDs. American mechanized forces by-passed Karl Marx Stadt (now Chemnitz) and drove hard for Dresden. At noon on the thirty-first, a brigade of the 3d MID entered Dresden from the west, while the West Germans moved into the city from the north. By nightfall, a combat group of the U.S. 2d Armored Division had reached Bautzen.

In Niedersachsen, NORTHAG, reinforced by fresh American units, most noticeably the 49th National Guard Armored Division, regained its lost momentum. In the early evening of 29 August, elements of the BAOR entered Luneburg, ending the nearly three-day-long see-saw battle for the Heath. On the thirtieth, the 49th Armored Division defeated the Soviet 27th Guards MRD in a swirling tank engagement near Uelzen and advanced eastward, capturing Salzwedel, just inside the East German border, before nightfall. Further north, a battalion of British paratroopers, veterans of the

Norwegian campaign, seized bridgeheads across the Elbe east of Hamburg at Ratzeburg and Boizenburg and held them into the evening until the arrival of British armored and mechanized forces. On the morning of 31 August, supported by RAF and Luftwaffe fighter-bombers, the BAOR broke out from its Elbe bridgeheads and sliced into the Soviet rear. By evening, the 3d Armored Division had reached Schwerin, the 4th Armored Parchim, and the 1st Armored Ludwiglust. To the south, the American 49th Armored Division entered Stendal, while the 4th Mechanized moved cautiously through Magdeburg, declared an open city by its mayor earlier in the day when the first American tanks rolled into the city's suburbs.

By the evening of 31 August, NATO forces on the central front had achieved a stunning victory over the Warsaw Pact and stood ready to continue the advance to the east. In his diary, MAJ Patrick Malley, commander of the 1st Irish Guards, a mechanized infantry battalion of the 4th Armored Brigade, 3d Armored Division in Schwerin, wrote:

> We are no more than twenty miles from Wismar, along the Baltic coast. If we get there, all the Russians and Poles in Denmark and north of the Elbe will be trapped. My Micks are straining at the bit; they're ready to go. I came across one of my companies in lager and found them working in the darkness, painting "on to Warsaw" and "on to Moscow," on their IFVs. Morale, despite some very heavy losses during the preceding weeks, is higher than I've ever seen it. But, of course, we've received the ceasefire order.

At 0200 on 1 September quiet descended upon the front in Germany and Czechoslovakia. The Soviet forces nearly trapped by the BAOR's advance—elements of thirteen divisions—withdrew along the E22 coastal highway. In East Germany and Czechoslovakia other Soviet divisions pulled out of line and began a speedy march to the east.

Newell Donohue, still commanding "Battlin' Betty II," the reserve M-60A3 he had received on 14 July, had led the 2d Squadron of the 2d Armored Cavalry Regiment to Gorlitz on the East German-Polish border in the final hours before the ceasefire. For the first

time in the campaign he felt he had the time to write, and penned
a letter to his father:

> We're positioned north of the town where we can watch the bridges
> over the Neisse. I can see the Russians moving east, and I can see
> the Poles, their tanks and guns at the ready, jeering the Russians as
> they pass. When the Poles first saw us they waved and cheered. I'll
> never forget, one Pole, he looked like an officer, was standing on top
> of a T-62, waving an American flag. Damn, it felt good, and I felt
> proud. But we've just received a ceasefire order. At first, I was pissed.
> But now I'm not so sure. We can very easily keep rolling east, but,
> hell, my crew's not all that upset by the order. We're tired. I'm awfully
> glad that my guys didn't die in vain. We've done our job; done it well.
> I guess I've had enough of this war. I think most of the other guys
> feel the same way. It's over, we've won, and we're still alive. What
> more can you ask for, Dad?

That very question, somewhat more elegantly posed, had been the
subject of debate within the NATO Council during 31 August. At
0800 that morning, the Swedish ambassador to Belgium met with
SACEUR and informed GEN Sexton that the Soviets wanted to
know under what terms NATO would agree to an immediate
ceasefire.

Early on the morning of 30 August, reports from the front had
convinced the Soviet general staff that the situation in Germany
and the Balkans could no longer be retrieved through military
means. Kaganovich found Marshal Durostnik unshaven, sitting in
a chair in a darkened room. The marshal asked the young colonel if
anyone at the front had suggested the use of chemical weapons. The
question surprised Kaganovich since Durostnik had rejected their
use earlier in the war when many thought they might have been
effective. The marshal had argued then that chemicals would slow
the advance and hinder Pact efforts more than they would hurt
NATO. Kaganovich had agreed, and still considered chemical use
out of the question, more so than before since NATO controlled the
air. Durostnik nodded in agreement.

Kaganovich then asked why, at such a late date, Durostnik was
contemplating the use of chemicals. The chief of the general staff's

answer shocked the colonel: the alternative might well be nuclear escalation.

The question of the use of nuclear weapons had come up at various times during the war. Convinced of their conventional superiority on the ground in central Europe, the Soviets had rejected the use of nuclear weapons, other than in a retaliatory role, at the start of the war. After their initial drive stalled, and operations on the flanks and in Asia had gone badly, some military and political leaders had proposed the use of tactical nuclear weapons to break the deadlock. But Soviet doctrine had never really embraced the idea of nuclear war confined to the tactical level. The expectation was that such a war would naturally escalate. There had been some not-so-veiled threats made through the Swedes that had NATO insisted on continuing its ground advance into the Kola, nuclear weapons might have been used. Of course, NATO had halted the advance in the north.

Now, with the Pact armies collapsing, Soviet leaders faced a difficult choice: either go nuclear, or give up their hold on eastern Europe. Durostnik was unsure which way the debate would go.

At 1300, the full general staff met and Durostnik recommended that political means be sought to bring the war to an end. "I am sorry, comrade president," the chief of the general staff admitted, "but I can offer no military way out of our debacle."

"What about nuclear weapons?" the president asked.

Durostnik looked around the room, but no one else appeared eager to speak.

"In my opinion, comrade president, I think . . . the answer's no."

Marshal Kubitskii shook his head.

"What are our alternatives? I just don't see what other alternatives we have."

"We give up," Durostnik replied, "we just give up."

"What are you suggesting," the president asked, "unconditional surrender?"

"Certainly not," Durostnik replied. "If the enemy insist on crossing our borders, yes, then we must go nuclear."

"You say our borders, my friend, but what about the borders of our allies? They've already been crossed." Kubitskii pointed out.

Durostnik leaned forward and looked directly across the table at the Soviet president.

"I think the issue is actually rather simple. We have to ask ourselves the following questions: are we willing to risk a nuclear holocaust so that we can retain our control of the Poles? Or of the Czechs? Or the Romanians? What about the Bulgarians?"

Durostnik turned to Kaganovich, who was in a chair off in a corner.

"Comrade president, our young colonel Kaganovich was recently at the front. Please, allow him to tell you some of what he saw regarding our splendid allies."

The president's eyes met Kaganovich who understood that he had leave to speak. He stood by his chair, seeking support for his shaking legs.

"Comrade president, the allied troops have been received as liberators, everywhere. And the mood of the people, especially the Poles, is ugly. I have to mention that, on the whole, they've let us down at the front. And I say that as a staff officer attached to the Warsaw Pact headquarters. If you will forgive me, I think it's appropriate to paraphrase Bismarck: eastern Europe's not worth the bones of a single Russian grenadier. It's only Russia that matters in the end. So, with regard to Marshal Durostnik's questions, in my opinion, I'd hardly risk nuclear war for the Poles, the Czechs, Hungarians, or the Bulgarians."

"What about the Germans?" Kubitskii asked.

"Or the goddamned Germans," Durostnik replied. "I'm not willing to risk nuclear destruction for the Germans. The hell with our allies; the hell with them all. I don't . . ."

"Without them we'll be weak," Kubitskii interjected.

"No, marshal, you have it backwards. We weren't strong because we controlled eastern Europe; we controlled eastern Europe because we were strong. We're just not as strong as we were."

"Certainly not after the events of the past few weeks," the president added. "I think I agree with what you've said. So, I ask you all: should we risk nuclear war to save our position in eastern Europe?" The Soviet president looked around the table at silent, sullen faces.

Kaganovich noted that the president appeared "unusually serene." After what seemed an eternity but was no more than thirty seconds he spoke: "We must work through the Swedes, as we did in Norway, and find a way to end the war as quickly as possible, before we are forced to escalate."

★ ★ ★

Within an hour, the general staff and the foreign ministry had worked out a proposal for the Swedes, who had already been alerted, to take to NATO. Moscow wanted an immediate, in-place ceasefire, following which negotiations would begin in Stockholm to bring the war to an end.

In Brussels, the NATO Council, after conferring with SACEUR, rejected the Soviet proposal. The allied counter-offer included an immediate, in-place ceasefire for NATO, but called for the withdrawal of all Pact forces, including those of the Soviet Union, back across their national borders before any formal peace negotiations began.

The Soviets recognized that the NATO proposal would undoubtedly lead to the overthrow of the Communist regimes in eastern Europe, a heavy price to pay, considering that NATO forces had yet to enter a single communist capital. But as the situation along the fronts in Germany and the Balkans deteriorated during the day, the Soviet president and his senior civilian and military leaders recognized that only two options remained: to agree to the NATO proposal, or to threaten escalation to nuclear war. That question had already been settled.

The Soviet president decided to accept the NATO proposal. The Kremlin passed word of that decision to the Swedes through their ambassador in Moscow, thence to Stockholm and Brussels. By late evening, still working through intermediaries, the Soviet Union and NATO determined that the ceasefire would go into effect at 0200 German time on 1 September. Fifty days after it had begun, the Third World War had come to an end.

Epilogue

THE WAR THAT WAS

"So, Yuri," Annie Taft at last spoke, "the allies win."

"That's right, the good guys win the big one," Yuri replied as he leaned back in his chair and reached into the vest pocket of his tweed jacket to extract a silver cigarette case. He flipped it open and held it in front of Taft. She just waved it away.

"No thanks. I don't smoke."

"Mind if I do?" Yuri asked.

"No."

"It's my house, Yuri," Hanson broke in, "you might ask if I care."

Yuri just smiled, picked up his Bic lighter, and lit the cigarette, blowing the smoke in Hanson's direction.

"For 15 percent, Fred, I smoke in your place."

Hanson shook his head, turned, and headed up the steps.

"If you don't mind, I have some work waiting for me in my office."

"Is there still some coffee in the kitchen?" Yuri asked.

"Brewing. Just help yourself."

"Annie, more coffee?"

"Sure. Thanks, Yuri."

A few minutes later Sinsukin returned with two fresh cups of coffee. He picked up his still burning cigarette and drew deeply.

"Yuri," Taft leaned back in her chair, trying to put as much distance as possible between herself and Yuri's smoke, "the war ends with the clear defeat of the Soviet Union. Were you, and the other Russians involved, surprised at how the war ended?"

Yuri took a sip of the still steaming coffee, drew again on his cigarette, and spoke as he exhaled.

"Some were. There were some of us who attributed everything to the fact that the Americans were running the game."

"What about you?"

Yuri shook his head.

"I wasn't surprised. In my judgment, had there been a war—a conventional war—about 1989 or 1990, we would have lost, and lost badly."

"So . . . you're saying what . . .," Taft remarked as she waved Yuri's smoke away from her face, "that the Soviet Union wasn't as strong as many so-called experts in the West had us believing?"

"In a way, yes, that's true."

Yuri watched as Taft scribbled furiously in her notebook. Without looking up she remarked: "The whole Reagan thing, the defense build-up, it was all a sham; the whole Cold War was . . . what . . . hype?"

"No, definitely not; that's not what I said," Yuri cautioned. "I was involved in military planning in the late 1980s. Us younger officers recognized what was taking place: a military revolution was underway—a technological revolution—and we weren't keeping pace. But you have to realize three things. First, not all of our military leaders saw this revolution for what it was. So I would hardly criticize your leaders for failing to recognize it. My guess . . . no, I know that their concerns were sincere. Second, had the West been weaker in the late '80s, who can say what would have happened. Believe me, the Cold War was real, very real, and there were leaders in the Soviet Union—both military and civilian—who were itching to play what they called our military card, rather than adopt the risky course of reform pursued by Gorbachev. And third, you have to realize that while what we used to call the correlation of forces favored the West in the late '80s, that wasn't true earlier. The technological revolution didn't begin to kick in until the late '70s or the early 80s. Had there been a war in 1980, or anytime earlier, we probably would have overrun Europe."

"So, then, you're saying the Reagan buildup was important?"

"Well, that depends on how you look at it. Reagan, of course, had nothing to do with the technology that made the buildup so effective. He just happened to be in the right place at the right time. But then again, that technology combined with his determination, that did have an impact on our thinking, and, especially, our fears for the future. The long-term trends were all running against us. It was becoming more and more obvious."

"Yuri," Taft asked, "why couldn't the Soviet military keep up?"

"Ah," Sinsukin replied, "that's what you Americans call the $64,000 question. The answer, believe it or not, is actually rather simple. Communism, or marxism if you prefer, is a set of ideas about political, social, and economic relationships, developed in the mid-nineteenth century, during the industrial revolution, at what appeared to Marx and others to be the height of the capitalist age. Marxism was a viable alternative to industrial capitalism. Perhaps not as efficient as capitalism, but viable."

"What exactly do you mean by viable," Taft asked.

"By viable," Yuri replied, "I mean that it could be made to work, albeit at a cost, both human and material, and that a society organized along those lines could keep pace with the capitalist world, more or less. To Marx, to Lenin, and the other communist leaders, marxism was . . . oh, what could you call it . . . a strategy for the end game of the industrial revolution. Marx and Lenin never foresaw a follow-on revolution, other than their own socialist and communist revolutions. And when this next revolution came, the technological revolution, the communist states found themselves being left behind.

"Let me give you an example. In the 1930s, you Americans built the best trucks. So, we Soviets bought ourselves a Ford truck, broke it down into its component pieces, copied them, and started producing our own trucks. That's what we called reverse engineering. Our trucks weren't quite as good, and we were always a little behind, but the system worked well enough. After all, truck technology didn't change all that often.

"But jump ahead a half-century to the computer. The West builds the best computers. So, we Soviets buy one, break it down into its component parts, copy them, and start producing our own computers. But, there are several problems. First, reverse engineering a computer processor is very different from reverse engineering an axle. Second, by the time we complete the reverse engineering process, the computer we're producing is not only inferior to the original, but the original itself is obsolete. Technological advance is moving too fast. And, quite simply, we couldn't keep pace. When that became obvious, we gave up. There were few other choices."

"What about a military option?" Taft asked. "You mentioned that a moment ago."

"Yes, it was considered. And, perhaps, it would've worked a

decade earlier, but not by the late '80s. By then, a war would have been pointless, as the Newport game demonstrated."

"Nuclear weapons: they aren't used in the book. Why not?"

"That's a tough question, Annie. You have to realize, that at Newport we were running a simulation, and then later, I was writing a book. Now, if the war goes nuclear, there might not be much to write about. Nuclear war is a touchy proposition."

"So Soviet plans called for a conventional war?" Taft asked.

"Some did and some didn't," Yuri replied. "In fact, most of our plans, especially before 1980, called for the use of nuclear weapons. Not so much because we wanted to use them, but because we knew that we were so much stronger than NATO on the ground, that we assumed that you would have to use yours if you hoped to stop us. In the 1980s that began to change and it appeared that you might not go nuclear, at least not right off the bat, because you had strengthened your conventional forces to the point that you might be able to defend Germany. The problem was, that as you got stronger, we began to doubt our capability to win conventionally, so there was a great temptation for us to use nukes because we were beginning to think that was the only way for us to win. So in either scenario, nuclear weapons figure prominently."

"So, Yuri, then, you're saying that the conventional nature of the war isn't . . . what . . . realistic."

"Well, I suppose you could make that argument. Keep in mind, though, that while planners often assumed that there would be nuclear use, there was always a tendency in war games for participants to refrain from first use. I know this was true in the Soviet Union, and I've been told that it was true in the United States as well. Hell, no one, even in a game, wants to be the first one to go nuclear. So I think that there was always a chance that restraint would win the day. Remember, no matter how badly things went during the Second World War, neither Hitler nor Stalin used their chemical arsenals. Then, beyond that, there's just the problem of writing a book about nuclear war. If you want to know what it'd be like, get a lighter and set the book on fire. There's your nuclear scenario!"

"So, Yuri, that's why in the end the Soviet president decides not to use nukes?"

"Right. Common sense. We weren't all raving lunatics, you know. Men like Gorbachev were calm, rational guys who could see the proverbial writing on the wall and drew the proper conclusions."

"Like Gorby who chose to pull back rather than fight a world war?"

"More or less. But, you know, Annie, in many ways we did fight the Third World War."

"What do you mean?" Taft asked, looking a bit surprised. "How'd I miss that one?"

Yuri laughed. "No, no, I didn't mean that there was ever a hot war. What I meant was that the Cold War was, actually, the Third World War. After all, what makes a war a world war? The first and second world wars were long, costly, bloody, global contests that pitted two camps, each led by at least one major power, against one another, right?"

Taft nodded.

"By that measure," Yuri continued, "the Cold War was a world war, pitting the United States and its allies against the Soviet Union and its friends. The Cold War was long, far longer than either the first or second wars. The Cold War was costly, far more costly than the two earlier world wars combined."

"But Yuri," Taft interjected, "how you can compare World War Two with the Cold War. So many died, and in such a short time."

"Ah! But you see," Yuri leaned toward the reporter as he ground his cigarette out in an empty coffee cup, "you can't let the lack of casualties color your perceptions. And besides, the Cold War was bloody, not as bloody as its predecessors, but certainly bloody enough. Over 100,000 Americans died in combat. And deaths numbered into the millions if you consider the proxy wars fought in Asia, the Middle East, Africa, and Latin America. You kept expensive armies and air forces poised along the German border, and enormous fleets cruised aggressively off our coasts.

"You see, Annie, too often we miss the significance of what occurs during large-scale conflicts. You can't just focus on battle lines and casualty lists. They're just two statistics to measure the progress of a war, and not always the most important. For example, because the battle lines of the First World War on the Western Front changed so little, we think of that conflict as a bloody war of indecisive battles, whereas we view the Second World War as a war of movement and decision, despite the fact that it lasted longer and cost more lives than the first."

"But Yuri," Taft pointed out, "there weren't any head-to-head battles between the Soviets and the Americans."

"Not necessarily true," Yuri replied. "Our navy and yours were always out there challenging each other. But that's beside the point. Modern nation-states rarely are defeated as the result of a single battle. Victory in modern war comes only after years of fighting, fighting that leads to the economic and psychological collapse of an enemy. Battlefield defeats accelerate that process, but they don't lead themselves to a nation's collapse.

"So you see, since the major antagonists of the Cold War avoided direct confrontation, the relative lack of combat drew out the processes by which the belligerents exhausted themselves. But those processes continued nonetheless. So, I would argue, between 1989 and 1991 the Soviet Union collapsed, its leadership, economy, and people exhausted by the forty-plus-year-long struggle—a Third World War, if you will."

Yuri could see that Taft was having some difficulty accepting what he was telling her.

"Annie, here, I think I can . . . make an analogy. I was watching television in my room one night. One of those nature shows was on. And they were showing sea anemones. Do you know what they look like?"

"Yes," Taft replied, "little sea thingies with lots of legs . . . or arms."

"Right. Now, think of the Cold War as the equivalent of a pair of sea anemones fighting for a rock. To the human eye, the two creatures appear to be waving their delicate little arms in the current, almost caressing each other. But your eyes deceive you. If you take a video of the anemones, and then you play it back at accelerated speed, you see the two animals lashing each other with poison tentacles in a life and death struggle for the control of that rock. What I'm saying is that the Cold War was a sort of slow-motion world war. But if it was on video, and if we could fast forward the Cold War, I would argue that we would see it for what it really was—a very deadly conflict."

Taft still looked unconvinced. "But your country was never defeated."

"We were! It's damned kind of you Americans to refrain from reminding us that we lost the Cold War, but the fact is that we did. How else can you explain what's happened to my country? Lenin's state collapsed, utterly, in defeat and despair. Our political, economic, and social systems disintegrated. As our economy collapsed, we retreated, on a global scale, we couldn't even prevent the breakup of the country we inherited from the tsars. We've managed even to lose Ukraine."

"But you weren't defeated, in a military sense," Taft replied.

"No, but that's irrelevant. What's amazing, Annie, is that what actually took place in the Soviet Union at the end of the Cold War was far, far worse than any of the scenarios dreamed up by your think tanks, or even the minds of your fiction writers. No one would have predicted such an utter collapse had the two superpowers actually fought a war! We were like the German Empire at the end of the First World War. Foreign troops hadn't yet crossed our borders, but we'd been defeated just the same."

"And now you're in what . . . your Weimar stage," Taft added.

"Yes, so to speak," Sinsukin admitted. "And who knows where that will lead."

"God forbid!" Taft exclaimed.

"Yes, there's the meat for another book," Sinsukin replied as he lit another cigarette.

"Yuri, in a purely military sense, what were some of the lessons that could be drawn from the Newport game?" Taft asked.

Yuri looked at his empty coffee cup then yelled toward the stairs.

"Dave, we need more coffee. The pot's empty."

"Tough shit!" came the response from Hanson's office. "I'm out of coffee. How about some tea?"

Sinsukin looked over at Annie and she nodded.

"Fine, we'll have tea."

As Hanson huffed his way down the steps and into the kitchen, Yuri gathered his thoughts.

"Okay, military lessons. First, I think the Newport exercise demonstrated what should have been obvious—the shortcomings of our, that is Soviet, military doctrine. Your analysts had always stressed the interconnection between military and society in the Soviet Union, but had nevertheless attributed to our military a degree of efficiency unparalleled elsewhere in our society. I never understood that. I was frequently astounded that your military analysts, who were so diligent in their efforts to explain how the Soviet system was meant to work, often avoided the question of whether it actually would work under the pressures of battle."

"Why do you think that was the case?" Taft asked.

"Two reasons. First, there seems to be a tendency in the West, in the democracies, to assume that dictatorships are more efficient when it comes to waging war. This just isn't true. Dictatorships, despite appearances, are terribly wasteful, even in the military sphere. After all, who won the Second World War? I also think that Western analysts envied the role our analysts played in developing doctrine through the 'scientific' study of history. It's true that the military historian was held in higher esteem in Moscow than in Washington. But was Marxist-Leninist history 'scientific'? Was it even history? Marxist-Leninist political science was fraudulently . . . puerile. Our economic concepts were absurd. Basically, once you stripped away the fancy marxist terminology, our military was little more than the old steamroller that had frightened Europe for centuries. It wasn't that we were so good, it was simply that there were so many of us. And until the technological revolution, that's what mattered.

"You know, Annie, setting aside the patriotic propaganda, our military's performance during the Second World War really wasn't all that impressive. That's not to say that we didn't improve during the war, or that our people didn't suffer heroically, but, unit for unit, we remained qualitatively inferior to the Germans. Look at the Middle East during the Cold War. Our proxies, armed with our weapons, trained and indoctrinated by our advisers, lost war after war. My God, look at how easily you destroyed the Iraqis in the Persian Gulf war. And those were our air defense systems, manned by our technicians. In our own Vietnam—located not half a world away, but along our own border—we couldn't even subdue the Afghans. It wasn't our military doctrine that threatened you and your allies, as I said, it was our numerical superiority in tanks, planes, and guns."

"Yuri," Hanson interjected as he set two cups of tea on the table, "we've another meeting in a half-hour. We're going to have to wrap this up."

"Just a few more questions, Yuri."

"Sure."

"What about the role of sea power. It plays a big part in the book."

"Well, Annie, I'll admit that I'm a former naval officer and the game was held at the Naval War College, so that certainly had something to do with it. But there's more to it than that. Have you noticed that since the end of the Cold War you don't hear much talk about geopoliticians, or discussion of the inherent strength of the Eurasian heartland. I think that the Newport game, and, more importantly, the end of the Cold War, highlighted the importance of your concepts of maritime power. I remember back in 1988, when I was attached to the general staff, one old general remarked that the West viewed the heartland somewhat mystically, sort of as interior lines on a continental scale. In fact, we saw ourselves quite simply as being surrounded.

"I also think that the global nature of the Newport game helped break the lock the central front had on many minds, both Russian and Western. The campaigns in the Kuriles, Korea, the western Pacific, the Indian Ocean, the Levant, Libya, Anatolia, the Balkans, the Atlantic, north Norway, and Denmark were basically maritime campaigns. In every theater of the war, the allies owed their success to the effective application of sea power. Even in Germany, where NATO brought the initial Soviet offensive to a halt in late July, allied naval victories on the flanks and in the Atlantic ensured that supplies and reinforcements reached the front, enabling NATO to seize the initiative and to destroy the Warsaw Pact. Keep in mind, Annie, the surface of this planet is 70 percent water!"

"What about the role of the Soviet navy?" Taft inquired.

"I think that our defeat demonstrated the bankruptcy of our naval policy. When our analysts pored over the results of the Newport exercise, they discovered that all of our defeats were related, directly or indirectly, to allied naval supremacy. One general lamented to me, 'Had our navy only succeeded in the Atlantic, we would've beaten NATO in Germany despite our early setbacks.' I think the *Tbilisi*'s impact on early operations in the Norwegian Sea surprised everyone and demonstrated what might have been accomplished by even a small number of capable Soviet carriers."

"So," Taft asked, "you think the Soviet Union should have built a larger navy?"

"Not necessarily. But if we were going to build a navy, we should have built a big, sea-going, blue-water navy, much like yours. If we weren't going to do that, we were wasting rubles, and lots of them. I think you could compare the Soviet fleet to the German fleet of the early twentieth century."

"There's a historian who called the Kaiser's navy a 'luxury fleet,'" Hanson interjected.

"Yes, that's about right, Fred," Yuri responded. "But it was a luxury we couldn't afford."

He drew heavily on the cigarette, then reached for the tea. Jet lag was catching up with him and he suddenly felt tired. Yuri stood up and stretched his back, signalling the end of the interview. Annie Taft took the hint, stood herself, and extended her hand toward Sinsukin.

"Thanks for taking the time. I enjoyed the interview. And good luck with your book."

But as Taft began to gather up her notes, she suddenly turned toward the Russian.

"Yuri, could I just ask one more?"

Sinsukin nodded, but remained standing.

"Why," the reporter asked, "was the war so short? Fifty days isn't much for a world war."

"No, it isn't," Yuri admitted, "and that's a good question. And there are two answers. This was just an exercise . . . a game . . . and once our defeat became obvious, there wasn't much reason to keep going. So we quit. Unfortunately, in a real war, the losing side rarely shows such foresight. After all, had the Kaiser drawn the proper conclusions following the battle of the Marne, the Hohenzollerns might still rule Germany today. And keep in mind what I said earlier about the Cold War being the Third World War. Don't look at those fifty days as the whole war; they were just the last fifty days of a fifty-year-long struggle. And, you know, Annie, those Cold War years of 'peace,' what we could call 'the war that really was,' wreaked far more havoc on your country and mine than fifty days of a fictional 'war that never was.'"

Abbreviations

AADS: Archangelsk Air Defense Sector

AAFCE: allied air forces, central Europe

AAM: air-to-air missile

ACG: amphibious combat group

ACE Mobile Force: Allied Command Europe Mobile Force (land)

ACR: armored cavalry regiment

ADCAP: advanced capability

AEW: airborne early warning

AFNORTH: Allied Forces, Northern Europe

AMPHIBSTRIKFOR: Amphibious Striking Force

AOR: area of responsibility

ASM: air-to-surface missile

ASWOC: ASW operations center

ASWSTRIKFOR: anti-submarine warfare striking force

ATGM: antitank guided missile

BALTAP: Baltic Approaches

BAOR: British Army of the Rhine

BMD: airborne armored personnel carrier

BMP: armored personnel carrier

BMS: battlefield management system

BTR: armored personnel carrier

CAG: commander, air group

CAP: combat air patrol

CARSTRIKFOR: carrier striking force

CARSTRIKGRU: carrier striking group

CASREP: casualty report

CDC: central digital computer

CDO: commando

CENTAG: Central Army Group

CENTCOM: Central Command

CEP: circular error probable

CFA: Combined Forces Army

CFC: Combined Forces Command

CHOD: chief of defense

CIC: combat information center

CINC: commander-in-chief

CINCCENT: (U.S.) Commander-in-Chief, Central Command

CINCEASTLANT: Commander-in-Chief, Eastern Atlantic

CINCENT: (NATO) Commander-in-Chief, Allied Forces, Central Europe

CINCHAN: Commander-in-Chief, Channel

CINCIBERLANT: Commander-in-Chief, Iberian-Atlantic Command

CINCLANT: Commander-in-Chief, Atlantic

CINCNORTH: Commander-in-Chief, Allied Forces, Northern Europe

CINCPAC: Commander-in-Chief, Pacific

CINCPACAF: Commander-in-Chief, Pacific Air Forces

CINCPACFLT: Commander-in-Chief, Pacific Fleet

CINCSOUTH: Commander-in-Chief, Allied Forces, Southern Europe

CINCUKAIR: Commander-in-Chief, United Kingdom, Air

CINCUSNAVEUR: Commander-in-Chief, U.S. Naval Forces, Europe

CINCWESTLANT: Commander-in-Chief, Western Atlantic

CJTFME: Commander, Joint Task Force, Middle East

COMAAFCE: Commander, Allied Forces, Central Europe

COMALFORGRK: Commander, Allied Forces, Greece

COMAMF (A): Commander, ACE Mobile Force (air)

COMAMF (L): Commander, ACE Mobile Force (land)

COMBALTAP: Commander, Baltic Approaches

COMCENTAG: Commander, Central Army Group

COMLANDJUT: Commander, Allied Land Forces, Schleswig-Holstein and Jutland

COMLANDSOUTH: Commander, Allied Land Forces, Southern Europe

COMLANDSOUTHEAST: Commander, Allied Land Forces, Southeastern Europe

COMNAEWF: Commander, NATO Airborne Early Warning Forces

COMNAVBALTAP: Commander, Allied Naval Forces, Baltic Approaches

COMNON: Commander, North Norway

COMNORTHAG: Commander, Northern Army Group

COMSEVENTHFLT: Commander, U.S. Seventh Fleet

COMSIXTHFLT: Commander, U.S. Sixth Fleet

COMSONOR: Commander, South Norway

COMSTRIKFLTLANT: Commander, Striking Fleet, Atlantic

COMSTRIKFORSOUTH: Commander, Naval Striking and Support Forces, Southern Europe

COMSUBACLANT: Commander, Submarines, Allied Command Atlantic

COMSUBEASTLANT: Commander, Submarines, Eastern Atlantic

COMSUBMED: Commander, Submarines, Mediterranean

COMUSJAPAN: Commander, U.S. Forces, Japan

COMUSKOREA: Commander, U.S. Forces, Korea

CONMAROPS: concept of maritime operations

CVBG: carrier battlegroup

CVW: carrier air wing

ECM: electronic countermeasures

ELF: extra low frequency

EMCON: emissions control

ESM: electronic support measures

EW: electronic warfare

FAR: Force Rapide Action

FGA: fighter/ground attack

FLIR: forward-looking infrared

GIUK: Greenland-Iceland-United Kingdom

GPS: global positioning

HARM: high-speed antiradiation missile

HAS: hardened aircraft shelter

HCOF: high command of forces

HSB: Heimatshützbrigade

IADS: integrated air defense system

IAF: Israeli Air Force

ID: infantry division

IDF: Israeli Defense Forces

IGB: Inner-German border

IPADS: improved processing-and-display system

JTFME: Joint Task Force, Middle East

KPF: Fleet Command Post

KPUG: ASW Striking Force (Soviet)

KUG: Surface Striking Force (Soviet)

LAAB: Leningrad Air-Assault Brigade

LANDSOUTH: Allied Land Forces, Southern Europe

LANDSOUTHEAST: Allied Land Forces, Southeastern Europe

MAC: military airlift command

MAD: magnetic anomaly detector

MAGTF: marine air-ground task force

MARINESTRIKFOR: Marine Striking Force

MEB: marine expeditionary brigade

MEF: marine expeditionary force

MEU: marine expeditionary unit

MFG: marinefliegergeschwader

MID: mechanized infantry division

MNC: major NATO commander

MPS: maritime prepositioning ships

MRD: motor rifle division

MRR: motor rifle regiment

MSDF: Maritime Self-Defense Force
NADGE: NATO air defense ground environment
NAVOCFORMED: Naval On-Call Force, Mediterranean
NCFN: NATO Composite Force for Norway
NEC: Northern European Command
NON: North Norway
NORTHAG: Northern Army Group
NSC: National Security Council
OKP: gunfire support force
OMG: operational maneuver group
OV: landing force
PACAIRFOR: Pacific Air Forces
PACOM: Pacific Command
PAP: preplanned activation point
PGD: panzergrenadier division
PGM: precision guided munitions
PLA: People's Liberation Army
POF: Pacific Ocean Fleet
POL: petroleum-oil-lubricants
PRC: People's Republic of China
PRIFLI: primary flight control
ROK: Republic of Korea
RPG: antitank rocket
SACEUR: Supreme Allied Commander, Europe
SACLANT: Supreme Allied Commander, Atlantic
SAG: surface action group
SLAM: standoff land-attack missile
SLEP: sea-life extension program
SLOC: sea lines of communication
SNA: Soviet Naval Aviation
SNFL: Standing Naval Force, Atlantic
SOC: special operations capable
SOUTHCOM: Southern Command
SOVINDRON: Soviet Indian Ocean Squadron
SOVMEDRON: Soviet Mediterranean Squadron
SS: diesel submarine
SSBN: nuclear-powered ballistic missile submarine

SSGN: nuclear-powered cruise missile-armed submarine
SSM: surface-to-surface missile
SSN: nuclear-powered attack submarine
STANAVFORLANT: standing naval force, Atlantic
STRIKFLTLANT: Striking Fleet, Atlantic
STRIKFORSOUTH: Naval Striking and Support Forces, Southern Europe
SUBEASTLANT: Submarine Force, Eastern Atlantic
SUCAP: surface combat air patrol
TACCO: tactical coordination officer
TAO: tactical action officer
TARPS: tactical air reconnaissance
TFR: terrain-following radar
TFS: tactical fighter squadron
TFW: tactical fighter wing
TLAM: tomahawk land attack missile
TMA: target motion analysis
TVD: strategic direction
TWOATAF: Second Allied Tactical Air Force
UK-NL AF: United Kingdom-Netherlands Amphibious Force
UNREP: underway replenishment
USKOREA: U.S. forces, Korea
VAW: U.S. Navy airborne early warning squadron
VAQ: U.S. Navy electronic warfare squadron
VERTREP: vertical (helicopter) replenishment
VLF: very low frequency
VF: U.S. Navy fighter squadron
VMA: U.S. Marine Corps attack squadron
VMF: U.S. Marine Corps fighter squadron
VMFA: U.S. Marine Corps F/A-18 Hornet squadron
VTA: Soviet military transport aviation

Tables of Organization

U.S. COMMAND STRUCTURE

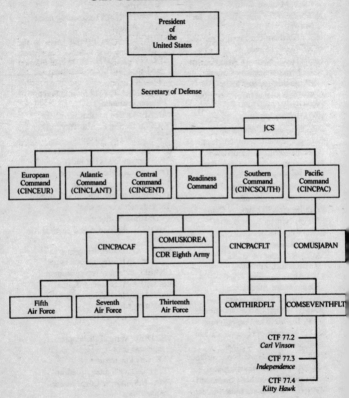

President
of
the
United States

Secretary of Defense

JCS

| European Command (CINCEUR) | Atlantic Command (CINCLANT) | Central Command (CINCENT) | Readiness Command | Southern Command (CINCSOUTH) | Pacific Command (CINCPAC) |

CINCPACAF

COMUSKOREA
CDR Eighth Army

CINCPACFLT

COMUSJAPAN

| Fifth Air Force | Seventh Air Force | Thirteenth Air Force |

COMTHIRDFLT

COMSEVENTHFLT

CTF 77.2
Carl Vinson

CTF 77.3
Independence

CTF 77.4
Kitty Hawk

SOVIET COMMAND HIERARCHY

Soviet command organization differed somewhat from NATO and U.S. practices. The Supreme High Command, unlike the American Joint Chiefs of Staff, was part of the chain of command at the highest, that is supra-theater level. The Soviets also had a plethora of "high commands" and "commands" of differing hierarchical authority. Readers may find the following chart helpful in establishing the relative seniority, or lack thereof, of a given Soviet command, an element that helps to explain numerous failures of coordination, especially on the Northern Flank.

For example, until shortly before the war, control of ground forces in the NWTVD rested with Arctic Detached Front headquarters, a sixth-echelon command (K). The establishment of a high command (GK) for the forces in the NWTVD in early July placed General Georgii Golikov in a fourth echelon post, giving him direct command authority over Soviet ground forces, frontal aviation forces, the Northern Fleet, and the air defense assets of the Archangelsk Air Defense Sector. Nevertheless, the Northern Fleet commander remained responsible for strictly naval operations in the Atlantic and Arctic Oceanic TVD, and reported directly to the naval staff of the VGK. He was also answerable to GKSNF for operations to protect SSBNs. The commander of the AADS likewise remained answerable to GKVPVO for the air defense responsibilities in the area. Both the commanders of the GKVPVO and the GKSNF outranked General Golikov and disputes over the operational control of naval and air defense assets could be settled only by the VGK in Moscow.

LEVEL OF COMMAND

1 State Committee of Defense (GKO)
2 Supreme High Command (VGK)
3 High Commands of Forces (GKs): e.g., SNF, VPVO
4 High Commands (GKs): e.g., NWTVD, FETVD
5 Commands (Ks): e.g., DA, VTA
6 Commands (Ks): Fronts
7 Armies/Fleets
8 Corps
9 Divisions

KEY

DA: Long Range Aviation
GK: High Command
GKO: State Committee of Defense
K: Command
SNF: Strategic Nuclear Forces
TVD: Strategic Direction, Northwest (NW), West (W), Southwest (SW),
        Southern (S), Far Eastern (FE)
VGK: Supreme High Command
VPVO: Air Defense Command
VTA: Transport Aviation

NOTE:

At the GK and K levels, globally deployed strategic forces outranked theater forces.

NATO COMMAND STRUCTURE

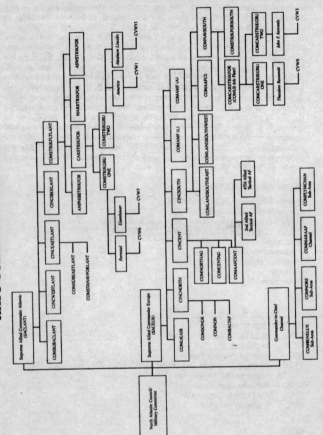

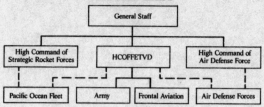

SOVIET COMMAND STRUCTURE IN THE FAR EAST

General Staff

High Command of Strategic Rocket Forces — HCOFFETVD — High Command of Air Defense Force

Pacific Ocean Fleet | Army | Frontal Aviation | Air Defense Forces

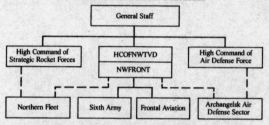

SOVIET COMMAND STRUCTURE ON THE NORTHERN FLANK

General Staff

High Command of Strategic Rocket Forces — HCOFNWTVD / NWFRONT — High Command of Air Defense Force

Northern Fleet | Sixth Army | Frontal Aviation | Archangelsk Air Defense Sector

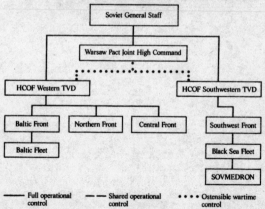

SOVIET COMMAND STRUCTURE IN WESTERN AND SOUTHWESTERN TVDs

Soviet General Staff

Warsaw Pact Joint High Command

HCOF Western TVD · · · · · HCOF Southwestern TVD

Baltic Front | Northern Front | Central Front | Southwest Front

Baltic Fleet | Black Sea Fleet

SOVMEDRON

——— Full operational control   – – – Shared operational control   · · · · Ostensible wartime control

Note: The Warsaw Pact High Command exercised ostensible control over alliance forces, but in practice the Soviet general staff directed the operations of all fronts within each of the TVDs and virtually all non-Soviet Warsaw Pact forces were subordinated to the various Soviet front commands.